AC

An elegant and hugely entertaining mystery set during Prohibition times in Galveston. Great style and a fantastic sense of authenticity....Well-written, cleverly plotted and very enjoyable.
  —*Christoph Fischer, Top 500 Amazon Reviewer (June 2014)*
  Author, Time To Let Go, Sebastian, etc.

Clever, authentic, and such a good read! It's hard to write in a time period other than your own, but Ms. Collier does it effortlessly. The dialogue was spot-on and the author's attention to detail was so perfect, I felt like I'd stepped into the 1920s. The characters and setting are genuine and intertwined so well into the story, the movie in my head was vivid and real. The combination of authenticity, mystery, and bit of romance make this book a winner.
  —*Amy Metz, A Blue Million Books Blog (January 2014)*
  Author of the Goose Pimple Junction mystery series

Ellen Collier's novel is set in one of my favorite locations, Galveston, Texas, during an era when the town was one of the wildest on the Texas Gulf Coast. Spunky society reporter Jasmine (Jazz) Cross gets involved with murder right off the bat, and her breezy voice carries the narrative along at a bright clip. Great Galveston period setting and atmosphere.
  —*Bill Crider, Author of the Sheriff Dan Rhodes mystery series,*
  and more than 50 novels (October 2012)

Collier's new series, set in 1927 Galveston, Texas, hit the spot for me, and is an entertaining bit of snappy summertime escapism.
  I was completely charmed by Jazz Cross, the spunky, intrepid flapper-reporter. Collier combines historical trivia with a cozy mystery beautifully, and I'm falling in love with her 1920s Galveston.
  —*Audra Friend, Unabridged Chick Blog (June 2013)*

ACCOLADES

What a sparkling gem FLAPPERS is. I was sucked right into the mystery and it captivated me. I loved Jazz's flapper-like attitude and her down-to-earth personality. She is a force to be reckoned with and no one, even gangsters, society madams or federal agents, can get her down. I promise this one will wow you and have you begging for more. I cannot wait to read *Bathing Beauties, Booze and Bullets* to see what Jazz and her friends are up to now.

  —*Kimberlee, "Girl Lost in a Book" Blog (July 2013)*

A wonderful mystery set in Prohibition-era Texas. This is fast becoming one of my favourite new series of mysteries.

  —*Rachel Cotterill (Book Reviews Blog, U.K), (May 2013)*
  Author of Rebellion and Revolution

I personally loved the historical setting, then-contemporary lingo and the lovely descriptions used to depict the atmosphere of the era. It kind of reminded me of a very modern Great Gatsby...with a proper balance of historical tidbits and fictional adventure. Definitely recommendable. I *loved* it.

  —*Summer Lane, Writing Belle Blog, (October 2012)*
  Author of State of Emergency and State of Chaos

FLAPPERS is fun and suspenseful and moves along at a good clip. Collier's cliff-hanger style keeps you moving. Hard to put down.

  —*Noreen Marcus, freelance writer and editor, former reporter and editor,*
  Sun-Sentinel newspaper (December 2012)

Fantastic! FLAPPERS really brings to life Galveston's glamorous past in a way that feels authentic and realistic. The mystery sucks you in immediately and leaves you fretting for the characters until the very end!

  —*Lauren George, Reader/Reviewer, Amazon (5 Stars) (September 2012)*

FLAPPERS, FLASKS AND FOUL PLAY

A Jazz Age Mystery (#1)

Ellen Mansoor Collier

E M Collier

Text Copyright © 2013 by Ellen Mansoor Collier

Cover Design Copyright © 2012 by Jeff J. Mansoor

Interior Page Design: Ellen Mansoor Collier and Gary E. Collier

Cover Artwork Illustration: George Barbier "Shawls" c. 1923

Alternate Cover: Photo (1920s): Photographer Unknown

Vintage Galveston Postcards

DECO DAME PRESS

All rights reserved. Published in the United States by Deco Dame Press
www.flapperfinds.com

ISBN: 978-0-9894170-0-6

Second Edition

The text of this book is Garamond 12-point

CONTENTS

Read the Complete "Jazz Age Mystery" Trilogy

By Ellen Mansoor Collier:

BATHING BEAUTIES, BOOZE And BULLETS
A Jazz Age Mystery #2 (2013)

GOLD DIGGERS, GAMBLERS And GUNS
A Jazz Age Mystery #3 (2014)

PREFACE

BY: ELLEN MANSOOR COLLIER

Before Las Vegas, Galveston, Texas reigned as the "Sin City of the Southwest"—a magnet for gold-diggers, gamblers and gangsters. Inspired by real people and places, **FLAPPERS, FLASKS AND FOUL PLAY** is set in 1927 Galveston, where businessmen rubbed elbows with bootleggers and real-life rival gangs ruled the Island with greed and graft.

During Prohibition, the Beach Gang and Downtown Gang fought constant turf wars for control over booze, gambling, slot machines, clubs and prostitution. To keep the peace, the gangs tried to compromise by dividing the Island into two halves: Bootleggers Ollie Quinn and Dutch Voight headed the Beach Gang, south of Broadway and on the Seawall. The infamous but long-gone swanky Hollywood Dinner Club on 61st Street and the Turf Club on 23rd Street (which became the gang's headquarters, renamed the Surf Club in the novel) were located in the Beach Gang's territory.

Colorful crime boss Johnny Jack Nounes and hard-boiled thug George Musey ran the Downtown Gang, the area north of Broadway. Nounes once partnered with Frank Nitti, Al Capone's legendary enforcer, who tried but failed to muscle in on the local turf.

Like many port cities, Galveston greatly profited from Prohibition—bar owners, businessmen and bootleggers alike—until it was nationally repealed in 1933. Enacted in January, 1920, the Volstead Act prohibited "the manufacture, sale, transport and possession of intoxicating liquor or distilled spirits containing more than 0.5% alcohol for beverage purposes." The Treasury Department employed hundreds of Prohibition agents to enforce the new law, but that proved futile as most local police and the public refused to follow the not-so "Noble Experiment."

PREFACE

The Maceo brothers, Rosario and Sam (Papa Rose and Big Sam), were Sicilian immigrants who eventually took control of the Island, known as the "Free State of Galveston" for its vice and laissez-faire attitude, for roughly 25-30 years, from 1926 on, until the Maceos' deaths. Sam Maceo died in 1951 of cancer and Rose Maceo passed on due to heart disease in 1954.

FLAPPERS, FLASKS AND FOUL PLAY is loosely based on actual and fabricated events, leading to the Maceos' gradual take-over in the late 1920s and early 1930s.

The *Galveston Gazette* is a fictitious newspaper, but the headlines in the novel are based on actual stories that appeared in *The Galveston Daily News,* the first and oldest newspaper in Texas, founded in 1842 and still in publication. Since many of the gangland crimes and activities went largely unreported and/or under-reported, the main characters and circumstances in the novel are fictitious and not intended to malign or distort actual persons or cases, but are purely the author's imagined version of possible events.

CHAPTER ONE

Everyone always warned me about Market Street after dark. Loud jazz played as I tapped a code on the unmarked wooden door. A muggy Gulf breeze shook the palm trees, plastering my silk frock to my body like a mummy's skin. Amanda and I jumped when a drunk flung a bottle out of a Model T.

"What's the hold up?" I tugged at the heavy door, peering into the tiny slot. It wasn't like Sammy or Dino to keep us waiting outside the Oasis at night. I knew it was risky to come, but I wanted, needed, to see Sammy, to keep a promise I'd made to my dad before he died.

Two winos wolf-whistled and made a beeline for us, leaning like twin towers of Pisa. "Get lost!" we shouted, trading anxious looks, relieved when they changed course.

"I've got the heebie-jeebies." Amanda shivered. "What if the cops show up?"

"Don't worry," I told her. "Sammy has friends on the force."

Still, how would it look if the *Galveston Gazette's* society reporter was thrown in jail after a raid? I'd rather write the news stories than be a headline. Besides, I couldn't afford to lose my job, even if it was just a fancy title for "stenographer and slave." But I kept coming back to Market Street, craving the thrill, the excitement lacking in my daily grind.

Finally the door panel slid open and cocoa eyes glowered at us. "Who sent you?"

"Sammy. Sammy Cook."

"What's the word?" A deep, familiar voice.

"Dino? It's me, Jazz. Jasmine Cross."

"The password?" His voice like a dare.

On cue, I recited: "Babe Ruth hits homers out of the ball park." The door groaned open and Dino's bulk filled the entrance, big as a baby grand. On weekends, Dino always stood guard at the door, checking for signs of trouble. His round, fleshy face reminded me of a hand-tossed pizza. Roughly he yanked us inside, clearly irritated that I'd passed "the test."

"What's the big idea? Why'd you give us the third-degree at the door?" I challenged him, hands on hips, my floral mesh bag swinging on my arm.

"Gotta be careful. Never know what can happen in a bar full of hooch hounds."

Amanda's baby blues widened. "A raid?"

Dino wagged a sausage finger at us, blocking our path.

"All I know is a gin joint's no place for ladies without escorts."

"Since when do we need escorts?" I pushed away his beefy arm, tattooed "Rosa" over a blood-red rose.

"Jazz, how do you always know the secret password?" Amanda sounded impressed.

"I've got friends in high places," I replied with a wink.

If I told her the truth, could she keep a secret?

"You mean in low places," she cracked as we rushed downstairs into the shadowy bar.

The Oasis hid in the basement of a brick Victorian building, a haven for sailors, oilmen, flappers and winos. As a front, it operated as a Mediterranean restaurant, serving food around the clock, day and night. Twice, undercover cops had stopped in for "a bite to eat" and almost shut it down. If Sammy heard rumors of a raid, he stashed the booze and served Coca-Cola in china teacups.

A hazy gray fog of cigarette smoke stung my eyes, scratched my throat. Brass ceiling fans did little to relieve the heat or sweet smell of gardenia perfume. Folks of all ages packed the room shoulder to shoulder, united in one quest: getting blotto. Busy night.

Doria, a beautiful life-sized figurehead Sammy rescued from a wayward ship, hung above the bar. Hands across her chest, she watched over us like a guardian angel.

"Doria is my true love," Sammy often joked. "When she comes alive, I'll get married. Knock on wood." That was Sammy—always a dreamer, chasing rainbows and mermaids.

A dandy in a top hat played "Ain't We Got Fun?" on the old grand piano, laughing with a group of chorus girls dancing the Charleston. In their glittering beaded gowns, they resembled brilliant butterflies. Even in my floral silk frock, I felt more like a moth.

Amanda disappeared to powder her nose, but I knew she wanted to survey the scenery—meaning the men. With her big blue eyes and long golden curls she refused to cut or bob, she reminded me of a Renaissance angel. Appearances can be deceiving.

I elbowed my way to the bar where Frank waited on customers behind the long oak counter. A beveled mirror reflected rows of liquor bottles lined up like soldiers. Model ships and schooners sat on the shelves, next to tinted photos of Sammy, the owner, surrounded by voluptuous vamps, hair bobbed, faces perfectly powdered and rouged. Women young and old swooned over his dark hair, hazel eyes and olive skin, calling him a "dead ringer" for the late Rudolph Valentino. Excuse the pun.

Frank looked spiffy in a red bow tie and suspenders.

"Hey, Frank. Where's Sammy?"

He shook his head, mixing a cocktail. "You just missed him, Jazz. He got a call and ran out in a hurry."

"What's so urgent?" I wondered. Sammy rarely left the Oasis on weekends, especially with a full house.

Frank eyed the guys sitting around the bar. "You know. Business?"

Monkey business, no doubt. Maybe Sammy was out with a dame or meeting a rum-runner on the docks or beach. Bootleggers often made deliveries on weekend nights—when the cops and clubs were hopping. Buzz, a freckle-faced orphan, helped out behind the bar. He was a bit slow upstairs, but did OK in a pinch.

"Hiya, Jazz! Can I getcha a soda?"

"How about a Dr. Pepper?" I tousled his sandy hair.

"A whiskey, on the rocks." A good-looking gentleman told Frank, pulling up a barstool by me with a smile. "Say, sport, have you seen Sammy?" he asked Buzz, who shyly shook his head 'no.'

"I'm looking for Sammy, too," I told the stranger.

"Join the crowd, little lady." He loosened his collar and tie. "Is he your beau?"

What beau? Sure, I'd had my dance cards filled a few times, but I'd almost given up on men since my last steady skipped town and headed for Hollywood. So far, no cigar—or movie star.

"We're just friends," I fibbed. "Not to worry. Sammy will show up soon. He's always here on weekends."

Buzz served our drinks and the man handed him two bucks. "Let me get that, doll. Keep the change, sport. Don't spend it all in one place." Buzz grinned and stashed a bill in his Levi's.

"Thanks, sir." I studied his fine features, pricey gray suit and navy silk tie. He seemed out of place here, like a shiny new Cadillac in a crowd full of jalopies. Where had I seen him before? Probably in the society pages—he was the bold-faced type.

"Call me Horace." His handshake was firm. "Any pal of Sammy's is a pal of mine."

"I'm Jazz," I said, wondering what they possibly had in common. No secret that Sammy's pals tended to have a lot more sass than class. "So how do you know Sammy?"

"Let's just say we go way back." Horace faced me, taking a swill of his drink. "Haven't we met before, Jazz? You look familiar. Do you come here often?"

Did he really think that corny line would work? I started to turn away, but he tapped my hand. "Say, if you see Sammy before I do, tell him Horace was here." I couldn't help but notice his red-rimmed eyes, the whiskey on his breath. "Tell him it's urgent. Life or death!"

Life or death? Was he serious or was the booze talking? Sammy always made it a point to stop serving liquor before his customers got too sloshed, but Frank didn't seem to notice or even care.

"Will do, Horace. Thanks for the soda." I could have dismissed him as just another drunk, but something about his tone, his high-class manners, set him apart from the regulars.

I excused myself and went looking for Amanda, who stood out in the crowd, her blonde hair bright as a beacon. She was flirting with an Italian sailor who twirled her long ringlets as she spoke. I doubt he understood a word she said, but he got the message all the same.

"Ciao, bella." He turned to me with a liquid smile. What a lounge lizard.

"Ciao," I replied, pulling Amanda away. "Arrivederci."

The sailor's face fell, but lit up when Amanda blew him a kiss. "Aw, don't be a killjoy, Jazz," she pouted. "I was just having fun."

"That kind of fun can end in heartbreak," I warned her. "Come on, let's get cocktails."

Who was I to give advice on men with my lousy track record? Amanda had so many suitors I needed a scorecard. I had to admit, at times I acted more like her chaperone than friend. We roomed at my aunt's boarding house, and felt as close as sisters, though we were a study in contrasts: She was tall and fair, while I was petite, with dark hair and blue eyes.

Circling the bar, we found a tiny table by the dance floor, and a bleached blonde strutted over to take our order.

"What d'ya want?" she drawled, sucking on a lollipop.

"A sidecar, please," we said in unison. Maybe a cocktail would help me relax, loosen up.

The pianist broke into a fast ragtime number, and I watched with envy as a sleek young couple danced the foxtrot. If only I could be so light on my feet, with a snappy partner to lead the way.

Miss Peroxide returned, slamming down our drinks while we fumbled in our bags for change. "Hope these ain't too strong for you girls." Gee, thanks. I faked a smile, ignoring her wisecrack.

"Say, have you seen Sammy?"

"What's it to you?" She gave me the once-over. "I'm his gal, not his babysitter."

"Oh, yeah?" Amanda's eyes flashed, revealing her not-so-secret crush. "Says who?"

"Ask him yourself. Tell him Candy sent you." She batted her lashes and scurried off.

"What a floozy!" Amanda huffed. "I think Candy needs a good dose of charm school."

"And how," I agreed, laughing as we sipped our sidecars, listening to a few flappers sing "Dinah" and "Always" by the piano. Some hangers-on sang along, swaying back and forth, a far cry from the church choir.

Across the room, a tall, dark and yes, handsome man caught my eye, lifting his glass as if toasting. Who, me? I blushed as he headed my way, tilting his head toward the dance floor. Sure, why not?

I smiled back, eager to dust off my dancing shoes. But I stopped and turned away when loud voices amplified, drowning out the jazz.

By the bar, I saw two "Mutt and Jeff" look-alikes having a row. A tall, wiry guy raised his arm to strike—blocked by a short, pudgy fella in a sailor's cap. Bar brawls were old hat: Beach and Downtown gangsters often faced off in public places to protect their turf.

The piano-playing stopped, and the scuffle around the bar expanded until all I could see were fists flailing, men shoving and fighting. Loud voices cursed each other, yelling at the top of their lungs: "Palooka!" "Clodhopper!" "Bohunk!" and more choice insults.

Dino thundered downstairs, arms out, pushing the men apart like a bulldozer. "Knock it off! What is this? A boxing ring?"

"I wonder what's wrong?" I tensed up, craning my neck to see the commotion. Tall, Dark and Handsome had disappeared. Just my luck. As the crowd fanned out, I heard a flapper cry out, "Help!"

Amanda and I squeezed through the crowd, and I froze in place when I saw Horace, the dapper gent I'd met at the bar.

He was lying on the floor, motionless, passed out cold.

CHAPTER TWO

"Is he dead?" Amanda whispered.

"I hope not," I replied, my stomach tight, looking around.

Where was Sammy when we needed him?

A hush fell over the Oasis, and a small group formed a half-circle around Horace, staring at his prone body as if expecting him to levitate. Dino bent down by his side and tried shaking him, to no avail. I hated to be a Nosy Nellie, but my reporter's instincts kicked in and I tried to observe everything.

"What happened?" I asked Frank. "Was that man involved in the fight?"

"Beats me." He fingered his suspenders. "One minute he's sitting at the bar, the next he's on the floor, out like a light."

Dino glared at the crowd. "Which one of you chumps knocked him out?"

The room was silent save for the creaking brass fans. "Don't look at me," snapped Mutt.

"I ain't touched a hair on his head," said Jeff, hands held high like a stick-up.

A few murmurs filled the air. Then Mutt and Jeff started pushing each other, yelling, "What'd ya do to him, huh? What made him keel over like that?"

A deep voice replied, "Lay off! The lush had a heart attack, plain and simple."

"So he got stinko," snickered a man. "He just needs to dry out."

How could they be so cavalier? My heart went out to him, this stranger, in such obvious distress.

Dino raised his voice for the crowd's benefit. "Looks like the poor sot couldn't handle his liquor. Got good and shellacked. We know how hard it is to find the real stuff." No one laughed at his lame attempt at a joke, but I knew he was only trying to help Sammy in his own bumbling way. "Go back to your seats, folks. This ain't no floor show."

"Fooled me," Candy drawled. If this was her idea of fun, maybe she thought visiting the old cemetery on Broadway was a good time.

I grabbed Dino's arm, trying not to panic. "Aren't you in charge? Do something!"

"What can I do?" Dino threw his hands up in the air. "I ain't no Houdini."

Sure, I wanted to help, but medical emergencies aren't exactly my strong suit. In a way, I felt guilty, as if I'd somehow let Horace down. I turned to the group of gawkers, blinking as if they couldn't see straight. It was a long-shot, but I called out, "Can anyone help? A doctor or nurse?"

A bespectacled young man spoke up. "I may be of some assistance." With his cherubic face and curly hair, he didn't look old enough to drink or drive, much less practice medicine.

"Are you really a doctor?" I frowned.

He nodded. "I'm a resident at John Sealy. I'll do my best."

"Big Red? Swell. We need your help."

We didn't have much choice. The group parted as he knelt by the body. Efficiently, the med student—I decided to call him 'Doc'—felt Horace's flushed face and loosened his tie.

Then Doc motioned me over. "You!"

Seems I was the only sober one in the bunch. Lucky me.

I squatted down, wishing I'd kept my big yap shut. Florence Nightingale, I'm not. I admit, I faint at the sight of blood. Fortunately Horace didn't appear to be bleeding, just blotto.

"Roll up his sleeves and unbutton his shirt," Doc commanded. "I'll check his pulse."

I obeyed, cringing at the cold clammy feel of Horace's skin, like raw meat fresh from a butcher.

"Why bother?" a man called out. "The guy's a goner."

Ignoring him, Doc checked Horace's face and neck.

"There aren't any obvious signs of bruising or indication of a struggle." Then he looked inside his mouth and stuck two fingers down his throat. "No obstruction in the airway," he muttered. Doc pressed his right fingers against Horace's wrist, and studied his silver pocket watch. "Perhaps it's a stroke or a heart condition. Could be diabetes or consumption. Now he appears to be comatose."

I felt nauseous as I watched Doc lift Horace's eyelids, one by one. His eyes had rolled back until you could only see the whites— actually more bloodshot-red than white. Doc held a small bottle of smelling salts under his nose, but Horace didn't blink or respond. Now what?

Then Doc looked up gravely. "This man is dying. Hurry, we need to call an ambulance!"

"Ambulance? Are you crazy?" Dino waved his hands in the air and swore in Italian. "Want your pals to see you guzzling gin in a juice joint?"

"If he's not taken to a hospital now, he may die," Doc insisted. "What'll it be?"

Dino folded his arms, facing Doc like David and Goliath. Guess who was Goliath.

"You made your point," Dino said. "We'll drive him ourselves."

"But it's not safe." Doc stood up, all five-foot six-inches. "He needs an ambulance."

"Take it or leave it, doc," Dino snapped. "If he dies here, it's on your head."

I couldn't think while Horace lay there helpless, with Dino and Doc trading barbs. His face had turned an ashen gray, the color of wet cement. Beads of sweat peppered his forehead and his lean frame was still, except for a few spasms.

Please don't die, not here, not now, I prayed to myself, and I'm not religious.

Holding my breath, I squeezed his arm, trying to stop the spasms. Then I noticed his gold wedding band and asked, "Does he have any ID? A wallet? Should we call his wife?"

"It's up to the hospital to notify his family in case of ..." Doc's voice trailed. He patted Horace's pants pockets, then drew out a sleek silver cigarette case. Sterling? "There's no wallet or money clip, only this empty case. Any idea who he is?" Doc asked, waving it around.

"He's a regular." Dino shrugged. "Most people won't give out their real names in a bar, get it?" He faced the crowd. "Let's keep this quiet, folks. Don't wanna embarrass his missus."

Dino was right. It wouldn't help business any if word got out about Horace's sudden collapse.

Looking for his missing wallet, I searched under the barstools, spying a silver hip flask—a common accessory these days—and a brass horseshoe key ring. After I palmed the flask and keys, a dirty work boot hovered over my hand.

"Drop it, missy," said a tall man with skin like worn leather, chewing on tobacco.

Shaken, I scrambled to my feet, the thug's craggy face inches from mine. I tried to stare him down, hard to do when he was a foot taller, and held the items out of reach, like bait.

"Back off, mister," I hissed, with more moxie than I felt.

The bully sized me up, grinning with tobacco-stained teeth, then spit out a wad, right by my new satin shoes.

Luckily Dino grabbed the jerk and gave him the bum's rush out the exit. "Beat it, buster!"

Just in time. "Thanks, Dino." I smiled with relief and studied the flask, engraved with "HCA" in a fancy scroll. "I found this with some keys on the floor, under the barstool. They must belong to Horace."

In a flash, Dino snatched the items, shoving the flask in his pocket. Doc noticed Dino's sleight-of-hand. "Wait a minute, mister. You need to turn over that flask to the doctors."

"What flask?" Dino grinned, and jingled the car keys. "Let's take him in his own wheels, so he'll be more comfortable. Look for a Bentley or a Studebaker."

Dino wasn't the brightest bulb, but he knew his cars. He tossed the keys to Doc. "You know how to drive, don't you, pal?"

A few thugs cornered Frank. "What kind of cheap hooch do you serve around here, huh?" Frank blanched as Mutt shook a fist in his face. "I'm not paying good money for this rotgut."

As they filed out, I heard someone yell: "Who wants to go blind in this blind pig?"

Stunned, I wanted to slap the slander right out of their mouths, but instead I stood there, dumb and numb, glad Sammy wasn't there to hear their lies.

Dino barked out orders to a few men who stood around like a motley barbershop quartet. Everyone else had left. Who could blame them? Drinking during Prohibition was bad enough, but a half-dead body in a bar—who wanted that kind of trouble?

If I was a smart cookie, I'd scram with Amanda. But my curiosity, or rather nosiness, won out, so we stuck around like barnacles on a sinking ship. Good thing I could swim.

The men clumsily lifted Horace by his limbs, and we followed them up the stairs to the alley. Outside, Market Street was filled with honking cars and strains of blues. The full moon illuminated a new Studebaker, waiting proudly for its owner: A ritzy maroon model with wood running boards and a roomy rumble seat, definitely out of our price range. Whoever Horace was, you knew he was a big shot just by looking at his hayburner.

"Poor sot was some high-roller." Dino whistled. "Musta been nice while it lasted."

We watched as the men hoisted Horace onto the back seat, long legs sticking out of the window like two loaves of French bread.

Dino shot me an anxious look. "I hope this won't make the papers. We don't want folks accusing us of spiking our Coca-Cola."

"He'll be fine," I snapped at Dino. "He has to be."

For Sammy's sake as well.

Dino signaled to Doc. "I'll follow in my car. Just in case."

Doc started up the Studebaker, which coughed and sputtered like an old wino.

"Thanks for your help," I told Doc, holding out my hand. "My name's Jazz. What's yours?"

"Never mind." He patted the passenger seat. "You wanna tag along? If you can stomach the ride."

"Sure, if I can help." He was cute—and a doctor to boot—but romance was the last thing on my mind.

As I started to climb in, Dino jerked me out of the car.

"You better stay put, wait for Sammy. You're good with words. Tell him what you saw."

"But I didn't really see anything…" I protested, but Dino cut me off with a crank of his Model T. Then the three men—rather, two men, one half-stiff—sputtered off like a sad parade.

I watched the red tail lights disappear, hoping Horace would revive and survive. I wished I had a car, so I could follow Doc to the hospital, make sure Horace was in good hands. If it was up to Dino, he'd drop him off in an alley like an old rug—or a mob hit.

Now all I could do was follow Frank downstairs, while Amanda chattered nonstop. "Jazz, are you OK? You were so brave!" She gave me a quick hug.

Brave? I'd felt like passing out, right next to Horace. "I'm peachy keen." I sighed and dropped in a chair. "Who needs the talkies when you can see the real thing?" I'd never forget the cold, clammy feel of Horace's skin, or his blank, bloodshot eyes.

Frank retreated into the kitchen with Bernie, the cook. Buzz hid in the corner, pretending to be invisible. Poor kid, witnessing such a frightening scene.

"Why don't we skedaddle?" Amanda shivered. "That whole spectacle gave me the willies."

"You said it. But let's sit tight. I need to talk to Sammy."

"Why not let Frank give him the bad news?" Amanda pouted. "Say, I wonder what's keeping Sammy? Tell me, Jazz. Why are you so worried about him? Are you sweet on Sammy too?"

I made a face. "We're only good friends."

She looked so skeptical that I decided to spill the beans.

"I'll let you in on a secret—if you promise not to tell anyone."

Amanda crossed her heart, eyes wide as portholes. "Sure, I won't tell a soul."

"Swear?" I felt like a worn-out tire, ready to burst. "Sammy is my half-brother, my father's illegitimate son."

So much for my spotless reputation as an upstanding young society reporter. Wouldn't my nosy editor—Mrs. I-Love-Gossip Harper—enjoy that juicy piece of scuttlebutt?

CHAPTER THREE

"Your half-brother?" Amanda looked shocked. "You don't say! I had no idea. Why keep it a secret?"

"Sammy doesn't want anyone to know. For my family's sake."

"Why not?" she wondered. "Because he owns a bar?"

"He's worried the gangs might come after us, try to use us as bait. Besides, if my snooty boss ever found out, I could lose my job."

I wasn't in the mood to tell her the long, sad story. Not now, not yet. "Let's talk later, OK? I need to ask Frank some questions."

I plopped down on a barstool. Doria floated over me, the perfect witness—if only she could speak.

"What a night!" I said to Frank. "Any word from Sammy yet?" Frank shook his head, hands trembling as he stacked glasses.

"I had him paged at the Grotto and the Hollywood Dinner Club, but there was no answer." He looked dazed, as if he'd been sampling the merchandise. Bad idea.

Tall and lean, with a thin serious face and spectacles, Frank acted more like a professor than a bartender. He'd attended college one year, but then his father got polio and Frank had to drop out to support his family. Too young for the war, too late for school.

"I hope Horace makes it," I told him. "Do you know why he wanted to see Sammy?"

Frank shrugged. "Said it was urgent. If I don't ask any questions, I don't hear any lies."

He wasn't much help. "What about that fight at the bar? Any idea what set it off?"

"Who knows? Two guys got into a shoving match, that's all. The gangs are always causing trouble." He avoided my gaze. "But that's not unusual on a busy Saturday night."

"So what happened right before Horace passed out? Anything suspicious?" I pressed.

"Like what? The fella was a heavy drinker, smoker—it happens." Frank stopped wiping the counter, eyes narrowed. "Hey, why the interrogation? Think something fishy is going on here? Not while I'm on duty. I run a tight ship." He snapped his suspenders for emphasis. Sure, I enjoyed the sea references, but he seemed nervous, on edge.

Like Frank, I had a strange sense of doom and gloom. I couldn't help it: Worrying was in my blood. Everyone in my family had a string of worry beads. Mine were mother-of-pearl.

"How about—?" I started to ask when Sammy burst in the room like a self-contained hurricane. He looked natty in a dark suit and white shirt, his straw boater tilted over his forehead. I smiled at Amanda, breathing easy now that Sammy was back.

"What's the rumpus?" He circled the empty room, flipping on lights, revealing the stained wood floors and scuffed tables. In the glare, the Oasis looked plain, washed-out, like an aging stage actress without her make-up. Even Doria looked lost.

"Frank, what's this emergency you called me about? Damn, this place is quieter than a morgue. Don't tell me we got raided! If those goddamn cops don't warn me next time..."

Frank motioned toward the back, but Sammy held up his hand when he spotted me at the bar. "Jazz—you're here!" His handsome face brightened like a neon sign, then flickered out, frowning at our glum expressions. "What the hell's going on?"

Sammy patted my back. "You gals have a soda while I discuss some business with Frank." He said *business* exactly like Frank, as if set in italics.

Reluctantly, I joined Amanda at a table adorned with wilted red carnations—I felt the same way. She stared into a teal enameled vanity compact, applying bright pink lipstick dangling from a finger ring chain. She never forgot to fix her face paint, even in a crisis.

"Glad Sammy's back. Now let's go." Amanda didn't like being ignored. Who did?

"Not yet." I motioned to Buzz, who had come out of hiding and was sweeping under the tables. "How are you?" I patted his back. "I'm sorry about that poor man."

"Me, too. He was nice," Buzz whined.

"Did you see the bar fight? Notice anything strange earlier?"

"Didn't see n-nuthin', didn't talk to n-nobody else." His lips started to quiver. "Am I in t-t-trouble? I did nuthin' wrong. Honest!" For a kid, Buzz knew how to keep his hands clean.

"Don't worry, Buzz." I tried to smile. "Sammy will take care of everything."

Sammy headed to our table, cigarette in hand. He'd stopped smoking two years ago. "Go ahead and lock up, Buzz." He tossed him the set of keys.

"Sure, M-M-Mr. Cook." Buzz rushed upstairs, holding the keys tight. Poor Buzz—rather, Buster—was short on brains but long on loyalty. Sammy nicknamed him "Buzz"—as in "buzz off"—because he was always underfoot, like a pesky puppy.

"So what brings you here tonight, Jazz?" Sammy's olive eyes looked troubled.

"I'm so sorry about Horace. He told me he had an urgent message for you. Life or death."

"Life or death?" Sammy frowned. "He called at the last minute. That's all I know." He puffed on his stick as a smoky cloud danced over his head. "And the less you know, the better."

I looked down, upset by his cold tone. Sammy's moods changed like traffic lights. He eyed Amanda, and she left like a good egg.

His voice softened. "If you must know, his name is Horace Andrews. Yes, we were supposed to meet tonight, but I got here too late—obviously." He rubbed his midnight shadow. "Tell me what happened. Did someone pick a fight with Horace?"

"I only saw two thugs come to blows, but I don't think Horace was involved."

"What else? Did anyone knock him out? Level with me," he demanded, eyes like slits.

Why the drill? "All I know is a nice man bought me a drink, and asked me to deliver a message to you. Next time I saw him, he was passed out on the floor."

Sammy took a deep drag off his Camel cigarette. "I put Dino in charge one night, and the whole place goes to pot. Glad he didn't lose his head completely." He'd once told me Dino had served time in Huntsville Prison for assault and battery, but now he was on the straight and narrow.

"Dino means well. He just panics during a crisis." As if I didn't.

"I know." Sammy shut his eyes, probably pretending he was on the high seas, anywhere but in the hot seat. "I'm trying to make sense of this whole mess, trying not to think the worst."

I stared at him, my stomach tightening. "What's the worst?"

"Frank told me what they said...about rotgut." Sammy worked his jaw. "Why would they say that? Why in hell would I poison my own customers?"

Frank and his big mouth. "I'm sure it was an accident, or heart failure, like Doc said." Sammy didn't reply, blowing smoke rings at Doria, like an Indian's signal for help.

I had to ask: "Do you think you got a bad batch by mistake? Even if you did, why was Horace the only one affected?"

"Who knows?" Sammy scanned the bar, shaking his head. "All it takes is one bad bottle."

Then Amanda appeared, giving him an excuse to clam up. "We missed you tonight," she said in her best debutante drawl. "Jazz...we...tried to help, but..." Her hands fluttered like falling leaves. Typical Amanda, always trying to get in his good graces.

"Thanks for sticking around." Sammy forced a smile.

"Don't worry, we won't desert you." I patted his arm. "By the way, where were you tonight?"

"On the docks," he admitted. Code for booze pick-up.

Suddenly noisy footsteps pounded the stairs and Buzz bounded into the room, waving his arms like a weather vane, yelling over and over: "The c-c-cops are c-c-coming!"

Police sirens wailed in the distance, getting louder, closer.

"Damn it—that's all I need." Sammy jumped up, cursing under his breath. He motioned to Frank. "Make sure all the doors are locked. Keep it down." What did he expect—a raid?

We all froze in place like park statues, afraid to move. As the sirens grew faint, we relaxed, exhaling in one loud sigh. False alarm— what a relief.

"I bet they're chasing those sex maniacs on Post Office," Sammy snorted. Everyone knew Post Office Street served as the popular red-light district, a haven for hoods and hayseeds, according to Sammy. He liked to brag that he never had to pay for company, the ladies always came to him. True, he was a regular Romeo.

"It's time to close up shop." Sammy tapped his watch and called to Frank. "Please take these ladies home. Party's over."

Before we left, I tugged on his sleeve, noting the nice gold cufflinks. Seemed sales were picking up, until tonight.

"Sammy, answer one question. Who's Horace Andrews?"

"Guess you'll find out anyway." Sammy swallowed hard, avoiding my gaze. "He's the vice president of Lone Star Bank—and a good friend."

"A bank VP?" I blinked in surprise. "Why was he here so late—on a Saturday night?"

"Business." That word again.

"It's not exactly banker's hours." I didn't buy it. "Horace told me it was life and death."

"Sorry, Jazz, that's all I know." He frowned. "Be sure to keep your lips zipped. Don't go spreading rumors at your paper."

Gee, thanks. Didn't he trust me by now?

Then Sammy ground out his Camel on a plate and walked off, dragging his feet, sad as Charlie Chaplin's 'Little Tramp.'

CHAPTER FOUR

Tonight's turn of events seemed surreal, like watching Lon Chaney in 'Phantom of the Opera.' That creepy movie gave me nightmares for weeks. Why did I ever let my friends talk me into seeing it at the drafty old Grand Opera House?

After Frank drove us home, Amanda and I tried to sneak in the back door, but my aunt Eva was waiting up for us. Curses, foiled again. With her graying hair and pale skin, Eva looked as tired and faded as her old print housedress.

"Where were you two, out so late? Were you at that speakeasy, that den of sin?" She shook her hands at me, refusing to mention Sammy by name.

"Relax. We were singing show tunes with some friends." I had a few white lies on hand.

"In a bar, no doubt. You both reek of smoke and alcohol." She turned away in disgust.

Frankly, I was sick of Eva's strict rules, tired of being treated like Little Orphan Annie. My mother was in Europe for the summer, not dead. We tiptoed upstairs and sat in my room with my favorite perfume lamp on, a half-nude Egyptian maiden, filling the air with a fresh citrus scent.

"Sorry about Eva," I said. "She can be a bit overprotective."

"I'll say! That's two close calls in one night." Amanda waved her arms around like a can-can dancer. "That poor fella. I still can't believe he's only a boring banker. In that fancy get-up, I expected a bootlegger or a loan shark, even a riverboat gambler!"

"Horace sure stuck out like a sore thumb," I agreed. "I wonder what started that fight?"

"Maybe it was only a ruse, so those creeps could pull a Mickey Finn." Amanda sounded like a gangster's moll. "He did look loaded—in more ways than one. A real sugar daddy!"

"Sugar daddy? He was barely breathing!" I rolled my eyes. "You think some thug spiked his drink and staged a fake fight just to rob him? That's screwy."

I was skeptical, but maybe she was right. Lots of fortune-hunters came to Galveston to gamble, but ended up on skid row.

"His money and wallet *were* missing," I noted. "What if it was a pickpocket? And did you see that bully try to snatch his flask out of my hands? But I need more facts before jumping to conclusions."

Thank goodness Dino had intervened. Still, what was Dino planning to do with Horace's things—hock them?

"Facts—isn't that your job? You could be like Sherlock Holmes, looking for clues."

Amanda had been reading my mystery novels again. "Sounds a lot better than covering those dull tea dances or debutante balls."

Exhausted, I wriggled out of my frock and shoes, ready for bed. But how would I get any sleep, worrying about Sammy and Horace?

"Wait. I'm dying to know." Amanda plopped down on my bed. "When did you find out Sammy was your half-brother?"

I took a deep breath, glad to finally reveal the truth. "My dad told me about Sammy right before he died. All this time I thought Sammy was only a clerk who worked in his store."

My heart seized as I recalled my dad's confession, a secret he'd kept all his life. "Keep an eye on Sammy," he'd told me. "He needs a family." I was too shocked to be angry, thrilled to have a big brother, never mind that we had different mothers.

Naturally, I felt protective of him, though he was almost 32, ten years older than me. Like my dad, he knew how to keep secrets.

"What did your mother do when she found out?" Amanda sat up. "Is that why she took off for Europe?"

I nodded. "She was devastated, especially since my dad left Sammy half his estate, enough to buy the Oasis. Aunt Eva thinks Sammy owes us, like it's all his fault. She hates to ask for help with the rent, but some months she doesn't have a choice."

Truth was, no one wanted to admit that we all depended on Sammy to make ends meet.

Finally an old family secret was out in the open, and I felt lighter, as if an albatross had flown away, across the Gulf.

"So Sammy helps support your whole family? No wonder you're so worried."

"I don't care about the money. He's my only brother, the last link I have to my father. I don't want to lose him too."

Sammy reminded me of a younger, wilder version of my dad with his big heart, his restlessness, his sense of humor. My mother always pressured me to marry a nice guy and have kids, but my dad had understood, even encouraged, my ambition and drive. As long as Sammy was around, part of my father was still alive.

While most good people were in church, the next morning I sat at my beat-up oak desk in the *Gazette* office, staring at a stack of papers to file. What a treat. Sundays were called "Dead Day" in the newsroom because of the skeleton staff. Even the editor, Mr. Thomas, hadn't come in yet. Probably overslept, as usual. I couldn't quite picture him singing hymns in a choir.

I held my breath when I read Sunday's headline: DOWNTOWN CLUB DESTROYED BY FIRE: POLICE SUSPECT ARSON. Who'd set the fire—the Beach Gang? And why? Fortunately the Lotus Club, located on the Strand, was empty, so no one was hurt.

Sadly, gangs in Galveston were a fact of life, like the tides in the Gulf of Mexico. We couldn't control or ignore the gangs, but we did our best to stay out of their way. Better for our health and well-being.

As I shuffled papers, I felt jealous of the male reporters hunched over their typewriters, clacking away, or yammering on the telephone, trying to follow a lead or badger a source for information.

All the newshawks in town wanted a scoop, but when journalists hung out with cops, gangsters and bootleggers, you never knew the real facts. Sort of a silent code of un-ethics: Everyone got something out of the deal—protection, publicity, or pay-offs.

To a reporter hungry for hot tips, half the truth—and a small bribe—was better than a blank page. As long as their stories sold papers, even the most honest editors tried to look the other way.

Still, the *Gazette* had a reputation for truth and integrity, thanks to its above-board editor-in-chief, Mr. Thomas. If the reporters only knew what I'd witnessed last night: a hot potato dropped in my lap.

For now, Horace's collapse was only a scandal, good gossip at best. Unlike the yellow journalists, I wasn't content with half-truths, fabricated stories or outright lies masquerading as facts. It was a story without an ending—yet.

I tried to type up some copy—of course my boss never had to work on Sundays—but Andrews' pale face kept floating across my blank pages. By 10:30, I couldn't stand the suspense, and asked the operator to dial John Sealy Hospital.

When a nurse finally answered, I asked, "What's the condition of Mr. Horace Andrews? He was admitted there last night."

A brief pause, then a curt, "I'm afraid that information is confidential." The line disconnected. Damn!

I slunk back to my desk and tried to imagine what news the real reporters were covering: crime, politics, raids, gambling, turf wars, murder. After last night, how could I get excited about the Galveston Garden Club or local Ladies' Library Group?

Before noon, Nathan, a junior staff photographer and all-around go-fer, stopped by my desk. A year younger than me, Nathan was my best friend and ally at work. As the youngest reporter on the staff, I felt sorely outnumbered in the mostly-male newsroom.

Despite his breezy manner, Nathan always provided a shoulder to lean on, a listening ear. Whenever I was late to work, he blamed it on his Tin Lizzie, saying it had stalled while he was driving me to work. Everyone knew I took the trolley, but my boss bought it anyway. A full-time photographer, Nate came and went as he pleased. A good pal to have, especially in a jam.

Today he looked keen in his blue and white seersucker suit. He tipped his straw boater and leaned over my desk.

"Hey, toots. How about lunch?"

I wheeled my old oak chair around. "There's no time to eat. Now I need to go to the hospital."

Concern flickered in his slate-blue eyes. "What's wrong? Want me to drive you there?"

"I'm fine." I smiled at his worried expression. "Why don't we take the trolley? We can talk on the way."

Glad for a break, I grabbed my hat and tooled leather bag, and we snuck out while Mr. Thomas was taking a nap.

The streets were quiet and calm, a typical Sunday. As we walked to the trolley stop, I told Nathan about Andrews, enjoying his animated expressions. "Sounds like a wild night." He whistled. "Next time I can go along for protection."

"Thanks, Nate, but we don't need a chaperone."

"Your loss." His face fell. "Who's this guy anyway? Why all the fuss for a stranger?"

"He's a friend of Sammy's. A real gentleman." I mulled it over, thinking out loud. "Maybe it's morbid curiosity. Or else it's the most exciting thing that's ever happened to me!"

"Exciting?" He frowned. "Sounds like you were in the wrong place at the wrong time."

"I just hope he's alive and well, for Sammy's sake." Nathan had no idea Sammy was my half-brother, and I wanted to keep it that way. Sure, I trusted him, but not his nosy newshound pals.

Luckily, the trolley car was almost deserted when we boarded. The balmy breeze cooled off the hot summer day. We got off near the Strand, passing a Baptist church as a chorus of bells pealed twelve times. A well-heeled crowd filled the sidewalk, all buttoned up in their Sunday finest, looking like limp oleanders. Short palms lined the streets, planted after the 1900 storm, providing little shade.

Nathan fanned himself with his straw boater, his face a bright pink. "What makes you think the nurses will tell you anything about this Andrews fella?"

"They can't ignore his family. After all, he's our uncle."

"Uncle, huh?" He looked skeptical. "What if that doesn't work?"

"Then we can always eavesdrop on the nurses. Maybe you can turn on the charm." I smiled at him.

"Piece of cake. Anything to help our dear Uncle Horace."

Distracted, I crossed the street in front of an old Ford, but Nathan grabbed my arm. The driver honked his horn, yelling: "Watch where you're going, girlie!" Yikes!

As we approached John Sealy Hospital, I admired the handsome red brick façade, and its graceful arches and towers. Locals loved to show off the imposing Galveston landmark, designed by the famed architect Nicholas Clayton, built in 1890—a Great Storm survivor.

Inside, the pale interior—creamy marbled floors, high ceilings, arched windows—matched the nurses' crisp white uniforms and caps. They seemed to float down the corridors like ghosts, silent and solemn. I took a few deep breaths as a plump nurse with silver mesh hair approached, working up my nerve.

"I'm Mrs. Pierce, the head nurse. May I help you?"

I let out a sad sigh. "We're here to visit our uncle, Horace Andrews. What room is he in? I hope it's not too late."

Was that convincing enough?

The other nurses stopped talking. Not a good sign. "Let me check my records," she said, retreating behind a counter.

Nathan was eagerly eyeing a cute young nurse, so I poked him in the ribs. No cheerful smiles for our nearly departed uncle.

Mrs. Pierce looked sympathetic. "I'm sorry, but he's still in a coma. No visitors allowed."

"A coma?! Thank goodness!" I almost jumped for joy. There went my poker face.

She frowned, baffled by my outburst. "I mean, I'm glad he's alive. So there's a chance he'll recover?" I felt relieved, yet surprised. To me, he'd looked half-dead.

"That's up to our Lord," she said gravely, her eyes cast upward. "And his will to live."

An idea flashed. "Wasn't Uncle Horace hospitalized here before, for his heart? Or was it his liver?" Curious, I watched her reaction.

"You should know, if you are indeed his relatives," she snapped. "Your family will be informed of any changes. Good day." She turned away, clearly uncomfortable discussing Horace's unseemly health problems in public.

I felt like clapping. Andrews was still alive! I couldn't wait to tell Sammy the news.

After the nurse left, Nathan pulled me to a quiet corner.

"Seems our Uncle Horace has a history of getting zozzled. No wonder he's out cold. That bathtub booze will get you every time."

"Bathtub booze?" I made a face. "Bunk! Sammy doesn't serve cheap hooch."

"Are you sure? Maybe he's cutting corners, trying to save dough…"

"Of course I'm sure." I stared him down. "Sammy only buys the best stock available."

"Says who? You can't be too careful these days." Nathan edged closer, his voice a whisper. "I hear there's a bad batch of liquor going around town. Wood alcohol. Pure coffin varnish."

CHAPTER FIVE

"Wood alcohol? Who told you that?" I frowned at Nathan, hoping it wasn't true.

"You know how reporters like to talk—and drink. And drink." He looked smug. "Not that they'd spill the beans to a dame. But I've got my sources."

"Your sources? You mean that lot of lushes they call reporters?" I snapped. "That's a load of hooey. Horace had heart failure, plain and simple, like Doc said." Where was Doc now?

Irritated, I stormed down the corridor, far away from Nathan, determined to prove him wrong. I veered toward a side hall, trying to avoid the staff while checking the names on each door. No luck.

I peered inside a few open rooms, but only saw older women with visitors or nurses. Crossing the lobby, I heard a young flapper crying, as a man tried to console her, speaking with an Irish accent.

In a separate wing, I noticed a man who seemed to be asleep. Andrews? But when I started to enter, Mrs. Pierce appeared, blocking my way, thick arms folded over her ample chest. "Where do you think you're going, miss? I told you, no visitors allowed."

Not her again. "I'm looking for Nathan."

"Then I suggest you wait for him in the lobby."

Luckily, the cute young nurse walked up then. "Nathan? He's visiting his father. Room two twenty-one."

His father? What was that lollygagger up to now?

"Thanks." I smiled and followed her down the hall, leaving Mrs. Pierce peeved. Served that old biddy right.

Nathan stood at the bedside of a middle-aged man, hat in hand, and looked up, surprised. "Jasmine?" The man's features were swollen and bruised, his head bandaged, but he sat upright, alert. "You remember Mack. This is Miss Cross, the society reporter."

Mack Harris, our in-house Hemingway. I hardly recognized him without his trademark safari hat and cigar. I tried to shake hands, but he winced in pain. His face looked blank, as if he'd never seen me before. Swell. I must have made quite an impression at the paper.

"What happened to you? Are you OK?" I blurted out. I'd heard rumors Mack was 'out of commission' for a while, but I figured he was chasing a big story, not laid up in a hospital.

"Do I look OK? I'm stuck in this godforsaken hell hole. It's like a prison in here." So much for tact.

Still, I had a lot of respect for Mack. A Great War veteran, Mack became a foreign correspondent after getting shot in the leg. He was considered a crackerjack reporter, always chasing down the most exciting news stories. Behind his back, the reporters called him 'Robin Hood,' trying to right wrongs, but they were just jealous because his articles always made front-page news. The editors thought he was a hero, a threat to the gangsters in pin-striped suits.

I noticed his dark bruises, his right arm in a sling. "Were you in an accident?"

Mack looked me over as if I'd trespassed on sacred ground.

"To be honest, I don't remember all the details. Guess I poked my nose in the wrong places."

"What kind of places? Were you doing a story?"

"Don't worry your pretty little head. I'll be fine." He gave me a condescending smile.

"Fine?" Nathan said. "Those bastards tried to kill you!"

What? Which bastards? Mack looked away, tight-lipped. Then Mrs. Pierce entered and stood guard by his bed like a scary watchdog.

Her timing was uncanny. "Mr. Harris needs his rest. Visiting hours are over."

"We're just leaving." Nathan tugged on my arm, winking at Mack. "See you later, Pop."

"Thanks for coming." Mack tried to smile. Clearly he didn't like being interrogated, especially by a dame. But wasn't persistence the hallmark of a good journalist? Or was I being *too* pushy?

Outside, I shielded my eyes from the bright sun. "Why didn't you tell me Mack was here?" I asked Nathan, feeling both annoyed and upset, as we hurried down the Strand.

He raked his fingers through his sandy hair, mouth tight. "Mack didn't want anyone to know. Hell, I'm not supposed to know."

I admired his loyalty to Mack, but I was dying of curiosity.

"So what's the big secret? I could ask around town and find out," I challenged him.

Nathan glared at me. "You do that and it's Mack's funeral."

"Is he in some kind of trouble?" I pressed, but Nathan avoided my gaze. "Fine, I'll ask him myself!" I did an about-face and headed toward the hospital. Would Mack even talk to me?

I was already ten yards away before Nathan caught up, holding up his hands in surrender. "OK, you win." He frowned. "Mack was attacked after bar-hopping with our fellow muckrakers."

"What? Why?" I stared in surprise. "Any idea who did it?"

"Mack won't say—at least in print. All I know is he was working on a hush-hush story about the Beach and Downtown gangs."

Nathan clenched his jaw, upset, since he looked up to Mack. "He started snooping around their favorite bars—the Surf Club, Murdoch's, the Kit-Kat Club—asking lots of nosy questions the gangsters didn't like. Last week, two thugs cornered him, and worked him over. He woke up in Big Red, black and blue, getting his stomach pumped out."

"Poor Mack." Despite his gruff and tough exterior, at his age Mack was no match for young hoods. "What's his angle? What got them so rattled?"

"Promise to keep quiet?" Nathan looked at me sideways. "Mack was trying to confirm rumors about a gang take-over. Word is, Ollie Quinn and Dutch Voight want to muscle in on the Downtown Gang. They think Johnny Jack is getting too reckless, too greedy. Turns out he pulled a double-cross on the Beach Gang recently. Now Ollie wants to even the score. It's a real turf war."

"A double-cross? Sounds like trouble."

Johnny Jack Nounes was the flashy flimflam man who controlled the Downtown Gang's turf north of Broadway, including Market Street, where Sammy's bar was located. The Beach Gang covered the Seawall and area south of Broadway, home of the swanky Surf Club and Hollywood Dinner Club.

Sammy somehow managed to get along with both gangs, hedging his bets like a gambler in a high-stakes poker game. But how long would that last during a turf war?

I wished he'd get out of the booze biz, but he was in too deep.

"The gangs are always fighting—over bars, booze, money." I let out a sigh. "They think they own the Island and everyone in town."

"You said it." Nathan nodded.

We stopped to admire a baby in a frilly pram while the proud parents beamed. The mother looked so young in her blue frock and cap, like a girl playing dress-up.

"One day..." He smiled as they strolled past.

Who didn't like babies? I changed the subject, fast.

"Say, did you see today's front-page story about the Lotus Club fire? I hear it's the Downtown Gang's headquarters. I wonder if Ollie Quinn is trying to run Johnny Jack out of town?"

"I wouldn't be surprised. But they're playing with fire. Get it?" Nathan snickered at his own joke. "Now it's payback time."

CHAPTER SIX

As Nathan and I walked down the Strand, I thought I smelled smoke, ashes. "Isn't the Lotus Club near here?" I said. "Or what's left of it. Why don't we go by, take a look?" I picked up the pace. What did I expect to find—gold coins? Buried treasure? The arsonist? Wouldn't that be convenient?

"What's to see?" He frowned. "A pile of rubble?"

Nearing the Lotus, I could smell burnt wood, paper, metal. Specks of soot and ash floated in the air, filling my throat, stinging my eyes. I stopped short when I saw the club's charred remains, resembling a pitiful funeral pyre: scorched remnants of brick, glass, and twisted metal. Half a brick wall stood like Roman ruins, surrounded by assorted debris: a metal ice box, a few tables and chairs, a broken door. I was tempted to look for clues in the wreckage, but cops had blocked off the area. A small crowd stared at the pile of blackened debris, transfixed.

I'd never been to the Lotus, but Sammy once told me it was Johnny Jack's favorite club, a hole in the wall where he liked to mix business with booze. Who'd set the fire? Were they trying to kill Johnny Jack or just send a message?

A born con man, Johnny Jack had a mile-long list of enemies who knew his soft spots. I'd heard he used to be partners with Frank Nitti, Al Capone's right-hand man, so he learned from the best. Beach Gang leaders Ollie Quinn and Dutch Voight had to stand in line for a piece of Johnny Jack.

As I scanned the rough-and-tumble group of rubberneckers, my heart skipped a beat: Was that Mutt and Jeff in the crowd? What were they doing here now? Did they go to the Lotus after Dino kicked them out last night? I nudged Nathan. "Do you see those two guys, who kinda look like Mutt and Jeff?"

He nodded. "Why, do you know those jokers?"

"They're the same jerks who started a fight at the Oasis last night. Strange they showed up here today." I turned away, getting the jitters. "Let's hit the road before they see me."

I made a mad dash across the street, looking over my shoulder. Was it a fluke those bums came by the Lotus the day after the fire?

On the walk back, I said to Nathan, "I wish we could help Mack while he's laid up. Maybe we can try to find out if the Beach Gang torched the Lotus—and why?"

"What do you suggest? Call Ollie and ask if he and Dutch set the fire?" Nathan snorted, shaking a finger. "Don't go looking for trouble. You saw what happened to Mack."

Maybe he was right. I couldn't just waltz into the Surf Club and demand to know who burnt down the Lotus. Did I want to end up like Mack, beaten black and blue—or worse?

By the time we returned to the *Gazette*, Mr. Thomas was circling the newsroom, waving his cigar, flicking ashes on the floor. He was a big bear of a man, more of a Teddy than a grizzly, with his bulging belly and easy-going manner. His hands and clothes were perennially smudged with black printer's ink. Today he had on a wrinkled brown suit, topped by the brown felt derby he always wore, despite the heat, to cover his bald crown—as if no one noticed.

"Where were you two?" he bellowed. Some sap must have interrupted his nap.

"Lunch." Nathan shrugged. "Since when is it a crime to eat?"

Ignoring his wisecrack, Mr. Thomas said, "Young man, you need to be on a photo shoot this afternoon. And Jasmine, I've got some stories that need to be typed right away. Make it snappy!" We were invisible as long as we remained in the newsroom, but the moment we left, we were in demand. On Sundays, Mr. Thomas didn't have many people to pick on.

Actually, I was fond of Mr. Thomas the way you'd regard an eccentric uncle. He was a customer at my father's general store, and after my dad died, he'd pulled a few strings to help me get this job at the *Gazette*. Female reporters weren't exactly in demand, so he stuck me in society news for my own protection, so he said—away from crime and corruption—and gave me an honorary (meaning fake) title.

Of course I was grateful for a job, but how could I ever become a first-class reporter or foreign correspondent like Nellie Bly if they always kept me trapped in this ivory tower?

After I typed up the copy, I walked to Mr. Thomas' office to get his approval. I took a peek at Mack's notoriously messy desk, and noticed a few file folders and a notepad scattered on top, as if he'd never left. Tempting. Was anyone watching?

Hands shaking, I flipped open his pad, studying his scribbles. The phone on Mack's desk suddenly rang and I jumped, knocking the notebook and files onto the floor. "I've got it!" I yelled to divert attention, but I quickly hung it up. Crouching down, I gathered his papers, glancing around at desk-level. Luckily the coast was clear: Mr. Thomas was on the phone and Nathan was probably in the darkroom. With Mack in the hospital and the newsroom nearly empty, this was my only chance get my hands on his notes.

Would anyone notice if I *borrowed* his files? Flustered, I shoved the papers under my stack of stories, feeling like a bungling burglar. Breathless, I rushed back to my desk and hid the evidence under the newspaper. Was I wrong to snoop?

True, this wasn't like swiping penny candy from Woolworth's, it was much worse: an invasion of privacy, a breach of trust. I might get struck by lightning or go to hell or get canned, *if* I got caught. But since Mack was a journalist, didn't he intend to make his findings public? And wasn't I part of the public?

I deposited my typed stories in Mr. Thomas' office, and rushed back to my desk. Hunched over Mack's notebook, I could barely decipher his illegible scrawling, but I did make out a few words: rum, Cherokee, J Jack, Beach Gang, Black Jack, hijacking, boat. I skimmed through his folders but they were mainly clips of his past articles.

In the last folder, I got lucky. There was a rough draft about the Beach and Downtown gangs written in long-hand, with several crossed-out words and misspellings. Seems Mack was sidelined before it got published. My pulse raced as I read the article: Turned out Johnny Jack Nounes recently hijacked a $20K shipment of rum from a Cuban bootlegger meant for the Beach Gang. What gall! He even managed to outrun the Coast Guard in his speedboat, the Cherokee—and to top it off, he paid the unsuspecting Cuban rum-runner with soap coupons!

I stifled a smile as I scanned the article. If it was all true, it gave the Beach Gang plenty of motivation to set the Lotus Club on fire as revenge. Was this story the real reason Mack landed in the hospital?

"What's so funny?" Nathan peered over my shoulder.

Caught red-handed. "Just reading the cartoons. Don't tell my boss." I covered the notepad with my arms, faking a smile. If Nathan told anyone I'd swiped Mack's notes, I could be fired on the spot. "So what's new?"

"You tell me. How about a lift after work?" he offered. "Beats walking in this heat wave."

"Sounds swell. See you later," I said to get rid of him. After he disappeared into the darkroom, I wandered over to Mack's desk, then pretended to drop a pencil. Luckily, I managed to scoot the papers back to their spot without alerting the staff or the National Guard. Mission accomplished!

On the ride home, I wanted to tell Nathan all about Johnny Jack hijacking the Cuban rum boat, but I knew he'd get suspicious, wondering how I found out. I didn't like keeping secrets from good friends. Instead, I said, "It was hard seeing Mack laid up in the hospital. Do they suspect Mack drank some wood alcohol by mistake? Is that why they pumped his stomach?"

"Either that or he was poisoned, accidentally on purpose." He swallowed hard. "Mack can drink like a fish so he must have downed some bad booze. Then they beat him up for fun."

I hated to think what they could do to Sammy. Johnny Jack often accused him of playing both sides, and knew how to apply pressure to get his way: withholding liquor, asking for extra protection money, causing fights and accidents. Was Horace Andrews an accident too?

Monday morning, I arrived late to work, almost tripping over the disheveled newsie who belted out the large thirty-six-point headline: POISON ALCOHOL CLAIMS LOCAL VICTIM! Snatching the paper, I scanned the article, but the poor victim's name was Stan Brown. Was it a coincidence that he died the same night Andrews had his so-called heart attack?

Mrs. Harper gave me a cold nod as if I was tardy to class. She wore her voluminous auburn hair in an upswept 'do straight out of the Edwardian era, with oversized hats to match. Her frilly frock did little to disguise the numerous circles around her widening tree trunk.

A couple of cub reporters straggled in like they were hung-over. No surprise. With their lined faces and dark under-eye circles, they looked much older than their years, but I knew it was their lust for late nights, ladies and liquor. I wondered: Where did they go bar-hopping with Mack?

I took a deep breath and sashayed over to the bull pen, where a few reporters huddled together like a bedraggled football team, bragging about their weekend, their dames and their benders. The group got quiet, treating me like the rival team's cheerleader.

Sadly, most of these Neanderthals thought all women should get married and stay home and raise children, not go to college or have careers or lives of their own. Hadn't they heard the news? Women now had the right to vote, and the right to be treated as equals.

"Morning, boys." I pasted on a sunny smile. "Working hard or hardly working?"

They jabbed elbows while one joker whistled under his breath, but it wasn't meant as a compliment. Their faces reflected condescension mixed with curiosity, resentment mingled with reserve. Since I was considered "the weaker sex," they tried to play nice. One reporter tried to ask me out recently and didn't appreciate being turned down, a fact he didn't let me forget.

"Say, I heard you really tied one on last week. Sounds like fun."

"Yeah, if you call upchucking fun," Charles, a beat reporter, said.

"Where'd you go?" I asked innocently.

"Never mind." Charles gave me the up-and-down, then resumed his conversation with Hank, a sports writer and resident know-it-all.

Hank flicked his cigar ashes on the floor by my feet, his face smeared with a patronizing smile. "Why don't you fetch us a cup of joe, toots?"

My eyes ran the length of his torso. "Something wrong with your legs?"

The reporters snickered while Hank, looking irritated, shoved the cigar back in his mouth.

Ignoring him, I sidled up to a young cub reporter named Pete. "Hey, aren't you new around here? Have these guys taken you to Murdoch's or the Surf Club yet? I hear they're a hoot."

"Not yet." Pete winked. "Wanna go sometime?" The reporters shot him dirty looks and swiveled their chairs around. So that's how they wanted it, acting like brats guarding a tree house: No Girls Allowed. I knew they didn't respect "girl reporters," but I was tired of always being locked out of the good-old-boys club. Still, I'd managed to eliminate two of the gangs' bars so far.

"Maybe I'll see you there." I smiled at his hopeful expression. "Better get back to the old grindstone." Head held high, I returned to my desk, refusing to throw in the towel. I knew I wouldn't get far with that bunch of blowhards, but at least it was a start.

As I worked, I tried to eavesdrop on the big mouths who bragged about their journalistic conquests. Reporters loved to compare war stories in the newsroom. Someday I hoped to contribute a battle tale or two of my own, but Mack and his cronies had access to sources and places I could only dream about.

Meanwhile, I had to earn my meager living. Mrs. Harper had asked me to do a short profile of the Galveston Garden Club's new president, due that day. How exciting. I snuck in a back office and did a short phone interview with Mrs. Wilma Bartholomew, who seemed delighted to be featured in the *Gazette*. After I pounded out a rough draft, Mrs. Harper read it, saying, "Good job, Jasmine."

Big deal. I'd been writing tidbits about the boring Garden Club all year, but they mainly ended up as captions next to photos of grinning gardeners by their petunias. I'd even memorized all the botanical names of the local flowers by heart. I highly doubted that a story on wisteria and azaleas and wilted Southern belles would ever make front-page news.

While Mr. Thomas took his afternoon nap, I decided to grab a bite to eat. Mrs. Harper already left for a fancy-pants "ladies luncheon," wearing long white gloves that conveniently covered up her ink-stained hands. Golliwog, a skinny black cat who hung around the *Gazette* building, followed me as I crossed the street. A Bentley roared past, kicking up black fumes, swerving so close I thought it would hit Golliwog.

"Watch out!" I yelled at the driver, shaking my fist. I picked up a ham and cheese on rye from a street vendor, then sat on a bench in a small shady park, sharing my sandwich with Golliwog. Some reporters pretended she was a pest, but I knew they secretly had a soft spot for the straggly stray. We named her Golliwog after the cute Negro cartoon character because of her big eyes and long black fur that stuck out at all angles. I even had a bottle of Golliwog perfume on my vanity, a monthly splurge.

Back at the office, I finished typing up Mrs. Harper's column for Tuesday, and placed it on her desk, but she still hadn't come back from her luncheon. Restless, I couldn't seem to concentrate on proofing and filing and all the mundane details that made me the glorified assistant to a critical and demanding boss. Glancing at today's headline gave me an idea. I stopped by Mr. Thomas' office, asking: "Can I type up the obits for Tuesday?"

"Why? That's Mrs. Page's job." He frowned and leaned back, his oak chair creaking under his weight. "Since when are you so interested in dead people? You're supposed to write about the cream of Galveston society, active folks who do lots of interesting things."

"Yeah, like watching their gardens grow," I mumbled.

"What?" He looked puzzled. "Never mind. Look on her desk, if you're so curious."

"Thanks, Mr. Thomas." I made a bee-line for Mrs. Page, an older woman who served as the receptionist/secretary and unofficial gossip columnist. Like Mrs. Harper, she had the dirt on almost everyone in town. Had she heard about Mack and the gin-guzzling reporters? Luckily, she wasn't at her desk, so I rifled through her papers until I found the obits.

My heart sank as I scanned the statement on top, with a small photo attached. I hardly recognized the black-and-white snapshot of a young Horace Andrews, looking dashing in his soldier's uniform, age 20 or 22. No surprise most people sent in early, flattering photos of their loved ones. I supposed even the deceased were entitled to their vanity.

I skimmed the notice, hands shaking: "Horace C. Andrews, 32, departed this earth after heart failure to be with the Lord…A native of Galveston, Andrews graduated from Texas A & M on a full scholarship. He served his country for two years in the Great War and married Alice Wright in 1922. Andrews worked for Lone Star Bank for eight years, and was promoted to Vice President in 1925. Survivors include his wife and three children. Funeral services will be held on…"

There it was in black and white. Horace Andrews was no longer an object of pity or scorn: he was a successful banker, a war vet with a family and wife, a full life. So Doc was right, it was heart failure, not alcohol poisoning. Thank goodness. Still, I had a nagging doubt: Could wood alcohol cause a heart attack?

Bad news travels fast, especially in small towns like Galveston. Had Sammy heard about Horace yet? I wanted to break the news to him in person, before word of his death hit the papers. In his underground watering hole, I wondered how much contact Sammy had with the outside world. I stuffed the mortuary notice in my purse and began typing up the other obits, but the words were a blur, black mingling with white until I only saw shades of gray.

I looked for Nathan and found him by the darkroom. He took one look at my face and asked, "What's eating you?"

"I need a favor. Are you busy tonight?" I saw heads pop up around the newsroom.

"A date? Sure." He flashed a smile. "Where do you wanna go?"

"It's not a date." My face flushed. "Can we talk privately?"

He grabbed my wrist and pulled me into the darkroom as a few reporters snickered. Hound dogs. The darkroom glowed an eerie red. Several photos dried on a wire like wet clothes.

"Alone at last." I stepped back as he moved toward me, grinning like a scary jack 'o lantern.

"Cut it out, Nathan." I turned away, not in the mood for his jokes. "I just found out Horace Andrews died. We got the mortuary notice today."

"Uncle Horace?" His face fell. "Can't say I'm all broken up since I never met the guy."

Was he dense? "If the Feds find out Andrews was at the Oasis before he died, they may get suspicious and shut it down. I need to alert Sammy before it hits the papers."

"Forget it. I wouldn't be caught dead in that gin joint." He smirked. "Get it?

I gave him a tight smile. "Very funny. Please, can you take me there tonight? Sammy may be in trouble." I hated having to constantly hitch rides with Nathan, but my family couldn't afford a car so I'd never learned how to drive.

"OK, I'll go as a favor." He pretended to gag. "Just don't make me drink the joy juice."

CHAPTER SEVEN

"Getting hot in there?" Hank wriggled his brows when Nathan and I emerged from the darkroom. A few reporters exchanged sly smiles and winks. Who cared? Let them have their jollies.

"Too hot to handle," Nathan shot back. I rolled my eyes, ignoring their juvenile jabs.

Finally Mrs. Harper appeared, all aflutter in her huge floral hat and pink frock, still giddy after her luncheon—no doubt aided by more julep than mint from her aroma. Solemnly, I handed her the mortuary notice. "Do, did, you know Horace Andrews?"

A freshly-manicured hand flew to her mouth. "What happened? Oh no!" She gasped and gripped the sheet, mouthing the words, as if in disbelief. "Poor Alice...all those children."

"How well did you know him?" I asked. Figured my nosy boss knew everyone in town. Still, I couldn't quite picture prim and proper Mrs. Harper at a smoky speakeasy with her ruffles and curls. But then again, you never knew who might turn up at underground bars.

"Only socially. He was so kind and generous at charity events. Alice is such a sweet young thing...Whatever will she do?" she wailed, blinking.

"I'll be glad to write a profile on him," I offered. "To honor his memory. He was a family friend, you see." Not a total lie. Maybe it was morbid, but I wanted to give him a final farewell.

"A family friend?" Her brows arched in surprise. "Fine, if you're sure you're up to it. I've hated writing up these horrible obits since the Great Storm. The stacks of bloated bodies rotting on the beach, all the debris and wood covering the island."

She shut her eyes, on the verge of tears. "I can still see those pitiful faces. So tragic. I had nightmares for years."

I'd heard the horror stories and seen the grisly photos of the 1900 storm that killed more than six-thousand people. Without warning, the winds and floods hit Galveston with such force that hundreds of homes and buildings were destroyed and thousands of families were torn apart; overnight, children became orphans.

Despite the Seawall and extensive reconstruction, Galveston had yet to fully recover. Fortunately, my parents had moved here years later, as the town was being rebuilt, so we were spared the suffering. Amanda wasn't so lucky—she lost her grandparents during the deadly storm.

"I'll need it right away," Mrs. Harper said. "Call the bank first, try to meet his boss and co-workers. Poor Alice may be too distraught to talk to any reporters yet." Then she waved her hand in dismissal. "I hope you'll do him justice, for Alice's sake. Please do give her my best."

The profile was a perfect excuse to do more digging, to try to find out the real reason a big-shot banker was at the Oasis on a Saturday night. Sure, a yellow journalist could write a sensational article—with a salacious headline like: BANK VP DIES AFTER GETTING BLOTTO IN BAR. But no matter how much I wanted that front-page byline, I'd never stoop so low to sell papers. Would I?

To prepare, I went downstairs to the morgue where decades of old newspapers and magazines were stored. The basement was dark and dusty, smelling of mold and mildew.

Mark, a Ball High student, waved his scissors at me, surprised. "Hiya, Jazz. What brings you here?"

"Hello yourself. Research for Mrs. Harper," I fibbed, sitting down under a dim light.

I flipped through the yellowing pages, blinking at the clouds of dust, and looked up Lone Star Bank. In the business section, an article declared: "Horace Andrews promoted to Vice President" next to a grainy photo of Andrews shaking hands with the bank's president, Mr. Earl Jones.

As I skimmed the "Society News," a photo of Mr. and Mrs. Andrews caught my eye, posing for posterity, with this caption: "Mrs. Horace Andrews named chair of the Firemen's Fund Ball." Was it a coincidence she'd chaired the fund-raiser right after her husband's promotion? The moment a man's clout rose in status, his wife's stock went up as well. Society cliques could be so predictable.

I felt a stab of guilt: Andrews was right. We *had* met before, at the Firemen's Ball. I'd gone with Mrs. Harper—my first formal society event—but she'd bossed me around like an errand girl. Worse, she'd paraded me in front of the firemen like a prize cow. She's worried I'll end up an old maid like my aunt—but unlike Eva, my heart didn't flutter over men in uniform. Then she'd edited my article beyond recognition and replaced my byline with hers, as usual.

Lost in thought, I was looking for more articles when the phone rang. Mark called out, "Mrs. Harper is looking for you. She seemed surprised you weren't at your desk."

Why was she keeping tabs? I rushed upstairs, trying to work up the nerve to call Horace's boss at the bank. I didn't want to use the communal candlestick phone by my desk, surrounded by nosy reporters and noisy typewriters. Even my Remington Noiseless didn't live up to its name. So I snuck into an empty office for privacy, and after expressing my sympathy, made an appointment to meet Phillip Clark, a vice president, later that day.

That afternoon, I arrived on time at Lone Star Bank, admiring the large lobby with its huge marble columns and streamlined glass light fixtures. I wished I was a more frequent visitor, but sadly, I had few funds to contribute to the bank's coffers.

The cranky receptionist ordered me to write down my name and pointed to the lobby. Yes, ma'am! I felt like saluting. Mrs. Harper rarely allowed me to do face-to-face interviews, and to date I'd only interviewed a few society matrons. I didn't want to let on that I was a novice, so I'd prepared a list of questions I studied like a pop quiz.

"You're too nice and polite," Nathan often told me. "You're afraid to ask nosy questions, to be aggressive."

Couldn't I be polite and be a good journalist? How could I ever get any experience if I remained locked up in the *Gazette* dungeon?

I drummed my fingers on my pad as I waited for Mr. Clark, who turned out to be a nice-looking chestnut-haired man, in his late thirties. As we shook hands, I smiled and discreetly glanced at his ring finger: no wedding band. He seemed to fit my aunt's type to a T, conservative and cultured.

"Thanks for seeing me on such short notice," I told him, trying to cover up my lack of experience with a confident smile. I sat down in a plush leather chair in his big corner office, admiring a black marble inkwell set adorned with a sleek gazelle.

"My pleasure," said Mr. Clark, nodding. "Andrews used to be my supervisor. Such a shame about his heart attack. A fine man, too." He seemed surprised, but pleased, that I was writing about Andrews for the *Gazette*.

I confirmed a few facts, wanting to add a personal touch, pretending I was a real reporter. "What was Andrews like as a boss? Were you two friends?"

"A good egg." He nodded, leaning back in his oak chair. "Always ready to lend a helping hand. Showed me the ropes here. Horace was by the book, a bit of a stuffed shirt, but we got on well."

His shirt certainly wasn't stuffed that night at the Oasis.

"What about his job history? His duties?"

"You'll have to talk to Mr. Jones," Clark said. "Sorry, but I've only been here a year."

"Where was his office?" I wanted to take a peek, curious about its contents. Most men considered office size and location a sign of prestige, a barometer of success.

"You're looking at it, thanks to our bank president, Mr. Jones." Clark beamed, puffed up with pride. "No use letting such a big office sit empty." Who could blame him?

He extracted a thin cigar from an enameled geometric box on his desk. "By the way, if you talk to Alice Andrews, please give her my regards." His concern seemed genuine. "She's too young to be left all alone. Such a lovely woman."

"I'll be glad to." I couldn't help but wonder: Was Clark carrying a torch for Mrs. Andrews?

He directed me toward Mr. Jones' office and as I crossed the lobby, I heard murmurs and voices whispering, "It's him. Rose Maceo." I turned to see a short stocky, olive-skinned man in a gray pin-striped suit shaking Mr. Jones' hand.

Everyone in town knew about the Maceo brothers, who were gaining a stronghold on Galveston society and politics. The Maceos were former barbers turned bootleggers, with Big Sam providing the public face, and Papa Rose, the behind-the-scenes force.

Mr. Jones smiled and patted Maceo's back like they were old buddies. The Italian thug strode through the bank, right by me, dark eyes squinting as if he wasn't used to bright lights. I was surprised that their friendship seemed so public, when we all knew how the Maceos earned their money. Even bootleggers and gangsters had to stash their cash somewhere.

Rose Maceo was close to my height, but built like a German tank: solid, broad and just as deadly. He brushed by me and gave me a cold glance. I shivered when I met his steely gaze, wondering if all the stories about him were true. How did he get his nickname, the "iron fist?" I'd heard his violent temper caused a few mysterious deaths, but they were never solved.

Despite Prohibition, as long as the bucks and booze were flowing, Galveston gangsters were bulletproof.

I rearranged my hat, trying to regain my composure before entering Mr. Jones' office, but my knees felt wobbly. "Wasn't that Rose Maceo?" I asked, forgetting my manners.

"Mr. Maceo comes here every Monday, like clockwork." He nodded, unfazed by the question, smoking a pipe behind his massive walnut desk. "How can I help you, young lady?"

"I'm Jazz Cross from the *Gazette*. I'm writing a profile on Horace Andrews for the business section." I quickly sat down, not waiting for an invite.

"Glad to help." Poor fat, bald, homely Mr. Jones resembled the frog little girls had to kiss before they found Prince Charming. "Horace was one of our brightest and best. He started as a teller almost ten years ago, and worked his way up. Never a complaint. Rarely missed a day. He was one of our shining stars here at Lone Star. Such a pity."

I nodded, and pulled out my pad of questions. "What were his responsibilities?"

"Three years ago, he was promoted to vice president. He'd started bringing in so much business, we even created a new position for him: 'Vice President of New Accounts.'"

"So he was a real go-getter." Very interesting. "What kind of accounts did he handle?"

"Too many to recall. Mainly small businesses. Groceries, dry goods stores, restaurants... you know, mom-and-pop type places."

I wondered what they'd consider the Oasis, since there wasn't a mom or a pop.

"Horace also managed a few foreign accounts, mainly shipping, import and export," Jones added.

"What did they import or export?" Any booze? I wanted to ask, but kept my trap shut.

"Dry goods, textiles, spices, and cotton, of course." He leaned forward, his face eager. "You're too young to remember, but Galveston was once the biggest port in the South, before the Great 1900 Storm. Over two-thirds of Galveston's buildings and homes were destroyed. Still, we bounced back.

"In only six years, several teams of engineers and builders helped elevate the city by several feet. They built the Seawall of solid concrete, over three miles long and seventeen-feet high. A true marvel of engineering." Jones boasted as if he'd reconstructed the city all by himself.

"Amazing," I agreed. Sadly, Galveston had never recovered from that devastating blow. Houston's Ship Channel was taking over as the area's biggest port, one more drain on the local economy—and the main reason why local bankers welcomed shady customers like the Maceo brothers.

Jones leaned back and plunked his black leather cowboy boots, tooled with bucking broncos, on his desk. "Did you know that Galveston was once the center of commerce in Texas? The Strand used to be called "the Wall Street of the Southwest" in the late 1800s. In fact, *The Galveston Daily News* was the first and biggest newspaper in Texas." He sighed. "Those were the good old days."

I smiled, familiar with stories of Galveston's glorious past. But frankly, I didn't want a history lesson. So I blurted out: "Did Andrews have any problems at work? Any conflicts with customers or coworkers? Was he depressed or upset about anything?"

Was that brazen enough for Nathan?

He frowned as he sucked on his pipe, filling the office with the aroma of cherry tobacco. "What? Why do you want to know?"

I blinked away the smoke. "Did Andrews have any health or personal problems? Anything unusual happen recently?"

"Say, what's going on?" His tone changed from congenial to confounded. "Why are you asking me all these nosy questions about Horace Andrews? Is this really for the paper?"

"I'm just doing my job, sir," I sat up, fidgeting with my pencil. "See, he was a family friend, so I've taken a personal interest in this matter." Who was I kidding?

"Well, your interest seems a bit *too* personal, young lady!" He slammed back his chair. "What business is it of yours? You'd better leave right now and stop wasting my time!"

"Sorry, sir." I avoided his glare, blushing beet red. Time to exit, stage right. I jumped up, fumbled with my purse and pad, and bolted out of his office. My face on fire, I darted across the lobby, avoiding the curious stares, hoping no one recognized me.

"What was your name again?" Mr. Jones roared out the door as I sprinted toward the exit like it was a finish line.

Jeepers! So much for my savvy interviewing skills. I hoped Mr. Jones wouldn't call my boss to complain and get me axed. Maybe Mrs. Harper was right—I'd better stick to society news and gossip.

I was too humiliated to go back to the *Gazette*, so I trudged home, my head down the whole way, hoping I still had a job.

Why did I think I could tackle this on my own? All I wanted to do was help Sammy, but I only ended up making a fool of myself.

CHAPTER EIGHT

To cheer myself up, that night I got dolled up in a gauzy rose frock, matching cloche cap and a long strand of pearls, faux of course. On my salary I could barely afford a powder puff. Still, it was better than no job. All evening I'd brooded, wondering if I'd get fired from the *Gazette*. Now would I have to change banks *and* jobs?

My aunt was at her quilting bee, so I didn't have to invent any excuses when Nathan picked me up. He eyed me up and down, acting like I was a banana split with cherries on top.

"You're the bees knees!" He whistled. "Why don't you dress like that for work?"

"Why? So I can get black ink all over my clothes?" I pretended to be annoyed, but was secretly pleased that he'd noticed my efforts at primping. Who else did I have to impress?

Nathan drove like he owned a race car, not a rusty old Ford, messing up my careful spit curls. "Say, why don't we go to the Hollywood Dinner Club instead, see some real entertainment?"

I frowned. "Don't be a spoilsport. You know I have to see Sammy. Why'd you agree to come tonight?"

"'Cause I don't want to read your obit in the *Gazette*, that's why," he snapped. "Why else would I risk my neck?"

"I appreciate it, Nate." My voice softened. "Eva would be upset if I came here alone."

He winked. "Maybe you can return the favor." What did that mean? Was he being fresh? "So how was your interview at the bank? Did you bowl them over?"

"Of course." I smiled, failing to mention that the bank president practically threw me out of his office. I'd never live it down at work—if I still *had* any work.

When we got to Market Street, Nathan parked at the Atlas Paint store nearby, and opened my door.

"Let me do the talking. I happen to know the right password."

At the Oasis, I tapped a code on the door. It was a formality, but Sammy and I thought it best to pretend we weren't family.

"What's the word?" I recognized Dino's growl.

Sammy changed the password—actually a sentence—weekly to trip up strangers. "My ma plays Mah Jong all night long."

"Never mess up, do you, Jasmine?" Dino sounded testy as he slid open the window.

"I have connections." I ignored his sour expression. "I'm looking for Sammy."

He cracked open the door. "It's a bad time to come by. He's not in a real good mood."

"Can you blame him?" I pushed past Dino.

"Who's the gutter-crawler?" Dino locked eyes with Nathan and crossed his sizable arms.

"Don't worry, he's a friend." I yanked Nathan inside before Dino could block his way.

"Looks like a snitch to me." Dino slammed the door and returned to perch on his stool.

"Sorry, Nate." What was his beef? "If you don't mind, I need to talk to Dino now. Meet me at the bar."

"Good luck. I doubt that dumb wop can even carry on a conversation," he said, barreling down the stairs.

Dino's face twisted in fury, like he wanted to smack us. Ouch.

"How's tricks?" I smiled to lighten the mood. "Keeping busy?"

He shrugged. "Folks aren't breaking down the door to get in, as you can see." True, Dino seemed to be gathering dust.

"Any problems since Saturday?"

"What's it to you?" He scowled. "You snooping for the paper or something?"

"Just curious. Excuse me for asking." I turned to go. Trying to get Dino to blab was like talking to a cigar store Indian.

Downstairs, I sat next to Nathan at the bar, feeling a strange sense of déjà vu: I almost expected to see Horace—perched on a bar stool, or passed out on the floor.

"Real friendly place they got here," Nathan griped, drumming his fingers on the counter.

"Dino's the resident bulldog. He's just jittery after…you know. Relax. Have a drink."

Nathan stared at me in mock-horror. "Thanks, but no thanks."

"How about a soda pop then? My treat," I offered.

"In that case, I'll take a Manhattan," he said, grinning. "I like to live dangerously."

"Make that two," I told Frank, who frowned at Nathan. "So what's new? Where's Sammy?"

"He's in the office, but he's been down in the dumps. Maybe you can cheer him up."

"Dump is right," Nathan said. "Look at this dive."

"Hush," I poked him, but I had to agree. Dirty dishes littered the tables and the stench of stale smoke, grease and sweat hung in the air. The grand piano stood silent in the corner, as if in mourning. A handful of customers nursed their drinks, whispering, afraid of their shadows. The whole place had as much activity as a funeral parlor after hours. Even Doria seemed depressed.

"So how's business?" I asked Frank, knowing the answer.

"It's been real quiet, too quiet." He wiped his glasses on his starched white shirt. "No customers, no problems. But we're still here, holding down the fort."

I gave Nathan the eye. "Hey, I can take a hint." He jumped off his barstool, saying, "How about some music? Isn't there a phonograph around here? A wireless radio?"

Leaning over the bar, I motioned Frank over. "Did you hear the bad news about Andrews? Doc was right—he had heart failure."

"I hope to God that's all it was." Sweat dotted his forehead but that was normal when it was humid as a swamp inside and out. Even the big blocks of ice by the bar had already melted.

"What do you mean?" I challenged Frank. "It was in the newspaper. I saw the mortuary notice myself."

"You know how people like to talk, spread rumors."

"Which rumors? You mean the one about a bad batch of booze going around town?"

"Hell, I don't know for nothing." His face looked blank, but his eyes gave him away.

"Did you see the headline yesterday—about alcohol poisoning?" Unlike Dino, Frank actually knew how to read. "You think it's a coincidence—that two men died in one week?"

"So what? They died of different causes—at different clubs. So far we've been lucky." He rapped his knuckles on the oak bar.

"What was Andrews drinking?" I lowered my voice. "Is it possible he got a bad bottle of booze?"

"Who knows?" Frank blanched, looking down. "I'll be honest. We can't always tell the good stuff from the bad. We don't make the liquor here, just mix it and pour it on request. Mistakes happen. Face it, we're not dealing with a bunch of Baptist preachers."

Was he pointing fingers? "But Sammy said he's always extra careful. He told me he pays top dollar for his stock, and only buys from the most reputable suppliers," I argued.

"Those snakes?" Frank snorted. "They'll stab their own brothers in the back to make a buck. When demand goes up, the suppliers get creative. Say this first-class bootlegger got low on stock and bought some moonshine from a farmer with an old still in his backyard. They got sloppy."

"Oh yeah?" I didn't want to believe him. "So why didn't anyone else get sick that night—or die?"

Frank shrugged. "Let's hope it doesn't happen again."

"You said it." Rumors about "bad booze" and "wood alcohol" could spread like a gasoline fire. Then Prohibition agents might try to shut down the Oasis—permanently. I heaved a sigh, looking around the empty bar. "Can you tell Sammy I'm here?"

"Stay put while I get him," Frank told me. "Buzz, come watch the bar, will ya, kid?"

Buzz bounded up like a gangly colt. "Hiya, Jazz! Wanna cold soda pop?"

"How about a Nehi?" I told him, wondering what happened to our cocktails. I sipped on my soda, surveying the dim room. What a contrast from Saturday night. The once-colorful scene was now awash in sepia.

Nathan sat by a hotsy-totsy harlot who wore a low-cut red dress, and fancy red satin shoes with bows. Her pink rouged cheeks formed perfect silver dollar circles; black kohl rimmed her eyes. Nathan could charm a sphinx if he wanted. Charm wouldn't get him very far with her type, but cash might do the trick.

What was keeping Sammy? Impatient, I walked over to his office, ready to knock. But as I stood outside, I overheard Frank say, "He was my friend, too. He lent me money when I needed it, no questions asked. Wish I'd paid him back, but I was working on it."

"How?" Sammy snapped. "By getting him plastered? You know how careless he got when he was all hooched up."

"Don't blame me," Frank said. "I tried to stop him, but…"

Slowly I backed away from the door. What was going on? Sounded as if Frank owed Horace money, but he was letting him drink it off instead.

Then Sammy walked out, his fine features spoiled by cuts and a fresh black eye. Upset, I rushed toward him, reaching out to examine his swollen face. "What happened? Were you in a fight?" His hot temper was legendary.

Sammy touched his eye and winced. "Had to deal with some tough customers, that's all." As usual, he was evasive so I didn't really expect a straight answer.

"Customers?" I raised my brows. "Did the Downtown Gang pay you a visit?" Both gangs demanded protection money from the bars on their turf, but they liked to call it "rent."

"Bunk." Shaking his head, he led me to a quiet table, collapsing in a chair like a lanky marionette. "So what brings you by? Thought our freak sideshow might close us down—for good." He seemed depressed, beaten down, as if he'd lost his life savings on a bad bet.

"I guess you heard about Andrews." That was obvious from everyone's glum demeanor. "He had heart failure, like Doc said. It's official. His obituary will be in tomorrow's paper."

"Thank God." Relief swept over his handsome face. "I had no idea he had a weak heart. I wish I'd been here to help."

Nathan walked over and whistled under his breath. "Wow, that's some shiner you got, pal." Seems he struck out with the lady in red.

"You should see the other guys," Sammy cracked, turning to me. "Who's your friend?"

What other guys? "Sammy, meet Nathan. He's a shutterbug at the *Gazette*. He's A-OK."

A shadow crossed Sammy's face, but he nodded at Nathan, who shook his hand hard, like they were long-lost pals. "How are ya?" He motioned toward Doria. "Really like that mermaid over the bar."

"Doria is a figurehead from Sammy's old ship," I explained. "She brings him good luck."

"Didn't help us much Saturday night." Sammy flipped his hand toward Doria in disgust. "Worthless piece of driftwood."

Now I knew he was in a bad mood.

Frank held out a metal tray, and set down two drinks in white china teacups. Nathan took a sip and sputtered, "Coca-Cola? Is this a joke? Where's my Manhattan?"

Sammy looked apologetic. "Not taking any chances now. Better stick to pop 'til this mess clears up."

"How about a real beer? Or at least a near-beer?" Nathan asked, heading to the bar.

"So how are things?" Sammy seemed so downcast, I was almost afraid to ask.

"How's it look? My customers go to Joe's next door. They can get soda pop from Star Drugstore." He ran his hand through his curly dark hair. "Still can't believe Horace is gone. When I left Saturday night, the joint was jumping. When I returned, it was a goddamned morgue."

I patted his arm. "It's a slow night. Your customers will return soon."

"Not soon enough. That's loyalty for you. Why do people assume something's wrong with my, uh, merchandise? I only stock the best. I don't buy crap off the street."

"That's what I said to..." Oooops.

"What? Who's talking behind my back?" His hazel eyes flashed. "What'd you say?"

"All I said to Frank was maybe you got a bad batch of booze, by mistake." I swallowed, trying to change the subject. "Say, I heard rumors that Johnny Jack hijacked a Cuban boat full of rum, worth twenty grand. Is it true?"

That did the trick. "I wouldn't be surprised." Sammy grinned. "He's got balls the size of coconuts."

Coconuts? What a picture. I blushed, but Sammy turned even redder. "Sorry, you know what I meant. Johnny Jack is hard-boiled. He thinks it's all fun and games trying to outrun the Coast Guard in his launch, but some day he'll get caught. And he'll pay, big-time."

"His speedboat, the Cherokee? I heard the rum belonged to the Beach Gang. Is it true?" He averted my gaze, which told me plenty. "So is that why they burned down the Lotus Club? As revenge?"

Sammy jerked upright. "Who told you that? Those bloodhounds at the paper? They should mind their own business." He shook a finger at me. "You stay out of it. Don't go spreading any gossip."

"I'm not a gossip!" I fumed, my face hot. I hadn't meant to get him so riled up, but now I knew the rumors were true.

Then without warning, a shrill buzzer sounded in the kitchen, piercing our ears. Saved by the buzzer.

Now what? I stood up, heart racing. "What's that? A fire alarm?"

"Stay calm. I'll go see what's wrong." Sammy leapt up, knocking over his chair.

Dino raced downstairs, waving his arms in the air. "Cops are coming! Pipe down!"

Nathan rushed over, giving me a worried look. "Just our luck. Geez, this place is jinxed."

CHAPTER NINE

"Cops? You sure?" Sammy asked Dino, who yelled back in Italian, as if Sammy understood. Then Sammy signaled to Frank, issuing commands like an Army general. Frank yanked the liquor bottles and glasses off the shelves, hiding them under the counter.

Then he lowered a thin wood partition, concealing the bar area. Sammy had designed and built it himself, modeled after his old roll-top desk. The rest of the liquor bottles were safe in a secret hideaway in his office. Without the telltale signs of booze, the Oasis could pass for any ordinary diner. All it needed was fresh red carnations and crisp white tablecloths.

Some bulbs flickered on, highlighting the worn wood floors and brick walls covered with old photographs. In a flash, the Oasis was transformed into a cozy, albeit smoky and dark, family restaurant—if you consider a few woozy sailors and floozies "family."

Calm and collected, Sammy walked around the bar like a kindergarten teacher soothing his students. "Keep quiet—this will all blow over soon." A man tried to sneak out by the kitchen, but Dino blocked the door. Buzz ran to hide in the office, his rubbery face animated and afraid.

"What's the gag?" I asked, panicky. "Another false alarm?"

"Who knows?" Sammy shrugged. "But I'm playing it safe."

He disappeared into the kitchen with Dino and Frank. Moments later, they emerged with plates of hot spaghetti, and distributed them to all the customers with a clatter.

Nathan glanced at the food, then at me, baffled. "Nice spread. Too bad I'm not hungry."

"Try to work up an appetite." I nudged him. "Just in case."

Suddenly a loud bang sounded, a crash, a door cracking. Heavy footsteps pounded down the stairs and three men in dark suits entered the bar, holding badges. Their pistols raised high above their heads, the trio circled the room like Wild West gunslingers. No place to hide. A stocky man shoved Dino against the wall and, for once, he didn't fight back. Sammy must have warned him to be on his best behavior. Frank crept toward the back like a spy, trying to disappear into the woodwork.

I'd never been in a raid before, but I'd seen them on news reels. My heart banged in my chest as I braced myself for the worst. What if we all got arrested and thrown in jail?

"Federal Agent James Burton, Treasury Department. Don't move and no one will get hurt!" yelled the tallest of the trio. Over six feet, he wore a fancy three-piece beige suit and felt hat. I didn't know flatfoots got paid so well.

Cool as ice, Sammy sauntered out from the kitchen, smiling at the coppers as if they were regulars.

"Welcome! How can I help you gentlemen?"

"You can tell us where you keep your booze," Agent Burton said, scanning the room.

"Booze? You're in the wrong place, boys. All we serve here is good food and soda pop." Sammy wiped his hands on a dirty red apron he'd thrown on for effect. "Hungry? How about today's special—home-made spaghetti?"

"We need a drink to quench our thirst," said Burton. "On the rocks, since we're on duty."

Sammy feigned surprise—not a bad job of acting for an amateur. "How about root beer or a Coke? The only cold drinks we serve here are soda pop. We're bone dry."

"That's not what we heard—Mr. Cook, is it? We hear this place is full of hooch."

I held my breath, trying to quell a bad case of the screaming meemies. How'd he know Sammy's name? Who mentioned any hooch? Agent Burton and his men slid between the tables, his eyes dancing back and forth, studying each customer, as if memorizing their faces.

A burly cop in glasses pointed to an older bald man cowering in his chair. "You there! What's that poison you're drinking?"

"It's lemonade," the man stammered. "I swear."

"Looks like a cocktail to me." The agent stuck his finger in the glass, tasted it, then threw it down. Glass splintered into tiny slivers as liquid seeped into the wood floor. The agents circled the room like hawks, glancing into the kitchen and behind the bar.

When Agent Burton opened the office door, Sammy froze.

"Say, who's this youth?" Burton pulled Buzz out by his collar. "Is he yours? Isn't he a bit young to be hanging out at a juice joint?"

I'd forgotten about Buzz. There were no laws against child labor, but naturally society didn't consider it proper to employ youths in a bar, especially during Prohibition. Dropping his friendly façade, Sammy marched over to Burton, his boots crunching on broken glass, and took Buzz's arm. "I told you it's a diner, not a bar. Leave him alone. Who do you think you are?"

"Like I said, name's Burton," he said, as if talking to a dim-witted child. "I'm the new head of Galveston's Prohibition enforcement office." He held up his badge like a shiny trophy.

The two men were polar opposites: With his tanned skin and thick honey-blond hair, Burton resembled a Golden Retriever ready to attack a Doberman. No contest, if you ask me.

"You're wasting your time here. No need to harass my help or my customers."

"Seems your customers like to play rough." Burton tapped his own cheekbone, indicating Sammy's black eye.

I nudged Nathan under the table, impressed by Sammy's bravado. But maybe this wasn't the best time to question authority. His big mouth could earn him a fat lip.

"What's going on?" I whispered to Nathan. My throat was so dry, I could barely speak.

"Who knows? Never been invited to a raid before."

Burton must have heard us because he strode over to our table, and draped an arm over my chair. "Evening, ma'am. What's a classy dish like you doing in this crummy gin mill?"

"Get your hands off me!" I gulped, shrugging off his arm.

He backed away, as surprised as I was by my response. Up close, I noticed how young he was, late twenties, face smooth and tanned.

Nathan stood up, a full head shorter than Burton. "Back off, buster. Leave my date alone."

Obviously Burton's gun and badge failed to impress Nathan. What he lacked in stature, he made up for with attitude. An attitude that could land us both in jail.

"Your date?" He raised his brows. "Lucky guy." Then he took a sip from my teacup, and spit it out.

"If you'd asked me politely, I could've told you it was Coca-Cola." Watch it, Jazz. In school, I'd often gotten in trouble for talking back to my teachers, but they hadn't carried a badge or a gun.

"Excuse my manners, miss. I can't resist a pretty face and a smart mouth." Why all the fuss—over me? I hate to admit, I felt a bit flattered, but I didn't want this kind of attention.

Then Agent Burton took off his hat, and strode toward Sammy. "Heard about an unfortunate incident the other night, and I was checking up on my leads." Did he mean Horace Andrews?

"Check your leads somewhere else," Sammy snapped. "I run a nice family restaurant."

"Oh yeah? What kind of family restaurant serves soft drinks in china teacups in the middle of the night?" He picked up my cup, then banged it down, Coke splashing over the sides.

"These folks can come here anytime they want." Sammy turned his back, picking up our plates. "We serve people who work all shifts, night and day—dames, sailors, wildcatters, doctors. Even if we sold liquor, which we don't, drinking booze isn't illegal, as you know."

"So you know your Volstead Act. Well, you can't be too careful these days. Lots of folks guzzling that bathtub booze. Sad to say, it can be fatal." He poked Sammy's chest, not once, but twice. "We'll keep an eye on you, Mr. Cook."

Then Burton tipped his hat at me. "Sorry to bother you, miss. Just doing my job, trying to protect the good citizens of Galveston from the ills of society. Hope I didn't ruin your date."

What date? "Not at all." I bit my lip so I wouldn't tell him off.

"Why let a little raid spoil our fun?" Nathan reached across the table and took my hands, but I yanked them away. Such an opportunist. He had about as much nerve as Agent Burton.

"I've got a business to run," Sammy told Burton. "You can show yourself out."

"You don't have to ask twice," he said. "See you later, Sammy." The trio turned on their heels, leaving as suddenly as they'd appeared.

"Good night, officers!" Sammy called out as they retreated, then muttered, "Good riddance."

No real harm done, yet. Still, I was skeptical: Where were the gun shots, the club sticks, the axes I'd heard about? Why didn't they arrest anyone, or at least toss the place? Was this a real raid—or a dress rehearsal?

Like a mass cattle stampede, the customers raced toward the stairs. Sammy followed them, waving his hands in the air like batons. "Come back soon, folks." He sounded upset, pleading for a second chance. "Drinks are on me next time."

A beet-faced man yelled, "Are you nuts? I'll never show my face in here again!"

Nothing like a little raid to spoil a cocktail party. Sammy walked over to our table, his smile forced, and patted our backs. "Close call, huh? We really showed those bastards. If those damn cops don't warn me next time, I'll break their scrawny necks."

"I wanted to punch that Fed right in the kisser," Nathan grumbled. "What a piker. Flashing his badge, strutting around like a damn peacock."

"You were swell," I told Sammy. "But what's the gag? They didn't even look for any liquor."

"You're right." Sammy nodded, his olive eyes clouding. "These jokers were the Welcome Wagon from the Treasury Department. This was no raid, it was a warning. A threat."

CHAPTER TEN

"What kind of threat?" I asked Sammy. "Why would the Feds come after you? There are dozens of bars in Galveston—and most cops don't seem to care." Was Sammy hiding something besides booze? Not only did he have to worry about the gangs' turf wars, now he had a Federal agent on his back.

"That's what I want to know." Sammy leaned back, blowing cigarette rings toward Doria. "I'm small fry. Why me? Why now?" His voice sounded far away, from another place, another time, perhaps sailing with Doria in the Mediterranean. "I have a feeling Burton's not only after booze—he wants to stir up trouble. Blame me for Andrews' death. Make a name for himself."

"But Andrews died of heart failure," I pointed out.

He cut me off. "So what? Feds read between the lines, draw their own conclusions. Say this Bruno snoops around town, asks questions, but he comes up empty-handed. He can always make something up, plant evidence, find a patsy—so he can get a gold star from Washington."

"Plant evidence?" I was surprised. I knew cops weren't always on the level, but I expected more from Federal agents. "I thought the Feds were after bootleggers, not bar owners."

"Right. That's what has me worried. No, I'm afraid that's not the only social call we'll get from Agent Burton," he scowled.

"You could close up shop here and open somewhere else," Nathan suggested. "Bars move around all the time. What about Texas City or Houston?"

"I like it here just fine," Sammy snapped. He didn't take orders from anyone, especially strangers. "What good would it do if I skipped town? They can still track me down."

Then Dino called out, "Sammy, come take a look at this door. Damn Feds nearly kicked it off the hinges." Guess they wanted to make a big impression.

Sammy jumped up, his face taut. "You kids better scram. Your aunt will be worried."

"Anything I can I do?" I fingered my necklace like worry beads, feeling useless.

He cocked his head toward the office. "Grab my keys so I can lock up. Nathan, come give us a hand." Nathan looked pleased, following Sammy up the stairs like a trained pet. Despite his earlier reprimand, I could tell Sammy had won him over.

I entered the office, a shabby cubbyhole with a few crates on the floor, and an old oak roll-top desk covered with papers, matchbooks and some change. Sammy was a regular pack rat—it's a wonder he ever found anything. Old Coca-Cola calendars and yard-long photos of Galveston's bathing beauty pageants adorned the walls. A small cot sat in the corner for Buzz.

Above his desk was a framed photo of Sammy in front of the Hollywood Dinner Club, posing with owners Ollie Quinn and the Maceo brothers on opening night in 1926. I was dying to go to the Hollywood Dinner Club—the first air-conditioned club in the country—known for its ritzy décor and world-class headliners.

Sammy raved about its opening night: the famous film stars, the bright searchlights on Sixty-first Street—and what a treat it was to watch Guy Lombardo and the Royal Canadians perform on stage. Lots of glamour and glitz. Invitation only. Lucky guy.

I rummaged around and found assorted calling cards, menus and silver dollars. The keys were in a center drawer, but I couldn't resist poking around the nooks and crannies in his desk.

As I was snooping around, opening drawers, something shiny caught my eye in a bottom drawer: a small silver hip flask. I had a flash of recognition, so I looked closely at the fancy engraving: HCA. No doubt about it—Horace Andrews' missing flask!

I was tempted to take it, but where could I hide it? My mesh bag was too small and I couldn't exactly drop the flask down my frilly knickers. I heard heavy footsteps, so I pulled off my cloche cap, wrapped it around the flask and shut the office door—just in time.

"How's the front door?" I asked Sammy, handing him the keys. Slowly I stepped back, holding tight to my cap, hoping no one noticed the flask.

"Bad," replied Nathan. "It almost cracked in two."

"We'll have to work all night to get this damn door ready for tomorrow," Frank grumbled. "Right, Sammy?" With his pristine attire and wire spectacles, Frank didn't look much like a handyman.

Sammy nodded silently, head down. He threw the keys to Dino, and retreated to his office without a word. I called out, "See you later!" But he shut the door and didn't reply. When Sammy got into one of his melancholy moods, it was no use trying to cheer him up.

"Time to lock up, kids," Dino told us. I waited until Dino went upstairs before I grabbed my purse, the flask still hidden in my cap. Frank led us through the back where Buzz was cleaning up, shoulders still shaking. He stopped sweeping, watching us leave.

"Bye, Jazz," Buzz said, ignoring Nathan.

"Be careful, Buzz," I smiled at his freckled face. "Don't take any wooden nickels."

"Sorry you had to witness this fiasco, but at least no one got hurt," Frank told us.

"Not yet. Frank, please watch out for Sammy and Buzz. You never know when the Feds may come back." Could I trust him after what I'd overheard? But even if he owed Horace money, would he resort to spiking his drinks?

In the alley, we walked around a rummy who'd passed out by the back door. Sad sot. The alley reeked of urine, vomit and rotting garbage. A few bar owners were hosing down their sections of street, nodding as we passed. A wino was bent over by the wall, upchucking. I stepped out of the way, then glanced at Nathan and made a face. I'd better wear long pants next time I came by.

In the car, I told Nathan, "Why don't we drive down Beach Boulevard awhile? I'm not ready to go home yet." I didn't want to face Eva, needing time to think, to clear my head.

"I'll say. It's one thing to read about a raid in the papers—it's another to be involved."

"I don't get it. Most cops watch Sammy's back, and he returns the favor. They know he's basically a good guy just trying to make a living." I shook my head, puzzled. Was Sammy in real danger or was this raid only for show? "This Fed seemed fishy, like he wanted something else."

Nathan stopped the car in a remote area by the beach. The sky was dark except for a crescent moon and a few shiny sprinkles of light. "Like what? Hush money? A bribe?"

I let out a sigh. "A scapegoat for Andrews' death."

"Why pin the blame on Sammy?"

"So he can shut down the Oasis, use his bar as an example. Case closed." I pictured Agent Burton and his men as they marched around the Oasis, conquerors staking out their claim. Again, I could see the sadness, the defeat, in Sammy's hazel eyes.

"Sure would make his job easier. But if the Oasis *had* gotten some bad booze, what about all the other bars in town? It's only a matter of time before more stiffs show up dead."

"Gee, thanks for that cheerful thought. Now I'll really have nightmares tonight." I looked away, watching the white foamy waves crashing on the jetties, like angry fists.

We sat in silence, listening to the waves. "Say, I've got good news." Nathan brightened, trying to cheer me up. "Mack is getting out of the hospital in a day or two. He was going stir-crazy in there, and can't wait to start working again."

I marveled at Mack's spunk. "Isn't he afraid to keep investigating the gangs, after getting beat up by those goons?"

"Compared to his horrible hospital stay, he said everything else is duck soup. To be safe, he's working behind the scenes, using informants. I think he's waiting for the Downtown Gang's next move. I'll bet Johnny Jack was really burned up about the Lotus Club fire," he said with a grin.

Nathan's jokes were wearing my patience. He rested his arm across my car seat, a bit too casually. To distract him, I pulled out the flask like a magic act. "Guess what I found in the office—Andrews' flask!" I showed him the engraving, hard to see by moonlight.

"What do you plan to do with it? Turn it over to the cops?"

"Applesauce! That would really get me in hot water."

Shaking the flask, I heard liquid swirling around. "Sounds half-full." I handed it to Nathan, warning, "Don't touch a drop. It's evidence!"

"Evidence?" He opened the flask and smelled it, then frowned. "Can't tell what it is off-hand."

"Say, do you know a chemist who can analyze the contents for me—pronto?"

"You're in luck." Nathan nodded. "There's a pharmacist the reporters always use. He owns a drugstore near the *Gazette*."

"Is he trustworthy? Can he keep his trap shut?"

"He'd better, for all the money we pay him. He's helped Mack on a few stories."

"The last thing we need is a tattle-tale. But don't tell anyone, not even Mack, OK?"

"Scout's honor. Why don't I hold onto the flask for now, so your aunt won't see it?"

"Good idea." I breathed a sigh of relief. The flask had felt like a live grenade in my hands. "We'd better head back. Eva would throw a fit if she found out the Oasis got raided."

"You gotta admit, it was an exciting night," Nathan said as we drove. "Glad we didn't end up in jail."

At the boarding house, Nathan parked and turned off the engine. He leaned toward me, angling his face for a kiss. I turned just in time so all he got was a peck on the cheek, and jumped out of his car. What did he think I was—a vamp?

Inside, I crept upstairs, hoping I hadn't hurt Nathan's feelings. To me, he was like a little brother, a pal, no more. I tapped on Amanda's door, and we sat on the bed as I described the raid in detail, dramatizing it with my hands.

"The raid seemed so routine, almost staged," I told her. "Thank God they didn't destroy the place." I slipped out of my frock and shoes, wishing I could forget the whole incident.

"Poor Sammy! Glad no one's hurt. Will they shut down the Oasis now?" She tugged on her curls, a nervous habit I knew well.

"I hope not." I sat down at my vanity, trying to ignore that possibility. As we talked, I smeared Pond's cold cream on my face, enjoying the cool feel on my skin. "Speaking of speakeasies, guess what I found hidden in Sammy's office? Andrews' flask!" I watched her surprised reaction in the mirror. "Nathan and I plan to take it to a chemist tomorrow, to get the contents analyzed."

Amanda looked worried. "Be careful, Jazz! What if you get caught? That's so dangerous! Not to mention illegal."

"You said it." I rubbed my eyes, exhausted. "But it's the only way to help Sammy."

That night, I had trouble sleeping, dreaming the flask was hidden under my mattress, and I was the proverbial Princess, tossing and turning on a huge flask-shaped metal pea. Was it worth the risk of taking it to a chemist—and did I really want to know the results?

CHAPTER ELEVEN

At the *Gazette* the next day, I kept my head low and tried to avoid my boss in case Mr. Jones, the bank president, called to complain about my nosy "interview." So far, it was business as usual, no immediate threat of dismissal. What a relief!

Before I started working, I scanned the front-page headlines: CUSTOMS MEN SEIZE $2K OF WHISKEY IN HOUSE ATTIC. I wondered about the naiveté of the homeowners, storing so much bootleg upstairs, if they even knew it was there. Who had tipped off the agents? My heart raced as I recalled the raid, and Burton's idle threats. If the agents were so anxious to get their hands on Sammy's stash, why didn't they padlock the doors and search the bar?

I couldn't wait to take Horace's flask to the chemist during lunch, but meanwhile I had a deadline to meet. As I reviewed my notes, I kept picturing Burton and his men circling the Oasis like blood-thirsty buzzards. What were they really after?

Restless, I got up and poured myself a cup of coffee, adding extra milk and four sugar cubes, the only way I could stand the stuff.

Hank watched my ritual with amusement. "If you can't even stomach black coffee, how could you handle real news? A crime scene? A murder?"

"You call sports real news?" I shot back. "Must take a lot of java just to stay awake."

"Better than the fluff you gals write." He gave me a smirk and resumed typing. We went through this song-and-dance routine once a week, like old vaudeville performers.

At my desk, I gulped down the coffee, almost scalding my tongue. Today I needed to call Mrs. Andrews, and convince her to meet me for an interview. I imagined her in a stately black mourning gown, gloves and wide-brimmed hat. What could I say? "I'm sorry about your late husband's death. By the way, I was there when he passed out Saturday night. No, he wasn't at church or bingo—he was getting juiced up in a gin joint. Care to comment?"

How could I face her, pretending to be objective, after what happened? Working up my nerve, I asked the operator to call the Andrews household.

When Mrs. Andrews came on the line, I expressed my sympathy and launched into my pitch, feeling like a pushy door-to-door salesman. Then I closed with: "May I come by for a chat?"

"A personal visit?" She sounded flustered. "Is that necessary? The funeral is tomorrow."

"Mrs. Harper needs the copy right away, so I promise to be brief," I persisted.

She paused. "I'll be accepting callers today after noon. Flo can prepare us hot tea."

When I gave Mrs. Harper an update, she said, "As long as you do Andrews justice," and shooed me away. What kind of justice?

At noon, Nathan stopped by my desk, jaunty in baggy brown pants and blue suspenders, sleeves rolled up, white shirt wrinkled as usual. "Are we still on for our appointment?"

The flask! "Of course. Do you have it with you?"

He smiled and patted his pants pocket. "Ready to go?" Nathan acted as if we were taking a Sunday stroll on the Seawall, not sneaking a stolen flask to a chemist for evaluation.

"Absolutely." I nodded and picked up my hat and clutch, hoping no one would notice our absence. Actually, I was having second thoughts: What did I expect to find out? What if we got caught?

Outside, the heat hit us like a furnace blast. The air was so heavy and moist that my hair started to curl up in corkscrews. So much for my hot oil hair treatments from Amanda.

"Where's this chemist?" I asked Nathan, feeling like a covert spy on a secret mission.

"A few blocks away. Let's drop this off, have lunch and come back later. It won't take long." He sounded so nonchalant, like this was a routine investigation for an article. Didn't he realize what this meant to Mrs. Andrews, to Sammy, to me? But to be fair, Nathan had no idea Sammy was my half-brother.

"If you're sure he's on the level." Half an hour to confirm or refute any suspicions, to find out the truth. "But I need to be back soon. Guess who invited me to tea this afternoon? Well, you can say I invited myself and she complied."

Nathan perked up. "Who—your boss? Mrs. Moody? Mrs. Sealy? Mrs. Kempner?" He named three of the most prominent, and richest, women in town. What a laugh.

"Right. Can't you see us now—society ladies at a tea party. Whatever would we talk about—our diamonds and pearls? Our charity work?" I smiled at the idea. "Alice Andrews."

"Andrews' wife?" He looked puzzled. "Why? You doing a story on her husband?"

"More like a follow-up feature." With an unresolved ending.

Golliwog trailed behind while we walked down the busy street, almost tripping me once or twice. When I stopped to pet her, she started purring and rubbing against my ankles. Her coal-black fur felt warm to the touch. Bet she was miserable in her fuzzy coat, poor cat.

Luckily the pharmacy was quiet and cool inside. Huge apothecary jars filled with brightly colored liquid—looking more like punch than medicine—lined the old oak counters. Colorful tin toys and fine-featured dolls filled the shelves. Ornate Victorian brass ceiling fans shook so hard that I was afraid they'd crash down on our heads. I hid behind a huge Mr. Peanut display, watching Nathan talk to the druggist: a spectacled old man in a white lab coat with hair to match, like a mad scientist in a movie. They shook hands and retreated to the back of the drugstore.

My hands shook as I pretended to peruse the latest Vogue magazine, eyeing the front door. Why did I bother coming here? What difference did it make? Horace was already dead.

Nathan reappeared after a few minutes, but it seemed like hours. "All set. He'll give us the low-down soon enough."

"What did you tell him?" I held my breath. "You didn't mention any names, did you?"

"I told him a city reporter was investigating an important story and to keep this quiet. Don't worry, he knows the score." He patted my shoulder. "Why don't we grab lunch by the ocean?" I tried to relax as we headed toward the Seawall, hoping to catch the trolley in time. Golliwog ran off when the trolley approached, no doubt afraid of the loud clanging bell. Poor thing looked so skinny, I decided to bring her back some fish scraps from lunch.

At Benno's by the beach, we ordered fish and chips, sitting at a wobbly picnic table on the deck. Nathan touched my arm. "Sorry about last night. I didn't mean to act like a masher."

"No need to apologize." I smiled at his sincere expression. "I'm flattered. But I'd rather not date coworkers. Too complicated." True, and it was nicer than saying, 'You're not my type.'

"So I've heard. I was just flirting, pitching a little woo. Friends?"

"Good friends," I assured him.

He grinned and it was over. One thing I liked about Nathan: He didn't hold grudges, unlike most people I knew.

As we ate, I enjoyed the salty Gulf air, watching a big brown pelican dip in the ocean, then land on a nearby pier. The lunch crowd had dispersed and only the birds remained, cleaning up the leftovers. Fishermen cast their nets from weathered boats while the lucky ones sorted through their catch like poker players. In Galveston, fishing was more than a competitive sport: it was a livelihood, a lifeline.

The wind whipped and whistled, and a gust of wind blew off my floppy peach hat. I had to chase it down the beach while it bounced and twirled. Nathan had a good laugh at my antics, pointing as if my hat and I were a carnival sideshow. Annoyed, I stuffed the stupid hat in my leather clutch.

"That's not such a good idea, Jazz." Nathan stared at my bare crown. "You know how seagulls like to use people for target practice. With your dark hair, I can only imagine."

"Thanks for the heads-up, Nate," I joked.

As we ate, a seagull landed nearby and I tossed it some scraps of fish, watching it dance around the deck in appreciation. Then I remembered Golliwog, and wrapped up my left-over lunch in a napkin. I was so nervous, I'd lost my appetite.

"Is that Eau de Catfish?" He held his nose. "You really need to get some new perfume, Jazz."

"Gee, thanks. Remind me to pick up a bottle of Chanel Number Five," I replied in a high-hat tone. "I can hardly afford toilet water from Woolworth's on my crummy salary."

"Crummy is right." He glanced at his watch. "Time to go. The verdict may be in by now."

We jumped on the trolley coming down 20th Street, but I felt queasy and uneasy during the bumpy ride. My stomach did flip-flops while we walked to the drugstore in silence. Nathan motioned for me to follow him as we approached the counter.

The chemist gave me a puzzled look. "Who are you?"

"She's OK, Mr. Baxter. She works with me at the *Gazette*."

The chemist led us to his back room where assorted jars and bottles were scattered helter-skelter over long oak tables. He looked at us solemnly, clutching the silver flask like a weapon.

"I'm afraid I have some bad news."

"Bad news?" I sucked in my breath.

"This flask contains almost ninety percent methanol—or as they call it, wood alcohol. Pure poison." The chemist sounded urgent, like a radio announcer. "It's half-empty—whoever drank from this flask should be dead by now."

CHAPTER TWELVE

If he only knew. My mouth felt dry, but I managed to ask: "How can you tell?"

"Didn't smell strange to me," said Nathan. "But I sure as hell didn't taste it."

"Pure methanol has unique characteristics," the chemist explained. "It's a lethal, colorless form of alcohol with a sweet taste. Hard to detect, especially in mixed drinks."

"So how do you know the difference between good and wood alcohol?" I wondered, worried about all the people who couldn't tell rotgut rum from Coke.

"That's the problem. Add it to a cocktail, you'd never know—until it was too late."

"What are the symptoms?" I asked, thinking of Andrews' red eyes and face.

"Everyone reacts differently," the chemist continued. "It all depends on quality and quantity—and the person. You know, their general health—age, weight and metabolism. In very small doses, you may simply feel nausea or get stomach cramps or blurred vision and eventually pass out. In larger doses, you can even go blind."

"That's how you get blind-drunk," muttered Nathan.

The chemist gave us a warning look. "It gets worse. You can become brain-damaged or paralyzed, and eventually it can be fatal."

As he spoke, I began to feel sick, and clutched my stomach. Why would anyone take that risk for a drink?

Mr. Baxter examined the flask. "Where did you get this? Who is HCA? You should dispose of it at once, for your own safety."

"We need it for research." Nathan nudged me. "For Mack."

"Sorry to say, I'm seeing more cases of alcohol poisoning these days. It's too easy to find methanol, especially in these parts, with all the refineries around." The chemist shook his head. "Between the government and the gangsters, it's hard to avoid wood alcohol."

I frowned. "Our government? What do you mean?"

"Indirectly they're responsible for this fiasco, but they call it upholding the Constitution." He let out a snort. "By law, denatured spirits like methanol must be added to industrial alcohol sold to the public. They're trying to deter drinking and make the pro-Prohibition supporters happy."

"Are you serious? You mean it's legal to poison people, just to enforce Prohibition?" I swallowed hard, staring at the chemist in disbelief. "I can't believe our own government would stoop so low."

Why was I so shocked? The Treasury Department was known for its blatant tactics in trying to enforce the Volstead Act. What had Agent Burton done to 'uphold the law'?

"Sad, but true." Mr. Baxter nodded. "Recently, there was a big fight in Congress between the Wets and the Drys since so many people are going blind or dying from drinking wood alcohol. Of course the politicians tried to cover it up, but the Prohibition Bureau finally had to come clean."

"I doubt the Eighteenth Amendment included poisoning the public," I fumed, shaking my head. "So what if folks drink a little booze now and then? They don't deserve to die!"

"Hey, I didn't make the rules." The chemist shrugged, looking frustrated. "Look it up yourself. The muckety-mucks tried to kill the story, but it's buried in the newspapers. Our government doesn't want to advertise the fact that the liquor lords are winning the whiskey wars."

"I'll think twice before I take a drink," Nathan said. "Don't worry, we'll be careful."

"If you really want to be careful, then try to trace the source— find out who's passing off this poison as the real thing." He thrust the flask at Nathan. "Before it's too late."

"Thanks for your help, Mr. Baxter," Nathan said, sliding the flask in his pants pocket. "Keep this under your hat, OK? Pretend we were never here."

I stepped out of the drugstore, my heart racing. Slowly I exhaled, feeling dizzy after holding my breath for so long.

"Is he telling the truth? Can you trust him?" I asked.

"Why would he lie?" Nathan frowned. "In fact, Mr. Baxter helped Mack with research on his story—before Mack got sick and had to rent a room at John Sealy Hospital."

My fears had been confirmed: No doubt about it, Andrews died of methanol poisoning. But in a way, it was good news because it meant he *hadn't* been poisoned at the Oasis.

I imagined Andrews adding spirits to his cocktails, oblivious that he was drinking pure poison. How could he, and all the thousands of saps like him, like any of us, be so foolish? Instead, it was obvious the Volstead Act had backfired and our trusty politicians, whom we elected and paid to protect us, were just as guilty.

"No wonder there's so much wood alcohol going around town." I shook my head, trying to make sense of it all. "Hard to believe our own politicians are no better than gangsters."

Now I couldn't wait to read the articles the chemist had mentioned, making a note to search our morgue files later.

Nathan and I caught the trolley to Post Office Street and rode back in silence, sweltering in the heat. My dress clung to my back like a wet bathing suit.

We took our time returning to work, ignoring the street noise, preoccupied. I couldn't find Golliwog, so I put the bag of fish scraps by her tin can water bowl in the alley. I needed to see a friendly face, even if it was a scraggly stray cat. Animals were trustworthy and knew how to keep secrets.

When we walked into the newsroom, Mr. Thomas raised his bushy eyebrows. Somehow he managed to keep a pencil wedged behind his ear, while holding the paper and circling the room. After decades in the newspaper biz, it was an old balancing trick.

"Where were you two?" he bellowed.

"Sorry we're late, sir. Out running an errand," said Nathan.

"What errand could possibly be more important than *work*?" Mr. Thomas roared.

"We're doing research for Mack," Nathan lied before disappearing into the darkroom.

"Is that true, Jasmine?" Annoyed, Mr. Thomas ambled over to my desk, but I looked away.

"Yes, sir," I fibbed, staring at my desk. "Excuse me. I've got an interview with Mrs. Andrews this afternoon."

At least the article gave me the perfect excuse to find out more about Horace's "hobbies." Still, how could I face her knowing how he'd really died—not of a heart attack, but of methanol poisoning? Wasn't it better to let her believe he'd died of natural causes?

My linen lilac dress and cloche cap were a bit casual for calling on grieving widows, so I slipped on a pair of long white gloves I kept in my desk for social emergencies. What would Mrs. Harper suggest? A floral bouquet—no doubt grown by the Galveston Garden Club.

Dreading our meeting, I took the trolley to Avenue L, an oak and palm tree-lined street of elegant, three-story Victorian homes. Flo, the elderly Negro housekeeper, answered my knock. After placing my calling card on the monogrammed silver tray, she ushered me into a handsome parlor, decorated with a rich burgundy brocade sofa and chairs, ivy wallpaper and Victorian walnut furniture. Wafts of lavender and roses filled the room.

Mrs. Andrews sat regally on the sofa, framed by bright floral wreaths lined up on stands like a daisy chain. Despite her formal black dress, she looked young and pretty, only 32 or so.

"I'm Alice Andrews. Thank you for coming." She held out a limp hand. I felt a pang of guilt, as if I'd invited myself under false pretenses. How in the world could I keep mum during our interview?

Flo carried in a silver tea service with petits fours, and poured us tea in porcelain floral teacups. "You work for Mrs. Harper? Will she be making an appearance?" Alice sounded disappointed that my boss had sent her lowly assistant in her place.

Was that a jab? "She's so sorry she couldn't be here, but she sends her condolences."

"I see." Alice looked skeptical. "Did you ever meet my husband? Perhaps at the bank?"

I nodded. "I met you both at the Fireman's Ball last year."

Her face was blank. Normally, I'd be upset that I was so forgettable, but for once, I was relieved.

To distract her, I motioned to the oil painting above the sofa: a stormy gray and white beach scene. "How lovely. Is this Galveston?"

"Yes, it is." Alice brightened. "I painted it myself. I used to paint quite a bit, but since the baby arrived I can hardly complete my daily chores. Now with Horace gone..." Her eyes misted, and she stared at the painting, as if in a trance.

"By the way, I met your husband's co-workers at the bank. Mr. Clark sends his regards." I hoped to cheer her up, wondering if she knew he had a crush on her.

Her face flushed. "Phillip Clark? Why would you talk to...oh, of course, your article." Abruptly she stood up, gathering her skirt. "Please excuse me while I get some papers."

Why was she acting so nervous? Was she shy or simply reserved? My mind worked overtime as I scanned the room. An old-fashioned Matthew Brady-style photo of the Andrews family sat on the fireplace mantel, their faces solemn as Victorians—save for the chubby newborn who beamed in Alice's lap. Such a handsome couple. The proud family man, Andrews rested his arm on his wife's Rococo parlor chair.

Slowly, I sipped my tea, trying to relax. Hot tea had such a soothing effect. When Mrs. Andrews returned, her face looked rosy, as if she'd pinched her cheeks for color, and she handed me a stack of papers. "These documents should have all the information on Horace you'll need."

I perused the papers, but the words were a blur. "Do you mind if we go over my notes?"

After she answered a few questions, she nodded her approval. "I see you've done your research."

"Thanks. I like to be prepared." I smiled, pleased that my Girl Scout training had paid off.

Proudly she rattled off Andrews' accomplishments: medals he'd won, job promotions, volunteer work, church duties. "I hope it doesn't seem like bragging," she said, blushing.

"Not at all." I took notes, trying to imagine a younger, ambitious Andrews, not the desperate man I'd met at a speakeasy. "What about his family—any brothers or sisters? Do his parents live here?"

"Sadly, Horace had no other family." She blinked back tears. "You see, his parents were killed in the 1900 storm. He spent most of his childhood in the Greater Galveston Orphanage."

"Really?" I sat up, surprised. Sammy never mentioned that fact.

"Horace preferred to keep it a secret. He thought people would think less of him if they knew he was an orphan, as if he was inferior, without social standing. That's why he worked so hard for us, to provide the things he lacked as a child." She smiled with pride.

"He managed to turn a distinct drawback into an advantage. His background gave him motivation, a sense of purpose."

"Good for him. I admire a self-made man." No wonder he'd craved status and wealth.

Her face flushed. "I'd rather that fact wasn't made public, please. Growing up in an orphanage wasn't his happiest memory."

"Of course. It's not needed," I agreed. "Do you want to add anything else?"

"Please mention that he was a good father and husband and will be greatly missed." She let out a sigh. "Honestly, I'm still in shock. One minute, he's here, full of life, then the next, I'm getting a call from the hospital." She tucked stray strands of hair behind her ears. "It all seems so sudden. Too sudden." What did she mean by that?

Mrs. Andrews studied me. "Do you mind if I ask you a question, miss Cross? Can I trust you, the *Gazette*? Are the articles they print factual and fair?"

"We try our best...Why?" The *Gazette* had been known to sensationalize a few stories now and then—which paper didn't?—but Mr. Thomas took great pride in the staff and its integrity.

"I read about all this crime and corruption in our city. Perhaps there's another side to the story, as they say?"

I shifted in my seat. What was she getting at?

"Please keep this a secret. Off the record." She leaned forward, her voice low. "I want to find out what really happened to my husband. Because I'm not truly convinced he died of natural causes."

CHAPTER THIRTEEN

I sat up, taken aback. Why was Alice Andrews telling *me* her suspicions? "But the mortuary notice said..."

"Guess who provided that information?" Her eyes narrowed. "Yes, I know the official cause of death was heart failure, yet something is bothering me. I can't help but wonder what else may have contributed?"

I sipped my tea, silent. What could I say—that I'd stolen her husband's flask and had the contents analyzed? Worse, it appeared that he'd been poisoned, perhaps on purpose?

Alice smoothed out imaginary wrinkles in her mourning dress. "Naturally, I wasn't willing to ask the hospital to perform an autopsy. That would raise too many eyebrows."

She was right. Not only could it cause a society scandal, I doubt she wanted to hear the truth. A brass fan whirred overhead and I was grateful for the cool air, as well as the calming noise.

"I know Horace had a few, shall we say, bad habits." The tea splashed as she set down her cup. "But to die when he was so young and had so much to live for. It's so unfair."

She stood up, pacing the plush Persian carpet. "I'll never forget his last night here. He got a phone call during dinner and rushed out in a panic. It was so unlike him to leave the family table without a word. So wrong."

What else did she know or suspect? "Do you have any idea who called, or where he went?" I prodded.

"I wish I did. That's all I'd better say for now." She crossed the parlor and opened the front door wide. I got the telegram. "Please call if you have more questions," she said, giving me a card.

"Thank you for your time." I shook her hand gently, and stepped outside, the heat and humidity hitting me like a wet towel.

On the trolley, I rode back to the *Gazette* in a trance, mentally replaying our conversation, trying to make sense of her suspicions. Was Alice distraught and delusional, or did she suspect foul play?

Back at work, Nathan stopped me in the hall. "How was your tea with Mrs. Andrews?

"Uncomfortable," I admitted. "She believes Horace didn't die of natural causes."

He shrugged. "Her husband was a boozer. He did it to himself. It's his own fault."

"That's not fair! No one should die that way." I frowned at him and walked off. No tea and sympathy from Nathan.

At my desk, I tried to write up Andrews' profile, but I felt guilty, as if I'd intentionally deceived Alice. I stared at my blank pages, hoping words would appear by magic. At a loss, I reviewed my notes again, but a crucial fact was missing: his true cause of death.

I went to get a cup of coffee, but the pot was empty. "Why don't you make us some fresh joe?" Hank called out. "Isn't that what you gals are *supposed* to do?"

Irritated, I shot him what I hoped was a withering look. "Make it yourself." A few reporters snickered and Hank glared at me, his jowly face in a permanent scowl.

Trudging to my desk, I tried to focus on my profile. The clattering of typewriter keys calmed me and I forced myself to write, to forget the day's events. The piece positively sang Andrews' praises, noting his awards and achievements. No one would have any idea what he had done behind closed doors, whatever that was. Afterwards, I dropped the story off on Mrs. Harper's desk, not caring if she rewrote it. Frankly, I was too close to the subject to be objective. I only wished it had a happy ending.

Finally finished, I snuck back downstairs to the morgue, and began rummaging through thick files, flipping through the yellowing pages of old papers. I spotted a few articles on "enforcement of Prohibition," buried in the *Daily News* and strained to read in the dim overhead lights.

Sad to say, the chemist was telling the truth. I was stunned to find out he was right about our lawmakers: In order to enforce the Eighteenth Amendment, the government required suppliers to *secretly* add poisons like methanol, anti-freeze and kerosene to industrial alcohol sold to the public, to make it less palatable.

A January 1, 1927 AP article said: Despite protests from the Anti-Saloon League, Andrew Mellon, Secretary of the Treasury, *"...declared he was not in favor of any denaturant which would fatally poison American citizens even to enforce the law."* That was swell of him. As I read the papers, my hands began shaking, and sweat dripped down my face, stinging my eyes, blurring my vision. Still, I couldn't stop digging for information, both repulsed and fascinated by the truth.

Then I found a January 5th article stating that Congress was debating the type and amount of toxins or denaturants to add to industrial alcohol, and seeking a new, "less injurious" formula.

Still, I was shocked to learn: *"the new formula contains twice as much wood alcohol as the old one."* A New York toxicologist found that: *"the new denaturant is apt to cause nothing worse than blindness....The main difference seems to be that a slow poison has been substituted for a fast one."*

What was worse than blindness, besides death? Personally, I'd rather die quickly than go blind first, and suffer a slow, painful death.

Naturally Congress became worried after they realized their own members could suffer the same fate as the lowly public: *"...If the government is putting poison in industrial alcohol, and if this same alcohol is liable to be redistilled and sold by a bootlegger under a deceiving label, a $10,000 a year congressman is just as apt to imbibe some of it as a $25. a week clerk."*

Talk about hypocrisy! Did President Coolidge actually condone poisoning the public?

How sad that our government had turned "a blind eye" to Prohibition. How would people react if they knew the truth? Even if they realized our government was at fault, would folks like Andrews ever stop drinking? A sobering thought.

Despite these dangers, most locals, even the "Drys," seemed to tolerate the "Wets" who drank to excess since Prohibition helped Galveston survive and thrive.

CHAPTER FOURTEEN

As I read the articles about the Volstead Act, my head spun like a roulette wheel. Hard to believe that our elected officials came up with this devious, deadly plan, then tried to keep it quiet.

Why couldn't the government admit that Prohibition was a colossal and futile failure?

By now, it was late afternoon and I was ready to leave. The day had been long and tiring—and full of unpleasant surprises. I spotted Nathan by the water cooler, and scrutinized his pants pocket for Andrews' flask. Somehow I needed to figure out a way to return the flask without Sammy or Dino knowing I'd snooped in their office.

"Don't you have a little present for me?" I asked Nathan. He'd insisted on holding onto the flask "for safekeeping," as if he didn't trust me. "Can you meet me in the alley in about ten minutes?"

Hope I didn't sound like a streetwalker!

"Is that an invitation?" He winked.

"Nathan!" How could he joke now? "You know what I meant."

"Just trying to have some fun," he said with a sly grin.

In the alley, Nathan blocked the entrance while he handed me the flask like it was a secret weapon. I leaned over and pretended to be petting Golliwog, who was licking her paws contentedly after devouring the fish. Even the paper bag appeared to be half-eaten.

"Be careful with that thing—it's lethal." He frowned. "If anyone catches you...well, you may get arrested and sent to jail."

I batted my lashes. "Who's going to arrest an innocent flapper?" I shoved the flask in a paper bag and stuck it in my purse. "Not to worry, I'll put it back soon."

"At least let me give you a lift home. Ready to go?"

"Sure, thanks." Driving with Nathan was like riding a roller-coaster, fast, thrilling and at times, dangerous—but better than walking home in this heat wave. We'd almost stalled on the railroad tracks once or twice, but his heap managed to make it just in time.

In the car, I couldn't wait to tell him about the articles I'd read.

"Guess what I found out? The chemist was right. Our politicians are as bad as gangsters. Worse in my book since they hide behind their so-called laws," I fumed. "Why do they have to resort to poisoning people to prove their point?"

"The way our government sees it, these folks broke the law—and they get what they deserve." Nathan shook his head. "Drinking has never been so deadly. It's not worth dying for."

"I'll say! Don't people realize how lethal industrial alcohol is? Why take that risk?"

"Lots of moonshiners don't know what they're doing and they don't care. Methanol is cheap and available. They can try to boil the toxins out, but there's no guarantee it will work. Sad to say, folks have no idea what they're drinking—if it's real or rotgut—until it's too late."

I had an idea. "Why not try to trace the source? Find out who's passing off hooch as the real deal. Bad booze hurts everyone."

"Good luck trying to track down the bootleggers," he snorted. "By the time anyone figures it out, those crooks are long gone."

I hated to admit, he was right. But while the gangsters profited from the politicians' idiotic laws, the public paid the price, literally, with their lives.

On Wednesday, I got into work a little late but luckily Mrs. Harper wasn't in yet. On my desk sat today's paper with the front-page headline: GANGS ACCUSED OF KILLING HOUSTON MAN IN SHOOT-OUT. I held my breath as I read about the slaying by the Seawall, the Beach Gang's turf. Would it ever end?

On page ten, I saw my article on Horace Andrews, his handsome face smiling at me from the business section. I had mixed feelings of guilt and pride: My first byline! Naturally Mrs. Harper had put her finishing touches on the piece and added her name, but my version remained intact. Not bad for my debut into print, if bittersweet. My society articles were mainly puff pieces that Mrs. Harper rewrote, taking all the credit.

Half the newsroom was empty, and the remaining reporters looked plastered. I felt hung-over myself, I was so tired. I shuffled over to the coffee pot, lids half-closed, and poured a cup.

"Congrats on your story, kid," Hank said. "Too bad it was wasted on a dead guy."

Was he serious or pulling my leg? I decided to take it as a compliment. "Why, thanks, Hank." I smiled sweetly. "I hope it's the first of many. Stories, that is—not dead guys." He grinned as he returned to his desk. It was the first time I'd seen that sourpuss smile.

Distracted, I wandered around the newsroom, looking for Nathan, but he wasn't there. Mr. Thomas motioned me over to his office, tipping back his hat. "I saw your piece on Andrews, Jasmine. He was my banker at Lone Star."

"Really?" I wished I could ask him questions without arousing suspicion. "What was he like?" Even tipsy, to me Andrews had conducted himself like a perfect gentleman.

"A nice man, generous, respectful." He paused. "Shame he died so young."

"It doesn't seem fair," I agreed, thinking of Mrs. Andrews.

"Life isn't fair." He looked stern. What was he trying to tell me? "I hope you've gotten that out of your system. Promise me you'll go back to writing about brides and society balls."

"Yes, sir." I nodded to pacify him. Did I have a choice?

My boss had left me a few stories to proofread, but I couldn't concentrate so I decided to stretch my legs. As I passed by Mrs. Page's desk, she called out: "Almost forgot—a Mrs. Andrews called looking for you. Want me to ring her up?"

"What did she want?" Did she have some news? Had I made a mistake in the article?

"How should I know?" She shrugged, and went back to filing her fire engine-red nails, scrutinizing each hand like a practiced manicurist. Sorry I interrupted her beauty routine.

Worried, I asked her to connect me to the Andrews' household. Flo's tone was much warmer this time. Alice Andrews was equally as pleasant. "I'm so grateful for the nice article you did on my husband. Horace looks so dashing in his Army uniform."

"Glad you liked it." I blushed, pleased by the compliment, so rare in my line of work.

"Jasmine, you must come for tea again, under more pleasant circumstances, I hope."

"I'd be delighted," I replied, surprised by her offer. "Thanks for calling." I stared at the phone, shaking my head in amazement. Could I really become friends with prim and proper Alice Andrews?

I'd started editing some copy for the wedding section—"Debutante to Wed Doctor"—when Nathan stopped by, wearing his trademark suspenders. He sat on the edge of my desk and thumped the paper. "Attagirl! Let's go out to lunch and celebrate your first byline—my treat."

"You mean half a byline." To be honest, I'd feel guilty celebrating while poor Alice was in mourning.

"So what if Mrs. Harper tried to take credit? It's a start. You should be proud."

"Thanks." I perked up. "Say, why don't we eat at Star Drugstore for a change?"

"Got something up your sleeve?" Nathan asked, brows raised.

"Someone." I smiled at him, mulling over an idea. "Amanda."

Outside, the sidewalks were busy with shoppers carrying packages and groceries. A couple of shopkeepers sat outside fanning themselves or smoking. Cars rushed past in a dark cloud of exhaust and noise. A Model T jerked to a stop when a few pedestrians crossed carelessly in front, the dark-haired driver cursing and shaking his fist out the window.

As we walked toward the diner, I filled Nathan in on my interview with Mrs. Andrews. "She seemed so suspicious that I'm starting to wonder if someone could have purposely added methanol to Andrews' flask," I confided. "But I have no idea who, or why."

"Think about it. Bankers have money, or at least easy access to money. Didn't you say you saw Rose Maceo at the bank? Maybe Andrews had some run-ins with the gangs."

"But he was such a gentleman. He wasn't the type to get involved with gangsters." Or was he? Why was I sticking up for a man I'd only met once?

"Why not? Look at our own corrupt government. You said it yourself: Our politicians are no better than gangsters."

Maybe Nathan was right. Were the gangsters threatening Andrews? Is that what he meant by "life and death"?

The Star Diner was known as a local hang-out for good coffee and even better gossip. Nice to have a pal like Amanda waiting tables there. The soda fountain was filled with children and young mothers, so we sat down at a booth by the window. Two elderly men sat at an oak table, playing checkers, drinking frosted bottles of Coca-Cola.

Low ceiling fans whirred over the horse-shoe shaped white marble countertop, the white tiled sides embedded with glossy red stars and green diamonds. The colorful designs brightened up the black and white floor and sparse decor. Who chose the color scheme anyway? The result was jarring, like Christmas in July.

Amanda waved across the room when we walked in. She rushed over, juggling a pile of plates, clearly glad for a break.

"Hi, y'all. Long time no see. What's new?"

"Plenty." I tapped the paper, showing her my article on Andrews. "What do you think?"

Her face soured. Like me, she couldn't forget that night at the Oasis, watching Andrews' downfall. Literally. "Poor man. It's so sad." Then she beamed at me. "But congrats on your story." No wonder Amanda had set her sights on Hollywood. She was a natural.

After we ordered sandwiches, I told her, "I need to go to the Oasis tonight. Want to go with me?"

Her smile lit up the room. "Do I!? I'm getting off early. Sit tight and then I'm all yours."

I leaned over the table. "Can you distract Sammy while I sneak into his office?"

"You bet I can! Finally I can show off my acting skills." I stifled a smile. She seemed to think she was auditioning for a big part in a play, not acting as my accomplice.

Nathan looked alarmed. "What if that Fed agent shows up again? I can go with you tonight, to be safe."

"Thanks for the offer, but Amanda is just the ticket I need." At least I hoped so.

That evening, Amanda and I freshened up our face paint, and changed into our glad rags. She was so excited, trying on one frock after another, acting like it was our homecoming dance all over again.

As we got ready, I described the visit to the chemist, and his guilty verdict. "I was scared to death! I was so afraid he'd turn us in."

"You don't say!" was all she could say, no doubt distracted by romantic thoughts of Sammy. Before we left, I carefully tucked the flask into my purse along with a copy of today's paper, my story on Andrews creased in half. I knew Sammy would be proud of me, even if the subject matter was maudlin, if not downright depressing. No sense in bringing up the flask tonight. I dreaded his reaction if he caught me "breaking and entering" into his office.

Luckily Eva was hosting her quilting bee, and for once didn't seem to mind that we were going out. She didn't even look up as we crept by, she was so engrossed in her handiwork.

"Don't be late!" she told us. The sun shone through the stained glass door as we went out, the colors reflected on the walls. I was glad Eva had a group of friends to keep her company, mostly spinsters and widows—women like her who'd lost their sweethearts in the Great War.

We caught the trolley to Market Street, holding onto our hats the whole way. After all her primping, Amanda looked like a disheveled doll by the time we arrived. As we waited outside the Oasis, she fiddled with her vanity compact, peeking into the tiny mirror while trying to touch up her rouge and lipstick. "This damn heat is melting my make-up!" she wailed.

"You look fine," I assured her, hiding my grin. I tapped a code on the door, but no one answered. Strange that Dino wasn't at his usual post. Anxious, I knocked louder, surprised to see Frank slide open the glass slot.

He stepped outside, putting a finger to his lips. "Feds are here. You gals better scram."

"Feds?" I frowned. "Where is everyone?"

"Dino's gone and Buzz is hiding—maybe at Joe's Bar? When the cops showed up, the place cleared out."

"What do they want?" I walked inside, motioning for Amanda to follow me down the stairs.

"Guess." He frowned as we passed. "Sure that's a smart idea?"

I waved him away as we tiptoed down the stairs, the steps creaking under our feet. The room was eerily still, except for two men's voices, arguing. I craned my neck to listen, my body stiff as an andiron. Their voices were muffled, but they came from the kitchen: one was Sammy, and the other sounded a lot like Agent Burton.

CHAPTER FIFTEEN

"Should we skedaddle?" Amanda whispered, her cheeks flushed.

Shaking my head, I considered our choices. Here we were stuck on the Oasis stairs, with a stolen flask hidden in my bag, and a Prohibition agent only a few yards away. Part of me wanted to run away like a scaredy-cat. But what I really wanted to do was eavesdrop—like a typical nosy reporter.

So of course I crept into the bar, holding my breath, as if that would help. I edged closer to the kitchen, trying to listen, but only heard a few words. Amanda hid on the stairway, arms waving, mouthing like a mime playing charades: "No! Stop! Don't!"

Why didn't I pay attention? The bar felt steamy, sweltering as a hot springs sauna. Beads of sweat ran down my back, my face. Ceiling fans creaked overhead, blowing hot air around the room.

Speaking of hot air, I strained to listen at the door. Then I heard Sammy say: "Why me? I mind my own business, pay my bills on time. Don't wanna cause any problems."

"I know. I know all about you, Mr. Cook," Burton's baritone voice boomed. "I asked around town. You're on the up and up—for a gangster."

"Hey, who you calling a gangster? I'm a legit businessman!"

I cupped my ear to the door, trying to control my breathing.

"Legit? This dive? It's a hang-out for hookers and hoods!"

"I'm trying to run a nice, quiet family business," Sammy snapped. "But you have a bad habit of showing up and scaring off all my customers."

Nice, quiet family business? OK, maybe Sammy was stretching the truth a bit.

"You think it's quiet now, wait till I shut this place down!" Burton yelled. "Then you'll change your mind." I heard a slight scuffle and the voices got muffled. Were they fighting?

Panicky, I stepped back, but the door swung open and Burton practically plowed into me. I dropped my purse and newspaper with a loud thud, my bag landing next to Agent Burton's feet. Good move, Jazz. I prayed the half-full flask wouldn't fall out and leak all over his shiny brown shoes.

"Pardon me," I stammered. "Hope my compact didn't get damaged." Did that sound convincing enough? In a flash, I grabbed my bag and shoved it under my arm.

"Fancy seeing you again." Burton eyed me, and bent down to pick up the newspaper—with Horace Andrews' face smiling up at us. "What are you doing here?"

"I—I think I lost an earring here last night…" I tapped my earlobe, pretending to look around. I saw Amanda's reflection in the bar mirror, frozen in place, dumbstruck.

"Oh, really?" He glanced at the newspaper. "What have we here? Special delivery?"

"I wanted to show Sammy today's paper…" I stopped, realizing I'd said too much.

"What's so interesting about today's paper?" He pulled it out, scanning the pages.

"Nothing," I mumbled, motionless as a store mannequin, clutching my purse, afraid he'd ask more questions.

Sammy stood next to me, olive eyes flashing, clenching and unclenching his fists. "Our business is finished, Burton. You should know the way out by now." Burton's jaw tightened and he started to say something, but changed his mind.

Amanda decided to make her entrance, as if she'd just remembered her cue from stage left. She breezed into the room, twirling her long curls, all Southern belle charm and manners.

"Hello, Sammy, how nice to see you." She reached up to kiss his cheek, and he smiled, looking surprised, his angry façade melting. Then she held out her pale manicured hand to Agent Burton.

"Why, I don't believe we've met, Mr.…?"

His mouth turned up, and he seemed to study her with amusement. "Federal Agent James Burton." I expected him to kiss her hand, but instead he leaned over and gave a slight bow. Very gallant. Amanda had that effect on men.

Then Agent Burton turned to me. "Isn't it past your bedtime? Why don't I give you ladies a lift home? Market Street isn't safe after dark, you know." He winked at me. "After you find your earring, that is." Clearly he didn't believe me, but was willing to play along.

"Why, thanks! I've never ridden in a cop car before." Amanda squealed like a child, batting her lashes, hands under her chin. You'd think she was on Broadway with that girly act.

"You must be a law-abiding citizen." He smiled at her, then gave Sammy a pointed look.

"I'll be glad to give these ladies a ride home." Sammy stood between me and Amanda protectively, his hands on our backs. "Aren't you still on duty, Burton?"

"Yes, unfortunately." Burton tipped his hat. "Well, some other time, ladies." He handed me back the paper and smiled. "Keep up the good work, Miss Cross."

I froze in place. "How'd you know my name?"

Burton grinned and strode toward the back door, like a regular. Yeah, a regular rat.

"Talk about a close call," I told Sammy after Burton left. "What did he want? I heard you two arguing."

"Never mind." He sat down, rubbing his forehead. "Harassment, that's all."

"Are you in trouble?" Amanda plopped down at his table.

"What gives you that idea?" He frowned. "I'm not afraid of Burton. But he's got the advantage—a gun and a badge to back it up. He can make my life miserable if he wants."

"Strange he showed up here again so soon. What did he want?" Burton was up to something, but I knew Sammy wouldn't give me a straight answer.

"Who knows? I don't trust his mug." Sammy stared at the table as if wishing it was a Ouija board with all the answers. "So what brings you here? Not that hooey about a lost earring?"

"I wanted to show you my story on Andrews—my first published article. Sort of."

I handed him the paper, waiting for his reaction like a kid with a good report card. "Nice job." Sammy nodded. "I've never seen Horace look so spiffy." As he skimmed my article, he said, "Heart failure—so they say. I wonder if Burton read this?"

"Why would he?" I frowned. "Speaking of Burton, how does he know my name?"

Sammy slumped in his chair, fiddling with his pack of Camels. "He asked me all about you, wondered if you had a beau. *Taken* is how he put it."

"What did you say?" I folded my arms, glaring at him.

He shrugged. "I told him you were an independent woman—a career girl—a moderne, whatever you gals like to call yourselves. Flappers? So he wanted to know where you worked, what you did—the whole shebang. I let him know my customers are above-board."

"I don't need a matchmaker. Thanks to you, now I have a Fed agent on my tail." I glared at Sammy.

"You and me both. May not be so bad, come to think of it." Sammy rubbed his chin. "May come in handy."

"Handy? What does that mean?" I faced him, hands on my hips.

He shrugged, looking away. "I only meant he might be a good contact, a source, for your journalism career." Yeah, right. He was more interested in using me as a buffer, or as bait.

"Sounds like he's got a crush on you." Amanda clasped her hands to her face like a love-struck loon and pretended to swoon. "Well, I think he's a sheik, especially for a copper."

"Why don't you go out with him then?" Exasperated, I threw up my hands.

Amanda squeezed Sammy's forearm. "He can't hold a candle to you," she cooed. "I like them tall, dark and handsome." She was laying it on thick, all right, and Sammy ate up the flattery.

He smiled at Amanda with new interest. But as we talked, she seemed uncomfortable—from the heat or our conversation?—and fanned her face with her floppy blue hat. "Jeepers, it's hot in here! Can we get a cold one, Sammy?"

"I'm fresh out," he griped, wiping his brow. "That damn ice truck didn't come by today. I had to send Dino over to borrow some blocks of ice from Joe's. Even Doria is complaining."

"How could the ice man miss you?" I wondered. "You're right next door."

"Good question." His eyes narrowed. "He must think he deserves a raise."

"Maybe he ran out of ice and plans to come back tomorrow."

"I hope so. I can't afford to lose any more customers. It was like an oven in here all day." Sammy mopped his face with a crumpled handkerchief. "Those damn fans are useless without ice blocks. They all melted by dinner time, so my customers left in a hurry. Can you blame them?"

"Sorry I mentioned it." Amanda squirmed, eyes downcast.

"Talk about rotten luck. First the ice truck skips my bar, then Agent Burton shows up again tonight." Sammy pounded his fist on the table. "Son of a bitch!"

We didn't dare say a word while we waited for him to calm down. Then he ground out his Camel and stood up. "Let me get some things in order before I take you gals home. Stay here a minute while I go lock up."

My heart sank as I watched him leave, his shoulders hunched, defeated. "Poor Sammy. I've never seen him so worried."

"He needs a night off from this place." Amanda's face brightened. "Say, I have an idea. Why don't I invite him over for a home-cooked meal on Sunday? We can make it a double date!"

Swell—which one of my many beaux should I invite? After my ex-boyfriend left town, I'd sworn off men for good, or at least for a while. "Sammy will enjoy that—but let me check with Eva." I hoped my aunt had plans for the weekend. Despite his generosity, Sammy was a persona non grata at her boarding house.

But first, I had a mission to accomplish. I was so flustered by running into Agent Burton, literally, that I'd forgotten about returning Andrews' flask. "Ready for your close up?" I nudged Amanda. The sooner I got rid of the flask, the better—especially since I almost got caught with it, red-handed *and* red-faced.

Amanda took her cue, then sashayed over to the kitchen to play her part. "Hey, good looking—what'cha got cooking?" she called out to Sammy. Corny, I know, but coming from her, it worked.

I edged toward Sammy's office and snuck inside, holding my breath and my handbag tightly. If only I could be as brave as Clara Bow in *Rough House Rosie*. The office was a mess as usual, and the lower desk drawer seemed to be stuck.

Then I heard Amanda call out, "Sammy, how about a drink?"

I figured she was trying to warn me. Too late.

Sammy swung open the office door and leaned against the frame, brows raised.

"Jazz, what are you doing here? Snooping around my things?" He crossed his arms, his expression guarded.

Now it was my turn to look sheepish. "I'm looking for my earring…" I pretended to search his desk, then decided to give up the act. My face flamed as I opened my bag wide, revealing the flask.

Startled, he held out his hand, almond eyes narrowed. "Where'd you get that? Whose is it?"

"It's a long story." I ignored his outstretched hand, stalling.

"Make it short." He thrust out his chin. "Amanda, why don't you check on Buzz? Jazz and I need to have a little chat." It was a command, not a request.

Her shoulders sagged, limp as a sock puppet, but she followed his orders. Sammy pointed to an old leather chair.

"Sit down. Tell me about the flask. Give it to me straight." He pulled out a Camel and lit it, glaring at me through the smoke.

"This belongs to your friend, Horace." I let out a sigh, handing him the flask. "After he passed out Saturday night, I found it under his barstool. Some bully tried to grab it from me, but Dino kicked him out of the bar. Then Dino took it that night, and I found it here, in your desk drawer." I paused, gauging his reaction. "Please don't tell Dino I have it, OK?"

"Leave Dino to me." He turned over the flask, studying the initials. "Why'd you swipe it?"

"I was there. I saw Horace lying on the floor, blotto. After what those men said about wood alcohol, I got worried." I waved my hands around, trying to explain.

"Why is this any of your concern?" He snapped. "It's my business, not yours."

"I was just trying to help…" I bit my lip.

Sammy squinted at me through puffs of smoke. "Help? How is stealing a stranger's flask helping?"

I flushed, avoiding his glare. "I wanted to find out if it was true. What they said about wood alcohol. So we took it to a chemist to get the contents analyzed."

"What? Who's we?" Sammy bolted upright, grinding his jaw. "What chemist? Jazz, don't you know how dangerous that is— besides stupid?" He slapped the table with his open palm. "Walking around town with a dead man's flask in your handbag?"

When he put it that way…stupid was an understatement. "Nathan says he's used to keeping things hush-hush. Don't worry, we didn't mention names or anything."

His hazel eyes flashed in anger. "Nathan? He's in on this? Who else knows? Jazz, you need to be more careful. I don't want you taking those kinds of risks." He took a few deep drags of his Camel, but his curiosity won out. "So tell me what this chemist said."

"You asked." I couldn't sugar-coat the truth. "Sorry to tell you that the flask was full of methanol. Seems your banker friend was poisoned by wood alcohol."

"What? It has to be a mistake." Sammy opened the flask and smelled it, making a face. "Can you trust this chemist?"

"I hope so. Nathan swears by him."

"If it's true, you did me a favor, in a way." He heaved a deep sigh. "That proves Horace didn't fill his flask here since no one else got sick. Thank God. It can take a while before methanol gets into your system. I know that much."

"Where did Horace buy his liquor? They must have sold him the methanol by mistake."

"That's what I'd like to know. But it brings up a lot more questions than it answers." He puffed on his Camel, shaking his head. "Poor Horace, that fool. Never knew what hit him."

"What are you going to do?"

"What *can* I do?" He shrugged. "I'd better hold onto the flask, just in case. For evidence. I'm no chemist, but maybe I can try to find the source, track down the seller. Wood alcohol hurts everyone, not only the victims. The sooner we get it off the streets, the better."

I nodded, recalling Nathan's remark, that Horace possibly had some run-ins with the gangs. "Did Horace have any enemies? Any reason someone might try to poison him?"

"Enemies? Not that I know of." Sammy shook his head. "Only the saps who lost to him at poker."

"Poker? Andrews was a gambler?" He didn't strike me as a big risk-taker, but you never knew who had what vice.

"He was a regular card shark. Trouble was, he lost as much as he made," Sammy said. "The Maceos hold a high-stakes poker game at the Hollywood Dinner Club every week. You wouldn't believe the big wheels who show up there to gamble their money away."

"Like who? The society set?" I perked up, hoping for a scoop.

"So I've heard, but I can't name any names. For Horace it was a hobby, a way to make extra money, hobnob with rich folks." He looked down, as if realizing he'd said too much. "Despite what you think, bankers don't get paid that much. And Horace liked to live the good life. The fancy car, big house, nice clothes. Plus he had other…expenses."

Sure, I'd seen signs of the Andrews' wealth on display, but gambling wasn't exactly a reliable source of income. I pictured his opulent home, nice suit and new Studebaker, and wondered if they were deep in debt. "What kind of expenses?"

"Personal." Sammy's eyes flickered. "Horace and I had a special arrangement. Whenever I needed cash up front, he lent me money— out of his own pocket."

"You didn't have to go through the bank?" I asked, surprised.

"Not officially. The bankers may hand out money to the Maceos or Johnny Jack or Ollie—with a hefty fee attached—but I'm small fry, not worth their time." True, I saw Rose Maceo there, best buddies with the bank president.

"So why did *you* get special treatment?"

Sammy blew out a smoky halo, watching it drift up to Doria. "You can say Horace took care of my books, and I took care of his…affairs."

"Affairs? You mean girlfriends?" Poor Mrs. Andrews. No wonder she was so suspicious.

"Not exactly." Sammy avoided my gaze. "A nephew."

"A nephew? But Alice never mentioned a nephew, or any other relatives for that matter."

"I may as well tell you, since Horace is gone." Sammy leaned forward, dragging on his Camel. "Buzz is Horace Andrews' nephew."

CHAPTER SIXTEEN

"Buzz?" I stared at Sammy in disbelief. Buzz and Horace were related? It didn't make sense. "But Alice said Horace had no family. His parents were killed during the Great Storm."

"Really? I figured he came from money, the way he put on airs." He knitted his brows. "All he told me was Buzz is his sister's son, that her husband was killed during the Great War, before Buzz was born. She wanted to raise him on her own, refusing to put him in an orphanage. But Horace said she got remarried and her new husband had no interest in raising Buzz, so she asked him to be his guardian."

"His sister? How sad." I sympathized with this young widow who struggled to take care of a baby alone, but questioned her motives. "Why didn't Horace take him in, raise him as his own?"

He shrugged. "I think he wanted to, but Alice just had a baby, and he didn't think she could handle him. Buzz is a bit... unpredictable. So he asked me to keep an eye on him here."

That explained why Horace was so nice to Buzz, why he'd given him special attention the night he collapsed. I'd heard a few Oliver Twist-type stories about orphanages, no better than prisons for juveniles. Still, the story seemed a bit dicey.

"Why keep him here, hidden away?"

"Beats me." Sammy sounded apologetic. "I got the feeling he wanted him out of sight. Horace was trying to sock away enough money to send Buzz to a private boarding school. Private as in pricey. Looks like those plans went up in smoke."

"I wonder why he never told his wife about his family. Why keep it a secret?"

"Who knows? Horace didn't volunteer much information."

"Does Buzz have any idea they were related? He seemed to get along with Horace."

"I doubt it." Sammy shook his head. "Horace tried to keep it that way. All Buzz knew is that a nice man showed up here once a week and gave him a treat, usually candy or a few coins."

"Maybe he felt protective of Buzz," I mused. "It's no wonder he wanted to keep him out of the orphanage, after his bad experience. Alice implied he had a rough upbringing there."

"That's all he told me." Sammy eyed me warily. "Let's keep this between us, hear me? I don't want your gossip mongers at the paper getting an earful."

"Don't worry." My face fell. "It's our little secret." Didn't he trust me by now? I wanted to ask him more questions, but Frank stuck his head in the office.

"Ready?" Frank held out the keys. Amanda signaled me, as if to say, "What happened?"

Sammy jumped up. "Let's go, ladies. You, too, Frank. I'll lock up behind us."

I walked over to say good-night to Buzz, who was wiping the tables with an old rag. "Good job, Buzz. You scared away that Fed agent. Again." I patted his back.

He thumped his scrawny chest, proud of himself. "I ain't scared of no cops."

I smiled at his bravado. "Keep an eye on Sammy for me, OK? He can use your help."

"You can count on me, Jazz," he said with a gap-filled grin.

Now I understood Horace's concern for Buzz, but that story had too many holes: Why did his mother seem so willing to give him up? And why in the world would a respectable banker want to hide his nephew in a Market Street bar? No offense to Sammy, but he was no father figure. Working in a blind pig wasn't exactly the ideal atmosphere to raise a sweet, sensitive boy.

During the ride home in Sammy's Packard, I tried to ask him more questions, but he clammed up. It figured. He still saw me as an immature tomboy, a pesky little sister, not as a peer or an adult.

Back at the boarding house, Amanda and I chatted a while, too jittery to sleep.

"Too bad Sammy caught you with the flask, but at least he knows the truth now." She looked down, then beamed at me. "Boy, am I glad I got to meet your Fed agent. What a looker!"

My agent? "He always turns up where he's not wanted, like a counterfeit bill."

"I wouldn't mind if Agent Burton carried a torch for me," she sighed. "Sammy barely knows I exist. Say, what did you two jaw about tonight?"

I was glad to change the subject. "You won't believe what Sammy told me. Can you keep a secret?" I paused, knowing it was a risk to tell Amanda. "Turns out Buzz is Horace Andrews' nephew."

"You don't say! I thought Buzz was an orphan?" After I filled her in, Amanda said, "Maybe Andrews was embarrassed by him, and kept him out of sight. Isn't he a little slow in the noggin?" She tapped the side of her head, voicing what I was ashamed to say or admit.

"I suppose a fine upstanding banker like him didn't want his poor past and his poor relations to haunt him." I nodded. "Still, the story sounds dicey. If Buzz really is his nephew, why did he try to hide him from his wife?" Perhaps Buzz was better off with Sammy, where he was at least protected and appreciated.

The next morning, I glanced at the paper, skimming through an article on Al Capone's latest exploits, making him sound like the patron saint of Chicago. Next to it was a small headline: COAST GUARD SEIZES TWO BOATLOADS OF LIQUOR WORTH $25K. I bet Johnny Jack was disappointed. For every booze boat the Coast Guard captured, dozens managed to slip by unseen. As long as the gangs controlled the island, the Feds didn't stand a chance.

I sorted through the stack of mail, invitations and telegrams waiting on my desk for Mrs. Harper. She'd left a new column to type up, along with scribbled notes asking me to fact-check her copy. The same old routine. Mrs. Harper was back to her bossy self, and I was relegated to typing and proofreading. Before my lunch break, the phone rang. A distinct male voice said: "Miss Cross? Agent James Burton. I'd like to speak with you. Are you free for lunch?"

Lunch? What could he possibly want? Did he want to badger me about Sammy, the Oasis? I brushed him off with: "I'm sorry, but I've made plans. What is this concerning?"

"I'd rather discuss this in person. I'll try you later. Good day."

Just like that, he hung up. Very formal, very abrupt. What did he want? Damn! How could I have a "good day" now?

His call made me so nervous, that I needed a diversion, a breath of fresh air—any excuse to go shopping. Tomorrow was payday and I couldn't do too much damage with my remaining "mad money." Didn't I deserve a treat, now and then?

I had my heart set on a ritzy enameled mesh bag or tango compact with bright colors and geometric or figural designs, like the ones I'd seen in color magazine ads. Sure, I'd gotten a couple of German silver mesh bags free with magazine subscriptions and ordered chrome compacts from the Sears catalog, but they were plain, nothing special.

I'd done my homework, and discovered that Eiband's department store had the best selection of ladies' accessories and perfumes. As I walked toward Post Office Street, Golliwog followed me like a shadow, but quickly lost interest when she realized I didn't have any treats. To her and all the neighborhood strays, I was mainly a food dispenser with legs.

Eiband's department store resembled a museum with its high ceilings, columns and oil paintings, filled with beautiful things—all for sale. Lucky me! I floated down the aisles, admiring the French perfumes standing at attention on glass shelves, their angular crystal bottles reflecting rainbows of light.

As I perused the beaded silk evening gowns, I thought I saw Mrs. Harper in the lingerie department, and stopped short. Her gaudy Edwardian hat was unmistakable, overflowing with faux fruit and frills. Was she following me? Ducking behind a column, I felt silly playing a grown-up game of hide-and-seek. My boss had a weakness for fancy hats just as I coveted chic purses and vanities. Now she was too busy buying undergarments to notice me. The image of my roly-poly boss squeezed in a too-tight corset made me laugh out loud.

Like a lady of leisure, I meandered over to the jewelry department, fingering the frothy frocks and wide-brimmed hats. Clothes came in and out of style so fast, I couldn't afford to keep up with all the trends on my paltry income.

To me, vanity cases and mesh bags were timeless, fashionable any season. Slowly I perused the showcases, marveling at the shimmering enameled mesh bags laid out on black velvet like perfect jewels, beckoning me, calling my name. Each bag was more radiant than the next—with escalating prices to match. Decisions, decisions!

A smart middle-aged saleswoman approached me, wearing long gloves and a navy linen suit and hat. "May I help you?" She extended her arms like a docent giving a grand tour of the Bishop's Palace.

In my blue cotton shift and cloche, I didn't look as sophisticated or wealthy as the older patrons, but didn't I deserve to at least admire, if not touch, the goods? I was tired of always window-shopping, counting my pennies. Nothing wrong with a small splurge!

"I'd like to see these bags, please." I pointed to my two favorites: a Whiting & Davis bag adorned with a bold cockatiel and a pink and teal Mandalian with a Persian rug design and drops.

"Very chic." She waved a white-gloved hand over the showcase and the bags appeared like magic. "Due to their delicacy, I'd recommend carrying these to operas, plays, weddings—not those wild parties or dance marathons or, heaven forbid, speakeasies frequented by the flaming youth and flamboyant flappers of today." Her hands fluttered to her throat.

Did she also consider me a flamboyant flapper? "No need to worry." I stifled a smile. "Do you take lay-away?"

"Certainly." The sales lady nodded. "You seem to be a nice young girl. As a working woman myself, I understand how it is to want the finer things in life. But sometimes they must be postponed—for a while." She smiled as if we shared a sisterly secret.

After studying the selection, I picked a stunning but less costly mesh bag: a glossy grapes design made of tiny baby mesh—so fine and supple, like silk, I couldn't resist. The cat's meow—and how! Handing the clerk my last dollar, I thought, Why not? I could go without lunch or new lipstick for a while.

She nodded in approval, no doubt calculating her commission. As I left, I admired the gleaming enameled compacts. A vanity case would be my next treat.

I rushed back to the *Gazette*, my head spinning, stomach rumbling. In my haste—and excitement—I'd forgotten to eat, but now I was too late and too broke. But the splurge was worth missing a few meals.

At the office, I slipped in my chair, while Mrs. Harper frowned in disapproval. She often disappeared for hours on end, but after one long lunch, I was given the cold shoulder. By her desk sat a huge striped hat box from Eiband's.

A few edited stories needed to be re-typed, so I started working furiously, trying to catch up before that day's deadline. An hour later, I'd made some progress but my back ached from hunching over my desk. While I stood up to stretch, I heard a commotion, loud whispers, chairs scraping.

A deep voice boomed: "Where can I find Miss Jasmine Cross, please?" All heads turned as I looked up to see Agent James Burton parade through the newsroom in my direction like the new sheriff in town—badge, hat, holster gun and all.

CHAPTER SEVENTEEN

Why in the world was Agent Burton here? Everyone stopped working to watch him make his grand entrance. People don't usually parade around in a newsroom: They sort of shuffle or stumble or stomp—unless a story's really hot, then they'll run. I felt like running away too, but I stayed glued to my chair, pretending to work, my heart racing.

Burton seemed to enjoy the attention as he headed my way. He was hard to ignore: Standing before me, all six feet-plus of golden skin and hair, he towered over my desk. Looking up, I noticed the curious eyes watching us in the too-quiet newsroom. The reporters stopped typing, fingers poised over keys, hoping for a scoop. Mrs. Harper stared with unabashed interest.

"To what do I owe this disturbance?" I adjusted my cloche, acting nonchalant.

He grinned at me, then looked around the suddenly still office. "I need to ask you a few questions. Can we go somewhere private?"

"What do you want?" I put on a brave face so the newsboys wouldn't see me sweat.

Burton scanned the hushed room. "You really want to discuss it here, out in public?"

He had a point. Did I want the whole staff listening in on my private conversation? He probably wanted to talk about Sammy, who was no one else's business.

"Let's go outside." Head down, I followed him past a leering Hank, feeling like a naughty kid going to the principal's office.

Nathan entered the newsroom, a camera slung over his shoulder, stopping to stare at Burton. "Jazz, is everything jake?"

"Everything's berries." I smiled to pacify him, but I admit, I had the jitters.

"I remember him. Your boyfriend?" Burton seemed amused.

"He's the staff photographer." I ignored his wisecrack. "And a good friend."

Outside, I felt safe among the throng of people and automobiles passing by in a rush. The hustle and bustle of the streets and sidewalks seemed almost comforting. I looked around for Golliwog, but she must have been making her daily rounds for scraps.

"How was lunch?" In broad daylight, Burton didn't seem quite as menacing or intimidating. Plus a group of hard-boiled reporters peered out the newsroom, spying on us.

"Fine." I crossed my arms, partly to cover my growling stomach. "So what brings you here?"

"Sorry to barge in that way." He smiled, tugging on his hat. "But I had to get your attention. You wouldn't give me the time of day the other night."

"Can you blame me? A raid isn't exactly the best way to meet new people."

"I think we got off on the wrong foot." Burton stuck his hands in his pockets, jingling some change. "Perhaps we can talk over dinner, instead of standing out here on the sidewalk?"

Was he serious? "Dinner? Just like that?" I snapped my fingers. "You waltz in as if you owned the place—like you did at the Oasis— and expect me to dine out with you, a total stranger, because of your badge? You've got a lot of nerve, mister."

"I wouldn't be a Prohibition agent if I didn't." He looked smug. "How about tonight?"

"Tonight? I usually work late."

"Every night?" He raised his brows. "Don't they let you off for good behavior?"

"For starters, I hardly know you and what I do know, I don't like at all." I squinted in the sun. "And I don't appreciate the way you bullied us at the Oasis that night. I thought people were innocent until proven guilty, not the other way around." I wasn't usually so bold and blunt with strangers, especially lawmen. Maybe it was his youth, or maybe I'd finally found my moxie.

"You must mean Sammy. Fair enough." He held up his hands. "If it makes you feel any better, my gun wasn't loaded that night."

"Small comfort now, after you scared everyone half to death." So it *was* all an act?

Burton looked down at his boots, as if reconsidering his options. "I hoped you could get to know me over dinner, but how about a quick bite now? I haven't eaten."

"Why not?" I nodded, not wanting to let on that I was famished. Burton stopped at a sandwich vendor on the corner, and tried to pay for my lunch and Nehi, but I pulled out a quarter before he did. It wasn't a date!

"Where can we talk, in private?" He motioned toward the newsroom. "Away from prying eyes and ears."

To be honest, I was curious. What did he really want?

I led him toward a city park and we sat on opposite ends of a bench, my clutch bag like a barricade, keeping my distance.

"What's the emergency? Why did you come by today, out of the blue? I hope I'm not under arrest!" I half-joked, gauging his reaction.

"I read your piece on Andrews. How well did you know him?" Burton was all-business.

I picked at my sandwich. "Not well at all. I met him once at a charity function."

He leaned back, taking a swig of his Coke. "I'm curious. Why would you write such a glowing article about a dead banker you didn't even know?"

Glowing? "I was just doing my job. It was a profile, not an investigative report." I chewed on my ham and cheese, but it tasted like cardboard.

"Where and how did you get your information—his wife, the hospital, the coroner?"

"Yes, I met with his wife, but why would I question the coroner?" I asked, my throat dry. "There was no crime, no autopsy. All I know is he died of heart failure." What was he getting at?

He turned toward me, frowning. "My sources tell me Andrews was a heavy drinker. Isn't it possible he got alcohol poisoning, perhaps at the Oasis?"

I shook my head. "The Oasis? If that was true, why was he the only person who got sick?"

"How do you know no one else got sick?" He challenged me.

"Say, what's the gag? Are you accusing Sammy of something?"

Angry, I sat up, ready to bolt. Then Golliwog began meowing, rubbing against my ankles in a desperate plea for scraps. Her timing was uncanny.

Burton eyed me over his sandwich. "I'm sure you know that a few locals imbibed some bad booze recently. I need to find the source and stop them before anyone else gets poisoned."

My heart skipped a beat. "That's your job, not mine. How does that involve me?"

"You tell me." He leaned forward, elbows on his knees. "I also heard a *Gazette* reporter had a recent mishap—in the Downtown Gang's area. Do you know which bar? What's the story?"

"News to me. I'm not a member of the good-old-boy's network. I'm a dame, remember?"

"I can see that." Burton looked me up and down with a grin like a drugstore cowboy. "Guess I'm wondering what a so-called society reporter was doing in a low-rent speakeasy—two nights in a row."

He moved closer, his voice accusatory. The sun highlighted a small scar, like a comma, across his cheek. "Can it be you're working on a new angle? An article about the dark side of Galveston society, where bankers mingle with bums?"

"You're all wet! I'm a society reporter. I don't cover the crime beat." Did he think I was actually working undercover, doing research for Mack? In a way, I felt flattered that he thought I was a serious journalist, not some silly society reporter.

He took a bite, wiping his mouth with a linen hanky. "So why hang around that dive?"

"The Oasis isn't a dive. Sammy is a friend of mine." My face felt hot as the fibs rolled off my tongue. I wondered if he could see right through my façade.

"How good a friend?" His eyebrows raised. "Is he on the level? Honest? Trustworthy?"

"He's no Boy Scout, but he always keeps his word. Why do you ask?" I shifted on the bench, the sun beating down on me like a spotlight. I may as well have been in a courtroom, being interrogated on the witness stand, with people gawking and whispering.

"Does Sammy ever discuss business with you?" Burton cut his eyes at me. "Do you ever hear any names of people he works with, like suppliers? You know, bootleggers? Rum-runners?"

"No, why would he? I'm not his employee." I was used to doing the interviews, and I didn't like having the tables turned. "Say, why are you giving me the third-degree?" If he was trying to grill me, he was as inept as I was, since I refused to answer any questions.

He shrugged. "I thought we could help each other, that's all."

"Help each other? By ratting on Sammy? No, thanks. You can do your own dirty work." I jumped up, pivoting like a gymnast on a high beam. That was my whole life—a balancing act.

I almost threw my sandwich in the trash, but instead dropped it before Golliwog, who devoured the remains. Then I stormed off, leaving Burton sitting there on the bench, his mouth hanging open. Served him right, ruining my lunch.

So I'd been right about Agent Burton all along. Inviting me to lunch was only a ploy, a way to find out what I knew, secrets about Sammy I wasn't privy to. Clearly he suspected there was a connection between Andrews' death and Mack's poisoning. But if he thought Sammy was responsible, why didn't he shut down the Oasis? Why hadn't he carried out his threats?

How ironic that Burton and Sammy, on opposite sides of the law, both had the same goal: to find out who was distributing the methanol, passing it off as the real deal, and try to shut them down—for good.

CHAPTER EIGHTEEN

I rushed back to the *Gazette*, and sank in my chair, breathing hard. My body felt tight, coiled up like a cobra. Did I say the right things to Burton? Did I help Sammy or make matters worse?

Mrs. Harper caught my eye. "How was your meeting? Who was your nice young man?"

"He's not my young man," I said, flustered. "He's a Federal agent." The newsroom grew quiet again. Why couldn't I keep my mouth shut?

"That's the new Prohibition agent?" She acted surprised, but I'll bet she knew exactly who he was. "Impressive. He's so tall and handsome. How did you two meet?"

What did she expect—a bodice-ripper? "We have mutual friends." Applesauce!

She nodded in approval. "He may be a valuable contact. Who knows where it can lead?"

Why was she so curious? Did she want some fresh gossip for her column?

Nathan walked toward the darkroom, ignoring me. "Hold your horses, Nate. I'd like to grab a soda after work." I admit, I used his nickname whenever I wanted a favor.

"I'm busy," he said, brushing by my shoulder. "Ask your new beau to take you."

"He's not my beau," I repeated loudly, for everyone to hear. "He wanted to ask me...."

"On a date? Hey, it's none of my beeswax. Sorry if I interrupted your plans." His face turned pink as he entered the darkroom and slammed the door shut. Was he jealous? Nathan?

Just my luck the staff had observed the whole scene. Pete, the cub reporter, walked by and it gave me an idea. "Hi, Pete, how's it going?" I twirled my curls. "Can we talk in private?"

"Sure, let's go to the break room." He winked. "Ready for that drink tonight?"

"How about later? I wanted to ask you about that night with Mack." I recalled Burton's remark, about the reporter who had a mishap in a Downtown bar. "I'm worried about Mack. Where was the last place you went? Do you remember the questions he asked? What got the gangs so spooked?"

His baby face turned to stone. "Why do you want to know? So you can tell the Feds?"

"Of course not." I blushed. "I'm trying to help a friend. He owns a bar on Market Street."

"You're pals with a barkeep?" His icy tone melted. "If I tell you, you owe me a drink."

"OK, it's a deal," I agreed. That was easier than I expected.

"Don't tell anyone, swear?" He looked around the newsroom. "Mack pretended he wanted to open a club in the Downtown Gang's area, so he asked the bartenders about liquor, suppliers, bootleggers. Guess he rattled their cages."

So that's how the reporters worked: Lied to get information. But didn't I do almost the same thing with Burton, lied to withhold information? "Which bar was it? Maybe we can go after work?"

"Too late." Pete shook his head sadly. "It went up in flames."

I was floored. "You mean the Lotus Club, on the Strand? We saw it the next day after the fire. What did Mack say to upset them?"

Pete nodded, and leaned forward, his voice low. "He tried to get the goods on Johnny Jack, his whole operation. Then he asked about some hotshot bootlegger and all hell broke loose. A few goons gave him the bum's rush, threw him out the door on his ass, the works. Poor old guy."

My breath caught. "What's the bootlegger's name? I won't tell anyone but my friend, I promise."

"OK, now you owe me two drinks. I think it's Black Jack." He pointed an ink-stained finger at me as he walked out. "Don't forget!"

Black Jack? The name didn't ring a bell. Did Sammy know him? I wished Mack was around to answer some questions, but doubted he'd spill the beans to me. I returned to my desk, grabbing my hat, purse and newspaper.

"I need to run some errands," I told Mrs. Harper. "Can I leave early? Please?" I hated to beg my boss, but I had to get out of the office, to clear my head.

"As long as your work is finished." She gave me a smug smile, as if I had a secret tryst with Burton. No, thanks.

Outside, I took a few deep breaths, trying to calm down. My "lunch" with Burton had me all balled up. True, he was only doing his job, following up on his leads—just like a reporter. While his motives were admirable, I found his methods underhanded, not to mention insulting: Flirting with me, pretending he was attracted to me, when I was merely a source, a means to an end. Luckily, I could see right through his tricks. I wasn't born yesterday!

Still full of nervous energy, I headed toward Star Drugstore, hoping to see a friendly face. Luckily it was quiet, too early for supper. Two men in overalls and faded plaid shirts sat on red barstools, eating burgers and drinking mugs of coffee.

I sat at my favorite booth in the corner, and waved to Amanda across the room. She frowned and sat down, a big no-no during her shift. "What's eating you?"

"Plenty. Guess who showed up at the *Gazette* today?" I made a face. "Agent Burton."

"I told you he had a crush on you!" She wriggled in her seat.

"Bunk. He treated me like a suspect in a case, asking me about Andrews and Sammy. He wanted to know the name of his bootlegger, his supplier. Hope I didn't get Sammy in any trouble."

"Tell me everything." She looked worried.

Talking to Amanda made me feel better, as if I wasn't to blame. Afterwards, she said, "You need to warn Sammy—in person. Say, why don't you invite him here for a piece of pie?"

Amanda thought pie was the answer to everything. If only it was that simple.

Eagerly she handed me the phone behind the counter, and after the operator connected me to the Oasis, I told Sammy: "I have some news. Can you come by Star Diner right away?"

"Now? What's the rush?" Soft jazz played in the background, and I heard loud laughter.

"I'd rather talk in person. Believe me, it's important." Sammy must have heard the urgency in my voice because he showed up ten minutes later, wearing an olive-green short-sleeved shirt that matched his hazel eyes. Women craned their necks for a better view, shooting us daggers of envy. Two matrons walked by our table, openly ogling Sammy. One lady swooned and crossed her heart: "He's even better-looking than Rudolph Valentino. May he rest in peace."

Amanda hurried over, giving Sammy a quick hug, and dropped off a piece of hot apple pie a la mode. It looked tempting.

"Are you still coming over for Sunday lunch?"

"Sure." He hesitated, glancing at me. "If it's all right with Eva?"

"She'd love to see you." I grinned at them both, before Amanda scurried off.

"Now I know you're lying." His face fell. Was it that obvious?

"What's wrong, Sammy?" I hated to add to his worries. "You seem upset."

"It's that goddamned ice man. He didn't show up again today. Two days in a row! It's hot as hell in there." He pounded his fist on the table. "I'm losing all my customers. Next time I see him, I'll break his skinny neck." An old coot turned to stare, his coffee cup poised in mid-air.

"Pipe down," I said, blushing. "Can't you borrow more blocks of ice from Joe's?"

"Joe says no dice, no ice." He let out a forced laugh, and took a bite of pie.

Glad he still had his sense of humor. "Why don't you order ice from somewhere else?"

"There's no one else in town. Johnny Jack controls the ice company too. He can make things hard on me if I complain."

Amanda reappeared with a cup of coffee, beaming at Sammy. He flashed her a manufactured smile, then turned to me.

"So what's the ruckus? Why'd you want to meet?"

Sammy had a hot temper, but a cool head when it came to giving advice. I leaned over the table. "You'll never guess who paid me a visit at work today. Agent Burton."

"Burton? That troublemaker. What did he want?"

"Information. He asked me lots of nosy questions about you, the Oasis, Andrews."

"Like what?" Sammy bristled. "What'd you say?" Before I could reply, he held up his hand like a stop sign. "Not here. Let's talk on the way." He gulped down his coffee and pie, then pulled out a money clip and handed Amanda a five dollar bill, enough to pay our tab for a month.

"Gee, thanks!" When we stood up, her smile turned upside down. "Leaving so soon?"

"See you on Sunday, doll." Sammy winked. "Around noon?"

"Can't wait!" Amanda called out. As we exited the diner, the waitresses' heads swiveled toward Sammy in a collective show of appreciation.

In the roadster, Sammy locked eyes with me but wouldn't start his engine. "Tell me about Burton. What did that bastard say?"

I fidgeted with my beads, then cleared my throat. "OK, here goes. He thinks there's a bad batch of booze going around town, and wanted to know the names of your suppliers. It's obvious he suspects Andrews died from alcohol poisoning." I decided not to mention the Lotus Club fire, or Black Jack, and make him even more upset.

"What did you tell him?" He gripped the steering wheel tight.

"What do you think? How should I know who your bootlegger is?" I shrugged. "Burton also asked about Mack, the reporter who got attacked. He seems to think I'm working on a story about bars."

"Bullshit. A nice girl like you?" Sammy snorted. "I bet it's a line, an excuse to ask you out. I know how these city boys operate." Then his face brightened like a bulb. "Why not humor him?"

"Humor him? Want me to tell him jokes?" I cracked. I doubted Burton even *had* a sense of humor.

"Come on, Jazz. You know what I mean." He shot me a stern look, his shoulders hunched as the car lurched away from the curb. "As they say: Keep your friends close, but your enemies closer."

"Think I should play along, pretend to be interested?" I shook my head. "I can't fake it. Amanda's the actress, not me."

"Why not? It can't hurt, only help." Sammy roared to a stop in front of the boarding house, and faced me, eyes like slits.

"You never know when you can use a friend on the force."

CHAPTER NINETEEN

A friend on the force? Sammy sounded just like Mrs. Harper. "Why do I need—?" But he revved his motor, speeding off like a fire truck. Was he mad at me for talking to Burton?

But I'd had no choice. So far Burton seemed to be all bark, no bite. Was he an enemy or a new-found *friend*? Was he on the level? When cops mingled with crooks, it was hard to tell the difference.

At home, all I wanted to do was take a warm bath and go to bed. I ate a quick meal of hot dogs and beans standing at the kitchen counter, a bad habit Eva detested. "Jasmine, where did you learn your manners? Certainly not from your mother!"

I was too shaken up to argue. "I'm turning in early," I said, to get her off my back. Yet I couldn't sleep, replaying my conversation, or rather *interrogation*, with Burton over and over in my mind.

The next morning, I arrived to work early—rare for me. Usually I showed up late to everything. Even back in school, punctuality was never my strong suit. Friday was payday, the one day the whole staff showed up on time. Even the crankiest reporters were in a good mood, including Hank and the office "football team."

Mr. Thomas made the rounds right before noon, passing out envelopes to the staff. Even Mack made an appearance, looking pale and bloated, but at least alert and upright. I made a mental note to talk to him later, but I doubted he'd remember my name. Strange that Nathan was missing. It wasn't like him to miss pay day.

When Mr. Thomas came by, he held my envelope out of reach like a carrot, or a bribe. "Can you come in to file on Saturday, Jazz?"

Did I have a choice? "Sure," I told him, pretending not to mind.

"I knew we could count on you." He handed me the envelope like it was a box of chocolates. I often ended up working on weekends—unlike the senior staffers—but Mr. Thomas always made it a point to ask me politely. Such a Southern gentleman. Of course they didn't pay me any extra, but he made sure I got a little bonus at Christmas. Emphasis on *little*. Still, who was I to pass up a few bucks?

During my lunch break, I went to Lone Star Bank, eager to cash my paycheck. As I walked down the block, I kept looking over my shoulder, expecting to see Agent Burton following me, but only saw Golliwog, my dark shadow.

The bank had the calm, hushed air of a library. Nervous, I stood in line along with the other worker bees, holding their checks, hoping Mr. Jones wouldn't see me and throw me out. I hid behind the newspaper as I scanned the offices for any signs of him. My eyes lit on Mr. Clark, but he was busy with a female client in his office.

After cashing my check, I felt rich with the new bills safely nestled in my handbag. Five bucks was a pittance to the Moodys or Kempners, but to me it was a small fortune. As I left, I walked by Mr. Clark's office and waved. He nodded and spoke to his customer, who stood up and smiled.

With a start, I realized it was Alice Andrews. I was surprised to see her at the bank so soon after the funeral, dressed in black from head to toe. Didn't we all have money matters to handle? She walked toward me, her hand outstretched. "Good to see you, Miss Cross."

"How are you, Mrs. Andrews?" I felt guilty for not keeping in touch, but we clearly didn't run in the same social circles.

"Call me Alice. I'm trying to straighten out our, my, finances." She sighed. "The bills never stop. I keep thinking Horace is away on a long business trip and he'll return any day now."

"I'm so sorry." We crossed the lobby and I held open the door. Outside, I blanched when I saw the Studebaker in front, a driver standing on the curb. Last time I'd seen the car, Andrews was barely alive. Alice motioned for the driver to wait, holding up a dainty hand.

"I need to ask a favor, Jasmine. Can you come by this evening?"

Now we were on a first-name basis? Must be quite a favor.

"I'll be glad to stop by after work. Is six o'clock OK?" I couldn't wait for hours to find out what she wanted, so I blurted, "Why?"

Her voice shook. "I'm afraid there was a break-in at our house."

CHAPTER TWENTY

"A break-in? Was anyone hurt? Anything stolen?" I asked Mrs. Andrews in surprise.

"No, thank goodness. Luckily, we were at the funeral." She took my hand as she turned to go. "Let's talk more later, in private."

My heart went out to her. First her husband passed away suddenly, leaving her alone, saddled with debts and three young children. Now she had to worry about break-ins and burglars and theft. So why in the world did she want to meet with *me*?

Cash in hand, I stopped by the same sandwich vendor I'd gone to with Burton, and ordered my favorite ham and cheese on rye. The grizzled old man grinned at me through his missing teeth. "Where's your fella today?" he asked.

I blushed. "My fella? He's only a f…" I was about to say friend, but decided on "Federal agent."

His eyes widened. "What's wrong? You in trouble with the law?"

I smiled at his concerned expression. "Don't worry, I'm not a jailbird." Not yet, anyway.

At the park, I tried to enjoy my lunch, but I was too worried about Mrs. Andrews. Why did she want to see me tonight? What was the favor? I returned to the office and worked through a stack of papers on my desk, trying to finish early.

Before I left, Mrs. Harper motioned me over. "You're in a big hurry. Any special plans this weekend?" She gave a knowing smile.

"Not really." I racked my brain, trying to think of any requisite society events I'd forgotten and might be forced to attend. "Why do you ask?"

"I thought perhaps you and Agent Burton…" She raised her penciled eyebrows slyly.

Not Burton again. "No, why?" I knew exactly what she meant.

"Oh, never mind." She waved me off, visibly disappointed. Was her column so devoid of scandal and gossip that she hoped adding our names as an *item* might spice it up?

After work, I took the trolley to the Andrews' home and waited in the parlor. The rooms looked forlorn without the colorful flowers and funeral wreaths. Outside, I watched a blond girl and boy chase a shaggy Sheltie in the yard. Alice came downstairs, pale and thin, holding a lace hanky. Flo carried a silver tray and poured two cups of tea, adding fresh mint. A nice touch.

"Thank you for coming, Miss Cross." Alice settled in a plush wingback chair. "Sorry to bother you with my problems."

"Not at all." I leaned forward. "You mentioned a break-in? Was anything stolen?"

"I don't think so. The back door was open, yet nothing seemed to be missing. But Horace's desk was a mess. Files and papers thrown out, drawers open, contents in disarray."

"His desk?" I asked. "Any idea what they wanted?"

"I'm not sure. His valuables were intact, but I wonder if these are significant? I wish I knew more about them." She opened the hanky and handed me a small notepad, a key and a Hollywood Dinner Club matchbook.

Was she playing dumb? "You think the burglars were looking for these? Where were they hidden?"

"In Horace's Sunday suit. They've been tucked away in my purse since then." She looked pleased.

The items reminded me of loot from a scavenger hunt, my favorite game we played as kids. I thumbed through the notebook, a ledger of some sort, then fingered the key. "What is this for?"

"It's a puzzle. I've tried all our locks and it doesn't fit." She let out a small, sad sigh. "I wonder if Horace was hiding something from me?"

Good question. I picked up the matches to distract her. "Did you ever go to the Hollywood Club?" I couldn't quite picture prissy Alice there, surrounded by gamblers and gangsters.

"That den of sin? Heavens, no! I hear it's just a cover for gambling and drinking, run by mobsters. I prefer the opera and theatre to jazz and Hollywood moving pictures." She stressed "jazz" and "Hollywood" as if they were curse words. Clearly she didn't share my taste in music or entertainment. "Besides, I don't approve of Horace consorting with those gangsters."

I smiled to myself at her high-hat attitude. Half of Galveston society wanted to pretend that people like the Maceos and Ollie Quinn and Johnny Jack Nounes didn't exist—the other half enjoyed doing business with the criminal element. Even the locals agreed they were good for the economy.

Blushing, she motioned toward the matchbook. "Please—take a look inside the cover."

I flipped it open and saw the name "Rose" scrawled in a man's handwriting along with a phone number. Could "Rose" mean Rose Maceo? "Do you know who it is? Did you ever call this number?"

Alice shook her head, uneasy. "Whatever would I say? What if Horace was having an affair with this Rose woman? He was never a ladies' man, but I began to wonder what he was doing, working late, going out at odd times. When I questioned him, he'd say, 'You take care of the children, Alice, and I'll take care of business.' " She wiped her eyes. "I ask you, what kind of bank conducts its business at all hours of the night?"

I knew from Mrs. Harper that "playing around" was a popular pastime in certain circles. Despite her pretense, Alice was a typical jealous housewife. "Did anything make you suspicious?"

"Worried more than suspicious. I hate to admit, I tried to search his wallet, desk, papers. I even checked his clothes for perfume, but they smelled like smoke and liquor." She stroked her teacup, as if in a trance. "He had a silver flask he took everywhere, like a best friend. How could I compete?"

I squirmed in my seat, feeling a pang of guilt. Why was she confiding in me? Did she suspect anything?

Alice stomped her tiny foot. "After all the work those Temperance ladies did to abolish that poison!"

Frankly, I'd heard enough lectures about "demon rum" to last a lifetime. Like Horace, some folks didn't know when, or how, to stop drinking until it was too late. Betrayed by his best friend.

"When did his behavior seem to change?"

"Right before little Tommy was born." She curled her pale hands around the tea cup. "You see, he was a surprise. Believe me, Jasmine, I love all my babies, but our finances were already strained with two young ones. I'm in no position to embark on a career, like you modern women. Whatever would I do?"

"You could sell your paintings at local galleries," I suggested, impressed with her talent. "Or perhaps you could illustrate children's books and periodicals."

"I paint purely for pleasure, not for profit," she huffed. Clearly the idea of making money was unfitting for a lady of her stature. Her brusque manner hinted that my nose had poked too far into her private life. True, I had a bad habit of giving unasked-for advice, as my friends often griped.

My face flushed, flustered by my faux pas. I shifted in my seat, trying to get comfortable. To change the subject, I picked up the small notebook and leafed through the pages, filled with cryptic letters and rows of numbers. Savings accounts? Or perhaps loans? "This appears to be a bank ledger of some sort. Was it for work?"

"I don't know. I can't make hide nor hair of it. I wanted to show it to Mr. Clark, but got cold feet. What was Horace hiding? What if he was up to no good? Then I saw you at the bank today, and it gave me an idea. As a reporter, I hoped somehow you could help."

What did she expect? Still, she seemed so fragile, I could only sympathize. "I'll do my best." I tried to reassure her. "May I borrow these items for a few days?"

"Yes, but please be careful," she pleaded. "I don't want them to fall into the wrong hands."

CHAPTER TWENTY-ONE

Wrong hands? What did that mean? Did Alice Andrews know more than she let on? Why get *me* involved? I wanted to ask more questions, but Flo appeared in the doorway, holding a chubby, rosy-cheeked baby, reaching out to his mother with tiny pink hands. "Excuse me, but little Thomas is getting fussy. Time for his feeding."

Alice sighed as Flo left with the squealing baby. "I can't bear to let Flo go. How will I manage without a nanny? She's been part of my family for years. She helped raise me." Alice pressed her fingers against her temples, squeezing her eyes, shutting me out.

I took pity on her. "I'm sorry. I wish I could do more to help."

"You are helping me." She managed a grateful smile. "Heaven forbid I air out my dirty laundry in public."

"I'll do my best." I felt flattered by her trust and faith in me, but I wasn't as confident in my abilities. I hid the items in my bag, and leaned over for a quick, awkward hug.

"Please keep this hush-hush," she said. "I don't want to tarnish Horace's good name."

"I promise to be discreet," I told her, gripping her hand as I left.

On the trolley, I mulled over her words, wondering why she gave me his items. I couldn't wait to examine them at home, alone. Had Horace spent his free time—and money—drinking and gambling in bars? Now Alice was stuck in a mansion she couldn't afford, caring for three fatherless children.

Was she in danger of losing her home? Unless she had family money, she'd be forced to join the growing ranks of working women like myself. Frankly, a job might do her some good.

Of course I felt sorry for her, but our visit brought back haunting memories. It had been a week since Andrews collapsed, and I didn't relish reliving that night or hiding it from his widow.

That evening, I arrived at the boarding house in time to eat supper with my aunt Eva. Old Mr. Hummel sat alone in the living room listening to the phonograph with his broken-down hearing aid the size of a tuba. Eva rarely went out, but preferred to stay indoors, taking care of the boarders, doing chores and handiwork.

At times she could be a real bluenose, acting like an old-fashioned Victorian spinster, not a moderne. She refused to cut or style her thick curly hair, but wore it pulled back in a severe bun. My mom told me Eva had been a raving beauty in her day, but now she insisted on downplaying her good looks, always wearing faded cotton dresses and big glasses that hid her dark eyes and long lashes.

"I was worried. Where were you?" she scolded, wiping her hands on her faded blue and white cotton apron. Corkscrews of graying dark tendrils framed her sallow face.

"I had to do an interview," I said, partly true.

In a way, Eva reminded me of Alice Andrews. When her fiancé died during the Great War, she was heartbroken and never recovered. I'd wanted to play Cupid, but she seemed resigned to being an old maid. Still, who was I to act as matchmaker? The only man after me was a Fed agent I detested who was more interested in arresting my brother.

"Say, this looks delicious." I reached in the pot for some stuffed grape leaves, my favorite dish, and piled them high on my plate along with yogurt and cucumber salad. I was too tired and hungry to be embarrassed by my gluttony.

"I made these for you," she said, pleased. "How was your day?"

Eva thought my life was all high-society gossip and glitz. I was tempted to fabricate a tony tea dance, or pass on the latest gossip, anything but the truth. "I worked on the obituaries."

She gave me a horrified look. "You call that a career?"

Clearly she wasn't interested in hearing any details of the departed, so I decided not to show her my article on Andrews.

"By the way, Amanda and I invited Sammy to lunch Sunday. Do you mind?" So what if she did?

"You know I don't approve of his business," she huffed. "That type of environment is a magnet for all sorts of scoundrels. Drunks, gangsters and criminals—and ladies of ill repute."

"That's not true. One day, he plans to open a ritzy place like the Hollywood Dinner Club."

"The Hollywood Club? It's only a gussied-up speakeasy!" Eva shuddered. "I've heard they have gambling and drinking in the back rooms. Even slot machines and poker games!"

For a reclusive old maid, my aunt was in the know. "I'm sure Sammy will be on his best behavior at lunch. I doubt he'll bring any of his gangster friends," I teased her.

Eva almost cracked a smile. "Well, I suppose it's all right if you and Amanda do all the cooking and cleaning. Turn off the lights before you go to sleep," she said and scuttled off to bed.

Since it was so nice and quiet, I decided to take a hot bath, a luxury I rarely enjoyed since Amanda and I shared a small bathroom with two ladies. One day we hoped to get our own flat closer to the beach, with our own rooms and a private bathroom. What a luxury!

In the bath, I couldn't relax and kept going over my meeting with Alice. What were the burglars looking for—the ledger? The key? Later I thumbed through the ledger, filled with rows of numbers and letters, like abbreviations or acronyms, written in pencil. Next to each listing were two dollar amounts, one high, one low. Were they gambling debts? Personal loans? The last page had one entry written in ink: RR628. What did it mean?

Saturday morning, I woke up late and after a quick lunch, I took the half-empty trolley to the *Gazette*. I'd promised Mr. Thomas I'd come in for a while to proofread and file. Not exactly my favorite duties, but I didn't mind working on simple tasks, to clear my mind.

I walked a few blocks to the paper, stopping to pet Golliwog, who lingered outside, looking for a hand-out. The newsroom was strangely quiet, even for a Saturday.

"Where is everyone?" I asked Mrs. Page.

"I'm not sure." She smacked a wad of gum. "Some big story."

Nathan rushed in and headed for his desk.

"What's wrong? Where's the fire?" I joked.

"No time to talk." He hesitated, looking down, as he gathered up his camera equipment and slung it over his shoulder. "Guess I'd better tell you…" Then he looked me straight in the eye. "There's been a murder on Market Street."

My heart stopped. "A murder?" Surely it wasn't Sammy or anyone I knew. "Who was it? What happened?" I was afraid to ask.

"All I know is Mack called and told me there was a murder and to meet him on Market Street." Nathan frowned, looking upset. "Sorry I blurted it out like that." He rushed toward the door.

"Wait. I'm coming with you." I grabbed my handbag and straw hat, and followed him outside.

"Sure you can handle it? It's no picnic."

"What am I gonna do? Read about it in the paper?" I tugged on his arm. "Hurry, let's go!"

In the car, Nathan stared straight ahead, driving as erratically as an ambulance. For once, I was glad he was speeding, holding onto the leather straps for dear life, my pulse racing.

Nathan turned on Market Street, parked near the Oasis, and we jumped out. A throng of people stood outside on the street—cops, reporters and gawkers—and we pushed our way toward the growing crowd. A truck with "Igloo Ice Company" painted on the side was parked on Market Street at an awkward angle, one tire on the curb.

What was going on? Did he have an accident? I held my breath as I recalled Sammy's beef with the ice man after he skipped his ice delivery—not once, but twice. A few reporters scribbled on pads, and a shutterbug jockeyed for position, trying to take photos.

We elbowed our way closer, and I stood on tiptoe, looking over the throng of people.

"Is that Sammy?" Nathan gasped in surprise, pointing.

"Sammy? What—where?"

In the midst of the crowd, I saw two cops flanking Sammy, clutching his arms. I froze in place, my heart beating so hard, my chest hurt.

Sammy was struggling, yelling, "Let go of me! I swear, I didn't do it!"

CHAPTER TWENTY-TWO

I began to sweat, not from the heat. Why were they holding Sammy? What did he do? Nathan took my arm and helped me push past the crowd toward the ice truck. Pale pink water dripped onto the street. Looking inside, I covered my mouth, trying not to scream.

The body of a young man, around 22 or 23, lay sprawled across several blocks of ice, streaks of blood on his clothing, congealing on the ice blocks. I cringed as I got closer, his pale blue eyes wide open as if in shock, an ice pick embedded in his chest.

My stomach lurched and I clutched my throat, trying not to upchuck. Not very professional. In the sweltering heat, the action unfolding seemed like a mirage, hazy and out of focus. The noise and commotion sounded far-off, surreal.

Everything was happening so fast, like a pulp movie. Police cars blocked both ends of Market Street, and a cop diverted traffic to Post Office Street. People milled around, gossiping, gawking at the ice truck, pointing at Sammy, as if he was the main attraction in a three-ring circus. Then Nathan gripped my arm, leading me toward the crime scene. "Let's find out what happened." He muscled his way into the crowd with me in tow, and a camera under his arm.

Moving closer, I caught Sammy's attention, anger and frustration blazing in his hazel eyes. I felt powerless, wishing I could help, wishing the chaos would stop. Was it possible Sammy was guilty? How could I talk to him in the middle of a crime scene?

"You've got the wrong guy," he yelled. "I've been framed!"

Framed? I tried to speak, but my mouth felt full of cotton. Then I spied Nathan, who'd eagerly set up his trusty camera, blue eyes shining like new pennies. I glared at him while he snapped away at the lifeless body, the ice truck, Sammy struggling with the cops.

When he looked over, he shrugged as if to say, 'Sorry.'

Yeah, right. Sorry he wasn't the first one on the scene.

In the crowd, I thought I saw Frank and Buzz, watching by the alley. Someone jostled me, almost knocking me over, but it was the wake-up I needed.

I rushed over to Sammy and the two cops, careful not to look at him directly. I took a few deep breaths, trying to calm my nerves. "What's going on?" I faced the cops. "Is this man a suspect?"

Sammy shot me a look, warning: 'Stay out of this.'

"What's it look like, sister?" A short cop stared at me, bug-eyed. He reminded me of a punk kid, with a round pink face, perspiring from the heat and the tight, buttoned-up police uniform.

"Seems to me you're jumping to conclusions. Maybe this man is innocent, like he said." I didn't think Sammy was capable of murder, but what if he'd lost his temper, acted in self-defense?

"What's it to you? Are you his squeeze? This is police business," the cop snapped.

"I'm with the *Gazette*." I squared my shoulders, and tried to sound authoritative. "I want to ask some questions."

"No joke? You're a reporter?" The cops looked me over, amused. "A girl?"

The tall one sported red hair and freckles. "I already talked to a guy from the *Gazette*. Are you his secretary? But since you asked so nice and polite, what d'ya wanna know?"

So Mack had already made an appearance. Figured. "When did you find the victim? Who called the police?"

The redhead became serious. "Half an hour ago, we got an anonymous tip. Guy said they heard a fight on Market Street. Gave us an address, then hung up. When we got here, this sucker was laid out cold. Cold as ice." He snickered at his own joke.

"An anonymous tip? He could be the real killer," I pointed out.

"Oh yeah? You're a cop now?" A few folks gathered around, trying to listen, including Pete and Chuck, our cub reporters. Sammy kept arguing with the police, avoiding my gaze, pretending we were strangers. Nathan was too busy taking photos of the poor stiff inside the truck to notice. Sensational sells papers.

I fired off more questions: "Are there any witnesses? What evidence do you have to hold this man? Any other suspects?"

What would Nellie Bly ask?

"The suspect sure looks guilty as hell to me. He was by the truck when we arrived. A source told us he had a big argument in the middle of the street with the deceased. I mean, before he got deceased." The redhead looked over at the short cop and laughed. Was murder a joke to them?

"I'm innocent, I swear!" Sammy yelled, wrestling with the cops.

If I had two cops yanking on my arms, accusing me of murder, I'd be yelling my head off too. "The guy showed up and tried to overcharge me for a few blocks of ice. We had a few words, that's all—no rough stuff. I made a deal with him, and I went to my office to get some dough. Honest Injun—it's the truth."

"That's not what we heard," the ruddy cop yelled in Sammy's face. "We heard you had a knock-down, drag-out brawl right here in the street. Got a bit of a temper, do you, sport?"

Sammy gritted his teeth, trying to control his anger. "How stupid do you think I am, huh? You think I'd try to kill some sap in public, right in front of my place of business?" He looked incredulous. "Like I told you, I was inside, getting some cash. I've been set up. Framed!"

"Framed? You sure?" A deep voice said behind me.

Agent Burton's tall figure cast a dark shadow. Now what?

The redhead let go of Sammy's arm and walked over to Burton, poking a finger in his chest. "Mind your own damn business, buster. Go find us some bootleg booze. Murder ain't on your dance card."

"I'm making it my business." Burton pushed him aside and grabbed Sammy's left arm. Sammy looked like a rag doll caught in a dog fight between a golden retriever versus a pit bull. "This man may very well be innocent. Could be a gangland slaying."

Did I hear right? Was Burton actually defending Sammy? He squinted, looking from the cop to Burton, then raised his brows at me, as if to say: 'What's going on?'

"Why don't you hit the road, city slicker?" The red-headed cop charged at Burton, but he shoved him backwards into the crowd. The cop tripped over the curb, his face flushed as he tried to regain his footing. "Damn you!" He took a swing at Burton, but he blocked the cop's arm, twisting it behind his back.

Why all the fisticuffs? I thought Fed agents got along with local cops, but that showed how little I knew.

"Hey, guys, I'm flattered you're fighting over me, but let's get this over with," Sammy said, now calm. "I've got nothing to hide."

"Sure about that, bud?" The redhead said to Sammy, then turned to Burton. "If you want to do something useful, go baby-sit the body. Let us real cops do our jobs."

He shook his fist in Burton's face, ready to slug him, but Burton stood his ground. Then the two cops hauled Sammy off, flaunting him in front of the crowd.

Sammy kept struggling, his head down, protesting, "I'm no killer! I swear, you've got the wrong guy!"

"Where are you taking him?" I demanded, following them to their squad car.

"Don't worry your pretty little head, doll," the short young cop smirked. "We're just taking him downtown for questioning. We don't want to pinch him—yet."

What kind of questions? I hoped it didn't involve sticks and fists, or worse. I'd heard rumors that some suspects taken in for "questioning" never made it downtown. Later their bodies washed up on the beach or were dumped on the docks, forever silenced.

The two cops pushed Sammy inside a paddy wagon, and I could hear him cursing under his breath. He squirmed and protested as they locked him in the back.

"I didn't do it!" he yelled, but the cops ignored him. My heart sank as they drove away, lights flashing, the crowd chasing behind.

Sammy held tight onto the bars, helpless, trapped like a caged circus animal, on public display.

CHAPTER TWENTY-THREE

My temples began pounding and wouldn't stop. I hated to think Sammy was capable of cold-blooded murder, literally in this case, but maybe it was self-defense? With his hot head and this heat wave, it's no wonder he was a suspect. He certainly had motive, means and opportunity. Or was he framed, a patsy, as he claimed?

"Sorry you had to witness that spectacle." Burton stood by me, watching the cops drive away. "I wouldn't wish that on my worst enemy."

"They should let him go, find the real killer." For once I was glad our father wasn't alive to see Sammy arrested in public, treated like a common criminal.

"Is there anything I can do?" Burton seemed sympathetic.

"Help Sammy." I blinked, refusing to cry. "Get him out of jail."

"Hard to reason with these palookas. These young guys have no experience, no street smarts."

"Then why don't you do something?" I must be desperate, asking for Burton's help.

"Don't worry, I will." He gave me a smug smile, then walked off toward the ice truck.

"I'll believe it when I see it!" I called after him, but he didn't reply. I tried to catch my breath before looking for Nathan. I found him by his car, calmly reloading his film.

"Why'd the cops arrest Sammy?" Nathan asked. "Do they really think he's guilty or is it just for show?"

"Who knows? They claim they're taking him in for questioning, that's all." I bit my lip. "So far he's their only suspect."

Nathan frowned. "They don't think he did it...or do they?"

"Looks that way." I glared at him. "And it won't help Sammy's case any if you splash his face all over tomorrow's front page."

"That's not my decision." Nathan looked down, shuffling his feet. "I know he's your friend, Jazz, but it's my job." He took my arm. "Tell you what. Let's go talk to Mack. Get his take on the whole situation. Maybe he knows something the cops don't know."

"Sure, thanks." Any information Mack dug up was bound to help clear Sammy's name, or so I hoped. Then I thought of Sammy locked up in a paddy wagon and Nathan taking picture after picture.

"Think you got enough photos? How about one of Sammy in handcuffs?" I couldn't resist. Still, this story, and the photos, could launch his fledgling career, and I had no right to make him feel guilty.

My dig went right over his head. "Plenty. Enough gore and guts for a whole spread." He noticed my squeamish expression. "Oh, sorry. But it could've been a lot worse. The ice kinda kept the victim—uh...well, nice and *fresh*, you could say."

"Nathan, please stop. You're not helping one bit." I made a face.

"Is that a smile I see? Good. Now let's go find Mack."

I felt dazed as he led me to the ice truck where Mack was talking to the coroner. Mack looked scruffy in a faded, crumpled khaki uniform, resembling a safari hunter. Now he was even dressing like Hemingway, his idol.

"Remember Jasmine Cross? She works for Mrs. Harper."

"Nice to see you. Hope you're doing well." I tried to put on a brave front.

"Anything is better than that jail cell. Speaking of jail, did you see that poor sucker get arrested?" Mack frowned at me. "Say, why are you here? Shouldn't you be at a tea dance?"

I ignored his jab. "What have you found out? Any ID or information on the victim?"

"All I know is what we saw. One man dead, the other a suspect." Mack frowned, impatient.

"But the so-called suspect is innocent," I protested. "They're only taking him in for questioning. He thinks he's been set up."

"Oh yeah?" His brown eyes narrowed. "Why do you say that?"

"I know him—he's a friend. He told me he was inside the Oasis when it happened."

Finally Mack looked interested. "How well do you know him?"

"Enough to know he wouldn't kill anyone, not in broad daylight, especially over ice." I shook my hands for emphasis. "The cops said they got an anonymous tip an hour ago, so there was a witness. Have they questioned anyone else?"

"Not yet, but if you hear anything, let me know." He gave me a condescending smile.

I figured he was teasing me, the naïve novice, but I pressed on. "What did the M.E. say?"

"I'll get the coroner's final report later. He said it won't take long since the body's been so *well-preserved*." Mack held his nose. "You know, like fish on ice?"

"Looks like a cold-blooded murder to me." Nathan nudged Mack, both starting to laugh.

How could they be so heartless, joking about a dead body?

"I take it you lady reporters aren't used to covering murders, are you?" Mack snorted.

No matter how much Mack tried to rile me up, I needed to stay on his good side. "Do me a favor. Please don't implicate Sammy— the suspect—in print before you get the whole story."

"Don't tell me how to do my job," Mack bristled. "I'm on a tight deadline today so this will be short, but I'll have more information by Monday."

"I'll be glad to stick around, try to find any witnesses who know what happened," I offered. "Anything else I can do to help?"

His expression softened. "Maybe you can snag an interview with your friend, Sammy? Hear his side of the story. Tell me what you find out."

What did he want—a miracle? "I'll do my best." I nodded. How did he expect me to question Sammy while he was in jail?

"I like your enthusiasm. Why don't we compare notes later?"

"OK," I said, hesitant. Was he baiting me again?

"For now I've got a story to file. See you at the *Gazette*." Mack saluted me like a general. "But be careful. Don't do anything stupid. We don't want you to get hurt. Coming, Nathan?"

Nathan looked over his shoulder. "I'll be right there, Mack." Then he patted my arm. "Gotta develop these photos. Sure you don't want a ride to the office?"

I turned around, surveying the crowd. "Thanks, but I need to find Frank and Buzz, see if they know or saw anything."

"That's the spirit." Nathan gave me a sympathetic smile. "I'm sure Sammy needs all the help he can get. Good luck."

Sammy needed more than luck—he needed a witness. After Nathan left, I wandered toward the truck, dreading the sight of the ice man. Yet I had to admit, I was morbidly curious. I steeled myself, pretending it was a routine assignment. The crowd had thinned out so I stood on tiptoe and peered inside.

A man in a white lab coat, the M.E. I assumed, was taking samples of blood and hair. The ice had melted and now the body seemed to be sinking into the blocks, his legs and arms drooping at an angle, his feet hovering over a pool of blood. Sawdust clung to the bottom of his boots, and a few sprinkles had fallen on the floor.

Why didn't they take the victim away, give the guy some respect, some dignity, in death?

"Got a good look?"

I jumped when I heard Agent Burton, flustered that he'd caught me ogling the ice man. He had a knack for showing up at the most inopportune times.

"I'll never get used to seeing a dead body." I shuddered. "He's my first murder victim."

"Tough, I know." Burton ran his fingers through his hair. "I feel bad for the kid. He's so young. Excuse me—*was* so young."

I snapped to attention. "You sound like you knew him."

"I did—in a way." He looked down. "Not well, but…I talked to him a few times."

"How'd you know him? What's his name?"

"Harvey O'Neal or O'Brien. Some Irish name like that. A young hood from Houston." Burton paced back and forth. "I asked him to do a simple job for me—and now this."

"What kind of job?" While Burton squirmed, I got more and more suspicious.

"Let's just say things didn't turn out as planned." His face flushed. "Guess I feel responsible, in a way. For everything—first, Harvey, and then Sammy."

"Oh really?" I held my breath. "What did you do?"

"Well, I probably shouldn't be telling you this…" He motioned me over to the side, away from the truck. "This is off the record, right? I'm telling you as a friend, not as a reporter."

"Friend?" Where'd he get that idea? "Come on, spill the beans."

"Well, I ..uh..suggested to Harvey that he skip Sammy's ice delivery this week. I never intended for it to go this far."

"You did *what*?" I fumed, hands on hips. "Why?"

Burton broke out in a sweat, avoiding my gaze, looking guilty as hell. "I only wanted to put the squeeze on Sammy—I didn't expect it to end in murder."

CHAPTER TWENTY-FOUR

"Put the squeeze on Sammy?" I flared up, my blood boiling. "Why in hell would you set him up like that?" I should have known Agent Burton was involved, the way he kept hounding Sammy.

"It wasn't a set-up," he insisted, pacing again. "I needed a favor, so I asked Sammy to help me out, but he refused. I thought a little pressure might work."

"What kind of favor? Why on earth would Sammy want to help you—after you threatened to padlock the Oasis?" I couldn't believe his audacity.

"I never shut it down, did I?" Burton turned away, eyes cold. "Sorry, but I can't discuss this with you. Not here. Not now. It's government business. Obviously I made a mistake."

"I'll say!" I wanted to slap him. "Your mistake got Sammy arrested for murder!"

He looked away. "I know I was wrong now. But it's all part of the job. People get hurt."

"That doesn't make it right." I stormed off, wanting to be as far away from Burton as possible. He'd mucked up things for Sammy so badly, I was afraid he could lose everything.

I raced toward the Oasis, anxious to find Frank and Dino. In the back alley, I noticed a bright red spot by the brick buildings: a red rose. It looked so out of place there, thrown out by the garbage cans, like an afterthought. When I bent down to pick it up, Burton caught up with me, taking my arm. "Jasmine, wait. Let me explain."

"I think you've already said enough." I pulled away from him, still holding the rose.

"Where did you get that?" He frowned.

"Right outside here," I said, motioning. "Not far from the ice truck. It's still fresh—as if it's been on ice." I began to feel hopeful. "Maybe it's a sign?"

"I bet some girl ditched the rose and broke her guy's heart." Burton gave me a pointed look.

I shook my head, lowering my voice. "No, I mean a sign from the Maceos. You know, Rose Maceo?" It was a long-shot, but I'd do anything to divert suspicion from Sammy.

He rubbed his chin, eyes darting back and forth. "That's possible."

"You said yourself it could be a gangland murder. And Sammy's not a gangster."

"I know that." Burton smelled the rose. "Maybe the Beach Gang is behind this."

I nodded. "What if they set up Sammy, as he said? Say, the killer was watching, and saw his chance to frame him? Sammy got caught in the crossfire."

"How about this scenario? The Downtown Gang may be trying to frame Rose Maceo, to create a rift in the Beach Gang," he suggested. "Sammy was in the right place at the wrong time."

"You said it." I pointed toward the truck, its wheels turned at a 90-degree angle. "Look how the truck is positioned, the wheels turned sideways, almost like he had an accident."

"Or was trying to avoid one," Burton agreed.

A bar owner opened a back door and threw a pan of water into the alley. He froze when he saw Burton, and slammed the door hard.

"Seems you're not too popular in these parts. Can't say I blame them," I razzed him.

"Fed agents aren't known as the life of the party." He smiled. "Say, why don't we discuss this in more detail, over dinner tonight?" It was a statement, not a request. "If we put our heads together, we can both help Sammy."

"Dinner? After you caused this fiasco?" I was dumbfounded. "It's Saturday night. Don't you have speakeasies to raid, innocent people to terrorize?"

"I'm off-duty tonight, luckily. You know worrying all night won't help you or Sammy." He smiled. "Besides, I have some ideas that might clear Sammy's name."

I crossed my arms, skeptical. "What did you have in mind?" The idea of teaming with Burton made my head spin, but I was desperate to help Sammy.

"Why don't we go to the Beach Gang's favorite bars, say the Grotto or the Surf Club? You can be my cover. I'm sure those hoods would rather see you than me across the table." He grinned. "Don't you want to watch Ollie Quinn and the Maceos squirm in public?"

Picturing those gangsters squirming made me smile. I recalled what Sammy said: "Keep your friends close, but your enemies closer." Maybe this was my chance to grill Burton, turn the tables, find out what *favor* he wanted from Sammy. I looked down the alley, watching a calico cat scurry away, trying to think.

"I wouldn't call this a real date. More like a mission."

"A mission it is." He tipped his hat. "I can pick you up at eight."

"You sure are cheeky. I never said yes."

He gave me a sly smile. "You never said no either."

I had a brainstorm. "Tell you what. I'll go out with you tonight if you do me a favor."

"Your wish is my command." He raised his brows. "If it's legal."

"Of course it's legal." I eyed him, almost pleading. "Can you get me in to see Sammy? I need to talk to him, find out the truth."

"That's a tall order." Burton rocked back and forth on his heels.

"If you can take me to see Sammy tonight, then I'll go."

Frankly, I didn't really feel like making whoopee while Sammy was stuck in jail, but it was worth a try. What did I have to lose?

"I can't make any promises. As you know, the police and I don't always see eye to eye." Burton held out his hand. "Why not give me the rose? I want to show this to the cops—may be evidence. Besides, a woman like you deserves a dozen roses, not just one."

Oh, brother! I rolled my eyes at him, wondering how many times he'd used that sappy line before. Yes, he could be a charmer, all right—or a silver-tongued snake.

"I'd better get back to the crime scene. See what the M.E. turned up. Sure you're OK?"

I nodded. "If I can't count on the cops, I'll have to investigate this case myself." Not one of my best ideas, but I was determined to help Sammy.

"Be careful." His face was grim. "There's a killer on the loose."

CHAPTER TWENTY-FIVE

True, but did Burton have to remind me of that fact? What if the killer was lurking nearby, watching us right now? I rushed to the Oasis and knocked on the back door, looking over my shoulder. When no one answered, I opened the door and let myself in.

Strange that it wasn't locked. "Frank? Dino? Buzz?" I called out, carefully climbing downstairs in the dark.

The Oasis was eerily quiet, as if abandoned. Where was everyone? Without Sammy, it was an empty, lifeless shell. I wandered around the dim room, feeling like a trespasser. Several chairs were overturned; dirty plates and glasses covered the tables. Was there a bar brawl—again? How could they be so careless—leaving the place unlocked, so messy and unattended?

I poked my head inside Sammy's office, but no one was there. This was my chance to snoop around, piece together the facts. A black metal cash box sat on the desk, wide open. No doubt Sammy was telling the truth about trying to pay the ice man. Buzz's burlap flour sack was strewn across a small cot where he often slept.

I noticed half of his prized possessions had spilled out— marbles, baseball cards, bubble gum, along with clean clothes. He hadn't run away, yet.

By the sack, I spied an old faded photo: A smiling young man, his arm draped across the shoulders of a boy, seven or eight years old, in overalls, with the year '1922' and 'Buster' scribbled on back. The boy clearly was a young Buzz, with the same goofy grin and wide-set eyes.

With a start, I recalled the photo of Andrews in his Army uniform. I felt a shock of recognition: The men were one and the same. Why did Andrews give Buzz this photo? Studying their faces side by side, the resemblance was unmistakable. I recalled the night at the Oasis, his interest in Buzz.

Then it hit me: Could Buzz actually be his son, born out of wedlock? What happened to the mother? Was she his girlfriend, before the war? Perhaps he'd created a sister as a cover. What an elaborate tale. No wonder he didn't tell his wife the truth.

The office door flew open and my heart skidded when I saw a shotgun slide out and take aim. I kept still, holding my breath, trembling. "Who's there?" A frightened voice said.

"Frank? Don't shoot! It's me, Jasmine," I cried out.

"Jazz, what in God's name are you doing here?" Frank walked in, his voice a mix of relief and surprise. "I thought you were…."

"Damn it, Frank! You scared me to death. Of all the nerve, pointing a gun at me!"

"Sorry, Jazz, I didn't mean to frighten you. I heard a noise and got worried." He put the gun down, exhaling loudly. "Did you know the cops arrested Sammy? Some bad luck."

I caught my breath. "Were you here when the ice man showed up? What happened?"

"I was in the kitchen, cleaning up." Frank looked upset. "Sammy said he had to pay the ice man—he was complaining about his high prices. Highway robbery, he said. Then he went to his office for some cash. Next thing you know, the cops are hauling him away."

"The police only want to question him. He'll be out soon."

Who was I trying to convince?

"Have you talked to any reporters?" Frank asked. "Do they know anything?"

"I talked to Mack, but he knows as much as we do." I glanced around in dismay. "This place looks like a hurricane hit. Where's Dino? Buzz? I saw all of you earlier in the crowd."

"Dino won't come in till later. I think Buzz disappeared." Frank shrugged. "He sure was upset about something, but he wouldn't tell me what was wrong."

"What if he saw Sammy get arrested and got scared? Any idea where he went?" I asked, anxious. "I'll be glad to go look for him."

"Try Joe's next door. He likes to play pool with the help."

I hated that grimy dive but it was worth a try. "Maybe somebody there saw the fight, even the murder?" I paused. "Say, are you planning to open tonight?"

Frank shook his head. "Not sure if it's such a smart idea, under the circumstances."

"But that makes Sammy look guilty. Why not stay open, act like nothing's wrong?" I suggested. "Business as usual. Don't let the killer think he's won." Sammy needed to save face—and how.

"Tough talk." He nodded, smiling. "OK, we'll do it. For Sammy's sake."

Outside, I shielded my eyes from the sun. Joe's Grill was a run-down hash house and bar next door that I tried hard to avoid. I'd heard the crowd was full of roughnecks, cowboys and grifters, not the proper atmosphere for a budding society reporter. Rumor had it Joe's operated as a bordello and flophouse on the side, if you counted the rooms upstairs, and from the looks of their "clientele," the two businesses often intermingled.

I knocked on the side door and waited. The sun beat down on my arms and legs and I covered my face, trying to shield my eyes. Maybe this wasn't such a good idea... Then a door opened slowly and a wrinkled old woman in a faded red hat peered out, her eyes dull as dirt.

"Who are you? What d'ya want?" She frowned.

Did I need a password? "I'm a friend of Sammy's next door. Is Joe around?"

"Sorry, missy. Joe's not here," she snapped, her smoker's voice raspy as a scratched record. She tried to close the door but I shoved my foot in and peered inside. I'd learned a few tricks from watching Nathan in action.

"Did anyone see what happened today? The ice truck? Sammy's arrest?" I asked politely. As my mother always said, you can catch more flies with honey than vinegar.

"We ain't seen nuthin'. Anything else?" The old biddy tapped her foot.

Why was she so quick to dismiss me? I got the hint, but refused to leave. "I'm looking for Buzz. A young boy, about twelve or thirteen, who works for Sammy. Is he here?"

"Buzz? Buzz who? Go ahead, girlie, look around, make yourself at home." She flung the door open, jerking her arm toward the bar.

Joe's Bar and Grill didn't even try to disguise the fact it was really a crummy gin joint, not an actual diner. Dozens of beer and liquor bottles and dirty glasses lined the counter. A thick layer of cigarette smoke cast a dingy gray fog over the room, mingling with the smell of grease and sweat and stale air. When was the last time they'd opened the windows?

I started to cough, and a few drunks laughed in response. One old geezer cleared his throat, a loud, hacking noise.

Upstairs, I saw a door open and a fat man in overalls stuck his head out, looked around, then slammed the door shut. I felt sorry for the hooker who had to entertain him for even one hour. Worse, assorted animal heads were mounted on the grimy walls: a few deer, a bear, a cougar, a majestic lion. I pitied these once-proud animals having to waste away in this hellhole.

Carefully I stepped over the broken bottles on the sawdust-laden floor. Wait, where had I just seen sawdust? Then I remembered the victim's boots were also covered in sawdust. Did he stop here first? Who tipped off the cops? I studied the men: was one a witness, or even the killer?

In the back, a few grizzled drunks in worn jeans and dirty work boots played pool. They stopped to eye me as I walked by, whistling loudly. Sorry, not my type. The pool sticks looked like weapons in their greasy hands.

"Buzz?" I circled the room, but saw no sign of him.

With a start, I thought I recognized Mutt and Jeff, the guys from the bar fight who showed up after the Lotus fire. They sat at the bar, beer mugs overflowing with foam, chewing tobacco. Just a coincidence or a stroke of luck? How did they manage to turn up at every crime scene?

I made a beeline for them, asking: "Say, did you guys see the ice man hit? Or his fight with Sammy? He owns the Oasis next door. Haven't you been there before?"

They didn't blink. "You look familiar, little lady," Mutt drawled.

"Were you here earlier?" I persisted. "They arrested Sammy, but he didn't do it."

"How do you know?" Jeff leered. "Why don't you ask Ollie or Dutch what they think?"

Was that a lead? "You mean the Beach Gang?"

"Maybe you should talk to Johnny Jack about the hit." He let out a snort.

"It was a hit? Are you sure?" Was he telling the truth or razzing me? "Sammy and Johnny Jack are good friends. He wouldn't set him up, or try to frame him for murder." Or would he?

"You sure? We hear Sammy likes to play both sides. Maybe they all ganged up on him?"

What a dimwit. "Thanks for nothing." I turned to leave when Mutt slid off his bar stool.

"Now is that any way to treat such a nice lady?" He punched Jeff hard in the shoulder. "I'll tell you what you need to know, toots, but we can't talk here."

Grateful, I followed him to a back room where a few grizzled geezers sat on barstools, dazed, plunking nickels and pennies into the one-armed bandits lining the wall. The constant clanging of the coins and bells rattled my brain, my nerves, but the men were so entranced, they didn't even notice we were there.

Eagerly, I turned to the tall, lanky man. "Do you know which gang put out the hit? Why did they frame Sammy?" The questions couldn't come out fast enough.

"You must have a soft spot for this Sammy," Mutt said. "Should I be jealous?" In a flash, he bent over me, his hot whiskey breath blowing in my face. "Pucker up, princess. How about a kiss?"

Ugh! I jerked away, but he grabbed my arm, his dirty nails piercing my skin.

"Let me go!" A jolt of fear shot through me, but I managed to squirm out of his grasp, kicking his shin before I bolted for the door. Too bad I wasn't wearing steel-toed cowboy boots.

"You bitch!" he yelled, holding his leg. I ran out, flinging open the door. Fresh air at last.

Shaking, I raced back to the Oasis, and leaned against the brick wall, catching my breath. I felt dirty all over, wishing I could jump in a hot springs bath, clean off the stench, the grime.

Thank goodness I got away from those dumb bastards. No longer did I feel safe—I felt violated, like a target.

I even began to feel sorry for Agent Burton: How did he deal with these lowlifes every day?

The back door was still unlocked, and I crept down the stairs, listening for voices, for any signs of life. What a contrast: The Oasis was the Ritz compared to that dirty dive. "Frank?" I called out. "Buzz?" I heard a muffled noise by the office and froze in place. "Hello? Who's there?" I reacted without thinking, creeping toward the sound. Slowly I cracked open the office door and breathed a sigh of relief: Buzz was curled up in a ball on the floor.

"J-J-Jazz? Is that you?" His face looked ashen and pale.

"Buzz, what's wrong?" I knelt down beside him, patting his arm. "What happened?" His whole body was trembling, his teeth chattering, as if he had a bad cold.

He looked up, blue eyes wide and frightened.

"I saw him k-k-kill the man. The ice man…They were fighting and yelling. Then he grabbed the ice p-p-pick. He st-stabbed him. Right in the heart."

CHAPTER TWENTY-SIX

"Who? What did you see?" I held my breath, afraid of the truth.

"D-dunno." Buzz sat up, hugging his knees, rocking back and forth. "N-n-never seen him before. He wore a c-c-cowboy hat and b-boots. He was short, but b-b-big. Like D-Dino."

"A cowboy?" So it wasn't Sammy, after all. What a relief!

Buzz was still shaking so I tried to calm him down, speaking in soft tones. "Want a soda pop?" He nodded, head hanging, scrambling to his feet. I handed him a cold bottle of Coke, motioning for him to join me at a table. He gave me a grateful grin and sat down, wiping his tear-stained face.

After he'd downed the Coke, he seemed to relax. "Where were you during the fight? Did you *see* the cowboy stab the ice man?"

Buzz nodded, chin quivering. "I went to the c-c-corner market to buy some f-f-food for Sammy. I was walking back when I s-s-saw the c-c-cowboy j-j-jump in the truck. They were f-f-fighting and yelling. I heard some b-b-bad words." He gulped in air.

"Then the c-c-cowboy stabbed the ice man, and ran away from the t-t-truck with blood all over his hands." His blue eyes darted around, his face and hands jerking like an animated puppet.

What a shock. No wonder Buzz was terrified. "Did you see where the man went?"

"He ran d-d-down the alley. It all happened so f-f-fast. I was so scared...I dropped my s-s-sack and ran away." His eyes began to water. "I d-d-didn't know they'd take Sammy away. Why Sammy? He had n-n-nuthin' to do with it."

Poor kid was stuttering so badly, I barely understood him.

"I know." I gripped his shoulder. "Did the cowboy see you? Did he try to follow you?"

"No, I d-d-don't think so…" He shook his head. "I was hiding the whole time. B-b-but I didn't say nuthin,' I just ran away. Didn't k-k-know where else to go, so I came b-b-back here."

"Stay inside the Oasis for now, to be safe, OK? Keep it between us, like a secret."

"A secret?" Buzz nodded. "I can k-k-keep a secret."

"Good." I smiled. "Hey, why don't you help clean up here? Make it nice for Sammy."

"Sammy's c-c-coming back?" His baby face lit up.

"Definitely." I looked around, unnerved by the silence. "Are you here alone? Where's Frank? Dino?"

"Dunno." He shrugged. "I'll g-g-get everything ready for Sammy. For t-t-onight."

Then I heard heavy footsteps coming down the stairs. Buzz and I exchanged looks, too afraid to move. But it was only Frank, followed by Dino, who carried two huge blocks of ice in a leather sling over his shoulder. With his bulging muscles and tight T-shirt, Dino looked like the strong man in a circus. Frank held a big tin tray piled high with chipped ice and rushed toward the kitchen. Buzz jumped up to hold the door open while they struggled with the heavy blocks. Then both Frank and Dino reappeared, grinning like wicked Cheshire cats.

"Jazz, you gave me a great idea," Frank smiled. "I thought, why let all that good ice go to waste? So we helped ourselves, as you can see. Free ice!" He and Dino chuckled and poked each other in the ribs. "A few blocks for the blockheads. Save a few bucks. It's the least we can do for Sammy."

"Are you sure it's clean?" I grimaced. "You know…all that dirt and blood?"

"Don't worry, we got the blocks from the cooler in back," Frank assured me.

"What about the cops?" I hid my smile. "Did they see you?"

"Hell, they didn't care," Dino said. "We did them a favor. The ice was melting so fast, it was dripping all over the place. All the barkeeps are out there, loading up."

"What about the body?" I shuddered, making a note not to drink anything on ice.

"The medics took him away," Frank said. "Unlucky son of a gun."

"Thank goodness," I said. "Poor kid. He gave me the creeps, with his eyes wide open." I turned to Dino. "So where were you when it happened? Did you see or hear anything?"

"I was on the docks. You know, running errands." He scowled. "What's it to you?"

"I'm trying to help Sammy." Why was he acting so guilty? Then I gestured toward Buzz, still in the kitchen. "Did you talk to Buzz?"

"Buzz told me a little," Frank said. "I'm not sure what to believe. Maybe he made it all up to protect Sammy. He does have a vivid imagination."

"I'm sure he's telling the truth," I said, annoyed. With Sammy gone, Frank and Dino acted like Amos and Andy. "He's scared to death, poor kid! Don't let him out of your sight. It's not safe."

Frank nodded. "We'll keep him busy tonight. Don't wanna let Sammy down."

"Make Sammy proud," I told them as I left. "But be careful."

I headed for the trolley stop, looking over my shoulder for Mutt and Jeff, trying to forget the whole disgusting incident. They seemed to pop up all over the Downtown Gang's area, like bad pennies. Was it possible that they worked for Johnny Jack or were they spying for Ollie Quinn? Was it a fluke they were at the Oasis the night Andrews passed out? What a coincidence that they showed up the day after the Lotus Club fire, and now at Joe's Bar. Was there any connection?

On the trolley, I could relax, glad for a chance to think. Naturally, I was relieved to find a witness to the ice man murder, but why did it have to be Buzz? I admit, I was worried about his safety, as well as his credibility. Even if he told the cops about the cowboy, could they be trusted?

At the boarding house, I'd just walked in when Eva waved me over, holding the telephone. "For you. A gentleman caller!" You'd think the call was long-distance, she seemed so excited.

"You haven't forgotten about our dinner plans tonight, have you?" Burton's voice boomed over the line. I turned my back on Eva, who hovered like a pushy sales clerk.

"Of course not." Did he think I was a dumb Dora? "Do you need my address?"

"I know where you live. Remember, I'm a Federal agent."

What else did he know about me? "Did you see Sammy? When can I talk to him?"

"Later. See you soon." Damn! I'd promised Mack an interview, but I hoped Sammy would get out before the story hit the papers.

After I hung up, Eva started banging pots and pans in the kitchen. "Jazz, who was your young man? Are we having a guest for dinner?" Her voice was lilting.

"Please don't go to any trouble. I'm going out tonight."

"Oh? What does he do for a living? How did you meet?" She was as nosy as Mrs. Harper.

"He works for the Treasury Department." Did she need to know that we met during a raid?

"Really? Is he a banker?" She perked up.

I tried to stall. "He's the new Prohibition agent." I turned to go, to discourage any prying.

Her face fell. "That's such a dangerous job, Jazz. Why can't you find a nice doctor or lawyer to date?" Despite her thankless duties of running a boarding house, she was truly a snob about jobs.

"It's only dinner, not a date." I smiled. "Don't worry, we're not getting engaged."

She gently pushed my hair away from my face. "I worry about you, honey, as if you were my own daughter. With your mother gone for the summer, I feel responsible for you."

"Thanks, but I can take care of myself."

Aunt Eva gave me this long lecture at least once a month. With a sigh, she returned to the kitchen and commenced banging pots and pans, this time with added gusto. What a life—cooking and cleaning for strangers. Things would be so different for her if only her fiancé hadn't died in the war, like so many innocent people.

Climbing upstairs, I felt sorry for Eva, leaving her alone tonight. Glad she had the boarders to keep her company. To be honest, I felt guilty going out while Sammy was in jail, but I planned to question Burton, to humor him, as he'd suggested.

Sammy was right: We *did* need a friend on the force.

Too bad Amanda wasn't home yet. For fun, I put on a teal beaded gown and shoes, adding a long necklace and cloche adorned with a small peacock feather. As I outlined my eyes in dark kohl, Eva entered my room without knocking. "Jazz, I've been thinking. Galveston can be a rough town at night. All that riffraff. I think I'd better chaperone you on your date tonight."

I stood firm. "I don't need a chaperone. It's more like an interview, not a date."

She frowned her disapproval. "You know the police here have a poor reputation, consorting with criminals, bootleggers, prostitutes and gangsters. Some of that bad influence is bound to rub off."

"Agent Burton is a Federal Officer. I couldn't be safer," I said. Applesauce! I didn't really trust him either.

"That's even worse." She knitted her eyebrows. "Federal agents raid those dangerous gambling parlors and speakeasies. You'll be forced to tag along!"

I turned away, ready to tear my hair out. Now I was dreading the evening even more: Instead of helping Sammy, we'd be fielding snoopy questions from my aunt. Like my mother, Eva often drilled my male friends to such a degree that they never returned for an encore. Too often, I felt humiliated by the implication that my date wasn't only an escort to a dance or a party, he was a suitor asking for my hand in marriage.

Worse, my mother thought my job was a waste of time, an amusing stepping stone until I met Mr. Right. She hoped that I'd give up my career , settle down and get married and have a brood of babies. No, thanks. I wanted to explore the world, experience different cultures, meet interesting people. Exasperated, I flung myself on the bed, wishing I could call the whole thing off.

Agent James Burton could be quite charming—when he pleased. He showed up promptly at 8:00 p.m. and managed to win Eva over completely by 8:15. After she answered the door, she invited him into the parlor as I watched from the hallway. In his striped shirt and three-piece navy suit and tie, he could pass for a doctor or a lawyer. A Joe Brooks buttoned-down guy: Just her type.

"You must be Jasmine's sister," he said to my aunt, kissing her hand. My sister? Who did he think he was—Douglas Fairbanks?

Eva sort of giggled, not correcting his faux pas. Faux pas my foot. "You must be James Burton," she said, blushing. "Please make yourself at home. Do you want some fresh lemonade?"

"Yes, ma'am, that would be swell." He smiled and sunk into the sofa, stretching out his long legs, his hat on his lap.

This could be a long evening. My aunt never served her prized lemonade to strangers—not even to her boarders, reserving it only for family and friends.

As I made my entrance, Burton jumped up, saying, "You look like the cat's pajamas!"— knocking his hat to the floor.

"Why, I'm flattered," I said in my best Southern accent. I admit, I'd taken extra pains to dress tonight. For once I felt like a fancy float in a Fourth of July parade. True, I had an ulterior motive: To disarm my source and get as much information out of him as possible.

He grinned. "I doubt flattery will get me very far with you."

"Flattery is fine as long as it's genuine." I didn't want to fall for his gimmicks.

Eva held out two frosted glasses of lemonade. "You look nice, Jazz. What's the occasion?"

"A date with a beautiful woman is always a special occasion," Burton said smoothly.

What a line! "Thanks." I blushed, feeling like it was my senior prom all over again, minus the corsage, but adding a badge. I took a few sips of lemonade, then stood up. "Shouldn't we be leaving?"

"Why don't you join us?" Agent Burton crooked his elbow toward Eva. I wanted to strangle him.

Did he really want my prissy aunt tagging along as we searched mob bars for mob bosses?

"Me?" Eva beamed and I could see any doubts she'd had about "shady Fed agents" melting away. I knew exactly what she was thinking: Husband material.

I shot her a warning look, relieved when she replied, "Thanks, but I've eaten. You two kids go have fun."

"Another time, then?" He tipped his hat as we left. Was he sincere? Taking my elbow, he led me to his late-model Ford roadster.

"Glad you could make it on such short notice tonight."

"I had my social secretary cancel my prior engagements."

Outside, I looked around, baffled. "Where's your posse, Agent Burton? Your paddy wagon? What, no raids tonight?"

"Call me James. No posse, no paddy wagon. Just me and you, painting the town red."

"Should I be worried?" I raised my brows. "Perhaps I do need to ask Eva to chaperone?"

"I can behave like a gentleman, if I want."

"Says you. One day you act like a bully, the next you're a real gentleman. You even managed to fool my aunt."

He flashed a smile. "Keeps thing interesting, don't you think?"

"You mean confusing." He reminded me of my ex-beau, a chameleon, changing moods to fit any situation. "So what happened at the police station? Did you see Sammy? Can I talk to him?"

"I'm sorry, but the cops said no visitors. Believe me I tried, but he's their only suspect." He stared ahead. "They claim he doesn't have an alibi, so they're holding him for further questioning."

"Alibi? But he's innocent!" I was crushed. There went my big plans to help free Sammy.

"Are you sure? I like Sammy too, but it doesn't look good. After all, he was on the scene when the cops arrived. And I certainly provided him with a valid motive."

"I'll say!" I hissed. "But that doesn't make him a killer."

"You told me yourself that he had a bad temper." Burton shrugged. "Maybe it was an accident—self-defense, not murder. So unless we hear otherwise..."

I had to act fast. "Before you hang him, I found an eyewitness who can swear Sammy didn't kill the ice man."

To be honest, I hated to get Buzz involved, but I felt I had no other choice: Sammy's freedom, even his life, could be in jeopardy.

CHAPTER TWENTY-SEVEN

"An eyewitness? No joking?" Agent Burton rubbed his chin.

"Why would I joke about that? I talked with him today. I'll take you to him—right now." Sammy was running out of options, and I'd do whatever it took to help him get out of jail.

Burton seemed surprised. "Who is it? Anyone I know?"

"Do you remember Buzz? A young boy, around twelve or thirteen, who works at the Oasis? He claims he saw everything."

"Oh yeah? Everything?" He frowned. "Are you sure?"

"Talk to him yourself—he'll be there tonight." I poked his shoulder. "It's the least you can do for Sammy."

"I doubt the Welcome Wagon will be on hand to greet me. How do you know he's a credible witness?"

"Let me do the talking. I know Buzz—he doesn't lie. You should've seen him earlier. He was scared to death."

"He should be." Burton sped up as he drove toward Market Street. It was still light outside so the street was half-empty. Some cars were boldly parked in front of the bars, but the more inhibited patrons parked down the alleys and side streets. Like rats and bats, most hooch hounds were nocturnal creatures who preferred to come out after dark.

A few people strolled down the block, singing off-key. A spirited young couple in glad rags was linked arm in arm, swaying back and forth—no doubt high from booze and romance. Strains of jazz and blues filtered out in the street, mingling with the traffic noise.

In the dusk, I watched Burton's reaction as he took in the scene, but he acted nonchalant. He parked on the corner of Market and 21st streets, and turned to me, blue eyes bright. "What now?"

"Wait in the car while I go find Buzz," I told him as I got out. "We can talk inside, in the kitchen."

"Yes, ma'am," Burton said, saluting me. "You'd make a good drill sergeant, you know that?"

My face felt hot. "I suppose I'm better at giving orders than following them."

He gave me a lazy smile. "I can tell."

I made a big show of walking through the alley and knocking on the side door.

A roughneck in dirty jeans and shirt sidled up to me. "Say, doll, can you get me into this gin joint?" he drawled, slurring his words. Obviously he didn't have any trouble finding gin earlier today.

"I'm waiting for a friend." I turned away, uneasy. Too bad Burton was out of sight.

"I'll be your friend," the rummy said, moving closer.

"Beat it!" I jerked back, pounding on the door. I'd had enough drunken advances for one day. Dino opened the sliding window, stared down the drunk, barking, "Leave the lady alone."

"Says who?" he challenged Dino, puffing his chest.

Dino stepped outside and faced the wino, 300-plus pounds of muscle and fat and intimidation. Backing away, the man ran off, cursing loudly.

"Thanks, Dino," I told him, surprised by his sudden chivalry. Dino rarely played knight in shining, or even tarnished, armor. "Say, is Buzz around? I need to talk to him."

"He's here, cleaning off tables. It's a busy night." He snorted. "Word spread about Sammy and the ice man. Folks got excited, wanting to hear all about the blood and guts."

"Murder must be good for business." I wondered what the customers would think if they knew the ice in their drinks came directly off the ice truck. Nothing like a little realism with their rum.

I took a deep breath. "By the way, I brought a friend who wants to talk to Buzz."

"What kind of friend?" Dino looked wary.

I paused, not sure how he'd react. "Agent Burton. He wants to help Sammy."

"Help Sammy?" Dino blocked the door. "You mean padlock the place? Tell him to scram. He can't show his mug in here."

"We need to see Buzz. He only wants to ask him a few questions about the murder, and clear Sammy's name." With Sammy gone, it seemed Dino was running the show—not a smart idea.

"Burton's not welcome here." Dino wouldn't budge. "He can stand out in the alley, with the rest of the gutter-crawlers. Wait here—I'll get Buzz. Make it quick."

I waved Burton over and he walked to the side door, hat in hand. "We'll have to talk out here. The restaurant is closed, because of Sammy."

He wasn't fooled. "Seems to me it's doing a booming business," he said dryly, watching people come and go.

Finally Buzz appeared, but when he saw Burton, he panicked and turned to go inside.

I held onto his T-shirt, pleading, "Buzz, don't be afraid. He only wants to talk to you."

"Why? Am I in t-t-trouble?" he asked, lips quivering.

"Not at all. He wants to help Sammy. Tell him what you saw today," I encouraged him.

"I doubt it's safe to talk outside," Burton interrupted. "Since he's a witness, he may be in danger." He cocked his head. "Let's go sit in my car. Better than standing here in plain sight."

"Fine," I agreed. Luckily the sky was deepening and in street clothes, Burton could pass for any regular Joe. I patted Buzz's hand to comfort him. "We need your help—it's important."

Burton opened the car door for Buzz and pointed to the passenger seat in front. Then he leveled a few questions—rat-a-tat-tat, like a machine gun—but Buzz hung his head, mute.

"Slow down. You're scaring him!" I told Burton. "Let me try. After all, I'm a journalist." Yeah, right, Jazz. Like Mack said, I was used to interviewing society ladies, not murder witnesses.

Still, I needed to protect Buzz, not frighten him. I leaned forward, touching his trembling shoulder. "Why don't you tell Agent Burton about the cowboy? How he entered the ice truck, and stabbed the ice man, then disappeared. Right?"

"Hey! You're coaching him." Burton sounded impatient. "This isn't helping one bit." He turned to Buzz, coaxing, "You want to help Sammy, don't you, sport? Tell Uncle Burton about the ice man. What did you see?"

Buzz mimicked the stabbing, acting out the killing, then whispered: "C-c-cowboy."

"He was dressed as a cowboy?" Burton frowned. "A cowboy stabbed the ice man?"

Buzz nodded, wide-eyed with fear, his body trembling.

"Are you sure it wasn't Sammy?" Burton persisted. "Are you hiding something, sport?"

"No!" His face was an explosion of red. "Sammy didn't do nuthin'!" Then he jumped out and rushed inside the Oasis. Poor little guy. I wanted to follow him, but knew he needed time to calm down.

Burton turned and smiled. "That's all I need to know. He may not be the best witness in the world, but I believed him. I'd like to take him to the station to make a statement, but..."

"That's not safe." I shook my head. "What if the gangs find out and go looking for him? Let's not jump the gun."

His eyes softened. "You're probably right. I doubt anyone will be there to take his statement at the station this late." He paused. "Anyone I can trust, that is."

I felt guilty, torn between trying to help Sammy get out of jail and wanting to protect Buzz. "What about Sammy? Are you sure he'll be all right there overnight?"

Burton nodded. "Actually, it may be better if Sammy stays in jail tonight. Let the killer think he's off the hook. Maybe he'll get careless, come out of hiding and brag about getting away with murder." He started the roadster, giving a slight shrug. "One night in jail won't kill Sammy."

I looked out the window at the gaily-dressed couples, enjoying a night on the town. By now, the sky had turned a peachy coral.

My stomach knotted as I thought about Sammy, locked up in a tiny jail cell. "I hope not."

CHAPTER TWENTY-EIGHT

"Let's go find some gangsters," Burton said, as we drove off. "We can try the Surf Athletic Club first. I hear Ollie Quinn and his boys usually go there on weekends. They like to make the rounds at all their bars, make sure the cash and booze are flowing."

"No raids, promise?" I said, half-serious. "I've had enough excitement for one day."

"Promise." Burton nodded. "Tonight we're just a couple of crazy kids out on the town. I'd want to see who all the big guns are, watch them on their own turf, so to speak."

I saw him smile, noticing his even profile—not unlike F. Scott Fitzgerald's photo on his book jackets. In his natty suit, Burton looked more like a gadabout than a Federal agent.

Still, somehow I had to get through this evening without revealing anything about Sammy or Andrews or the methanol found in his flask. We turned onto 23rd Street and Burton parked directly across from the Surf Club. Bold move. Several husky-looking men, no doubt security guards and bouncers, stood outside the three-story building, watching the entrance, scrutinizing the guys and dolls lined up outside. The Beach Gang didn't take any chances.

Everyone knew the "Surf Athletic Club" was a euphemism, a cover for the Beach Gang's swanky headquarters. It was a class act, all right—complete with a bookmaking parlor on the first floor, a lavish nightclub on the second floor, and a gym on top, sporting a boxing ring. These gangsters even had their own baseball team, the Surfers. How all-American. I hated to think about the way they punished their players if they ever lost.

I couldn't wait to get inside, curious to see how Agent Burton was going to fast-talk his way into the club. But I lagged behind, expecting to be turned away or tossed out like gate-crashers. To my surprise, the door opened wide, as if by magic.

"What did you say?" I asked, impressed. "Open sesame?"

"Like you journalists, I've got my sources," he said with a sly smile. "Most of them prefer to remain anonymous, if you get my drift. Tonight I'm incognito, only an average sport."

Once inside the door, a platinum blonde hostess held out her hand. "Welcome to the Surf Club. May I take your hat?" She looked familiar, but I couldn't quite place her.

"Thanks, but we may not stay long." Burton held his hat over his chest, like a shield. "Say, do you know if Ollie or Dutch are here tonight? How about Papa Rose or Big Sam?" He dropped the Beach Gang leaders' names as if they were old pals.

She looked uncomfortable, as if she'd swallowed a fly, and motioned for the maitre d'. This was it! I was afraid they'd give us the bum's rush, but instead a short Italian host appeared.

"The Studio Lounge? Right this way." He escorted us to an elevator operated by an old Negro man in a red uniform and hat that opened out onto the second floor. The elevator man held the door open as we stepped into a different world. Stylized murals and zebra fur-trimmed mirrors decorated the walls while the black lights cast a mystical, purple glow over the nightclub.

A few heads turned as we crossed the polished hardwood floors under the mirrored dance ball. Even in my bias-cut silk teal beaded gown, I felt sorely underdressed compared to the sophisticated older crowd, probably rich oilmen and tourists on a toot. Sure, I could fake it for one night, save for one big difference: I wore costume jewelry, but I knew their pearls and diamonds were real.

The host led us to a plush wine leather booth shaped like a half-moon, with a clear view of the bandstand. A crystal vase held a single blood-red rose, like the one tossed in the alley.

"Is this satisfactory?" The host bowed politely.

"Yes, fine." Burton nodded, acting like a man about town. The moment I sank against the cushions, a tuxedoed waiter arrived, his pencil poised. In such a swanky club, I was tempted to order lobster and caviar and make Burton pick up the tab. Wouldn't that be swell?

But I behaved myself, saying, "Lemonade, please." Burton smiled in approval.

The waiter frowned, then looked hopefully at Burton, who said, "Make that two."

I stifled a laugh as the waiter turned away, muttering, "Teetotalers!" When he returned, he banged the glasses on the table. Luckily, the lemonade was cold and tart, the way I liked it. "Nothing to start? No hors d'oeuvres?" he sniffed, his beady eyes blinking, but I shook my head no. I'd lost my appetite since Sammy was arrested.

"Not tonight." Burton sounded disappointed. Maybe we *should* have ordered the lobster?

Under the mirrored ball, I watched a few elegant couples glide across the dance floor, the ladies in flowing beaded gowns shimmering in the muted lights. I couldn't take my eyes off one couple, the woman in a sleek backless bias-cut gold gown and matching beaded headdress with long pearls and blonde spit curls across her forehead, dancing with her movie star-handsome date. He reminded me of the suave actor Ramon Novarro, with his thin moustache and slicked-back hair.

"Enjoying yourself?" Burton smiled at my awed expression.

"Absolutely." I struck a pose, fantasizing I was the film siren Louise Brooks.

"I'm glad." He edged his arm across the booth, a bit too close for comfort. Sure, he was attractive, but I had no interest in a double-crosser who wanted to put, and keep, my big brother in jail. Still, it was hard not to be dazzled by the lavish décor, the lively music and exhilarating atmosphere. Surveying the club, I envied the couples on actual dates who were talking and laughing, their heads together, their bodies close, intimate.

Tonight Burton seemed more refined and respectable, like a proper gentleman. But was it all an act? A means to an end? "Have you ever been here before?" I asked him.

"Once or twice, only on business. Not with a date."

"It's a mission, not a date. Remember?"

"What's wrong with friends having fun?" I shifted in my seat as he moved closer, getting a manly whiff of musk cologne.

"Friends? After what you did to Sammy?" I shook my head.

Burton looked perturbed. Or was it jealousy? "What's with you and Sammy anyway? He almost looks old enough to be your father."

"We're just friends. He worked for my dad, who died two years ago." Why did I blurt it out? He didn't need to know my life story.

"Sorry to hear that." His face softened. "I know so little about you—your personal life. One thing about Sammy, he knows how to keep his mouth shut. That's why I wanted his help."

I eyed him. "What kind of help? You never told me what favor you wanted."

He watched the band play, drumming his fingers on the table. "Let's try to have a good time tonight, shall we? We'll talk about Sammy later."

"A good time? Is that all you care about?"

"I'll explain later," he whispered. "I don't want to get you involved."

"I'm already involved." I fell back against the booth. "Whether you like it or not." His leg grazed mine, but I pulled away like a goody two-shoes. Aunt Eva would be so proud.

A cute cigarette girl with a short skirt and red curly hair came by and blatantly beamed at Burton, leaning over to show her big white teeth and even bigger cleavage. "Cigars? Cigarettes? Or perhaps something else...not on the menu?" She purred, winking at Burton.

Fake date or not, I was annoyed. Boy, she had some gall, flirting with him right in front of me. Who was I, a bug-eyed Betty? For all she knew, Burton was my beau.

He smiled and shook his head. "No, thanks. But can you tell me if Ollie Quinn is here tonight? Maybe the Maceos?"

The cigarette girl's smile vanished. "Why do you want to know?"

"Just want to say hello," he replied calmly. She walked off in a fit, as if he'd offended her girlhood. I admit, I was secretly pleased. What a vamp!

While the band took a break, I heard a buzz going around the room, people staring toward the entrance, muttering, "That's Sam Maceo." I noticed a handsome, dark-haired man in a spiffy striped suit, escorted by a pretty young blonde in a floral bias-cut gown. Her plunging neckline revealed her ample assets, as the crowd noticed. When they passed, I got a quick glimpse: It *was* Sam Maceo.

I recognized him from news photos and pictures of the Hollywood Club's opening night. The dapper gangster walked upstairs to a table, but it was hard to see in the hazy purple lights.

"Isn't that Sam Maceo?" I turned, pointing him out. "Do you know him?"

"I've met Sam. Nice guy." He nodded. "He's A-OK for a gangster. I'll stop by his table later."

What? When? Why? I wanted to know. How in hell did a Prohibition agent know the biggest bootlegger in town? I had to bite my tongue to keep quiet, since this wasn't exactly the time or place.

When the band started playing, "Side By Side," I hummed along, enjoying the upbeat tune, tempted to ask Agent Burton to dance. Would I dare? Would that be asking for trouble?

Suddenly the Italian host reappeared with two fluted wine glasses and a bottle of chilled Champagne, set in a zebra-striped ice bucket. With a flourish, he uncorked the bottle and poured two glasses of the bubbly.

"But we didn't order any Champagne," Burton said, puzzled.

"Compliments of Ollie Quinn," the host said with a smile, smoothly replacing the cork. "Enjoy your evening with your date, Agent Burton."

CHAPTER TWENTY-NINE

My heart stopped. Our cover was blown. How did the gangsters know Burton was actually a Federal agent?

"What a nice surprise," Burton said graciously, studying the label. He acted as if receiving a complementary bottle of Champagne was the most natural thing in the world for a Prohibition agent. "Please give Ollie my thanks. Where is he sitting?" The host gave a sly smile, tilting his head toward an upper balcony behind a brass rail where Sam Maceo had been seated.

After the host left, Burton exhaled, refusing to look around. "So much for being incognito."

I squirmed in my seat, eyeing the bottle like it was a live bomb. "What should we do?"

"Like the man said, I'm going to enjoy my evening."

I had to hand it to him, Burton didn't miss a beat. He lifted his glass, nodding toward Quinn's table. But he never took a sip.

"Let's make a toast—to us."

To *us*? There was no 'us.' I forced a smile, clinking our glasses.

Then, a short man in a beige suit and hat appeared out of the shadows holding a camera, flashing a bright light in our faces. Caught off guard, I swallowed, feeling exposed, literally. A few people turned and smiled, no doubt thinking we were young lovebirds or newlyweds on their honeymoon. If they only knew Burton was a Treasury agent, and I was what? His undercover spy?

"Want a souvenir of this special night?" The shutterbug quickly snapped a second photo before we could set down our glasses. For once, Burton looked surprised, blinking at the bright lights.

"What was that for? Why do you need *two* photos?" I asked, my face flushed.

"We like to keep tabs on our customers," he said, smirking. "We often display the photos in our foyer so we can remember your faces, and our guests can recall the good times." He winked at me, then added, "I'll be back later with your memento."

Swell. That's all I needed: My photo plastered on the walls of the Surf Club—a popular casino and club owned by the Beach Gang—drinking with a Prohibition agent, no less.

"Was that a threat?" I gasped, feeling light-headed. The local gangs had powerful friends, and I didn't want any trouble. Who knew what they could do?

"Apparently," Burton said, strangely calm.

I fidgeted with my frock, my hair, trying not to panic. If Mrs. Harper heard about these photos, I'm sure she'd be tinkled pink to print the photo in the society pages—as pink as the pink slip she'd no doubt give me. Burton patted my arm. "They don't scare me. Don't let them scare you." Then he edged closer, saying, "Or at least don't show it. Pretend you're having fun."

Fun? This was getting too dangerous to be fun. But I played along, laughing out loud, as if he'd told the most hilarious joke. To be honest, I was afraid—for both of us as well as Sammy.

"In that case, I think I'll have a drink," I taunted him, wanting to see his reaction.

"Wait a minute." Burton picked up the bottle and rolled it around in his hand, studying the label, examining the cork. "I've heard this place gets their booze straight from Canada and Cuba. Looks like their fine wine and Champagne come from France. Only the best for these hoods." He gently put his hand on my arm. "Seems jake to me, if you want to have a glass."

"Really? Don't mind if I do." I took a few sips, enjoying the bubbles and fizz, already getting a buzz. I was used to watered-down cocktails or cheap wine, not the expensive stuff.

Burton winked. "Is that all? I've given you a free pass for tonight."

"I'm not used to fancy French Champagnes," I admitted. "Or any liquor for that matter. I don't want to commit a federal crime."

"You don't strike me as a dumb Dora, or I wouldn't be here."
Burton pointed at the Champagne bottle. "Legally you can drink to
your heart's content. Prohibition only enforces the sale, manufacture
and transportation of alcohol." He tapped the bottle label. "These
gangsters are smart, too smart."

"Glad I'm in the clear." I could get used to drinking fine
Champagne—and how!

He held out his hand. "Let's take a spin around the dance floor,
get a better look at our host. I'm a fair dancer, if I say so myself."

"Says you. We'll see if it's true." The band was playing a slow
waltz and he cocked his head toward the dance floor, but I put him
off. "Let's wait for a fast number." To stall, I opened my beaded
reticule and took out my tango vanity compact so I could apply fresh
Rumba Red lipstick.

"You look swell." Burton pulled me out onto the dance floor,
while I still clutched my vanity by the finger ring. The band played a
bouncy jazz song, perfect for doing the Charleston. Burton sure
knew how to cut a rug, twirling me around the dance floor, watching
the crowd as we danced. Then he nodded toward the balcony,
imperceptibly so that only I'd notice. When a slow song began, he
held my wrist. "Waltz with me."

Dizzy from the Champagne, I didn't quite trust myself in the
arms of Agent Burton, dancing under the glittering chandeliers.
Sadly, I hadn't been out with a handsome man, or any fella, in ages.
"Let's sit this one out. I'm getting a bit blotto," I admitted.

"You seem fine to me, Jasmine. Besides, we have no choice.
They're watching us."

My back tensed up and I surveyed the room. "Who? Where?"

"Our fan club." Burton pulled me close, his breath on my neck.
He smelled like a mixture of Ivory soap and musk cologne. Not bad.

I tried to focus as he whispered: "Notice the top tier of tables by
the Greek statues. Some wiseguys are flirting with gals half their age."

He glided me around in a half-circle and I saw the group sitting
at a big round table, elevated above the dance floor. The bright lights
obscured their features, but the flappers looked young enough to be
their daughters.

"I can't see them clearly. Can we get closer?"

Holding me tight, Burton waltzed me backwards until I faced the top row and peered over his shoulder. "Now I see Sam Maceo. Who's the man on the right? Ollie Quinn? The other guys look familiar, but I can't quite place them."

"No, Quinn is on the left. Where have you seen the others?"

I turned sideways to catch a better glimpse of the group. The music changed tempo to a Latin song and I tried to keep up, but sambas weren't my specialty. When a silver-haired man dancing the tango with a buxom blonde bumped into us, I blushed while Burton apologized. "Pardon us. She's leading again." He smiled at me. "You'd like that, wouldn't you? Being in charge?"

"Of course." I smiled back. With a firm grip, he attempted to teach me the tango, pressing my cheek against his clean-shaven face. I admit, my heart quickened along with my steps. Such a smooth operator. As we danced, I glanced up at the top tier of tables, then stopped in place, swallowing hard. "Wait. I think I recognize two of those men."

"Let's keep dancing. It takes two to tango." Burton winked, pulling me closer. "Who are they?"

"Jones is president of Lone Star Bank, and Clark is vice-president." Why were two bankers socializing with the Beach Gang?

"You don't say." Now it was his turn to stop. "Are you sure?"

"Looks like them. I interviewed Jones and Clark for my story on Andrews earlier this week. That's when I saw Jones talking to Rose Maceo at the bank." Clearly neither man was shy about being seen in public with well-known gangsters.

"Interesting. Tell me more. What about the other two?"

"Probably politicians." I shrugged. "The Maceos have been known to grease a few local palms."

When the song ended, Burton led me back to the booth and our still-fizzy glasses of Champagne. "It's not safe to talk here." His eyes darted around the room. "We seem to be in the spotlight."

I nodded. "I feel like we're in a fishbowl, being watched from every angle." My mouth felt dry and I took a sip of my lemonade. "Why don't we do the twenty-three skidoo?"

"Not yet. I think I'll stop by Quinn's table and thank him for the Champagne. Nice and polite, like a good Prohibition agent." Burton stood up and put on his hat, straightening his collar and bow tie. "Besides, I want to find out what he plans to do with our photos."

"Smart idea." I tugged on his sleeve. "But be careful. Please don't do anything foolish."

He cupped my chin. "Don't worry, doll face. I'll make my move when the time is right."

Doll face? What was I—a gangster's moll? I watched as Burton climbed the stairs to Quinn's table, shaking his hand as if they were old pals. What was he up to? The shebas got up and left in a hurry, crestfallen as kids banished from the adult's table.

As I waited, I watched a chic young couple expertly dance the fox trot, the woman's pink beaded gown and cloche glistening like jewels. Long pink crystal earrings dusted her shoulders, catching the light as she moved. Her whole outfit reminded me of a prism, sparkling from head to toe.

When the band took a break, I looked around for Burton. What was taking so long? I didn't want to sit there like a limp centerpiece.

On impulse, I rushed up the steps, heart racing, hoping to catch Quinn and his banker buddies off-guard. They'd already taken our photos, so what else could they do to us?

Behind a column, I got a sneak peek: Ollie Quinn sat between Sam Maceo and Dutch Voight with Jones and Clark across the table, next to two Brooks Brothers types. Politicians or mob lawyers or thugs? Hard to tell them apart these days.

The gangsters had some nerve, grandstanding with their pricey call girls, while Sammy was stuck behind bars. I took a deep breath, wondering if I should confront them in public. But what could I say? I had no proof they'd ordered the hit—my only clue was one rose in an alley.

Burton towered over their table, deep in discussion. Whatever he was saying, the hoods didn't look too happy, their faces hard as granite. They didn't see me as I approached, but then the bleached blonde hostess appeared out of nowhere, blocking my view.

Guess I wasn't important enough for the big-shot section.

"May I help you?" she snapped, then stared at me in recognition. "Wait. I know you. Aren't you a friend of Sammy's?" Her hair was freshly marcelled, but I couldn't forget her face.

"Sure—you're Candy, right? Didn't you work at the Oasis?"

I tried to act friendly as she led me down the steps.

"Right. Candace." Then she whispered, "Did you hear about Sammy's arrest today?"

"I'll say! I was there." I nodded and followed her, glancing back. Had the mobsters seen me?

She plopped down at my booth, face tight. "What happened? Is he OK? I'm so worried!"

"You said it." I let out a sigh, glad for a sympathetic ear. "He's in jail, and I have no idea when he's getting out."

"Those rotten bastards. I swear it's a set-up," Candy hissed, her eyes flashing.

I leaned forward. "You sure? How do you know?"

She nodded, talking low. "I overheard some guys talking tonight in the Western Room about a hit." The band began playing a samba, drowning out our conversation. "They were laughing about the poor sap who got pinched today on Market Street. One jerk said he was waiting for the ice truck and got lucky when Sammy showed up, just in time to take the fall."

I perked up. "Who was he? Did you hear any names? Are they still here?"

Before she could reply, the host appeared and yanked Candy by the arm. "Scram! Don't you have work to do?" he snapped. "Stop socializing with the patrons."

"She's not bothering me. I was asking about the bands," I piped up. Was he watching us?

The host dipped his head. "I didn't mean to interrupt. But we're getting busy and you're needed up front." He scowled at Candy.

"Yes, sir." She gave me a grateful smile and rushed to the lobby.

"Is everything OK?" The host frowned. "You barely touched your Champagne."

"Everything is fine." Without warning, Burton appeared behind him, a full head taller than the host. "We'd like to take this Champagne with us—as a souvenir."

"By all means—it's yours." He sized up Burton's lofty frame as he scurried away.

Burton replaced the cork. "No sense in letting perfectly good Champagne go to waste."

"Why take it if you won't drink it?" I hinted.

He hadn't touched a drop all night.

"Evidence," Burton said, tucking the bottle under his arm. "Maybe we can save it to celebrate later."

Celebrate what, I wondered?

Then he held out a firm hand, helping me up from the plush booth. "Ready to go?"

"Sure." I grabbed my teal beaded bag, its long fringe` swaying under the lights.

"I saw you talking to the blonde," he said in my ear. "What was that all about?"

"Oh, she's an old friend," I stammered.

In a way, I wanted to tell him what she'd overhead about the "hit" on the ice man, but I still didn't quite trust Burton—or Candy, for that matter.

As we crossed the lobby, Candy waved at me from the hostess stand. The Italian host hovered near the entrance, greeting guests and shaking hands, polished as a politician.

"Here's our schedule," she said, handing me a brochure. "We have big bands every weekend night." She leaned close to my ear. "Tell Sammy I said hello—when he gets out."

"I'll be sure to mention I saw you." We traded clandestine smiles, sharing our concern for Sammy.

Burton tapped me on the shoulder. "Remember me? Let's go." What was eating him? He led me to the elevator, and waited while the elderly Negro operator opened the door.

"Hope you folks are enjoying your evening." The Negro man smiled wide when Burton gave him a quarter.

In the elevator, I glanced at the program while Burton stared at the ceiling. What was so interesting up there anyway? The elevator man hummed a Louis Armstrong song I'd heard earlier that night.

I peered inside the program, inhaling when I saw one word hand-written in blue ink: "Cowboy."

CHAPTER THIRTY

Cowboy! Candace must have also seen the killer close up. Luckily, this proved Buzz wasn't imagining things or making up fairy tales. Quickly I stuffed the program into my purse, hoping Burton hadn't noticed. I didn't want to tell him anything yet, for Candy's sake. No need to get her involved until I could question her, verify her information. Maybe she'd be willing to give a statement to the police, help clear Sammy?

Outside the Surf Club, a group of flappers and their fellas had lined up trying to get inside the club, but the door man turned most of them away. One floozy in a sheer frock and rolled stockings looked me up and down, slurring her words.

"What's she got that I ain't got?"

"A bottle of booze!" one joker yelled, pointing to Burton's Champagne. Was that all?

"Hope the cops don't see me here tonight," he said. "I'd have a lot of explaining to do."

"No kidding," I agreed. "You and me both."

He opened the car door and held my elbow as I got inside. "How about a stroll on the Seawall? It's a nice night and we can talk freely there."

"As long as we're only walking and talking. No funny business." I didn't want to lead him on.

"Don't worry. I got the telegram." He gunned his motor as we left, screeching around the corner, like a Keystone cop chasing a bank robber.

Sorry if I'd hurt his feelings, but I had to keep my wits tonight.

"What's the rush?" I held onto the door straps while he sped toward the beach. In the distance, I saw the bright lights of Murdoch's Bath House, a huge pavilion housing Gaido's restaurant, a news stand, gift shop and amusements.

As we neared the ocean, the salty sea air bathed my face, whipped my hair in the wind. Burton parked by the Seawall across from the Hotel Galvez and helped me out. Palm trees swayed like fan dancers, the wind blocking out any street noise.

While we walked along the Seawall, I was dying to know: "What happened with Quinn? What did you say?"

"I thanked him for the Champagne, and asked if they knew anything about the *incident* on Market Street today. Of course he played dumb. I said I wanted to keep the peace, that the gangs should respect each other's turf." He gave me a sideways glance. "They got my message."

"It was that simple?" I figured he had opened up a Pandora's box of trouble.

"We'll see how long it lasts. Now I need to talk to Johnny Jack, see what he knows."

"Good luck." I chewed on my nails. "What about our photos? Can we get them back?"

"Quinn claims they're still wet—but I think he's the one who's all wet." Burton smiled at his own joke. "He says I'll get the pictures back if I behave like a good sport." His face flushed with fury. "Cooperation, he called it. Quinn even handed me an envelope filled with bills, like I'm some kind of pushover. He thinks he can buy me off with a bribe and some fancy Champagne?"

"Boy, he has some nerve!" I had new respect for Burton, turning down such a blatant bribe. "Can't you report him to the Treasury Department?"

"Sure, but why bother? It's my word against his. And he has pals to back him up."

"You're new in town. Maybe they're trying to rile you up, see if you pass the test."

"Hope so." He scowled. "They must take me for a rookie."

"I'll bet half the cops in Galveston are on their payroll," I said with disgust. I'd heard rumors from the reporters about crooked cops who worked with both gangs, as long as they paid up.

"I may be new, but I'm not naïve. And I'm not for sale." He shook his head, working his jaw. "The gangs are getting too cocky, too violent. They think they can get away with murder."

I was impressed by his resolve, but wondered if a Prohibition agent had any clout in a murder case? Unfortunately, most gangland crimes went unresolved and unreported. Gangsters weren't known to be chatty, especially when it came to protecting their own.

As we strolled along the Seawall, Burton grew silent. Was he feeling shy? Couples passed us, arm in arm, and Burton touched my arm once or twice, but I pretended not to notice. The breeze felt warm on my bare arms and legs, but it wreaked havoc on my curly hair. In the distance, the Crystal Palace pavilion rose like a huge layered wedding cake. I'd been there lots of times with friends, swimming in their huge indoor pool, surrounded by onlookers watching on balconies. On the beach, couples in bathing suits played in the waves, screaming like children.

Bright stars glittered like rhinestones in the dark sky. If I was with a beau, I would have thought they were diamonds. Foamy white waves beat against the pale sand. The night might have been more romantic, if only I was with a real date. Considering the starry backdrop, I wondered what might have happened if we'd met under different circumstances?

All night I'd been trying to work up the nerve to ask him about the ice man. Finally I tapped his arm. "You still haven't told me much about Harvey, the victim. How did you know him?"

"I met him at a diner in town," he said. "A customer was grabbing a waitress there and Harvey tried to defend her. The guy beat him up pretty badly so I took him to the hospital. Poor lovesick fool. He changed jobs later, went to work for the ice company, and we kept in touch."

"That was nice of you." I took a deep breath and faced him. "So tell me—why did you ask him to stop delivering ice to the Oasis?"

"This is all off the record, right? We're just talking as friends." He ran his fingers through his thick blond hair. "It all started with your pal, Horace Andrews. I'd heard that he'd passed out at the Oasis and was taken to the hospital from there. We both know what happened next."

My stomach lurched, recalling that night. "Who told you?"

"I work with cops, remember? Dirty or not, they talk. Plus I've got a few well-placed friends around town. They give me information here and there, no questions asked."

"You mean informants? Snitches?" In school, we considered them tattle-tales.

"Whatever you want to call them. They do me favors, and I do the same for them." He eyed me. "Like it or not, that's how this business works—friends helping friends."

"That's a good way to get your friends killed," I retorted. "So what about Andrews?"

"I'd heard there was a bad batch of liquor in town, so I started raiding all the bars on Market Street, trying to find the source," Burton explained. "That's when we met."

"How can I forget? Was that a real raid or a dress rehearsal?"

He ignored my jab. "As you know, the raids weren't working so I asked Harvey to help me out, to keep his eyes and ears open. Since he made daily deliveries anyway, no one suspected that the ice man worked for me. Or so I thought. I figured he'd hear something eventually since he was hitting all the bars in the area."

Burton looked out at the waves, eyes clouding. "I'm sorry I ever got him involved. It seemed like a good idea at the time."

"So why put the squeeze on Sammy?" I studied his face in the dark for clues.

"I tried to pressure him, get him to reveal his suppliers, his sources. I assumed he also wanted to stop the flow of wood alcohol." He shook his head. "But he refused to cooperate."

"What do you expect?" I threw up my hands. "Want him to wind up dead—like Harvey?"

"Don't insult me." His mood turned stormy. "I didn't expect Sammy to end up in jail. And I never thought Harvey would get whacked. All I wanted was a small favor."

"A small favor? If the gangs even suspected he was a snitch— that's like asking him to commit suicide!" Angry, I turned away, but he grabbed my wrist.

"I'm sorry, Jazz. I'm trying to find out who—or what—killed Andrews and the other victims, so I can stop the bootleggers before they hurt anyone else. Don't you understand?"

"Yes, but how do you know he got poisoned at the Oasis? I'll bet he went to a few other bars earlier that night."

"I don't know anything for sure—no one wants to talk." His shoulders sagged. "My so-called sources make up false leads to throw me off track. I'm back to square one."

I considered sharing what little I knew—about the methanol in Andrews' flask, Mack's poisoning, the turf wars—but changed my mind. Sure, he seemed sincere, but could I trust him?

Burton darted ahead of me, head down, walking so fast he bumped into a wino stumbling along the Seawall. When he stopped to help him, I caught up. "Watch where you're going, sir," Burton said. "You could fall off the Seawall onto the rocks."

"Rocks? I can't see in this fog," the man said, rubbing his eyes. "It's so thick."

"There's no fog tonight, mister," I told him, trading worried looks with Burton.

"How much have you been drinking?" He frowned.

"I'd say a whole barrel full." The rummy started chuckling. "I've been drinking since last night. Got good and zozzled!" Talk about digging your own grave.

"Where did you go?" Burton asked. "Do you remember?"

"I went up and down the Seawall." The man slurred his words, swaying with the wind. "Ended up at Murdoch's." His weather-beaten face was as crinkled as an old map. "Why—you a cop?"

Burton took his arm. "I think you need help, mister. Let me find someone who can take you to the hospital." He turned to me, urgency creeping into his voice. "Jazz, go find a cop who can take care of this man. And hurry!"

"Why don't we drive him? It's not far," I suggested, recalling Andrews' sudden collapse.

"Trust me, we don't want to get involved." He brushed me off. "Just go—now!"

I raced down the Seawall, hard to do in heels, and found a uniformed cop patrolling the area by Murdoch's. After I told him about the wino, he blew a whistle and signaled for another cop. They both raced toward the drunkard, and Burton identified himself as a Treasury agent.

"Take this man to Sealy Hospital. Immediately." He sounded upset. "Tell them it's an emergency. I'm no doctor, but I think this man is going blind—from wood alcohol poisoning."

"Poor old sot. I hope he'll be OK," I said, touched by Burton's concern. I watched the cops help the drunk into their squad car. He may have broken the law but their expressions showed only sympathy, or was it pity? "I've never seen anyone go blind from drinking. Have you?"

Burton watched the police car traveling down Seawall Boulevard toward the hospital until the lights faded. "I have, unfortunately, and it's not a pretty sight."

"What happened?" I thought of Andrews, wondering if he also had gone blind, before he passed away. In contrast, Mack was a tough old bird, recovering from his ordeal unharmed.

"Sad story. Never mind," he said. "Want to get some ice cream or snow cones?"

"Sure." Frankly, I was puzzled by his curt reply. Sooner or later, I thought all cops got used to the seamy side of their jobs. Despite his show of bravado, maybe he was still wet behind the ears.

As we walked down the Seawall, I watched the jovial crowd milling about, dressed in everything from bathing suits to the finest frocks. A few couples waded in the Gulf between the tall pilings under Murdoch's. I had so much on my mind, so many questions. But I asked him a question I thought was safe: "How did you end up becoming a Prohibition agent?"

"My father was a cop," he said, his mood darkening. "That's all he talked about while I was growing up. Violence, crime, murder. He was a barrel of laughs."

"Why work as a Treasury agent? Isn't it more dangerous?"

Burton stopped and looked at me, wild-eyed, gesturing toward the hospital. "You want to know why I put myself in this shit job? To help people like that half-blind sucker. To stop the criminals who sell poison and call it pure liquor. To stop the idiots from ruining their lives with every damn drink they take."

His emotional outburst surprised, even frightened, me. Clearly I'd managed to touch a nerve beneath his cool, calm demeanor. "Thanks for being honest. I didn't mean to pry."

"And I didn't mean to get on my soapbox." He looked away. "Sorry I got so riled up."

"That's OK. I've got more questions, if you don't mind." Even if he did mind, I wanted to ask anyway. "I read a few articles that have me worried. Is it true that our government legally forces suppliers to add poison to industrial alcohol? Isn't that why so many people are going blind and dying—because our government is trying to enforce a law that's a losing battle?"

Who better to ask than a Prohibition agent?

Burton stared at me in amazement. "How did you find out? Congress tried real hard to cover that up, so the public wouldn't put two and two together."

"I found a few obscure articles in the paper. Sad to say, their underhanded scheme is working. And it's killing lots of innocent people." Curious, I turned to face him, crossing my arms.

"What I want to know is, what's *your* honest opinion? Is it right to purposely poison people to uphold a stupid law?"

"Of course not." He stared at me, eyes wide, obviously agitated. "You want to know the real reason I became a Prohibition agent? Because the Eighteenth Amendment is a farce. A deadly game of Russian roulette."

CHAPTER THIRTY-ONE

"My thoughts exactly. Prohibition is only helping gangsters get rich, and punishing the public." In one night, my opinion of Burton had changed. He didn't seem opposed to social drinking—he wanted to prevent senseless deaths from alcohol poisoning. All of a sudden, his actions began to make sense: Maybe that's why he hadn't shut down the Oasis despite his threats, why he was so hell-bent on finding the bootleggers passing off poison as pure liquor.

"So how about that ice cream?" he asked, not-so-subtly changing the subject.

"Sounds good." A fitting diversion from all this talk of gloom and doom. Some people craved liquor, but my real downfall was my sweet tooth.

Silent, we walked over to a vendor across from Murdoch's, and each ordered a chocolate cone. I bent over my cone, trying not to drip on my silk dress, making a mess on the Seawall. Burton laughed as he watched me try to lick the ice cream before it melted— impossible in this heat. The ice cream seemed to soothe him, both of us. For once, I felt like we were simply two kids having fun.

Burton reached over with a napkin, and I blushed while he carefully wiped my cheek, hoping he didn't notice my red face. Reluctantly, I checked my watch: it was already 11:40.

"It's getting late. We'd better go back." I had to admit, I was enjoying his company.

"I hoped you wouldn't notice." He grinned. "Do you turn into a pumpkin at midnight?"

"Eva will have a fit. She stays up waiting for me when I'm out late at night."

"So you're a night owl? No wonder she has so many gray hairs."
He teased. "What do you do during all those late nights?"

"Wouldn't you like to know?" I said over my shoulder as we
walked to his car.

"Yes, I would." He tried to grab my arm, but I slid out of reach.
"Tell me why a sweet society reporter spends so much time in
speakeasies—when she hardly drinks a drop. And why is a nice girl
like you so curious about gangs and the criminal side of Galveston?"

Was he gunning for my job? "Why the third-degree?" I asked
nervously, since I didn't quite know how to reply.

Perhaps it was my sheltered upbringing, my rebellious side, the
hypocrisy I saw in high society that piqued my interest in journalism.
Did I think working at the *Gazette* might really make a difference?

I met his intense gaze, his hat silhouetted against the tall
Victorian street lights. "Now what I'd like to know is: How will you
get Sammy out of jail?"

"I'm not sure," he admitted. "But I'll do my best."

Like a gentleman, Burton helped me in his roadster. I rolled
down the window and took a last look at the soapy waves crashing
against the shore. I couldn't help but wonder: Was he as balled up as
I was this very minute? Were we crossing over the line? Had I said
too much, or not enough? My head felt so muddled, I needed some
distance, and time, to absorb everything.

When we arrived at the boarding house, Burton walked me to
the door and stood there, shuffling his feet. He was so tall, the porch
light shone on his honey-blond hair. I couldn't help but smile, he
looked so uncomfortable. James Burton—flustered?

Finally he said, "If I wasn't a gentleman, I'd try to kiss you."
Then he turned and rushed down the brick walkway to his car.

Kiss me? Now I was really confused.

Luckily, he'd escaped just in time—Eva peered out the curtains,
then opened the front door wide. "Where's Agent Burton?" Her face
fell as she looked around. "I was going to invite him in for
lemonade." Following me inside, she asked: "Did you two have fun?
Will you go out with him again? He seems too dashing to be a cop."

I feigned nonchalance. "It wasn't a date. We're only friends."

"I don't get that dolled up for my friends," she teased. "Too bad
he left so soon."

So soon? She didn't even scold me for staying out past midnight. Maybe Eva had a crush on Agent Burton? I knew she wanted to chat, but I begged off. "I'm so tired. Can we talk tomorrow?"

I hugged her good-night, then tiptoed upstairs to my bedroom. Amanda flung my door open, and rushed in, like a melodramatic opera singer. "I heard all about it—that murder! How they arrested Sammy in the middle of Market Street! What happened?"

"Be glad you weren't there," I fumed. "It was so humiliating for Sammy, getting arrested in front of everyone. He claims he was framed by the gangs."

"Good-for-nothing gangsters!" she said. "What did Sammy ever do to them?"

"Burton thinks it may work to our advantage, that with Sammy in jail, the killer may get careless and start bragging about getting away with murder." I didn't want to reveal that Burton was partly, or all, to blame, that he'd hired Harvey to snoop on Sammy. She always saw the glass as half-full, and I didn't want her to get sore.

"Don't worry, Burton will get Sammy out soon," Amanda tried to reassure me. I sure hoped she was right.

Her sunny disposition never failed to cheer me up. When I was despondent after my star-struck beau, who shall remain nameless, left town, she lifted my spirits, boosted my ego, telling me that I could focus on my career now. True, but it wasn't much fun snuggling up to a job.

"Now I wanna hear all about your hot date with the handsome copper. What happened?"

"We went to the Surf Club and danced the Charleston and he tried to teach me to tango. You won't believe this: Ollie Quinn had a bottle of Champagne delivered to our table!"

"With Burton sitting there? Of all the nerve!" She giggled. "What did you do?"

"I took a few sips, what else?" I grinned, enjoying her shocked expression. "I enjoyed it, too."

She laughed, and covered her mouth. "Get to the good part: Did he kiss you?"

"I'd like to see him try. If he ever made a move, I'd slap him." Or would I? "Honestly, I think he's only using me to get to Sammy."

"You're daffy!" Amanda shook her head. "Even if that was true, aren't you doing the same thing to Burton—going out with him to help Sammy?"

She was right. "So what? Like he said, we're friends helping friends." I couldn't believe I was quoting Burton, after only one "date." As I recounted the evening's events—my exchange with Candy, the walk on the Seawall, the old rummy—her eyes widened.

"Jeepers, you've had some day. I wish mine was half as exciting. All I did was work at the diner."

I gave her a sympathetic smile. "That's not all. I went to visit Alice Andrews today and she gave me a few of Horace's things. She'd just had a break-in and I think she wanted to hide them."

"She must trust you," Amanda said, after I showed her the ledger, matches and key I'd hidden in the vanity. "Or else she's trying to get them out of her house to protect herself and her family." She flung out her arms like a Ziegfeld Follies showgirl. "Maybe she poisoned her husband and wants to get rid of the evidence!?"

"You're nuts! She's not the type." I frowned at her.

I'd never even considered the possibility that Alice Andrews could be involved. "You think she was putting on a big act, trying to cover her tracks? Applesauce!"

Amanda sat up, twisting her hands. "Suppose she only wanted to teach him a lesson, and never intended to kill him?"

I mulled it over. "What if you're right? Say, she was angry about his drinking and his so-called affair with Rose and tainted his booze as revenge? Who had better access to his flask?"

Maybe it was all a big mistake? Perhaps that explained why Alice wanted to send me on this wild goose chase, to divert suspicion from her own dirty deed. No wonder she was so eager to ask for my help, to turn over Horace's personal items to me, a virtual stranger.

Was the break-in even real or concocted for my benefit? I felt sick at the idea that Alice could be so devious, so deceptive.

"What do you make of these?" I asked, handing Amanda the items, now worried.

"Looks like a boring old ledger and key." She tossed them onto the pink velvet slipper chair. But she perked up when she flipped open the matchbook. "Who's Rose? His mistress?"

"That's what Mrs. Andrews suspects." I nodded. "But I think it may be Rose Maceo."

"Only one way to find out." Amanda clutched the matchbook. "Let's call the number!"

"Now? It's after midnight." Still, the idea was tempting. Besides, I was dying of curiosity. An affair would certainly give Alice Andrews a valid motive for adding methanol to Horace's flask, then trying to make it look like an accident. "OK, why not?" I agreed.

We used the downstairs phone and after the operator connected me, a woman answered. She sounded as young and fresh as a co-ed. Poor Alice—so Horace *was* having an affair. Who else but a tart would answer a phone call so late?

"Is this Rose?" I asked in a fake French accent.

"Who's calling?" In the background, I heard loud music and laughter. A jazz band?

"A friend." I deepened my voice.

Then a man with a heavy Italian accent, came on the line. "Who is it? How did you get this number? Don't ever call on this line again. Or else!" The phone disconnected. I put down the phone, shaken. Was it Rose Maceo, or one of his many goons?

"What happened?" Amanda sat up. "Did you talk to him?"

"I think it was Rose Maceo, but I'm not positive. I've never heard his voice."

"So is that good news or bad news?"

"Both," I told her. "What I really want to know is, why did Andrews have Rose Maceo's private number?"

The next morning, I woke up late to the high-pitched barks of the Sheltie next door. I'd tossed and turned all night, worrying about Sammy and the ice man, Harvey, frozen in time—literally.

The boarding house seemed quiet, usual for a Sunday, except for some banging in the kitchen. Eva was at church and the boarders usually spent weekends with their families and friends. Sadly, I found Amanda at the kitchen table, tears running down her cheeks.

"What's wrong? Is it Sammy?" I patted her back, concerned.

She forced a smile. "I'm only chopping these damn onions. Getting ready for our lunch today. Sammy is supposed to be here by noon. I told him to be on time, before Eva gets home."

"I'm sure he'd break out of jail to be here." I had to admire her positive attitude, acting as if nothing had happened. Burton assured me he'd use his pull with the police, but I had my doubts about his powers of persuasion.

Meanwhile, I decided to pretend all was well, for her sake. "Whatever you're making sure smells delicious," I said. "What is it?"

"While you got your beauty sleep, I splurged on some pot roast from the butcher and fresh vegetables I found at the farmer's market. Wanna help?"

"Sure," I said, eager for a distraction. As we worked side by side in the kitchen—chopping celery, carrots, potatoes and onions—we chatted as if it were any ordinary Sunday.

"Need anything else from the store?" I asked when we finished.

Amanda brightened. "How about some red apples? I want to bake an apple pie."

"Wouldn't it be easier if I bought a fresh pie from the bakery? My treat. I just got paid."

"Thanks! That'd be swell, Jazz." She gave me a grateful smile. "I'll wait here for Sammy. He promised to be here by noon."

Poor Pollyanna. She could be waiting for days.

Outside, the muggy air felt like a moist washcloth on my face. As I walked the few blocks to the Camel Stop, I mulled over my evening with Burton. One moment he could be kind and thoughtful, the next, arrogant and abrasive. I thought of the careful way he held me on the dance floor last night, yet so firm and commanding. Despite my reservations, he continued to surprise and confound me.

Was I attracted to him—or was he mainly a challenge?

I was so deep in thought, I hardly noticed the gleaming gold Bentley that seemed to keep time with me, its windows opened a crack as it hummed down the street. Was it my imagination—or were they following me? I stopped to window-shop at a millinery store, looking over my shoulder. The Bentley also slowed down, its' motor purring a few feet away. I glanced over to see two men in front, their hats blocking the sunlight, but I couldn't make out their faces.

This was silly. Maybe they were looking for someone else, perhaps a specific shop or address. Why would they come after *me*? Then I recalled the shutterbug at the Surf Club, and his veiled threat.

Preoccupied, I practically plowed into a young couple walking their black Scottie down 22nd Street, getting tangled in the dog's long leash. Flustered, I stepped out of the way, while the young couple, giddy as newlyweds, profusely apologized. Grateful for the interruption, I looked over to see the Bentley roar past. What a relief.

I'd almost reached the corner when I heard a young newsie standing in front of the Camel Stop, shouting, "Read all about the ice pick murder! Local man arrested!" I handed the boy a coin, and grabbed Sunday's paper, holding my breath.

Sure enough, Sammy's picture was featured on the front page above the fold, next to Mack's story, with a bold 36-point headline: "ICE MAN ICED: LOCAL SUSPECT ARRESTED FOR MURDER."

CHAPTER THIRTY-TWO

I grimaced as I studied the graphic photos of the bloody victim under the ICE MAN ICED headline, the ice pick eerily silhouetted against the ice blocks. A dramatic photo of Sammy's arrest was juxtaposed next to the crime scene, making him look guilty as hell. The *Gazette* covered gore and guts as well as the next yellow rag.

No doubt an eager beaver copy editor concocted that salacious headline to attract readers, but did they have to exploit Sammy?

Nathan expertly captured his expression of anger and humiliation as he was handcuffed. My face flamed, feeling Sammy's shame all over again. He was so proud, so private, that I doubted he'd ever live down this public disgrace.

Of course, I was upset by the sensational spread, but how could I blame Nathan or Mack? What did I expect, a Joe Palooka comic in its place? After all, murders sold newspapers.

My hands shook as I skimmed the article. Mack identified the ice man as: *"Harvey O'Brien, 22, a member of a notorious Irish gang in Houston. He had allegedly left that life behind when he moved to Galveston in January."* Allegedly was right. At least Mack wrote that: *"Sammy Cook, owner of a local diner, was arrested and taken in for questioning as a potential suspect, but wasn't formally charged."*

So why was Sammy still stuck in jail?

I wished I could tell Mack about Buzz and the cowboy, but what would I say? That a young boy, his employee, witnessed the crime? And a club hostess—his former flame to boot—overheard some goons talking about a hit? There was no real evidence to prove a 'cowboy' was the real killer. Not only were the facts dicey, Candy and Buzz weren't the most credible sources.

I folded the newspaper under my arm, as if that could erase Sammy's haunting image plastered all over the front page. Glad for a distraction, I selected a nice, fresh pie bursting with apples. I hoped Amanda was too busy getting lunch ready to read the paper. Despite her theatrics, she could hide her true feelings quite well. I trudged back to the boarding house, reluctant to face her or Eva, or anyone else. Now Eva's poor opinion of Sammy would really be sealed.

After I arrived home, I handed Amanda the boxed pie, hiding the telltale paper behind my back. "Thanks—it looks swell!"

I rushed upstairs and shoved the paper under my bed, then joined her in the kitchen. Amanda was in a good mood, singing "Jeepers, Creepers, Where'd You Get Those Peepers?" I hated to burst her bubble, so I kept quiet about today's headlines and the ominous Bentley. She was determined to pretend everything was fine, even cutting pretty pink roses from the garden as a table centerpiece.

The phone rang, and we both ran to get it, but it was only someone calling for old Mr. Hummel. Still no word from Burton or Sammy—nothing. While Amanda was busy getting ready, I did a few chores before Eva returned. We didn't dare spoil the illusion that all was well.

When the doorbell sounded, Amanda and I looked hopeful and rushed toward the front. I peered through the window, then flung open the door. On the steps stood James Burton, alone.

"Where's Sammy?" I frowned, not even bothering to hide my disappointment. "I thought you said…"

"I did my best." He shrugged, shuffling his feet. "I offered to get Sammy released into my custody, but he said 'no thanks,' that if word got out I sprung his bail, he could be killed."

"That's true." I nodded. I was so upset, I wasn't thinking straight. "What happens next?"

"The cops want to hold Sammy indefinitely. He's still their only suspect. I told them we had a witness, but they said to 'prove it.'" Burton tilted his head. "Think Buzz would be willing to come downtown to testify? He may be our only chance to get Sammy out of jail."

"Buzz?" I stalled. Frankly, I was torn: In my own haste to prove Sammy's innocence, I'd possibly put Buzz in danger. "If he did testify on Sammy's behalf, won't he be a target?"

"Maybe, but he's our only chance. Besides, I'll protect him."

"Oh yeah? Like the way you protected Sammy?" I snapped. "He's in jail 'cause of you."

On cue, Amanda rushed to the door, opening it wide. "Nice to see you again," she smiled. "We're expecting Sammy for lunch. Why don't you come join us?"

She tried to keep up appearances, well-versed in the etiquette and charm I lacked. My mother had told me to "bite my tongue" so often that it would've fallen off long ago if I'd taken her advice.

Burton hesitated, as if waiting for my consent, then walked inside, taking off his hat. "Sure, thanks. I'm starving since we didn't eat dinner last night." He gave me a pointed look.

"Make yourself at home." I motioned half-heartedly to the faded Victorian settee, sprouting several lumps and bumps in its worn-out cushions. Burton shifted in his seat awkwardly, as if trying to avoid the squeaky springs, to no avail.

Inside the kitchen, I hissed to Amanda, "Why did you have to invite him to lunch?"

Amanda looked hurt. "I thought he was our friend? Isn't he trying to help Sammy?"

She was right, as usual. Lashing out at Burton wouldn't help Sammy get released. In the moonlight, it was easy to get carried away by the romantic beach setting, but today was Sunday and Sammy was still behind bars.

Feeling guilty, I brought him a glass of lemonade, setting it on a doily on the end table. I forced a smile. "Glad you can join us. How's Sammy holding up?"

"I saw him at the jailhouse, and he was doing fine. He fits right in with the inmates."

I bristled at his insult. "You make it sound like he's on holiday." True, Sammy had a knack for adapting to any situation, as comfortable around high-society types as lowlifes.

By noon, the dining table was covered with a fancy floral embroidered linen tablecloth and napkins. As we sat in the parlor making small talk, I noticed Amanda kept glancing at the grandfather's clock. Still, she managed to keep up a lively conversation about everything but the arrest, an amazing show of restraint. I stole a few glances at Burton, who avoided my gaze.

"Can I help?" he asked. "I feel useless just sitting here."

You said it, I thought, upset.

Amanda was more gracious. "Sure. Follow me."

He returned with a box of our good silverware and began neatly setting the table. This domestic scene made me want to scream.

Finally I jumped up, grabbed my things, and stood by the front door. "I'm going bonkers, doing nothing, waiting for Sammy. Burton, can you please drive me to the police station? I'll go bail out Sammy myself!"

"Oh yeah? How?" Burton frowned, and followed me the door.

"I'll think of something." I glared at him, hands on my hips.

"Hold your horses, Jazz. How would it look if a society reporter showed up at the jailhouse, bailing out an alleged killer?"

"He's not a murderer," I snapped. "Don't bother, I'll take the trolley. I'll find a way to get him out of jail!"

Exasperated, I flung open the door and my face instantly lit up.

There stood Sammy on the porch, his clothes rumpled, dark circles under his eyes, but still looking as rakish as ever.

CHAPTER THIRTY-THREE

"Sammy—you're back!" I dropped my bag and hugged him. "What happened? I was on my way to see you. How'd you get out of jail so soon?"

"Not soon enough. My friend Andrew bailed me out." His smile stretched from ear to ear.

"Andrew?" Whoever he was, I was grateful.

"Andrew Jackson." He rubbed his thumb and forefingers together. "Lucky for me, I had some cash on me for the ice man. Money talks."

"And Sammy walks." I returned the smile. Sure, some cops could be bought for a twenty. A bargain, if you ask me. "So does that mean you're off the hook?"

He nodded. "For now. They said the evidence was circumstantial, so they let me go."

"I'm so relieved!" I held open the door. "Come in! Lunch is ready, if you're hungry."

"I'm starved. Jail food isn't fit for a dog."

Amanda rushed out, squealing "Sammy! You made it!" She threw her arms around his neck. He clearly enjoyed her display of affection, but shook her off when Burton appeared.

"Glad you got out OK." Burton reached out to shake his hand, but Sammy ignored him.

"What in hell is he doing here?" His face fell, looking betrayed.

"I was invited." Burton's eyes narrowed. "What's your excuse?"

"I lost my appetite." Sammy turned to leave, but Amanda tugged on his arm.

"You're both our special guests." She patted both men on their backs. "I've made enough for everyone."

"Come on, let's have a truce." I tried to ease the tension. "This calls for a celebration."

Maybe inviting two sworn enemies, on opposite ends of the law, to break bread together wasn't such a good idea. But I knew the meal would be far from dull. Wouldn't Mack and Mrs. Harper be jealous if they found out I'd invited a murder suspect and a Fed agent over for lunch today? Talk about a scandal!

"How are you, Sammy? How did they treat you in jail?" Amanda couldn't mask her concern, watching his face with anticipation. We'd set the dining table buffet-style, so we could help ourselves.

"Piece of cake. Except for the grub and the rock-hard bed." Sammy grimaced. I couldn't tell if he was serious or sarcastic, putting on a front for our sakes. He looked around the parlor, scratching his day-old beard. "Where is everyone? Where's Eva?"

"Don't worry, the boarders are gone and Eva's at church all day," I reassured him, dying to ask a laundry list of questions. He and Amanda sat down across from us, like a double-date.

"I know I've been gone less than twenty-four hours but it feels like a week." Sammy smiled at Amanda as he piled hot food on his plate. "This looks great, girls. I could eat a horse."

Sammy wasn't kidding, digging into his meal like a starving stray dog. In contrast, I couldn't help but notice Burton's impeccable table manners, acting more like a Rockefeller than a rookie Fed agent. Burton and Sammy shuffled their silverware, avoiding eye contact, only interacting when necessary.

I leaned forward. "Tell us what happened. Start at the beginning." It was worth a try.

"Not in front of your Fed friend," Sammy snorted. "He'd have me behind bars if he could."

"Bunk. I tried to help you," Burton replied. "Besides, murder is out of my jurisdiction."

"Oh yeah?" He looked wary. "OK, you asked for it. Remember how I was complaining 'cause Harvey was skipping my place? After two days without ice, I decided to confront him. So Saturday I waited for him in the alley, and when he tried to drive by, I stood in the street, blocking his way. He had to swerve to avoid hitting me."

Nervously, I glanced at Burton, who looked poker-faced.

"I noticed the ice truck was parked on the curb at a sharp angle," I told him.

"Right. I tried to stop him before he drove by. I swear, I had no intention of hurting Harvey." He exhaled. "I only wanted to know why he refused to deliver any ice. I'll admit, I lost my temper and roughed him up a little, but nothing serious."

"What was his excuse?" I wondered.

His eyes looked like pale jade as he glared at Burton. "All he said was: 'Ask Burton.'" Sammy leaned over the table, shaking his fist in Burton's face. "What in hell is that supposed to mean? 'Ask Burton'? What business did you have with Harvey?"

Burton flinched, but he managed to block Sammy's arm. "Let's talk about this later."

"Later?" Sammy shook off his grip, angrily. "I want to hear what you have to say. Now."

I held my breath, trading worried looks with Amanda, afraid Sammy might blow his top.

"What happened next?" I broke in, trying to keep the peace.

Sammy shot daggers at Burton but sat down. "When I offered to pay, he doubled his rates." He scowled. "'Highway robbery,' I told him. 'Extortion.' I wanted to know why in hell he was charging twice the price for the same damn ice he sold me last week."

No wonder he'd lost his temper. "You think he was pocketing the extra cash?" I asked.

"Hell, yes. I'll bet he was skimming off the top, that greedy little Mick." He pounded his fist on the table, rattling the dishes. No one spoke, riveted by his story, all eyes on Sammy.

"Finally we agreed on a price so I went inside the Oasis to pay him. By the time I got back, I found Harvey in his truck, his blood cold, that damn ice pick planted in his chest. Swear to God, I tried to help, to see if he was breathing, but he was already dead." He blew out a burst of smoke.

"You didn't see or hear anything?" I asked.

"Hell, no. That's when the cops showed up out of nowhere, accusing me of murder. I tried to explain what happened, tell them the truth, but they didn't believe me."

"They released you, so the cops must know you didn't do it," Amanda pointed out.

"I'm just the fall guy. The killer is still out there." His olive eyes flashed in anger.

"Guess what?" I piped up. "Buzz saw everything. He said a cowboy killed the ice man."

"A cowboy?" Sammy exhaled. "That's a relief. At least Buzz backed up my story, even if he is a kid."

"The cops may have some new leads by now," I said. "Maybe the cowboy is in custody?"

"Why don't you ask your new boyfriend?" He gave Burton the once-over.

My face flushed, and I glanced at Burton to watch his reaction.

"Me?" Burton shifted on the couch. "What do I know?"

Sammy ignored him. "Well, I did manage to find out a few more things about our good friend Harvey. I knew a couple of Joes in the slammer, and we sat around shooting the breeze for hours. Kept the guard up all night." Slowly Sammy pulled out a cigarette and lit it, taking his time.

"What about Harvey?" Burton's back stiffened.

"Most of it I can't repeat in mixed company." Sammy took a long drag, enjoying our attention. "Turns out the victim wasn't your ordinary ice man."

"What does that mean?" Burton narrowed his eyes.

Sammy paused, watching Burton as the words sunk in.

"Word is, Harvey worked as a snitch for the Downtown Gang. He was on Johnny Jack's payroll."

CHAPTER THIRTY-FOUR

"Harvey was an informant for the Downtown Gang?" Agent Burton swallowed hard, bolting upright. "How well do you know these guys? I doubt jailbirds make reliable sources."

"They have no reason to lie." Sammy scowled at him. "Especially to me."

So Harvey was double-crossing both Burton and Johnny Jack? No wonder he was murdered. It was only a matter of time before the gangs found out, and had him killed.

The men locked eyes, but Burton looked away first. "Interesting. Who else knew?"

Sammy shrugged. "Poor sucker had it coming to him. Messing around with the gangs. What burns me is both gangs let me take the rap." He rammed his fist on the table. "They needed a scapegoat, and I was the perfect patsy. My arrest was just for show—to make the gangs happy." Sammy fixed his gaze on Burton. "Everyone knows that gangsters dole out a lot more dough than a cop makes in a year. Or for that matter, the Feds."

"What are you implying?" Burton glared back at him. "I'm not for sale."

"Good for you." He gave Burton a smirk. "Too bad all the cops aren't as clean as you."

I moved in my seat, afraid to say a word. The fireworks had begun. Amanda and I got an earful, but Burton and Sammy didn't seem to notice we were even in the room. While they sniped at each other, our heads swiveled back and forth as if watching a heated tennis match at Wimbledon.

"It's getting stuffy in here." Sammy suddenly stood up, then stormed out the door, with Amanda following on his heels, loyal as a puppy. I watched as he stomped around the yard like a rodeo bull.

After they went outside, I sat down next to Burton, his legs almost a foot longer than mine. "You need to tell Sammy about Harvey. About your arrangement."

"What good would it do now?" Burton bristled. "The poor sap is already dead."

Yes, but shouldn't Sammy know the whole truth? "So what did you tell the cops? Did you mention the cowboy?"

He shook his head. "I said we had a reliable witness, but I didn't want to alert the killer."

I sat up. "You didn't mention Buzz or the Oasis by name, did you?" If so, Buzz was a sitting duck.

"Of course not. I said the witness had to remain anonymous for now, for his own safety. I didn't mention the fact that he's only a young boy." He took a sip of lemonade, staring at me over the glass. "I also didn't bring up your friend at the Surf Club. What's her name—Candy?"

I blinked, caught off guard. "Candy? What about her?"

He smiled. "You forget how tall I am. I saw the word *cowboy* written on the program she gave you. If two different people claim the killer was a cowboy, that's no coincidence."

I breathed a sigh of relief. Honestly, I was glad he'd found out on his own, so I didn't have to betray Candy's confidence. "Any idea who he is? Do the cops have any new leads?"

"Not yet," Burton said, tight-lipped. Then he stood up, put on his hat and held out his arm. "Why don't you walk me to my car?"

Curious, I followed him outside where Sammy and Amanda sat on the porch swing. "Thanks for the delicious feast, ladies. My compliments to the chef."

Then Burton turned to Sammy. "Can I give you a lift?" No doubt he wanted a private audience to discuss the ice man murder.

Sammy scowled. "Are you nuts? How would that look—me riding around town in a Fed agent's breezer?"

Good point. Burton leveled his gaze at Sammy. "Fine. Let me know if you find out anything else."

Then he took me by my elbow and we walked to his car, out of earshot. "I swear, I had no idea Harvey also worked for the Downtown Gang. That no-good double-crosser."

"I'm surprised, too." This was getting complicated. "You think the gangs found out and had him killed?"

Burton nodded. "Johnny Jack probably knows everything I do— and more. I should've figured that punk kid would sell himself to the highest bidder." He kicked his shoes into the dirt, scuffing the toes.

"You went to a lot of trouble for nothing. And Sammy had to wind up in jail." I also felt frustrated, like a dog chasing its tail but only getting dizzy. "Did you see today's paper? Sammy even made the front page."

He whistled. "Your reporter pals did a number on Sammy. But maybe it wasn't a complete waste of time. Why don't you stick close, see what else he found out in jail?"

"Forget it. I won't be your spy. Look what happened to your last snitch." I exhaled loudly.

His face fell. "That's not what I meant. Sammy could have overheard something else that might help both of us." Perhaps he was right, but I didn't want to get between him and Burton. I'd have better luck getting rival gang leaders Ollie Quinn and Johnny Jack to smoke a peace pipe together.

Down the block, I heard a loud motor start and saw a shiny gold Bentley ease down the street, slowing to a crawl, taking in the view. Shaken, I asked Burton, "Have you ever seen that gold Bentley before?" I tried to memorize the license plate numbers, but it sped up and roared past.

"No, why?" He watched it drive away.

"The same car was following me today, when I went to the store." Now I knew it wasn't a fluke.

"Following you?" He frowned. "That Bentley? Where? Did you see anyone?"

"The windows were dark. Maybe I imagined it all," I fibbed, not wanting him to worry or consider me a ditzy dame like in 'The Perils of Pauline.' I turned to go, adding, "Thanks for last night."

"My pleasure. I hope we can do it again soon?" He started to lean over, but I pulled away. What would people think?

As I walked back to the house, Sammy razzed me, saying, "Getting chummy with the local Probie, are we?"

"No, we're only friends." I blushed. "Besides, this was all your bright idea. You said to *humor* him, remember? Or was that only hooey about keeping your enemies closer?"

"I don't mind you getting close, but don't get *too* close. You never know who you can trust in this town. Anyone can be a snitch, like Harvey." Sammy gave me a warning look. "Say, how did he know your pal, Agent Burton? I can't figure out what he meant by, 'Ask Burton.' Did he tell you anything?"

What good would it do to reveal the truth now? Still, my first loyalty was to Sammy. Didn't he have a right to know?

On impulse, I said: "Burton told me this in confidence, but it may not matter, now that Harvey's gone. Turns out that Harvey was also Burton's informant."

"What? So Burton was behind this mess?" Sammy shot up and paced the porch, eyes blazing. "That son of a bitch! Why doesn't he mind his own damn business?"

"He's only trying to help. He wants to find the source of the wood alcohol, just like you." True, I didn't like Burton's tactics either, but I didn't want Sammy getting in trouble 'cause of me and my big mouth.

"Now you're defending that asshole?" Sammy eyed me. "Well, I'm not surprised Harvey tried to work both angles. That no-good double-crosser. He was always poking his nose into my business, hanging around like a goddamn spy."

"I bet that's why the gangs put out a hit," I told him.

"Maybe they found out he was on the take from your new beau." Sammy scowled and stood up to leave. "Thanks for lunch, ladies. I'd better go check on the Oasis."

I overlooked his jab, tapping his arm. "Before you go, I forgot to mention the rummy we saw last night on the Seawall."

"So what? Rummies are a dime a dozen in this town."

"This was different. He seemed to be going blind after an all-day bender. Wonder where he got his liquor?" After I described the situation, Sammy looked alarmed.

"That's what I'd like to know. Jazz, can you show me where you ran into him? I want to question the barkeeps in the area, try to find out who's delivering their booze. Besides, I could use some fresh air after being cooped up all night." Sammy headed toward the door.

"What about the apple pie?" Amanda looked disappointed, running after us. "Hey, don't forget me!"

The three of us caught the trolley to the Seawall, and got out by the Hotel Galvez. As we crossed the busy street, I noticed how different the crowd was during the day, compared to last night. Now the beach was filled with families picnicking by the shore, and children riding bikes on the Seawall. To me, it looked dangerous, but the cyclists seemed fearless as they pedaled down the long, wide stretch of concrete, oblivious to the jagged granite rocks below.

Arms linked, Amanda and I flanked Sammy as we walked along the Seawall, enjoying the salty sea air. A warm breeze brushed my face, my frock; the crashing waves sounded soothing. Sammy's good mood returned, and he told us amusing stories about the other inmates: one man who crowed like a rooster at dawn, the other who sang the blues all night and beat on his cell bars using his shoes like drumsticks. Sounded more like a funny farm than a jail.

Sammy stopped and faced me. "So how was your date with Burton? I hear you two tied one on." Gee thanks, Amanda. "Did he try anything? If he did, so help me..." He raised a fist in warning.

"Relax. Believe it or not, Burton was a gentleman. He wanted to confront the Beach Gang at the Surf Club, find out about the ice man hit. But Quinn beat us to the punch. He had the host deliver a bottle of fancy French Champagne to our table."

"You don't say." In retrospect, the story seemed almost humorous. Even Sammy stifled a laugh. "Wish I could've seen Burton's face. Did you drink any?"

"Naturally. Why pass up a chance to enjoy fine French Champagne?" I smiled. "Say, guess who I bumped into last night? One of your old flames, Candy. She works there as a hostess."

Sammy blinked a few times. "I wondered what happened to that dame. She quit without giving us any notice."

Amanda made a face. "Good riddance. Who needs her?"

"Think she left because of Andrews?" I asked Sammy.

Sammy shrugged. "Maybe it was my fault. She was upset because I wouldn't give up my 'harem,' as she called my lady friends. What did she have to say?"

Nervously I looked around, but the wind and waves helped drown out our conversation. "Candy said she heard someone bragging in the bar about the hit on the ice man. Sounds like he was waiting for the right moment to attack, but got lucky when you took the fall. Then when we left, she gave me a program with the word *cowboy* written inside."

"Cowboy?" His face fell. "That's all? No name, nothing else?"

"The host was hovering around so she couldn't say much, but it confirms Buzz's story."

"We need to pay her a visit at the Surf Club right away. I'm sure they'll let us in since you're a regular. I hear they took your picture and everything. You're famous now," Sammy said with a smirk.

"Want my John Hancock?" I shot back. "Don't blame me! A shutterbug snuck up and took our mug shots with the Champagne, trying to blackmail Burton."

"Too bad you can't keep them as a souvenir of your romantic date," he said dryly.

"It wasn't a date. The only reason I went out with him in the first place was to help *you*!" I hated fighting with Sammy, especially over Burton. I stormed off toward the Crystal Palace, then pointed at the spot where we saw the wino. "The man was there, stumbling down the Seawall."

Sammy stopped, scanning the area. "Wait here," he ordered before he entered a seedy-looking bar. Typical tourist traps, luring suckers craving cheap liquor and even cheaper women.

After he left, I turned to Amanda. "Sorry I lost my temper. Glad you two seem copacetic."

She beamed, as if nothing had happened. "I think everyone had a really swell time at lunch, don't you?" Only Amanda could pretend our lunch was a cakewalk, despite the obvious fighting and friction.

A few minutes later, Sammy reappeared with a grin on his face. "I knew the bartender so he gave me the name of a rum-runner they use. Also there's a joint nearby I want to check out. Let's go have a look." As we walked down the Seawall, I trailed behind Sammy and Amanda, feeling like a fifth wheel.

On the beach, I heard children laugh as they splashed in the water, arms flailing while they tried in vain to outrun the tide. A creamy white seagull squawked overhead, its graceful wings outstretched like a ballerina. We'd almost reached Murdoch's when a loud scream carried over the roar of the waves. Several bathers had gathered on the beach, forming a semi-circle.

A woman cried out: "Help! Call the cops!" Holding onto our hats, we ran toward Murdoch's and rushed down the concrete steps to the beach. A small group surrounded a body lying on the sand. A drowning victim?

As we got closer, my knees buckled and I tried to steady myself, feeling faint. Amanda shielded her eyes and leaned against Sammy.

A stocky man lay face-down on the beach, in soaking-wet blue jeans and a denim shirt, wearing soggy cowboy boots.

CHAPTER THIRTY-FIVE

"Is he still breathing?" A young woman in a frilly bathing outfit ogled the lifeless body.

"Looks dead as a doornail to me," a big man in wet trunks snickered. "Was he looking for his horse in the Gulf? Hard to swim in cowboy boots."

I gaped at the body, recalling a neighbor boy who, on a dare, tried to swim across a lake but ended up drowning. What a horrid way to die, gulping for air, calling for help that never came. Edging closer to Sammy, I whispered, "Think it's him? The cowboy?"

Sammy squinted in the sun, nodding. "Must be. It's too much of a coincidence." He bent down and turned the body over, then wiped his hands on his jeans.

The frilly bathing suit lady let out a high-pitched scream and ran down the beach. I wanted to follow her, but I forced myself to watch as Sammy examined the cowboy, bloated and puffy, like a blue beached jellyfish. His ruddy face was swollen, his thick copper-colored hair plastered against his forehead, his pale fingers like fat cigars. Vacant blue eyes seemed surprised, staring out into space.

"I'm going to be sick," Amanda muttered, her eyes half-closed.

"Me too." I stood there, speechless, unable to move or breathe. Two bodies in two days....Too much violence, too many deaths. Feeling woozy, I leaned against Amanda for support. We stood together in the sand, like a pair of crumbling pillars.

Sammy studied the cowboy's face and neck. "Looks like rope burns around his throat. Maybe he was hung by a rope—but his neck doesn't seem broken. Probably strangled."

I lowered my voice, swallowing hard. "You think he was murdered, not drowned?"

He nodded. "Seems he was strangled somewhere else, then dumped off in the ocean."

"You a doctor?" A short pipsqueak of a man in a black bathing costume challenged Sammy. "You don't look like no doctor to me."

"Says who? You?" Sammy stood up to his full six feet and crossed his arms, facing down the diminutive bather until he walked away, anxiously looking over his shoulder.

"I'll go get the cops," a heavy-set older man said. "Too late for an ambulance."

After the crowd left, Sammy said, "He looks familiar. I'll check his pockets, see if I can figure out who he is." He pulled out a soaked train ticket and poker chips from the Surf Athletic Club—marked SAC. "Take a look at this," he said, handing me a chip. So Candy was right— the cowboy *was* gambling at the Surf Club last night, after the murder. Did we miss him?

"Where have you seen this guy before?" I asked Sammy, trying not to stare.

"Maybe at Joe's Bar. The cowboys seem to like that run-down saloon, with all the sawdust on the floor. Makes them feel right at home." That made sense. The cowboy may have been waiting for the ice man at Joe's, and followed him to his truck after he made his delivery there.

"There's no wallet or ID?" I doubted hit men used their real names anyway.

"Nothing." Sammy studied the wet ticket. "One-way to Houston. Poor sucker got a one-way ticket, all right, to nowhere." He stuffed the items back into the cowboy's pockets. "Too bad he can't tell us who put out the hit."

"What about the Surf Club chips? You think the Beach Gang hired him?" I whispered.

"Looks that way." He nodded. "It must be the last place he went. Maybe he stopped by there to collect his payment—or gamble it away."

Mention of the Surf Club gave me an idea. "What if the Beach Gang had both guys killed?" I said. "Say they strangled the cowboy so he wouldn't talk. Could be symbolic, a warning to rival gang members and hired guns."

"I wouldn't be surprised," Sammy said, wiping his forehead. "But we may never find out who's behind the hits. Gangsters know how to cover their tracks."

"I'll let you know what the reporters dig up. Now I should call Nathan so he can take photos before they move the body."

Too bad I couldn't send Mack a postcard: 'Wish you were here.' But was stumbling over yet another dead body really such a feat? To be honest, I felt more like upchucking than gloating.

"I'd better scram. After Burton, I can't stomach any more cops." Sammy turned to Amanda with a grin. "I need to make a few stops. Want to come?"

Amanda nodded. "You bet! Beats standing around this funeral."

"Be careful," I called, waving good-bye, tempted to follow them.

After they left, I climbed the stairs to Murdoch's, clutching the banister for support, and found a public phone.

When Mrs. Page answered, I described the crime scene on the beach and asked her to locate Nathan. "Oh my! You poor dear! Want me to call Mack, or one of the city reporters?"

Who did she think I was—a Gibson Girl? "No thanks, I can handle this," I bristled. "Let me talk to Mr. Nelson, get his OK."

While I explained the situation, Mr. Nelson sounded skeptical but gave me a few pointers: "Take lots of notes, get accurate quotes and keep your facts straight. Make it snappy—the shorter, the better." I figured he couldn't turn me down since I was already on the scene, and Nathan would be taking photos. Didn't dead bodies still make front-page news?

On the beach, I watched a roly-poly cop with a handlebar moustache examine the body. Word had spread about the cowboy and only a few gawkers remained. Terrified mothers gathered their children and fled the beach. The heat, the bloated body, the whole scenario made me nauseated, but I couldn't pass up this opportunity—a hot scoop dropped in my lap.

"How long has he been dead?" I asked the corpulent cop.

The cop looked me up and down, taking in my street clothes. "Who are you?" He sounded suspicious. "Why are you so interested in this young man—did you know him?"

"No, sir." I tried to stand tall. "I'm a reporter for the *Gazette*."

"Oh yeah? Where's Mack? He usually follows stories like a stray on a steak."

"Since it's Sunday, I'm filling in for him."

"You don't say? Well, I'll be. A lady reporter?" He stroked his moustache. "I'd guess this poor fella has been in the water less than a day, from the looks of him. He's not too swollen or decomposed like some of those bodies we fish out from the bay."

I grimaced, trying not to picture the unfortunate folks who ended up as shark food. Still, the time frame made sense. If the cowboy had spent Saturday night gambling at the Surf Club, then he may have been strangled and dropped into the ocean after midnight.

"Any idea who he is? Any ID on the body?" I played dumb.

The cop squatted down and dug into the man's pockets, producing the same items Sammy had already found. "Here's a train ticket and some gambling tokens." Then he turned him sideways and looked behind his shirt collar. "He's wearing a shirt marked with the name MacDougal," the cop noted. "If that's his real name. Maybe he's a roughneck or rodeo cowboy. I'd best call the M.E. to come down, take a look."

We hadn't thought of looking under his collar. Strange that both the ice man and his killer had Irish surnames. Was it a fluke? Were they in rival gangs, or the same gang? Or was it a hit? I was tempted to contact Burton, get his take, but for now I had a story to report.

As we waited for the M.E., I studied the corpse, wondering how he was involved. Was he a novice or an experienced hit man? He looked so young, too young to die. Did he work for the gangs or was this a personal vendetta? I felt dizzy from the heat, so I walked toward Murdoch's for some shade, to catch my breath. Was someone calling my name or was I hallucinating? Then I saw Nathan wave at me from the Seawall, then rush down the concrete stairs with a smile. Dead bodies didn't seem to faze him at all.

"Thanks for the tip, Jazz. I was so tired of taking photos of fat babies and their doting mothers at the church picnic." He studied my face. "You don't look so hot. Are you OK?"

"I've seen enough corpses to last a while." I shuddered. "Hurry, shoot your photos before the M.E. takes him away." Keeping my distance, I pointed to the cowboy's neck. "See these red marks? Sammy said they looked like rope burns. Maybe he was strangled with his own rope?"

"Sammy was here? He's out of jail?" Nathan grinned. "Attaboy! What happened?"

"There was no proof. He was innocent. Just bad luck." I wanted to rub it in, saying, 'I told you he was framed,' but bit my tongue.

Nathan studied the man's neck, and took a few close-up shots. "They look like rope burns, all right. Sammy would make a good cop, you know that?"

Interesting idea, Sammy going semi-straight.

Nathan cocked his head. "I'll have to move fast. He won't keep long in this heat, like the ice man." Did he have to bring that up? "Say, why don't you try calling Mack at the paper?"

"I can do this on my own," I insisted, pulling out a pencil and pad from my bag.

"Sure? No offense, but you're used to covering society stories, not murder." He changed angles to get various shots. "You seem so uncomfortable around crime scenes, especially dead bodies."

Who isn't? "How can I learn to be a real reporter if I don't try new things? I can't wait forever for my big break." Clearly covering murders wasn't my forte, but neither was stupid society gossip.

"Fine. I get it." He held up his hands in mock-surrender. "Did you examine the body?"

"No, why?" I made a face. "That's what cops and coroners do."

"Yes, but when they're not around, it's a good chance to do some digging on your own." He smiled. "I learned a few tips by following Mack around. Have you looked in his boots yet?"

"His boots?" I frowned, puzzled. "Why?"

"You've heard of lead boots? How about lead cowboy boots?" Nathan pulled the cowboy's pants leg up and peered inside the boots. "Just as I thought—they're filled with sand. The next best thing to concrete or rocks, especially on the beach." He tapped the side of his head. "Quick thinking. Could be the killer has done this before, or was in a tight spot."

I'd heard of cement shoes, but this was a new trick. "Doesn't the sand wash away?"

"Eventually, but it works for a while. The killer has enough time to get away before the body floats to shore," Nathan explained. "Do the cops know anything about him?"

"Not yet. But we think he murdered the ice man."

CHAPTER THIRTY-SIX

"Two murders for the price of one?" Nathan cracked. "Why do you think he's the killer?"

"Buzz told me he was a cowboy. And the timing, the place, everything seems to fit." I described what Buzz told me, not mentioning my chat with Candy at the Surf Club.

"You don't say…" He shrugged. "I guess one dead body deserves another."

I glared at him. "How can you joke about murder now?"

"It's the only way to stay sane. You see enough of this stuff and it's bound to make you crazy. The newspaper business isn't for the faint-hearted."

"I realize that. Two dead bodies in a row is two too many for me." I looked away, my cheeks hot.

"Think you can cut it as a news reporter? After all this?"

I met his gaze. "We'll find out."

He had a point. Clearly I wasn't hard-boiled enough to cover hard news. Maybe Nathan was right: I should focus on society events and weddings. Sigh.

When the M.E. arrived, I watched, fascinated, as he checked the cowboy's airway and neck, then removed his boots. I felt an eerie sense of déjà vu, recalling Doc examining Andrews' body at the Oasis. "I'm with the *Gazette*," I told him. "How long do you think he's been dead?"

"Less than twelve hours, I'd say. The victim was dead before he hit the water, sometime after midnight." He pointed to the cowboy's neck. "Appears to be death by asphyxiation, probably strangulation, by these red marks on his throat."

"I see. Do they look like rope burns to you?" I asked innocently.

The coroner frowned, giving me a quizzical look. "Very likely."

"When will your report be ready?" I needed to rush the story out before Mack took over.

"Give me a few hours." The M.E. gave me his name and a few more details, including his office number.

"Thanks for your time," I told him.

He looked amused. "You must be new. I don't usually get thanked for doing my job. Wish more people did."

"You might score a few points with the dead guy, too." Nathan nudged me with his elbow. "Come on, Miss Manners, let's hit the road." As we walked to his car, we tried to shake the sand off our clothes and shoes, without much luck. After cranking up his engine, he opened the car door for me. "So where were you last night? I tried to call, but your aunt said you were out."

"Really? Eva never told me you called." I looked out the window, biting my lip. "I had last-minute plans." Did I have to tell Nathan every little detail of my life?

"Too bad she can't keep track of all your gentleman callers. Guess she lost count."

"You're all wet!" I turned away, my face flushing.

"So what's the big deal?" Nathan eyed me. "Where'd you go?"

"If you must know, I went to the Surf Club with Agent Burton. He thinks the Beach Gang put out the hit on the ice man, so he wanted to confront Ollie Quinn and the Maceos."

Nathan let out a whistle. "I've got to give the Yank some credit. Bet he worked hard to come up with that line. Seems he'll do anything to get a date."

"It wasn't a date. We were undercover, doing research."

"Is that what they're calling it now? Research?" He raised his brows. "Whatever you call it, it's still hanky-panky in my book."

I rolled my eyes. "You know me better than that." Why did I care what he thought?

"Yes, but I know his type just as well." Nathan shook his head. "These city slickers don't take no for an answer. Maybe at first, but not for long."

"I didn't ask for your advice." I knotted my fists, ready to blow my top. "By the way, I sure as hell didn't appreciate the front-page spread of Sammy's arrest in such graphic detail. You may as well plaster his mug on a 'Wanted' poster all over town!"

He tried to look apologetic. "I'm sorry if Sammy got hurt, but that's news. No one is off-limits. You need to learn to be more objective if you want to become a real reporter."

"A real reporter? So I'm a fake?" I admit, my emotions often clouded my mind. But how could I be detached about family? Seems I couldn't protect Sammy in print or otherwise.

"You know what I meant, Jazz." Nathan tried to take my hand, but I pulled it away. "So tell me, how did Sammy get out of jail? Did your boyfriend spring him?"

"They found a witness," I said, not wanting to explain. Why couldn't he dry up? Glumly, I stared out the window, watching the churchgoers in their Sunday best stroll down the street, children playing hopscotch. I clammed up as he drove to the *Gazette*, entering the building without thanking him for the ride. He looked hurt and sat in the car a while before going inside.

A stack of mail sat on my desk, piled up over the weekend. Swell. I had skipped my weekly filing session due to the ice man's murder. Now the tedious task seemed welcome compared to writing about yet another unsolved hit.

The cowboy's bloated body seemed to float before me like a Halloween ghost. I tried to write a lead but I only knew the 'what and where.' I wasn't sure about the 'who' or the big question: 'why.' So far, all I had was speculation and hearsay.

I slipped into a back office and asked the operator to call the M.E.'s office. "The coroner? Whatever for, Jasmine?"

"For Mack," I replied, to shut her up. After the coroner got on the line, he confirmed what we'd suspected on the beach: that the cowboy died of asphyxiation by strangulation.

As a hunch, I asked, "What else? Is there a toxicology report?"

He was silent a moment. "I haven't had time to work up the toxicology, but I can tell you the victim put up a good fight. He showed definite signs of a struggle: scratches, bruises, a nasty knot on the head—plus the rope burns on his neck. It will all be in my formal report tomorrow."

"Can I quote you on that? I'd like to make Monday's edition."

"Sure, but you can call it speculation and say my findings are inconclusive," he instructed.

After writing up my draft—all three paragraphs—I handed it to Mr. Nelson for approval. "If we print the article along with the photos, someone could ID the body," I offered.

"Sounds rather lurid to me. I don't want the *Gazette* to get a reputation as a yellow rag. We'll have the photos on hand, just in case." He skimmed the copy and marked it up with a red pen. "A bit dramatic but it's fine now. Just in time for Monday's paper."

I looked it over, frowning. "Only two graphs?"

"Jasmine, by the way, don't expect a byline for this." Mr. Nelson was polite but firm. "It's little more than a mortuary notice."

My face fell. "I understand, Mr. Nelson." Some thanks I got for covering a murder on my day off. What did I expect, flowers? It wasn't front-page news, but it was better than nothing.

As I waited for him to proof my whittled-down copy, I poked through the pile of envelopes on my desk. A large brown manila envelope caught my eye, with: MRS. HARPER, SOCIETY EDITOR crudely printed in big black block letters. Not the flowery handwriting of the social climbers.

Curious, I opened the sealed envelope and pulled out two 8 x 10 black and white glossies: Photos of me and Prohibition Agent James Burton celebrating at the Surf Club, raising our crystal fluted glasses filled with bubbly French Champagne, toasting to the moon.

CHAPTER THIRTY-SEVEN

I froze in my seat, heart racing. Who'd sent the photos? I spun around, expecting to see the Surf Club shutterbug lurking nearby. Hands trembling, I shoved the photos back into the envelope.

Clearly the Beach Gang wanted to threaten Agent Burton—or was it a warning to me? Where else did they send the photos? The *Galveston Daily News, Houston Post* or *Houston Chronicle*? I hoped the editors would realize the gangs wanted to intimidate, if not incriminate, Burton and refuse to publish the photos—or would they? He'd become a laughingstock—and I'd get the ax. Still, he might get off scot-free, while my budding 'career' would be ruined.

Panicky, I took a quick look around the newsroom: Luckily it was quiet, save for a sportswriter who was describing last night's baseball game. I pulled out the photos again and sneaked a peek. If the gangs wanted to scare us or try to blackmail us, they did a great job. I had to admit, the photos weren't half-bad, clear and in focus.

If you hadn't known Burton was a Prohibition agent and I was a rookie reporter doing "research," you'd think we were any two sweethearts on a date, celebrating with fizzy Champagne.

"What's that you got there?" Nathan peered over my shoulder.

"Nathan, you scared me!" I almost jumped out of my chair.

"Out on the town with lover boy, I see," he said. "I don't think that's such a bright idea, flashing those photos around a newsroom."

"Pipe down!" I hushed him. "I was opening Mrs. Harper's mail as usual, and found this on my desk. Obviously the gangs are gunning for Burton, but I don't want to be involved."

"I don't blame you," he warned. "It doesn't look good—for either of you. I can see the headlines now: Society reporter caught getting sloshed at gin joint with new Prohibition agent."

"Go jump in the lake," I snapped. "Besides, that headline's too long for page one."

"You get the picture. I mean pictures," he cracked. "Just watch your back, Jazz."

"Nate, I'm in a real jam." I sighed. "What should I do: Hide the photos or come clean?"

He leaned over my desk, lowering his voice. "If it was me, I'd take the photos home and keep them out of sight. Pray no one else has copies. Who knows what the gangs will do next?"

"Good advice, thanks." Nathan was right. No one else had to see the photos. Maybe I was overreacting. I had done nothing wrong. Why should I worry about some dumb goons?

"Speaking of photos, can I see your close-ups of the ice man? Maybe I missed something."

"Sure." He returned holding a short stack of photos of the ice man, laid out cold.

"I'll never get used to seeing a dead body. It's so sad, so final."

I studied the gruesome photos, scrutinizing each scene. In one shot, I noticed a long object on the truck floor. "What's that by the ice blocks?"

"Wait, I may have a better one." He shuffled through his stack of prints. "Will these help?" These photos were a bit fuzzy and off-center, but I saw what I needed: One photo showed a full shot of the truck's interior. Below the dead man's feet lay a long-stemmed rose.

My stomach clenched, and I tapped the photo. "Who put the rose there? Was it red? Where was it before?"

"All I know is the rose was on the victim's chest when I showed up. I moved it so I could take close-ups of the stab wound." He shrugged. "Why? I figured someone left it to be nice—so he could rest in peace."

"You moved it? Why didn't you mention the rose before? It could be important."

"It was only a red rose—so what?"

"Could be a clue, a sign from the Beach Gang. The red rose might mean Rose Maceo is behind the hit, like a calling card. Or some rival may be trying to pin the murder on him."

"That's interesting. We'll see what Mack has to say tomorrow."

Mack, always Mack, the ace reporter. No one seemed to take my opinions or my work very seriously.

"By the way, do you have any photos of the cowboy? I can show them to Buzz, confirm he's the killer."

"Not yet, they still need to dry." He paused. "Hey, how about a lift home while I wait?"

"Thanks, I'll be ready soon." Nathan had a short fuse, but luckily was quick to make amends.

In minutes, I'd rewritten my copy, all sixty or so words, and placed it on Mr. Nelson's desk. With any luck, the piece would appear in Monday's paper. I hoped someone would come forward with information about the dead cowboy—MacDougal, if that was his real name.

Before I left, I gathered up the Sunday paper and hid the brown manila envelope in the middle. Now my boss would never see the incriminating photos—possibly harmful to my health *and* my career.

On the way home, I told Nathan about our experience at the Surf Club, leaving out a few choice details. "That was some evening you had." He let out a whistle. "So the Beach Gang made good on their threat. Better hope they don't use you to squeal on Burton."

"They don't even know who I am," I protested. "For all they know, I was some floozy."

"Says you. You think it's pure coincidence that the photos happened to land on Mrs. Harper's desk?"

"Jeepers, what if you're right?" My stomach knotted, recalling the menacing Bentley. "Maybe it was a warning. Now what?"

"Hey, you're the one involved with Agent Burton, not me." Nathan shrugged.

"I'd hardly call it involved. More like entangled."

"Ain't that the truth?" Nathan walked me to the door, like a gentleman. Hard to believe that I'd stood on these same steps with Burton only last night. So much had happened in the past 24 hours.

"Thanks for the ride, Nate. Why don't you come in? I want to show you some things."

"OK, but I can't stay long. I need to make sure I get credit for my cowboy photos."

Eva met us at the door and smiled at Nathan, looking surprised. "Hello, Nathan." She glanced outside, no doubt looking for Burton. "Why don't I get you some fresh lemonade?"

In the kitchen, she asked, "So how was your lunch Sunday? Where's your Fed agent fella?"

"He's not my fella, but he joined us for lunch." I gave her arm a light squeeze and quickly changed the subject. "Guess what? Sammy was released today!"

"That's good news," she said, smiling. "What happened?"

"They let him go for lack of evidence. I knew he didn't do it."

I noted her relieved expression as she filled the glasses with lemonade and chipped ice. "Sammy may be rough around the edges, but I can't quite picture him as a killer."

"I'll say." Glad she agreed. I excused myself and stepped out to give Nathan a glass of lemonade. "I'll be right back."

I rushed upstairs to my room, eager to show him Andrews' mystery items, and stuffed them in my purse. As I headed down the hall, I saw old Mrs. Miller struggling with her luggage. Her quaint Edwardian hat was straight out of *Godey's Lady's Book*, with its colorful bouquet of flowers and fruit.

"Going out of town?" I tried to pick up her overnight bag and suitcase. "Can I help?"

"Why, thank you, Jasmine. I'm taking the train to Houston to see my oldest daughter. She just had her third baby and I'm beside myself. It's a boy!" She beamed with pride.

"Congratulations." I almost dropped her bag on my foot. What was in it anyway—a cannon ball?

Downstairs, she brightened when she saw Nathan. "You must be my cab ride."

"Sorry, Mrs. Miller, he's not a cab driver. He's a friend of mine."

"Beg your pardon," she said, flustered. "I'll wait on the porch."

After Eva and I helped her get settled on the porch swing, Eva whispered, "Keep an eye on her. Make sure she doesn't fall asleep and miss her cab."

I propped open the stained glass door with a heavy flowerpot so I could watch Mrs. Miller through the screen. She was hard to miss with that gigantic gaudy centerpiece perched on her head.

Then I put on a Duke Ellington record and turned the phonograph up loud. While Eva washed dishes in the kitchen, I dug into my purse, handing Nathan the key, ledger and matchbook. "What do you make of these?"

Nathan fingered each item, studying them one by one. "Where did you get them?"

"They belonged to Horace Andrews," I said, my voice low. "His wife gave them to me."

"Really? Why?" He thumbed through the ledger with a frown.

"I think she wants me to figure out what they mean, see if they have any significance. Truth is, she doesn't want anyone in her social circles to know she suspects her late husband of wrongdoing."

I pointed to the rows of cryptic numbers and letters. "Look at these entries. I think they might be personal loans, gambling debts or secret accounts. Underground businesses—like the Oasis."

Nathan examined the ledger. "Could be all of the above. Looks like a private record, maybe a listing of his off-the-book clients. Why else would he hang around places like the Oasis?" He grinned. "That gave him an excuse to get smashed on weekends."

"You may be right. Plus it explains why he worked so late, the secretive phone calls, the odd hours. A banker isn't as conspicuous in a crowded club at night." While Horace was out wheeling and dealing, poor Alice was left alone at home with the children.

"Now you're on the trolley! What better time to collect cash from bars and bookies?"

"So you think he was keeping their accounts on the side, so the bank wouldn't know?"

"Of course. But I suspect that's not all Andrews did for his clients." Nathan lowered his voice. "I'll bet he cleaned up their accounts, made them look legit."

I hated to think the worst, but the signs were obvious. "You mean money laundering?"

"You said it." He nodded. "How else will these gangsters stash all their cash?"

"Makes sense." I pointed to the name "Rose" in the matchbook. "Seems Rose Maceo was one of his clients. Poor Mrs. Andrews thought he was having an affair with a tart named Rose."

I described seeing Rose Maceo at the bank Monday, how the crowd parted as he passed.

"Interesting that a straight arrow like Andrews had a pipeline to the Maceo brothers."

"He wasn't exactly a choir boy, as you can see," I said, thumbing through the ledger. To me, it all looked like alphabet soup.

On the last page, I pointed out the bottom line written in large letters: RR628.' "What's strange is it's the only entry written in ink, so he wouldn't forget it," I mused. "I wonder if it's an address or a city or place—say, Round Rock? Or a code name—like Rough Riders or Round Robin. Maybe it stands for rum-runners?"

"Good guess," Nathan said. "What about a speakeasy or a gaming parlor? Didn't you say he was a gambler? Maybe it's a betting hall or casino or code for a bookmaker. Or a racetrack address?"

He scratched his head as he studied the page, puzzled, repeating over and over, "RR628."

Outside, a car honked loudly and Mrs. Miller scrambled to her feet, holding her valise, the other hand on her enormous flower basket hat. As the cabbie got out to help with her luggage, she yelled, "I'll be back this Friday! Don't forget, Eva—I'll be on the 5:35 train."

A brain bulb flashed. Nathan and I traded smiles, saying in unison: "Railroad!"

CHAPTER THIRTY-EIGHT

Finally, a clue. I shook Nathan's arm, saying, "Do you think this may be a date or the time of a train stop?"

He nodded. "Maybe Horace was going to pick someone up at the station?"

"What if he was going to catch a train himself? Maybe he had an important meeting out of town." I leapt off the couch. "Say, let's go to the train station and try to figure out what the numbers mean. I'm sure Eva won't mind."

"Now? Hold your horses, Jazz." He tapped his watch. "I've got photos drying in the darkroom, remember? We're on deadline."

"Oh, Nate," I pouted. "Can't they wait? They're not going anywhere."

"Neither is the train station." He stood up and put on his hat. "Why don't we go there during lunch tomorrow? Sunday is too busy with all the trains coming and going."

"It's probably a dead-end anyway." I walked him out reluctantly. What I really wanted to do was rush down to the train station and question the station master. Too bad I couldn't drive.

"Thanks again for the tip about the cowboy." He winked. "See you tomorrow."

"It's a date." I forced a half-smile, and watched him walk down the brick path, waving good-bye as he got into his car. Here we were, making progress, then it all fell flat.

"A date?" Eva rushed out of the kitchen. "You haven't even told me about last night!"

"There's no date, Eva. We can talk over the dishes. You want to wash or dry?"

Eva and I stood over the sink filled with soap suds and dirty dishes, gabbing as we did the dishes, a regular ritual for us on weekends. Naturally she asked me routine questions about my "date" like: Where was Burton from? Was he a good dancer? What did his father do? What kind of car did he drive? Then out of nowhere: "Did he try to kiss you?"

What? That was a question I expected from Amanda, not my spinster aunt. "Of course not!" I felt my face flush. "I told you, we're only friends."

"I wish my friends were tall, blond and handsome," Eva said with a sly smile. Nice to know she still had an eye for good-looking men. Perhaps one day we'd both find real romance.

"Want me to see if he has an older brother or uncle?" I teased her as she turned beet-red.

After we'd finished half an hour later, Amanda burst in: "Hello? Jazz, are you there?"

I hurried out of the kitchen, glad to escape the monotony of housework. If this was the life of a homemaker, I wanted no part of it. I was afraid I'd die of boredom—or go bonkers.

Amanda had that happy, flushed glow of a girl in love—or smitten. Her long blonde hair looked windblown, and her face was sunburned. "How was your afternoon with Sammy?"

"Loads of fun. We went to one bar after another, up and down the Seawall. He said I was a 'good distraction.'" She laughed. "I hope he meant it as a compliment."

"Sure he did." I pulled her aside. "So did he find out anything about that bootlegger? Or the cowboy?"

"Not much." She shook her head. "But I overheard the name "Black Jack" a few times. He said it like it was all one word: blackjack. Like the card game."

"Sounds familiar." Wasn't he the "hot-shot bootlegger" Pete had mentioned?

"Afterwards, he was all anxious to go to the Surf Club and see that hussy, Candy."

"You went to the Surf Club?" I admit, I was disappointed since I'd wanted to question Candy myself. Amanda was all wound up, twirling her curls as she talked. "What did she say?"

"Nothing." She paused for dramatic effect. "Turns out Candy no longer works at the Surf Club. She never showed up there today."

"That's strange." I frowned, concerned. "I wonder if they overheard her discussing the ice man murder...or talking to me. Did she get axed or what?" Was it my fault?

"I don't know and I don't care," she admitted. "But guess what? I saw you and your handsome Fed agent there, painting the town."

"What are you talking about?"

"Your photos, silly." She froze in a pose like Lillian Gish, her idol. "They were plastered on the wall, right in front by the entrance. Like you were some big high-rollers. Imagine that!"

Just peachy. I could imagine the look on my boss's face if she had seen the photos on her desk. So they weren't kidding about posting our pictures at the Surf Club. What if the bankers saw them? One more strike, and I was out. On my can. "Swell. Come upstairs, I've got a surprise."

"I love surprises!" Amanda said, following me to my room. Nervously, I pulled out the glossies of me and Burton, our glasses raised to the sky.

"Well, what do you know? Here they are! I thought they refused to give you the photos?"

"They showed up on my boss's desk today, so I swiped them before she could see them."

Amanda stared at me in surprise. "No fooling!? Are they trying to blackmail you and Burton or what?"

"Blackmail?" I shook my head. "It's got to be a warning to Burton. I'm merely the arm piece."

"Maybe you're the mouth piece," she retorted. "What if the gangs are trying to get the goods on Burton? If you don't snitch, then they'll force the papers to publish those photos."

"Snitch? Me? I don't know anything!" Then I got worried: What if she was right?

"Be careful, Jazz. You'd better watch your step from now on." Amanda paused, studying the photos. "But you've got to admit, you sure do make a cute couple—with your dark bob and his wavy blond hair. You look like movie stars, holding your wine glasses and all."

Oh, brother!

Monday morning I got ready for work earlier than usual, and gathered the ledger, key and matchbook, slipping them into my purse. For once, I couldn't wait to get to work: Not only did Nathan and I plan to visit the train station during lunch, I also hoped to see my short piece on the cowboy in print.

Short was right—my copy had been cut down from two graphs to two sentences, buried in the obit page, only mentioning that an unidentified man had washed up on shore, an alleged murder victim. What had happened to the M.E.'s findings, my description of the cowboy's clothing, his bruised neck, the sand in his boots? All that work I'd done was for nothing. Didn't the editors trust me enough to publish my piece the way it was written? I'll bet they were saving the main headliner for Mack, and didn't want to risk riling him up with my two-bit tidbit.

Still, it wouldn't accomplish much, edited or not. How in the world could I prove the cowboy had killed the ice man, and help clear Sammy's name, once and for all? Weren't the items in the cowboy's pockets considered clues?

Despite Sammy's release from jail, I knew Mack's story about the arrest had hurt his reputation as well as his pride. A cloud of doubt would always hang over his head.

I knocked on the darkroom door, hoping to see Nathan's photos of the cowboy, worried I'd missed something. Had Burton heard about his death yet? I doubted he dealt in murder or homicide cases, but wasn't it related because the cowboy had allegedly killed Burton's informant?

Fortunately, Mrs. Harper was late so I had a few minutes to myself before my slave-driver boss chained me to my desk. Boy, was I glad I'd swiped the Surf Club photos and taken them home! The Beach Gang had no right to distribute our photos to the press or use them to threaten Burton or for that matter, me.

I wanted to question Mack, sitting behind a mound of paper at his messy desk, typing away. Did he know anything new about the cowboy? Dark raccoon circles sagged under his eyes and a cigar dangled off his lip. As I approached, he leaned back in his banker's chair, fingers laced behind his head, elbows pointed like triangles. "What's cooking, little lady?"

I took a deep breath. "I saw your story on the ice man murder with that flashy headline. Those photos were real doozies."

Mack puffed up with pride. "I just report the facts, and Nathan brings the article to life."

Ironic choice of words. "Speaking of facts, I found out that the victim was also an informant for the Downtown Gang. It wasn't mentioned in the article." Take that, Mack.

"You don't say. How do you know?" His bushy brows reached his forehead.

"I've got my sources." Why didn't he believe me? No need to mention the dicey ice man also snitched for Agent Burton. "Who do you think was behind the hit?"

He shrugged. "I've got a few calls out to my buddies, so we'll see what they dig up."

"By the way, did you hear Sammy Cook was released yesterday?" I gave him a smug smile.

"The suspect? Why?" Mack leaned forward, scratching his head.

"Lack of evidence." I lifted my chin. "I know he's innocent. Besides, there's a witness."

"Who? Anyone I know?"

"It's all very hush-hush."

"Well, I hear you had a run-in with a dead cowboy yesterday. Nathan told me he died with his boots on," Mack snorted.

"Good thing I happened to be on the Seawall when he washed up on shore." I crossed my arms, wondering what else Nathan and his big mouth had to say. "Did you hear anything new?"

"I also found out he died of strangulation." Mack wrapped his big bear paw around his throat. "Seems somebody wanted to shut him up forever."

"Who told you that?" I asked, getting more and more irritated with his best buddy, Nathan.

"I have a pal at the coroner's office." He leaned back, his chair squeaking. "He always calls me if a dead body turns up under suspicious circumstances. Whenever an alleged drowning victim shows up with all his clothes on, that's no accident. And the red marks around his neck kind of gave it away."

"They looked like rope burns to me."

"That's what the coroner told me, too." His eyes narrowed. "How did you know?"

"A lucky guess." I shrugged. "Remember, I was on the scene."

"What a coincidence." He scowled at me.

Frankly, this cat-and-mouse game was becoming old hat. Despite being a chauvinistic snob, Mack was an experienced journalist whom I admired and respected. "Say, I'm writing a short article about the victim. Can I get your opinion?"

"The cowboy?" He blinked, as if trying to decide whether I was a dingbat or a smart-aleck. "Why don't you show me your little story later? I'm on a tight deadline."

I didn't need my walking papers.

As I turned to go, Mrs. Harper motioned me over with a stern frown. When did she get here? Was she mad that I was gabbing with Mack instead of working?

"We need to have a little chat, Miss Cross. Come with me." She pointed at Mr. Thomas' office like the Grim Reaper.

Across the newsroom, Nathan cut me one of his "You're in trouble now" looks. Seems I was getting into a lot of trouble lately.

Silently Mrs. Harper led me to Mr. Thomas' office and shut the door. I glanced from one frowning face to another, feeling like a delinquent caught skipping school. What was wrong? Were they upset that I wrote about the dead cowboy without their permission?

Mr. Thomas opened a desk drawer and pulled out a familiar-looking big brown envelope with MR. THOMAS, EDITOR crudely written in block letters. Without a word, he withdrew two glossy photos of me and Agent Burton holding our glasses of fizzy French Champagne at the Surf Club, and dropped them face-up on his desk.

CHAPTER THIRTY-NINE

"How do you explain these photos, young lady?" Mr. Thomas demanded. My heart dropped as he stared at me with those sad, heavy eyes, the same let-down expression that my dad had when I'd misbehaved as a child. It was worse than a spanking.

I fumbled for words. "I was out with a friend and they took our picture." That was the best I could do?

Mrs. Harper tapped her foot, arms crossed. "You mean Agent Burton? Don't forget, we all had a good look at your young man. A date is one thing, but don't you think it's irresponsible to be seen drinking at a notorious gang's nightclub with a Prohibition agent?"

"Agent Burton—we—were sort of undercover, doing research," I stammered, my face flaming. "We wanted to get inside the Surf Club, so we acted like we were on a date."

"Undercover? Doing *research*?" Her dark eyes pierced through me and my story. "Looks to me you were doing more drinking than any actual research."

"We didn't order any cocktails, honest. See, we're not really drinking, only holding up our glasses, toasting for fun. Ollie Quinn gave us a complimentary bottle of Champagne," I babbled, pointing to the photo. "Agent Burton thought it best if we played along, pretended to drink."

"Ollie Quinn, the *gangster*? *Pretended* to drink?" Mr. Thomas echoed, exchanging disapproving glances with Mrs. Harper. "Frankly, I'm disappointed in you, Jasmine. You were seen out in public *drinking* with that new Prohibition agent. Here's the proof." He slapped the photo on his desk, shaking his head.

I felt like a puppet in a bad "Punch and Judy" show, getting pummeled by both Punch *and* Judy. "Honest, I was only doing some research. I was Agent Burton's cover, that's all."

"What do you mean by research? I didn't assign you to write any articles about cocktails and criminals. That's not fitting for the society section, as you well know," Mrs. Harper huffed.

I wrung my hands, panicky, blurting out, "Burton was trying to gather evidence for an investigation." After all, he *did* take the Champagne bottle as evidence.

How could I tell her the real truth? That my half-brother was arrested for murder in a gangland hit, allegedly, but in order to clear his name, we wanted to confront the Beach Gang. Wasn't that worse than drinking Champagne? Not quite society news, but plenty of material for the gossip column.

"I'm afraid your Agent Burton is a bad influence." She raised her brows as high as her voice.

I racked my brain for an escape. Outside the office, I saw Nathan talking to Mack, both watching us with curious stares.

"To tell the truth, I was on an assignment, helping Mack get some inside information for an article." I tried to sound convincing, hoping they'd believe my bluff.

"What kind of article? Of all the excuses you've made so far…" Mrs. Harper challenged me, eyes on fire, then opened the door and motioned for Mack to come into the office.

Now what had I gotten myself into?

Mack saw our dour expressions and smiled. What a guy—I was about to get the boot and he thought it was funny. Then he glanced at the photos and took in the situation.

"Miss Cross here tells us she's helping you with a story," Mr. Thomas said hopefully.

I held my breath, waiting for Mack's response.

Mack glanced at me, then down at the photos and finally at Mrs. Harper. "That's right, she is." He nodded, not blinking an eye.

My hero! I felt like cheering, I was so grateful.

"Pray tell, what kind of story involves going to sleazy bars? Are you researching the criminal element? The Beach and Downtown gangs?" Mrs. Harper demanded.

Mack's eyes shifted from one frozen face to another. "If you must know, I'm doing a series on local gang activity and I don't like to advertise my work. You never know who could leak out important information around here." He tapped the photos with his ink-stained hands, right on Burton's smiling face. "Miss Cross has sources that could prove to be a real asset."

"Thanks for clearing that up," Mr. Thomas said, looking relieved. "But please make sure our Miss Cross is not put in any more danger." He seemed to think that, "sleazy bars" or not, it was fine for me to go as long as I was properly escorted in public—and working with Mack.

My boss folded her arms, skeptical. "In the future, I'd appreciate it if you'd ask my permission before you used my assistant for help with your articles," she scolded, implying her fluffy society stories were of far greater importance than Mack's award-wining journalism.

"Your *permission*? Excuse me?" Mack locked eyes with Mrs. Harper in a battle of the senior staffers. Mr. Thomas shrunk down in his chair, trying to remain as neutral as Switzerland.

Then Mack opened the door to leave, giving me a quick wink behind her back. Relieved, I turned to follow him, but Mrs. Harper blocked my way. "Not so fast, Miss Cross. What do you suggest we do with these incriminating photos?"

"Nothing," I challenged her. "If you print them, then you're playing right into the gangs' hands. It's obvious they want to undermine Agent Burton's authority, and ruin his reputation."

"You're right." Mr. Thomas picked up the photos and hid them in his desk drawer. "For now, let's keep this unfortunate incident under our hats. I'll call my friends at the area papers and see if they've received any similar photos."

Oh no. I'd forgotten about the other newspapers. "I'd appreciate it if you didn't mention our names."

"Don't worry, Jazz, they owe me a few favors," Mr. Thomas said to reassure me.

I gave him a grateful smile. "Thanks, Mr. Thomas." I turned to go, then added, "You too, Mrs. Harper."

"Glad to help." Mr. Thomas smiled, ready to forgive and forget. "I'm sure Mrs. Harper can keep you busy the rest of the day."

My boss scrunched up her face, as if she'd swallowed a lime. "Let's pray there are no more indiscretions, Miss Cross. Or you'll be out of a job faster than you can say *sorry*."

No kidding. After our confrontation, Mrs. Harper wouldn't let me out of her sight all day. While I worked, filing and typing and proofreading, I could hear her long nails tapping impatiently on her desk. She seemed to be punishing me for having a life, and goals, beyond her boundaries.

Finally, I had time to talk to Mack, who was smoking a cigar while typing, ashes dropping on his keys. He looked up, a glint in his eye, his smile smug.

"Thanks for backing up my story, Mack. You really helped me out of a jam. And how!"

He pointed his cigar at me. "I know it. You owe me one, kiddo. Don't forget."

Then he shoved the cigar back in his mouth and resumed typing. What did he want—a full-time typist? Inside information from Burton? A personal slave?

Across the newsroom, Mrs. Harper gave me the evil eye. Great—that meant I'd have to work twice as hard tomorrow.

CHAPTER FORTY

After finishing for the day, I finally got my boss' permission to escape the lion's den. What a nightmare!

Nathan stopped by my desk and offered me a ride. "What was that all about?" he grinned.

"Not now," I hushed him. "Let's talk on the way home."

Outside, I took a deep breath. "That was a close call. Mrs. Harper was ready to feed me to the sharks."

"Hate to say I told you so. Good thing Mack bailed you out." Nathan didn't even try to hide his smile. I think they enjoyed seeing my public humiliation.

"Mack was a lifesaver. If he hadn't lied for me, I'd be out of work." For once, we both agreed about Mack.

As Nathan drove, I described my debacle in detail, imitating Mrs. Harper's shrill voice and Mr. Thomas' bark. "The gangs have some nerve, using our photos to blackmail a Federal agent. I hope the editors don't fall for it next time." I heaved a sigh. "Guess they won't let me off my leash anytime soon. And I doubt I'll be seeing much of Agent Burton."

"Better stay away from Burton, for your own protection." Nathan gloated. "Obviously the gangs are trying to send a message or better yet, run him out of town."

"Sounds like the Wild West to me. A lawless society."

Nathan nodded. "The gangs like to call the shots without any interference. It's all about control, power, leverage."

"You said it. What if the gangs go after Burton next?"

Nathan shrugged. "He should have thought about the consequences before he took the job."

He was right. Didn't Burton realize what he was getting into?

Nathan turned on 25th Street, slowing down by the train station. "Remember our plans? Got everything we need?"

How could I forget? We still needed to figure out the cryptic RR628 notation in Andrews' ledger. As Nathan parked across from the train station, I marveled at its imposing façade, its geometric carvings and towering columns. Inside, I admired the stylized black and white glass light fixtures hanging low from the high ceilings. I'd never been to New York City, yet, but I imagined that Grand Central Station was at least twice as nice.

"Let's look around, get some ideas," I told Nathan. "I'll go get a train schedule from the station master, and see if it's a train number." I found the daily and weekend schedules, and we sat on a carved wooden bench near the trains. Then I pulled out the ledger and compared the arrival and departure times, but it was a dead-end. "These don't seem to match anything here."

"Maybe it's a date? That's over a week away," Nathan said. "What do you suggest we do—sit here all day and wait for a mysterious stranger to appear? Sorry, doll, but I don't have that kind of time—or patience."

We wandered around the station aimlessly, studying trains and platform signs, departure times, whatever had a number. "We may be going up a blind alley," I admitted. Is that what Alice intended?

Frustrated, I watched the travelers rushing around, laden down with trunks and luggage. A few women struggled with young children, trying to hold their hands while carrying, or dragging, their suitcases. Nathan offered to help one pretty young mother of four with her luggage, lifting each child onto the steps of the departing train. I knew he'd make a great dad one day.

"That was nice. Must be hard to handle all those kids alone."

"She's in for a long train ride. I wonder what happened to the father?" He looked around the station. "Say, I'm starving. How about a bite to eat?"

We found a snack bar located near the clock tower, chiming 6:00 p.m., and sat down facing the ticket windows. Nathan ordered our sandwiches—ham and cheese on rye for me, roast beef on sourdough for him—while I watched the flurry of activity all around. A young flower vendor approached, smiling at Nathan, but I shooed her away, not in the mood for flowers or flirting.

As we ate, I complained: "What a lousy day. First, my story gets cut down to two sentences, then my editors bawl me out for the Surf Club photos. My personal life is none of their business."

I heaved a huge sigh. "Then I have to depend on Mack to rescue me, like a dumb damsel in distress. Worse, now I have gangsters tailing me in gold Bentleys."

"What do you expect?" He threw up his hands. "You were seen at the Beach Gang's swankiest club, photographed drinking with the new Prohibition agent! I say Mack deserves a medal."

"Go chase yourself," I griped. Where was *my* medal? I almost got fired!

A Negro shoeshine boy with baggy pants held up by red suspenders had positioned himself by the snack bar. When he wasn't polishing shoes, he energetically tap-danced for change. I threw a few coins in his hat and he beamed at me with nice white teeth. Hard to be down in the dumps with such an enterprising entertainer nearby.

At the next table, an old man with wavy white hair and a long beard stood up to leave, pulling out some change to pay the waitress. I watched as he picked up his satchel and hat and walked off, leaving his spectacles and keys on the table.

"Sir, you forgot your things!" I called out but he didn't hear me. In a flash, I grabbed his items and followed him as he headed to the trains. For an old codger, he was fairly agile. I rushed to catch up and tapped him on the shoulder. "Excuse me, sir, but you left these on your table."

He stopped and patted his pockets. "Well, I'll be. I couldn't get very far without my keys or reading spectacles. Thank you, miss."

I watched him walk over to the train lockers, shoulders hunched, select a loose key and pull out his luggage.

"Do you need any help with your bags?" He was short and stout, like my grandfather with a Santa Claus beard.

"No, but thank you for asking, miss. I've been managing all these years on my own."

"Take care, " I told him, missing my grandfather, who still lived in Europe.

When I returned, Nathan joked, "Got a thing for old-timers?"

"Only trying to do a good deed, like you. But he gave me an idea." Eagerly, I pulled out the key and laid it on the table. "His key looked just like this. I think it may open one of these train lockers."

Nathan's eyes widened in anticipation. "Let's go find out."

I felt like a giddy kid on a scavenger hunt as we darted through the rows of train lockers, looking for number 628. The lockers were arranged in a maze of blocks, but finally we found it in a remote corner, away from the hustle and bustle. Nathan and I exchanged hopeful glances as I inserted the key into the keyhole and turned the lock. Voila! A perfect fit.

The metal door opened without a hitch, and we peered inside. A long black bag almost two feet long and a foot wide, resembling a doctor's satchel, sat inside the locker.

Suddenly I got cold feet. Should we open it there or take it straight to Alice? But shouldn't we check it first, to be safe?

"Hurry up! What are you waiting for?" He nudged me. "Come on, open it."

"Hold your horses, Nathan. I feel funny opening a stranger's bag," I protested. Still, curiosity won over courtesy. I squatted down and turned my back to the main room, trying to block any nosy Neds or Nellies from view. I tugged on the zipper and opened the bag wide so we both could get a good look inside.

My breath caught when I saw the contents: The bag contained several stacks of crisp, neat bills—tens, twenties, fifties and hundreds—filled to the brim.

CHAPTER FORTY-ONE

Nathan and I stared at the bag of cash, then each other, in stunned silence, afraid to move, to breathe. "That's a hell of a lot of loot," he said finally, whistling under his breath.

"I'll say!" I gulped, starting to panic. "What should we do?"

"I know what I'd like to do—take the money and run," he smiled. "But for now, I wouldn't mind at least counting it."

"Not here!" I scanned the station, slamming the locker door. "I'll bet someone is looking for it."

"So what? We're the only ones who know about this treasure chest." He smiled and rubbed his hands together like the mustachioed villain in a corny melodrama. "Finders, keepers, I say."

"Very tempting, but if it's Horace's money, it belongs to his wife and family." Including Buzz.

"All right, be a spoilsport. Just think what we could do with all that dough! Quit our jobs, run off to Mexico or Europe. I could live on the French Riviera and paint all day."

"Wouldn't that be swell?" I agreed. "I'd love to go to Europe. Ever since Charles Lindbergh's flight in May, I've wanted to travel to Paris, London and Rome."

As we eyed the bag of crisp bills, I fantasized about all the things money could buy: Eva could pay off her debts and hire a housekeeper, and Sammy could open a gourmet restaurant. For starters, I'd splurge on a bright enameled compact and a scenic beaded purse, plus a few frocks. What I really wanted to do was travel the world, racking up adventures in Europe and Egypt.

Now I surveyed the station, nervous as a train robber. "Let's shake a leg. Someone might get suspicious," I told Nathan.

"You don't want to leave the money behind, do you?" He stood in front of the locker like a security guard. "Lots of gangsters go through here. What if the station master or a stranger got hold of it? They'd keep it, that's what. They sure as hell wouldn't turn it in to Lost and Found."

Suddenly everyone at the train station looked like Al Capone or Frank Nitti or Rose Maceo—and just as dangerous. "How about taking it to Sammy? He'll know what to do."

Nathan shook his head. "That's not safe. What if it's gang money? Sammy's up to his neck in hot water. How would it look if hundreds of brand-new bills turned up in his bar?"

Didn't he trust Sammy by now? I poked his ribs. "Thanks to you, he's a famous face in Galveston."

"I say we take the dough and satchel back to the boarding house right now."

"My place?" I frowned. "Are you sure it's safe? What if we're followed?" I felt guilty, as if Andrews and Mr. Thomas and Burton were all watching us try to escape red-handed.

"Now you sound like a dime novel," he teased me. "Relax and pretend nothing's wrong."

How could I relax? I took a quick look at the bag of cash to make sure I wasn't dreaming, and zipped it up tight. Then I lifted the bag—it weighed a ton—and pressed it into Nathan's arms. "Here you go. Since it's your cock-eyed idea, you get to be the chump."

"So I'm left holding the bag." He grinned. "Sure you don't want to sail to Cairo or Rio?"

"How about sailing down the Seine?" I sighed. "I'd love to, when we're both rich and famous." Wouldn't that be swell?

As he darted through the lobby, avoiding the crowds, I followed close on Nathan's heels like a loyal Border Collie. Once I swore someone was following us, but they were rushing to catch a train.

Outside, we dashed to his Model T and jumped in, like thieves on the lam. "I can't very well hide this big bag from Eva. What should I tell her?" I fretted.

"Tell her it's for work. And quit acting so damn guilty. You act like we robbed a bank!"

"Maybe we did, indirectly?" I let out a worried sigh. "I can't help but wonder, what if Andrews robbed a bank? His own?"

"You mean embezzlement?" Nathan drove slowly, giving us time to think. "That makes sense. Plus it explains why the bills are so crisp and clean." Sadly, he'd voiced my worst fear.

Still, I refused to believe it. "If he did, he must have had a good reason. I'll bet he planned to return the money soon, but died before he had a chance." Sappy, sure, but I liked to give people the benefit of the doubt.

"You're absolutely right! That's why Andrews kept the satchel hidden away in a secret locker no one knew about, not even his wife," Nathan scoffed. "If I were him, I sure as hell wouldn't hang around town. Looks like he was planning to run away and start a new life, maybe with a new wife."

My heart sank, thinking of Mrs. Andrews. Did she have any idea? "What if it *is* mob money? Say the gangs knew he'd swiped their cash and planned to escape?" Is that what Horace wanted to tell Sammy that night? Is that why he was poisoned?

"Say, why don't we go by the Oasis after we drop off this bag?" I suggested. "I bet Sammy can decipher this ledger, find out where the cash came from."

"Good idea." Nathan parked in front of the boarding house, and threw his arm across my seat. "Want me to go with you? Why don't we run away together, hop on the next ship?"

Such a joker. "I wish. Come on in. I need help carrying the bag. I almost pulled a muscle lifting this thing."

Sadly, sitting at my desk all day surrounded by smokers didn't offer much fresh air or exercise.

"Here, let me help you." He hoisted up the bag and reached in, taking out a twenty dollar bill. "A small reward for my troubles. Call it a finder's fee. What's one twenty when you've got a whole sack full of jack?"

"Nathan!" I frowned, but didn't stop him since the money wasn't mine either.

The squeaky screen door announced our entrance as we walked inside. "I'm home," I told Eva. "But we need to go back to the office to work on a story. We're on a tight deadline."

"This late?" Eva glanced at the clock, then at the satchel. "What's in that bag?"

"Books for work." I lugged the bag upstairs, casting worried glances at Nathan. I hated to put Eva or anyone in danger. Whose bright idea was it to bring home a huge bag of stolen cash?

I tiptoed upstairs to my room, taking a quick peek inside the bag. If my aunt only knew. I rifled through the stacks of brand-new bills, bundled together, mixed with loose bills—a small fortune! Heart pounding, I shoved the bag under my bed, hoping no one would snoop in my room while I was gone.

Downstairs, my aunt had persuaded Nathan to sample her roast beef, not that he needed much convincing. He seemed perfectly at ease sitting at the dining table, eating contentedly, as if finding big bags stuffed with cash was an everyday occurrence.

After we said good-night to Eva, Nathan gunned his engine and raced to the Oasis while I held onto the straps for dear life. "What are you going to tell Sammy?"

"Everything. He knew Andrews well so I hope he can make sense of this mess."

"Everything?" He frowned. "What about the cash? Can you trust him to keep quiet?"

"Of course. He's no angel, but he's honest." Why did I need to defend my own brother to Nathan?

At the Oasis, Dino slid open the window, glaring at Nathan. "What d'ya want?"

What, no password this time? "Dino, it's urgent. I need to talk to Sammy. Now."

Grudgingly, he opened the door, turning his back on Nathan. Downstairs, a few sad sacks with time and life on their hands sat at the tables nursing their drinks. I waved to Frank and Buzz who stood behind the bar, their smiles forced, formal. Everything appeared to be back to normal, except...I couldn't explain it, but there was a tension in the air, threatening like a hurricane. Even Doria, our good luck charm, seemed on guard tonight.

Sammy came out of his office, arms wide, and hugged me, happy for once. Nathan stuck out his hand, but he ignored it, his eyes cold as jade. "Looks like you made me a household name, kid."

"Sorry, sport. Just doing my job." Nathan sounded sincere, since I knew he genuinely liked Sammy.

"No hard feelings, kid." Sammy finally shook his hand. He appeared more cheerful now, less melancholy, as if he appreciated life a bit more after his ordeal. "What brings you here?"

"I've got something to discuss," I said, voice low. "It's private."

"Why don't you wait in my office? Frank, fix this man a drink. Whatever he wants."

"I'm not thirsty," Nathan mumbled, eyeing the liquor bottles with apprehension.

"Just got some rum straight from Cuba. No hooch. The guy barely speaks English but he knows his liquor." Sammy patted Nathan on the back. "Only the best for my customers!"

Was it the same rum snatched by Johnny Jack when he hijacked the Cuban rum-runner?

"Sure." Nathan brightened. "How about a rum and Coca-Cola?"

"I'll take the Coke," I told Frank. He handed me a cold bottle, but averted his eyes. Even Buzz seemed more fidgety than usual, stacking glasses haphazardly, bumping into Frank. What was wrong with everyone? Did the place get raided again?

I entered Sammy's office, swiveling around in his shabby oak banker's chair, trying to mentally rehearse the right words, to predict his reaction to the stash of cash. His office was messy as usual, with bills and knick-knacks stacked haphazardly on his desk. The clutter was so tempting, I poked around his papers, looking for clues.

My breath caught when I spied a small pad with a note scribbled on top: 'Black Jack, 9 p.m. Wed.' Black Jack, the bootlegger Pete and Amanda mentioned?! It had to be. But why was he planning to meet a dangerous bootlegger? Wednesday was only two days away.

Nervously, I began pacing Sammy's office, trying to think. Was now the best time to tell him about the cash? Should I bring up Black Jack? In the corner, I noticed a coat rack covered with various hats and a few coats, probably lost from last winter. Then my eyes lit on a beat-up beige cowboy hat in back—odd since the local cowboys preferred Joe's next door.

Before Sammy returned and caught me snooping, I rushed over to the rack and picked up the hat, a rather sad and scruffy thing, stained and spotted. Curious, I turned it over and looked inside.

On the brim was a name scribbled in faded black ink: *MacDougal.*

CHAPTER FORTY-TWO

MacDougal, the ice man's murderer? Hands shaking, I almost dropped the hat when I heard noises and placed it back on the rack. Where in hell did they get his hat—and why was it here? Sammy had left the beach early, so maybe he was unaware it belonged to the killer cowboy.

Sammy burst into the office with a big smile. "Good to see you, Jazz. So what brings you here tonight with Nathan? I thought you and Burton were getting pretty tight." I knew he was teasing me, but he sounded more than curious.

"Nathan and I are good friends," I stammered. "Agent Burton and I are friends, too." Couldn't we all be friends?

Flustered, I changed the subject. "Say, I need to talk about something serious." I walked to the coat rack and picked up the cowboy hat. "But first, where'd you get this hat?"

He shrugged, his face blank. "Never noticed it before. Bet a customer left it here."

"Remember the cowboy who washed up on shore yesterday?"

"How can I forget? Not a sight you see every day."

"After you left, the M.E. checked for ID and saw a name written on his shirt collar, MacDougal." I pointed to the band inside the hat. "It's the same name, in the same handwriting." Only a few people knew that the cowboy's name was allegedly MacDougal.

"Damn it!" Sammy frowned at the hat, as if trying to come up with a logical explanation. Then he snapped his fingers. "I'll bet Buzz found it by the ice truck and left it here."

"You're probably right." I relaxed my shoulders. The cowboy hat had likely been knocked off during the struggle with the ice man and Buzz found it outside, tried to hide it in Sammy's office. "Sure you want to keep it here, in plain sight? May be incriminating."

"What do you expect me to do? Turn it over to the coppers?" Sammy bristled.

Why was he acting so defensive? "No, but I'd keep it hidden to be safe."

"Good idea." He studied my face. "So what's eating you? You seem rattled."

How to begin? I cleared my throat, and pulled out the ledger from my bag like a rabbit in a hat. "Have you seen this before?"

Sammy leapt up, snatching the book. "Is that Horace's bank ledger? Where in hell did you get it?"

"Mrs. Andrews gave it to me. I wanted to come by on Saturday, but that's when the cops..." I swallowed, trying not to upset him. "This is my first chance to show it to you."

"Alice? I don't understand why she gave it to *you*?"

Good question. I jerked back as he waved it around.

"Do you realize how dangerous this is?" He scowled. "People are searching all over for this book. They can't get their cash out of the bank without this information."

"Which people?" My heart began a slow thud. "What cash?"

Sammy glanced over his shoulder, as if looking for a quick exit. "You probably figured this out by now, but Horace was managing our accounts at the bank, keeping our records straight."

I eyed him, gauging his reaction. "You mean laundering money."

"Fine, he was cooking the books." He avoided my gaze. "After Horace passed, some goons came by and roughed me up, trying to get their greedy mitts on this ledger." He rubbed his jaw, wincing at the memory. "I did some fast talking, but it wasn't fast enough."

"Is that when you got the black eye?" I grimaced. "Why did they suspect *you*?"

"They found out Horace came by my place before he kicked the bucket. So the gangs assumed I was hiding it here. I had no idea Alice had it all along." He lit a Camel, inhaling with deep breaths.

"Horace was their own private banker? So how did it work?"

"This is just between us, right?" Sammy looked around the office, as if it was bugged.

"Of course." I frowned. "I'm not a Treasury agent or a snoop."

For once, Sammy was in the mood to talk and I was happy to listen. He spoke non-stop, as if releasing months of pent-up anxiety.

"Every week Horace picked up our take and deposited it under some dummy accounts. I'm sure the bank knew what was going on, but no one complained. It was a win-win deal. A good way to keep our cash safe. Legit. He promised to invest it, make it grow."

Sammy exhaled and leaned back, taking a drag off his Camel. "But without the names and numbers of these fake accounts, we had no idea where or how our money was stashed."

Finally, the truth. "You couldn't access the accounts directly?"

"Not without Horace. He said it was safer that way. It was never a problem before. He held all the cards—literally."

Now I understood why he kept Alice in the dark. He wanted to protect her, as well as himself. "Did he launder cash for both gangs?"

Sammy nodded. "That's the problem. I'm sure they'd love to get their hands on this ledger, steal all the dough. The gangs will do anything to destroy each other."

"I'll bet." I shook my head. "How could he take such a risk, laundering money for two rival gangs?"

"Horace was a gambler. He liked to live dangerously. It's in his blood." Sammy eyed me over his Camel. "What I want to know is— why did Alice Andrews give the book to *you*?"

I took a deep breath, glad to share the burden. "When I bumped into her at the bank, she told me there was a break-in at her house and invited me over. That's when she gave me the ledger, along with a key and a Hollywood matchbook with Rose Maceo's private number. I think she hoped I'd do the legwork, find out if any of the pieces fit. Clearly she didn't want to arouse any suspicions herself."

"Papa Rose, huh?" Sammy rubbed his chin. "My guess is Alice wanted the ledger out of the house, for her own safety. Sounds like she got scared after the break-in, and tried to protect her family by getting rid of Horace's things."

"Do you think she knew what he was up to?" I hated to think Mrs. Andrews was involved in any way. But why would she give the ledger to me if she'd planned to use it and cash in herself?

Thank goodness Sammy shook his head 'no.'

"Alice is as straight-laced as a nun. Even if she knew, I'm sure she wanted nothing to do with Horace's get-rich-quick schemes." He exhaled a plume of smoke. "Don't worry, I doubt anyone will connect you to the Andrews."

"I hope not." My mind shifted to the satchel of cash—was it mob money? Or did it belong to the bank? Would I put Sammy in danger if he knew I was literally "holding the bag"?

"What's wrong, Jazz? What's got you so spooked? You act like you've seen a ghost."

Yeah, the ghost of Horace Andrews. "Promise you won't get upset?" There was no easy way to broach the subject. Sure, finding a sack of money was like discovering a pot of gold, but not if it was stolen from the bank or worse, from gangsters.

"You know the key I got from Mrs. Andrews? We found out it fit a locker at the train station." I took the ledger, turning to the last page. "See this entry written in ink—RR628? We went there tonight and opened the locker."

"Who's we, you and Nathan?" Sammy shook his hands with impatience. "Well?"

I nodded and leaned forward. "Inside we found a huge black satchel—filled with cash."

"Cash? How much dough are we talking about?" Sammy shot up, pacing around the tiny office.

"A lot. I didn't have time to count it, but the bag looks full."

"Where is it now—at the train station?"

I glanced away, whispering, "It's in my room, under my bed."

"Your room?" He dropped in his chair, bowing his head in his hands, as if praying for salvation—or me. "Damn it, Jasmine! I can't begin to tell you how much danger you're in."

"Danger? What else could I do? I didn't have much choice." Why did I let Nathan talk me into taking it home? "Do you have any idea whose money it is? Does it belong to the gangs?"

"That's a good guess." His eyes were narrow as key holes.

"What's strange is half the money looks like brand-new bills. Seems fishy to me…" I had to ask: "Was Andrews embezzling money from Lone Star Bank?"

"Embezzling?" His eyes blinked rapidly, like Morse code. "It's possible. Never thought he'd resort to stealing from his own bank. Maybe he used the extra cash to gamble, pay off his debts. Plus he had to care for a wife and four children. Horace was determined to send Buzz to that fancy-pants boarding school."

"He must have been desperate. For all we know, he gave himself a temporary loan, and planned to pay it all back," I suggested, trying to rationalize.

"Who knows? I doubt he was thinking straight, and got in over his head." Sammy flipped through the ledger, squinting while he studied the entries. Scowling, he pounded his fist on the desk.

"Son of a bitch! Horace was stealing, all right—from his own customers. That's why he kept this ledger out of sight."

"Are you positive?"

"Take a look." Sammy pointed to a page. "My account is OSS—for Oasis. I gave him the same amount every weekend, about $250., to keep it simple, for both of us. Notice by the entries, there are two columns. See? One is for the amount I gave him each week—the other must be his fee."

He was breathing hard, trying to contain his anger. "We'd agreed he'd charge ten percent of our weekly profit as his take. But this column shows he collected twice that much, twenty to twenty-five percent." Sammy shoved his chair back, his face twisted in fury. "That goddamn piker. After all I've done for him and Buzz!"

My heart dropped, knowing Sammy felt hurt, not to mention betrayed. "Did he take the same amount from all his clients?"

I looked over the columns, trying to do the math in my head.

"That much and more." He jabbed his finger on a page in front. "Look at this entry, HDC for the Hollywood Dinner Club. They raked in over ten grand a month, and Horace was helping himself to a good portion of the profits, around two-thousand, twenty percent. Not every week, but enough to make a dent."

I was floored. No wonder the gangs were so eager to get their hands on this ledger. "How did he get away with it?"

"It's obvious he didn't—Horace is dead, isn't he?" Sammy slapped the ledger on his desk. "That greedy bastard was skimming off the top, cheating us all along."

CHAPTER FORTY-THREE

I held my breath. "You think the gangs found out and ordered a hit? Maybe they hired a goon to fill his flask with methanol, to make it look like an accident?" Mobsters killed each other over a few barrels of beer, but poisoning a prominent banker was risky business.

"I'll bet Ollie or Johnny Jack got wise and wanted revenge." Sammy pounded the wall. "Horace must've thought we wouldn't notice the skim, that we're all a bunch of dumb palookas."

"Hard to believe he'd be so careless. There's got to be a valid reason. Didn't his clients need Horace as much as he needed them?"

Why was I defending a shady banker who lied to his wife, who stole from gangsters, from Sammy? His life was so full of secrets, it got him killed.

A knock sounded, and Sammy stood up, making a zipper motion across his mouth. But it was only Frank. Was he eavesdropping outside, like I'd done earlier?

"Let's talk more later." Sammy's face was tight with worry. "Your pal looks lonely."

I'd almost forgotten about Nathan. "What should I do about—you know?"

"Leave it there for now. We'll figure something out. I'll keep the, uh, notebook here." In one swift move, Sammy palmed the ledger and held it behind his back so Frank wouldn't notice.

Still rattled, I joined Nathan at his table, avoiding his gaze. Tapping his watch, he griped, "What took so long? I got bored sitting here by myself. Even the help is giving me the cold shoulder."

"Sorry." I patted his back. "Why don't I get us some drinks?"

I walked over to Buzz, who was hiding behind the bar. "How about a Coke? Bet you're glad that Sammy's back now."

He nodded shyly, handing me a frosty bottle. "Sure am. I f-f-feel safer now."

"That's good." I smiled. "Well, you don't have to worry about the cowboy anymore. He's gone and won't be coming back."

Did Sammy already tell him the cowboy was dead?

"I know." His lips started trembling. "But it wasn't my f-f-fault."

"What wasn't your fault?" I frowned. "You mean the cowboy?"

Buzz nodded and his fingers shook as he opened his shirt collar, exposing dark bruises around his neck. I felt the blood drain from my face. The marks looked like rope burns, the same ones on the dead cowboy's neck.

"What happened? Did the cowboy come here?"

"Nothing happened." Frank rushed behind the bar, giving Buzz a warning look. "You need to go clean up. Now." He pointed to the tables, and Buzz obeyed like a faithful mutt.

"Never mind Buzz." I tried to read Frank, but his eyes were dull as coal. "We had no choice."

"No choice?" I studied his face. "What did you do?"

He motioned for me to follow him into the kitchen, leading me to the back.

"Tell me what happened," I demanded. "Did the cowboy show up here? Did he try to hurt Buzz?"

"Hurt him?" Frank slapped a dish towel on the sink. "That bastard tried to kill him!"

My heart stopped. "What? When? How?"

"I'll make this quick, in case Sammy comes in." Frank looked around the kitchen.

"Sammy doesn't know? Why keep this quiet?"

"It's for his own good," Frank said. "I don't want to make him feel guilty. For now, let's keep this between us. Don't go telling all your boyfriends, especially that Burton."

"I told you, he's not my boyfriend." My face felt hot. "So what's the story?"

"Off the record, right?" He exhaled. "Saturday night the joint was jumping 'cause of the murder. Made us famous for a few days. That's why we were sucker-punched, unprepared for the big crowd."

"I'll say!" I hissed. "How in hell did the cowboy sneak in past Dino? Or you? How'd he get to Buzz?"

"We never saw him before, remember?" Frank bristled. "He came by, all liquored up and ordered some whiskey. Hell, we had no idea he was the killer. We didn't notice him since it was so crowded, but later he must have slipped out through the kitchen."

His breath came out in spurts. "Buzz was in the alley, throwing out some trash. Luckily, Dino was watching the door and heard him scream for help. He ran outside and saw the cowboy trying to strangle Buzz with his rope."

My stomach knotted as I pictured scrawny Buzz trying to defend himself against the burly cowboy. Talk about an unfair fight.

"Poor Buzz. What did Dino do?"

"You know Dino, big as an ox. Dino said they struggled, but he fought back, choked the cowboy with his own rope." Frank was breathing hard, his words tumbling out. "Buzz ran to get me, but the poor kid could barely speak. By the time I got there, the cowboy was unconscious. So Dino and I tied him up and dragged him out back, out of sight, behind the trash cans. I thought he'd revive after a while. But when we came back later, he was already dead."

"Dino choked him to death? Are you sure he was alive when you left him?" I stared at him in shock. Frank had implicated Dino in a homicide—or was it murder?

"I think so, but it all happened so fast." His voice caught. "Dino won't talk about it—he wants to pretend nothing happened. The big baboon was only trying to protect Buzz. I'm sure he didn't mean to kill the cowboy. He only wanted to scare him away. In any case, it was self-defense. But I say that asshole got what he deserved."

"You said it. What a bully, picking on a kid half his size."

I didn't condone violence or believe in taking the law into your own hands, but in this case I thought Dino was justified. Then it came to me: Dino was Italian, like the Maceos. Was he working for the Beach Gang? Was it a hit? Did the Maceos hire him to kill the cowboy and make it look like an accident? I hated to think the worst of Dino, but it was a possibility.

"What did you do next?" I played dumb, knowing the answer.

"We took him to the beach, loaded his boots with sand and threw him over a pier. Some bright idea I had, huh? I didn't think he'd wash up so soon." He wiped his face with a dish rag, his hands trembling. "That makes me an accomplice. An accessory to murder."

"Sounds like you had no other option. I can't believe that cowboy had the nerve to come here and try to kill Buzz!" I fumed, breathing hard. "How'd he find out where Buzz worked?"

"He must have seen him or was tipped off by the cops." Frank gulped, sweat dripping down his face, clouding his glasses. "I didn't expect this to happen, never on my watch."

"Who else knows?" I tried not to panic. How would Sammy react if he knew?

"Just us. Bernie suspects too, since he came out with his frying pan, ready to do battle." He smiled. "But Dino got to the cowboy first, the yellow-bellied bastard. Beating up a little boy."

"Thank God Dino was there. You'd better tell Sammy before Buzz spills the beans."

"Tell me what?" Sammy appeared behind us like a mysterious genie, arms crossed.

"I'd better talk to Sammy alone." Frank eyed him nervously.

"Good luck." He needed it. I gave Sammy a shaky smile, and a quick hug before I left. I didn't want to be in Frank's shoes now.

At the bar, I tapped Nathan's shoulder. "Going my way?"

I projected a lightness I didn't feel, wishing I could tell him the truth. He had a matter-of-fact way of interpreting things, seeing the black and white, while I saw all the shades of gray.

"What was that all about?" Nathan asked. "Why all the secrecy?"

"They had a break-in," I told him, which in a way was true. As we left the Oasis, I smiled at Buzz, who watched us with apprehension. But I avoided looking at Dino, not sure what to think.

Of course I was grateful that he'd saved Buzz's life, but did he have to kill the cowboy? Now we might never know the whole story.

On the way home, I was silent, staring at the shuttered shops and people wandering along the streets, marveling at the carefree revelers who pretended Prohibition didn't exist. How could I keep this quiet, knowing that Dino had strangled the cowboy to death—and, with Frank's help, threw him in the ocean to cover it up?

But if I told anyone, especially the authorities, it could end up hurting everyone I cared about.

"What's eating you? What did Sammy say about the cash?" Nathan eyed me in the dark.

"I showed him the ledger, and told him about the money, that's all." I hated keeping secrets from Nathan, but I was afraid he'd run off to tell his pal Mack about Buzz and the cowboy. First him, then the whole world would know.

"That's all? I'm sure Sammy wanted a big piece of that pie."

"Bunk. He didn't ask for a dime," I bristled.

"Oh yeah? Give it time."

Now the bag of cash was the least of our worries.

At the boarding house, Nathan tapped his mouth. "Remember: 'Loose lips sink ships.'"

"So do icebergs. Remember the Titanic?" My head was reeling with other people's secrets and I felt like I'd explode if I didn't confide in someone. "Can't I even tell Amanda?"

"I wouldn't. She's such a chatterbox." He raised his brows. "Just think of me, your *poor* friend, literally, while you're counting all those clams."

After talking to Eva, I went upstairs to my room and closed all the windows and drapes. I pulled the satchel out and dumped the cash on the bed, marveling at the sheer volume. After I locked my door, I started arranging stacks of bills, making piles of tens, twenties, fifties and hundreds. What a pot of gold! Strange that roughly half the bills seemed to be new, fresh from the bank, while the others were crumpled, worn currency. Poker winnings?

Slowly I counted the money, not once, but twice. My palms were clammy by the time I finished: There was over $12,000. in the bag— $12,568 to be precise. Nathan was right—that was a lot of jack.

Sure, it was tempting to palm a few bills, but the money didn't belong to me, and probably not to Horace Andrews either. The bag wasn't safe under my bed, so I looked around for a hiding place.

Then I remembered an old steamer trunk my mother's family used when they traveled on an ocean liner to the U.S., via Galveston. New York was too cold they decided, based on relatives' reports, so they headed to Galveston: the Ellis Island of the Southwest.

Galveston Island had gotten quite a reputation over the years, including the "Wall Street of the South," and a less flattering description: the "Sin City of the Southwest."

And this illicit bag of cash proved the point.

I pulled out the heavy trunk, removing all the quilts and linens while a few moths fluttered away. The satchel fit neatly into the trunk, and I used both legs to shove it back in the corner. Shaking out the quilts, I placed them over the trunk, feeling like a shady crook hiding incriminating evidence.

That evening, I went to bed early, but tossed and turned all night. When Amanda tiptoed into my room later that night, smelling of burgers and bacon, I pretended to be asleep.

Finally I nodded off, dreaming I was dancing with Burton in a fancy satin gown at a high-society ball at the Hotel Galvez. Suddenly he arrested me and handcuffed me to Sammy and Horace Andrews.

Then Nathan appeared out of the blue, shooting countless photos as Burton took us away in a paddy wagon, while Mrs. Harper, Mack, Hank and the other reporters pointed and laughed.

Did I say I was dreaming? It was more of a nightmare.

CHAPTER FORTY-FOUR

The next day at the *Gazette*, I stayed glued to my desk, avoiding any of the reporters. Mrs. Harper seemed pleased that I was working so diligently, our Surf Club crisis blown over, for now. Even Nathan and I barely made eye contact.

Around noon, Mack came by, leaning over my desk. "Hey, kid. You've been awful quiet today. Cat got your tongue?"

I forced a smile. "I'm just tired. How's the story coming along?"

"Fine. Thought you'd like to take a look, since you seem so interested in all this gangland activity. Here's a rough draft. My deadline's at five so if you have anything to add, make it snappy."

Did he really want my input or was he fishing for information?

I didn't like his condescending tone, but I nodded anyway, anxious to read his article. Mack wrote: *"In addition to the turf wars between the Beach and Downtown gangs, sources say internal fighting exists within each gang. Apparently two prominent Beach Gang members are attempting to wrest power away from current leaders Ollie Quinn and partner Dutch Voight."*

Strange that the gangs sounded as structured and organized as bankers or lawyers. Guess that's why they called it organized crime.

Still, I wasn't sure if Mack was smart to mention the gangsters by name, but I figured he meant the Maceos were the "prominent gang members." So had they left the rose on the ice man's body?

As I read further, I was impressed by how much Mack knew regarding the gang activity in Galveston and Houston. Who were his sources, I wondered?

Mack wrote: *"Patrick MacDougal, a part-time rodeo cowboy and roustabout from Houston, reportedly worked as a hired gun for the Beach gang. There is strong speculation that MacDougal stabbed and killed Harvey O'Neal, an alleged informant for Johnny Jack Nounes' Downtown Gang. An employee of the Igloo Ice Company, O'Neal serviced clubs and restaurants in the areas controlled by both the Downtown Gang and Beach Gang.*

"On Sunday, MacDougal was found dead on Galveston beach. Sources claim the victim was strangled to death by a member of the Beach Gang, but Ollie Quinn and Dutch Voight deny any involvement in the killing. The Downtown Gang's leader, Johnny Jack Nounes, also denies any knowledge of the alleged murder. As demand for bootleg grows, so does gang-related violence."

Thank goodness they suspected the Beach Gang had the cowboy murdered. What a break! That let Dino and Frank off the hook, for now. Fortunately, the Beach Gang didn't seem to know that the ice man was also Agent Burton's informant. Or did they?

Still, was I wrong to withhold vital information in a murder case? Should I tell Mack the truth or keep quiet? As I weighed the pros and cons, I jumped up when I saw a familiar face, heading my way.

Why was Agent Burton here? What did he want now?

The newsroom grew silent as all eyes rested on Burton, in full cop mode with his badge, holster and gun. I tried to smile, covering my panic. "What brings you here, stranger?"

He grinned back, then resumed his professional stance. "I'm here on police business. I need to talk to a friend of yours. Can you take me to see him?"

"Now? Can this wait?" I tried to stall, turning my chair around so the staff couldn't stare. Mack watched from his desk, his head raised high for a better look.

Burton leaned over, lowering his voice to a whisper, aware everyone was eavesdropping. "It concerns the victim who was found dead Sunday. A cowboy named MacDougal."

Damn! Who did he suspect—Dino or Frank, or both?

"I've got lots of work to do," I stammered. Dumb excuse, but it was the best I could do under pressure.

Burton's eyes bore through me, hard as marble. Then he turned to Mrs. Harper, hat in hand. "Mrs. Harper, may I borrow your assistant for an hour? It's urgent. Police business."

"You know my name?" She perked up, forgetting Burton was such 'a bad influence.'

"Of course, ma'am." He nodded. "Jasmine, I mean Miss Cross here, speaks highly of you."

She shot me a skeptical look. "Of course, Agent Burton." She smiled sweetly, batting her lashes like a debutante at a tea dance. "Take your time. Who am I to interfere in police business?" Was she flirting with him—a man half her age? The Surf Club fiasco must have slipped her mind.

"You know *my* name?" Burton turned on the charm. "I'm flattered." With a firm grip, he took my elbow and guided me toward the door like a dog on a leash. "I'll have her back to you later today."

I had no choice but to go along. The newsroom began to buzz as we walked out the door. Nathan stood by the darkroom, shaking his head, as if to say, "Here we go again."

Outside, I felt self-conscious when Burton opened the door to his police car, boldly parked in front of the *Gazette*. All I needed were handcuffs to complete the picture. The sandwich vendor stood with his mouth open; the Italian grocer stared, arms folded on his big belly, taking in the scene. Even Golliwog ran out to watch the spectacle. Maybe I should've sold front-row tickets.

In the car, I asked, "Why do you need me to tag along? Can't you handle this alone?"

"Sure, but this is a lot more fun." He grinned. "I enjoy watching you squirm in public."

"Glad you find me so amusing. What is this really about?"

His tone became serious. "I need to see Buzz right away. The police want him to ID the body, see if he's the same guy who killed the ice man, O'Neal."

I breathed a sigh of relief. Honestly, I was happy to accompany him since I was worried about Buzz. Who knows what he'd blab about the cowboy and Dino or Frank? I wished I could warn Sammy in advance, but I had no time.

"I'm curious. Why are *you* working on a murder case?"

"You mean a homicide? Murder is premeditated and there's no proof, yet. I volunteered my help, since I'd already met with the witness." He shot me a glance. "Besides, it's an excuse to see you."

Hogwash! His charm may work on Mrs. Harper, but not on me. "Admit it, you want me to pave the way, to make your job easier. You know Buzz may not talk to you or the police directly."

"Right." Burton nodded, avoiding my gaze. "But if Buzz can positively ID this man, we can begin our investigation into who—or what—killed him."

I sat up. "What do you mean by that—*what* killed him? Wasn't he strangled?"

His head snapped around. "How do you know? That's not public knowledge. Our reports say he drowned."

Me and my big mouth. "Nathan told me."

"Oh really? I heard a certain female reporter was on the beach where the victim washed up on shore. "A pretty young thing was how the M.E. put it." He raised his brows. "You seem to have a knack for always showing up at crime scenes, Jazz. Is there anything I should know about you?"

"Just doing my job." I shrugged. "The killings are all gang-related. It's in Mack's article."

"Did he get his facts from his so-called informants? You know how reliable they are. Can he trust the word of gangsters? I'm sure they rat each other out, lie through their teeth."

Burton parked in front of the Oasis, watching a new Cadillac speed by. "How should we do this?"

"Let me talk to Sammy and Buzz first." I held up a hand. "Why don't you wait here?"

Before he could refuse, I rushed inside the Oasis, wondering why Dino wasn't guarding the door. A few tipsy customers sat scattered around the bar, watching me with interest. Buzz was waiting tables, and gave me a shy half-smile.

"How are you, kiddo?" I pulled him aside. "Buzz, I need you to do me a favor. Agent Burton wants to talk to you about the cowboy, OK? Remember, he's our friend. He needs to take you to a morgue."

"What's a morgue?"

Poor kid. He should be going to the circus, not viewing corpses. I made a note to treat him the next time Barnum and Bailey was in town. "It's a place where...people go to sleep for a long time. We need to find out if this man is the same cowboy you saw stab the ice man. Don't be scared. Just tell Burton yes or no, nothing else, OK?"

Buzz nodded solemnly. "He won't t-t-try to hurt us?"

"No, he wants to help us. Don't say anything about Dino or Frank, and you'll be all right." Then I noticed the red marks still visible on his neck. "Buzz, you need to button your shirt all the way to the top, to hide your neck. Keep it closed tight. Don't let him see your bruises. You understand?"

Buzz's fingers shook as he buttoned his shirt collar. "Wait here for me," I told him, heading to the office. I knocked on the door, wanting to warn Sammy and Frank. "It's me, Jazz."

They looked surprised to see me, their faces strained. "What are you doing here? Why aren't you at work?" Sammy frowned.

After I explained the situation, Sammy stood up. "Buzz is my responsibility. I'll talk to Burton myself. Where is he?"

"Parked in front. He said he'd wait in the car." Secretly I hoped Sammy would chase Burton off and leave us all alone.

"Let's both talk to Burton. It's better that way," Frank said.

"Where's Dino?" I asked. He took up so much room, the place felt empty without him.

"He's running an errand," Sammy said. "In Houston."

"Houston?" Not a bad idea. To be safe, Sammy must have told him to skip town—pronto.

Sammy motioned for Buzz to follow us upstairs, shoulders tense. Outside, Burton leaned against his police car, acting like it was a social call. "How's it going, Sammy?" He reached out to shake his hand, then smiled at Buzz. "Hi, buddy."

"What do you want?" Sammy crossed his arms, ignoring Burton's outstretched hand. "Still trying to scare away my customers?" I stood by Buzz, hoping Sammy wouldn't go off half-cocked and assault Burton.

"Not at all. I need Buzz's help in a police matter. Did Jazz explain everything to you?"

"Why involve Buzz in your business? He's just a boy." Sammy faced down Burton, hazel eyes narrowed.

"So far, he's the only eyewitness we have to the O'Neal murder. The rest is just hearsay and rumors." Then he patted Buzz on the back. "Ready to help with a major police case, son?"

Jittery, Buzz nodded and jerked his shirt collar up to his chin.

Frowning, Burton reached over and opened his collar. "What's that on your neck, son?"

"N-n-nuthin'." Buzz backed away, his shoulders hunched, hand at his throat.

Sammy stood in front of Buzz, blocking Burton. "That's none of your business."

"It *is* my business if someone tried to hurt this boy. He's our sole witness in a murder investigation. What's the beef?" His eyes darted from Frank to Sammy, daring us to tell him the truth.

"I'll tell you what happened." Frank finally spoke up. "The cowboy slipped in late Saturday night. He cornered Buzz in the alley and attempted to strangle him with his rope. Buzz yelled for help, and Dino fought him off." He crossed his arms. "No doubt about it. The cowboy came here with the intent to kill Buzz."

"Dino was just trying to p-p-protect me!" Buzz blurted out. "It was an ac-c-cid-d-dent."

"The cowboy attacked Buzz?" Burton raised his brows. "And where's Dino—inside?"

Sammy shrugged. "He took off this morning, didn't say where or when he's coming back."

"Dino disappeared in thin air?" Burton snapped his fingers. "How convenient."

"He's my doorman, not my property." Sammy moved toward Burton. "What of it?"

"I only wanted to ask him a few questions," he said, exasperated. "Damn it, Sammy! Don't you understand I'm trying to help you?"

"How do you plan to do that?" Sammy frowned. "By arresting Dino for murder?"

"Who mentioned murder? Sounds like self-defense to me," Burton said. "I doubt any jury would fault a man for trying to save the life of a young boy, especially a material witness in a murder."

All eyes were on Burton as we collectively held our breaths.

Burton paused, fanning himself with his hat, watching our guarded expressions. "Besides, if Dino choked that cowboy to death, he did him a favor."

"A favor?" I piped up. "What kind of favor?" I'd been holding my breath so long, I thought I'd pass out.

"I may as well tell you since you're bound to find out anyway. But keep this quiet for now." Burton glanced at me, then looked Sammy right in the eye.

"That cowboy was pumped so full of methanol, it would have killed a horse. He only had a few hours left to live, if that long."

"Methanol?" I repeated, trying not to get my hopes up.

Sammy looked skeptical. "Do you have any proof?"

"Of course." Burton nodded and gave me a sly smile. "A young female reporter mentioned a toxicology report to the M.E. that made him think twice. The M.E. hadn't done a full exam, since it appeared the poor bastard had been strangled and drowned, no questions asked. But with all the local poisonings and the Surf Club chips in the cowboy's jeans, he wanted to do more digging. And it paid off."

"Really?" I swelled with pride. Was he serious? Did I actually help solve a crime? A murder, no less!? "Is that why you're helping with this case, because of the methanol?" I asked, still in shock.

"Yes, that and my personal interest," Burton said, nodding.

"That changes everything." Frank exhaled, patting my back. "Doesn't it?"

"Appears to be one more unresolved gang slaying." Burton shrugged. "What a pity."

He was full of surprises. Was it finally all over?

CHAPTER FORTY-FIVE

"So where'd the booze come from?" Sammy crossed his arms.

"We're not positive, but it was no accident," Agent Burton said. "The wood alcohol had been in the cowboy's system a few hours when he died. Your friend Candy was right: He was at the Surf Club Saturday night, gambling and drinking in the Western Room. Turns out Ollie Quinn had his drinks mixed with methanol, so he couldn't squeal." His gaze lingered on me. "We just missed him that night."

"Too bad. It shows your hunch was right." I smiled, still elated.

"Wish we could've gotten a confession out of that weasel before he drowned," Burton said, half-joking. "Ready to go, Buzz?"

"Want some lunch first?" Sammy asked Burton, his stone-faced demeanor softening. "It's the least I can do."

"Thanks, but we'd best be off to fight crime, right, son?" Burton opened the car door for Buzz and patted the passenger seat. "Here, buddy, you ride up front with me."

"I'll go too." Frank climbed in back, beaming at me. "Attagirl!" Buzz waved to us out the window, looking like the kid he was, playing cops and robbers—or rather, killers.

"You and Frank take good care of Buzz." I leaned over Burton's car door, flashing my best smile. "Thank you."

"My pleasure." He tipped his hat. "See, Jazz, there are happy endings after all."

"That was some close call." When Sammy smiled, his rugged features lit up like candles on a birthday cake. "Gotta hand it to Burton, he came through in a pinch. Shocked even me."

"I'll say!" I nodded. "I thought he was so by-the-book."

"At least Dino is in the clear. Glad that's all settled, thanks to you and Burton." He squeezed my arm. "Come inside and have some lunch. We need to talk."

"Sure, I'm not ready to go back to work. I feel like celebrating."

For once, Burton seemed to be on our side, an ally instead of a foe. But if he was no longer my enemy, what was he—a friend, or could he be more?

Sammy retreated to the kitchen and returned with heaping plates of hot lasagna. Famished, I dug in, grateful that Dino's grandmother had taught them how to cook real Italian meals. While we ate, I could tell Sammy was preoccupied, the way he picked at his food like a spoiled child.

"There's no polite way to ask, but I need a favor." He looked away. "I've got a big business meeting coming up and I hope you can help me out… with a small loan. Hell, part of the dough belongs to me anyway. Says so in Andrews' ledger."

I looked up, my fork in mid-air. Sammy was so proud, he had to be desperate to ask *me* for money. "Now that you have your account number, why don't you just get it from the bank?"

"Believe me, I've already tried. I went to the bank this morning to get some cash, but no such luck. Some bigwig told me I had to provide proof of identity and ownership. What bullshit." He said it in a formal, high-hat tone, trying to mimic the banker.

"Imagine that—I can't even touch my own hard-earned dough till some stuffed shirt gives me the A-OK."

"I'm sure it's just a formality," I said, stalling. "I doubt anyone can waltz into the bank and withdraw money, especially if they don't know you."

"What a tightwad. He gave me some forms to fill out, but said it takes a few days to be approved. Trouble is, I need the cash right away. It's an emergency." He slapped his knee for emphasis.

"What for? Liquor?" I asked dryly.

"You can't very well run a bar without booze, can you? Consider it an investment."

"Sorry, Sammy." I shook my head, my heart sinking. "It's not my money to lend. If I gave you cash that belongs to the bank, we'd both be in hot water."

Truth be told, I hated being put in this predicament, having to turn down my half-brother when he'd never asked me for a dime. But I couldn't hand out cash like carnival prizes. Still, the false sense of power and control the money gave me made my head spin.

"Jazz, it's only a temporary loan. I'll get it back in a week or two." Holding his arms out, he did a half-turn, indicating the empty bar. "Look at this place. Ever since Horace passed away, the Oasis has been quiet, like it's cursed. People seem to believe I'm serving rotgut rum to cut costs."

"That's bunk!" I fumed. "You'd close shop first."

"You said it." In the dim lights, Sammy looked tired, weather-beaten, like an old abandoned schooner. "See my problem? That's why I need the loan, so I can buy the best from the best."

I leaned forward. "You mean Black Jack? How can you trust a dangerous bootlegger?"

His head whipped around. "What gave you that idea? And how do you even know his name?"

"I've heard his name mentioned at work," I mumbled. That was partly true.

"Well, then you may have heard he requires big bucks before he'll do business with anyone. I need to buy stock directly from him, not his greedy goons."

"Is that all?" I paused. "Aren't you planning to confront him about the wood alcohol?"

"Why not? That's the whole idea. I'm sure he wants to put a stop to this supply of bad booze as much as I do. Whoever it is, this asshole is giving every barkeep in town a bad name."

"How do you know Black Jack isn't to blame?"

"I've known Black Jack a while. We're not exactly friends, but he trusts me and vice versa. You may not believe this, but for a bootlegger, Black Jack is fair and square." He lit a cigarette, staring at the match. "As long as I pay cash up front, then I'm in the clear. But if I show up empty-handed, that's the kiss-off."

The kiss-off as in *dead*? I wished I could change his mind, but he was determined. "Why should you get involved? It's too risky."

"I got involved the minute Horace died." Sammy flung out his arms. "This bar is all I have. If I don't straighten out this mess soon, more people could die. I need to talk to Black Jack, find out if he knows anything about the bad hooch."

"You're not going alone, are you? Sounds dangerous." Not to mention stupid.

"Those are his rules." He shook a finger in my face. "Don't you dare tell Nathan, and especially not that Fed. That's all I need, Agent Burton on my tail. They'll accuse me of being a snitch. Then I'm a dead man." Scowling, he blew smoke rings at Doria. "So what about the dough? I need at least a grand or so."

"A thousand bucks?" I whistled, trying to stall. "Let me think about it. For now, I need to get back to work."

"Let me give you a ride, Jazz." Sammy seemed to take my hesitation as a good sign. "When do you think I can get it? I need it by tomorrow evening at the latest."

"Sorry, Sammy. I can't make any promises."

Sammy drove a new Packard roadster with the top down. I held onto my floppy hat as he raced down the streets, tires squealing when he turned the corners. I knew he was upset, but I didn't feel right about handing over so much money. I wasn't a big shot or rich banker, free to disperse cash at will. What if it was embezzled? What if the bills were marked—or counterfeit?

As we slowed to stop for a trolley, Sammy turned to me, curious. "I don't get your boyfriend, Burton. One minute, he accuses me of selling bad booze, the next he's making excuses for Dino. What's with him? He must be sweet on you."

"You're daffy." I made a face. "Believe it or not, he wants to work *with* you, not against you. Obviously you have a better chance of finding this dirty bootlegger than he does. He hopes if you locate the source, you'll give him enough information to shut down his operation." After Burton had helped Buzz and Dino, I thought the least I could do was try to explain his motives.

"Squeal to the local Fed? That's a good way to get whacked. Just like our pal, Horace Andrews."

"No one has to know but us. You don't even have to see Agent Burton. Find out who it is, and I'll pass the name on to him."

"No dice." He shook his head. "Then we'd both be in danger."

In my heart, I knew Sammy was right. If the gangs thought we'd complied with Agent Burton, we could both end up like the cowboy.

CHAPTER FORTY-SIX

Sammy parked a block down the street from the *Gazette* building, got out and opened the car door for me. "Sorry, kiddo, but it's not a good idea for us to be seen together. I may be recognized, thanks to your newshounds." His expression soured.

"Sammy, that's old hat. Everyone knows by now that you were innocent." I tried to reassure him. "It's all blown over."

"What about the Oasis? Hate to ruin your reputation, even if we *are* family." Was he ashamed or trying to make me feel guilty about the money?

"Who cares if you own a bar? Half our reporters live in gin joints. Their home away from home."

He grinned, looking hopeful. "So how about that grand, just this once? No one has to know."

I mulled it over: Wasn't Sammy entitled to the cash? After all, Horace was his friend and banker, but he'd already paid for his greed. Besides, it was only a temporary loan. How could I refuse my only brother? How many times had Sammy paid our rent or bailed us out? Finally I had a chance to return the favor.

"OK, I'll come by the Oasis tomorrow after work," I agreed.

"Swell! I knew you'd come through for me. Thanks, Jazz."

"Glad I can help." He gave me a grateful smile, and honked his horn as he drove off. My heart turning over, I stood on the sidewalk, watching him drive away, hoping I'd made the right decision.

After he left, I raced to the *Gazette*, bumping into a newsie near the steps. I needed to talk to Mack, to ask him about Black Jack. Was he as ruthless as I'd heard or "fair and square" as Sammy believed?

I crept into the newsroom, placing my hat and purse on my desk, smiling at Mrs. Harper. She didn't miss a thing. "How did everything turn out with your agent friend?" She glanced at the clock, specs dangling off her nose. "Nothing serious, I hope?"

"All is well." I knew she hoped I'd spill the beans about our rendezvous, but I wanted to find Mack first. I spied him in a corner office talking to Mr. Nelson, so I picked up his manuscript and walked by the office, trying to get his attention.

When Mack saw me, he excused himself and came over. "What's new, kid? I just finished my article and wanted to run it by Dave before it's typeset."

"About your article..." I lowered my voice. "You should call your coroner friend first."

"Why? What's the scoop?" Mack crossed his arms over his barrel chest.

I paused, hoping Burton wouldn't mind me spilling the beans.

"I have an update, so you may want to revise your story before it goes to press. My sources tell me the cowboy was at the Surf Club on the night he died."

He frowned. "So what? Isn't that where you went with your Fed agent beau?"

Would I ever live that down? "According to the toxicology report, the cowboy's blood contained large quantities of methanol. Apparently someone poisoned his drinks, probably at the Surf Club."

Mack stared at me a minute. "Oh, yeah? How do you know?"

"Like I said, call your M.E. pal to verify it."

"I'll do that," he nodded, looking skeptical.

I stood by his desk while he dialed the coroner, trying to listen. After a brief conversation, Mack hung up in a daze. "Guess what? Your information checked out. I'd better go rework that angle before the story goes to press." He grinned around his cigar. "Good job, kid. You may get a front-page byline yet."

"Thanks, Mack." That was high praise coming from him. "But before you go, I'd like some information." I took a deep breath. "What do you know about a bootlegger named Black Jack?"

"Black Jack?" His eyes widened. "Nothing I'd want to print. He's bad news, kid. He's the biggest supplier in the area—sells to both the Beach and Downtown gangs and all of South Texas."

My stomach knotted. "You don't say."

"I hear he'll sell his own brother to make a buck—and throw in the dog for free." Mack looked alarmed. "Why? You're not investigating this crook, are you? You don't want to mess with the likes of him."

"No, but his name came up, and I figured you knew something." Did I really want the truth?

"Sure, I heard some rumors about this rotgut rum going around. Word is, Black Jack's goons may be responsible for distributing the hooch." He waved his cigar. "These palookas buy low-grade alcohol from any cheap supplier—moonshiners, farmers with stills, refineries, industrial plants. They dilute the good liquor, cut the cost and pocket the cash. That stuff can be deadly if it's not manufactured right."

I nodded. "I've heard lots of bootleggers cut corners, add cheap filler, to stretch their stock."

"Right, but if they don't distill the liquor properly and boil away the methanol, it can turn into wood alcohol. Worse, they recycle old liquor bottles, fill them with this poison, and pass it off as the real thing." He leaned forward, his voice low.

"Did you ever hear about my run-in with the gangs? The minute that I mentioned Black Jack, two thugs took me out to the alley and beat me senseless. Luckily they didn't touch my hands and fingers or I'd be out of work by now." He wiggled his hands.

So Pete's story checked out. "Glad you're OK." I stood up, shaken. Mack had just confirmed my worst fears about Black Jack. "Good luck with your story. Thanks for your help."

"Thank *you*," he said. "You can read all about it tomorrow, on the front page."

Now I was really worried. What was Sammy getting himself into? Could I convince him to change his mind or was it too late?

When I returned to my desk, Mrs. Harper refused to look up. Clearly, she was angry by the way she typed, long nails clicking with extra force. So I stayed put all day, but kept worrying about Sammy's meeting with Black Jack, knowing he was too stubborn to put it off.

Around 6:00, I was still at my desk, mentally and physically exhausted, when Nathan stopped by. "I see you're out on bail."

"Funny." I smiled, glad for a break. "Say, can you give me a lift? I've got some news."

"Sure, I always like good gossip," he teased.

On the drive home, I filled him in on the day's events, starting with Burton and Buzz, and MacDougal's death by alcohol poisoning. Just recounting the facts made me dizzy.

"So the cowboy tied one on, literally." He grinned.

"In more ways than one. I gave Mack the update and he seemed appreciative. When I asked him about Black Jack, he gave me an earful, told me to stay away."

"That bootlegger? Why'd you bring up such a sore subject to Mack? Get it—sore?" Boy, he was full of one-liners today.

"Can you ever be serious? Nathan, I'm in a real bind." I looked out the window. "Sammy asked me for a thousand dollars cash, to buy booze from Black Jack. What should I do?"

"Hate to say I told you so. You don't owe him any favors. He just wants easy money."

I bristled at his jab. "It's only a loan. But if I do give him the cash, am I doing the right thing?"

"That's up to you. I'd have no trouble helping out a friend in need, especially with a dead guy's dough. There's plenty to go around." He eyed me. "Sammy has no idea whose cash it is?"

"He said it was Horace's take from the gangs, but turns out he was skimming off the top, keeping the change for himself."

Nathan let out a whistle. "You'd think a banker would know better. That's a deadly game."

"Deadly is right." I chewed on my nails. "The gangs probably found out and put a stop to it, permanently. I think Sammy's asking for trouble if he confronts Black Jack and his thugs alone."

"Give Sammy some credit." Nathan honked his horn at a mother pushing her baby carriage into the street. "Maybe he just wants to buy some booze so he can check it out, get it analyzed, find out if Black Jack is selling hooch to suckers."

"What if they catch on and try to hurt Sammy? Mack told me when he mentioned Black Jack, the goons threw him out of the Lotus, then later jumped him in the alley. He's heard rumors that his men sell diluted hooch at cut-rate prices." I let out a worried sigh. "Can you believe they'd try to undercut their own boss?"

"I'm not surprised." Nathan stopped in front of the boarding house, his face grim. "But Sammy's a big boy, Jazz. He wouldn't have lasted so long in this biz if he wasn't hard-boiled."

"I know. But I'd feel better if I knew he had some back-up tomorrow night, to be safe."

"Planning to call Burton?" He frowned. "Why not call the mortician while you're at it? He should bring Dino along. That big Bruno would scare anyone to death."

"Sammy said no cops. He has to come alone."

"You can't talk him out of it?"

"He won't change his mind." I mulled it over. "Say, you gave me a brainstorm. Why can't *we* be his back-up? Go on a stake-out?"

"A stake-out? Are you screwy?" Nathan snorted. "Sorry, Jazz, but we're no match for a bunch of cut-throat bootleggers. Can't you see us now? We'd be more like the Katzenjammer Kids. "

"I'm worried about this meeting with Black Jack." I knotted my hands. "Sammy's such a hot-head, he could be in real danger. We can be his look-out, behind the scenes, make sure he's OK."

"No, thanks." He shook his head for emphasis. "If you insist on going through with this hare-brained scheme, maybe Burton is the man for the job. It's right up his alley."

"Burton? He'd alert all the cops around and before you know it, the circus is in town." I clasped my hands, pleading, "Come on, Nathan, do it for Sammy, if not for me."

He crossed his arms, skeptical. "What did you have in mind?"

"After I give Sammy the cash, we'd secretly follow him, and look for a place to hide. Then we wait and watch to make sure everything goes smoothly." Sure, it sounded simple in theory.

"Is that all? I don't know if it's brave or stupid or both," he admitted. "But I'm willing to take a chance. Sounds kind of exciting. Want me to bring a gun?"

CHAPTER FORTY-SEVEN

"A gun?" I didn't know Nathan even owned a gun. Were we getting in over our heads? But I couldn't back down now, after Nathan finally agreed to help Sammy. "Sure. Can you also bring along some pants and a shirt? Casual, nothing fancy."

"What for?" Nathan looked puzzled.

"For me." I smiled. "I'm going incognito. Today I'm Jazz Cross, but tomorrow night, I'll be in disguise as your kid brother, Jason."

"Role-playing." He grinned. "I like it. I can't wait to see how you look in my clothes." His expression became serious. "If I'm caught aiding and abetting, will you visit me in prison?"

"Don't worry, I'll be in the cell right next to you. I'm your kid brother, remember?"

"I'll take my camera. I may get some good shots for the paper."

I frowned. "How can you hide that monstrosity? We need to be inconspicuous. Better yet, invisible."

"I'll keep it in my car, just in case we catch the bad guys."

"Maybe you can take a few shots from a distance," I suggested. "No flash or lighting."

"How can I take pictures in the dark?" he complained.

"You're the ace photographer, not me. I doubt Black Jack and his goons are willing to pose for pictures." I smiled and added, "Don't forget to bring your gun." What was I getting us into?

After he drove off, I saw Eva waiting outside in a full apron embroidered with ducks and geese, like a farmer's wife. "Was that Nathan? Why didn't you invite him in for pot roast?"

"Maybe later?" I hated to brush her off, but tonight I had more on my mind than a home-cooked meal, though it smelled delicious.

Anxious, I went upstairs and pulled out the trunk from the corner, opened the satchel, and counted out ten one-hundred dollar bills for Sammy. Still, I began having second thoughts: Was I wrong to give him this money? I'd never seen so much cash in my life.

At my father's general store, he only kept twenty dollars in the cash register and less in his pockets. A few robberies over the years taught him to always be careful, on guard. He always kept a gun handy in case of a hold-up.

Without warning, the door flung open, and Amanda gasped, eyes big as pies. "Jazz, what in hell is going on?" She shut the door and gaped at the money spread out on the bed. "Where'd you get all that dough? Looks like you robbed a bank!"

"Don't look at me." I felt a pang of guilt for keeping her in the dark. "But maybe Horace Andrews did. I meant to tell you..."

"That poor banker?" She sat on the bed, excited. "I knew he was a high-roller, all dressed up in his Sunday clothes, drinking like there was no tomorrow. So how'd *you* end up with his cash?"

"For him, there *was* no tomorrow." I didn't have any choice but to confess. "OK, I'll fill you in, but you have to keep it quiet. Nathan and I are in enough trouble as it is."

Amanda threw her hands in the air. "Nathan is involved, too? Jeepers! Leave me out, why don't you?"

After I told her the long story, she pouted, "You've been sitting on this goldmine for two whole days without telling me?" She pointed to the big wad of bills I clutched. "What's that for?"

"Sammy. Remember that bootlegger he was asking about— Black Jack?"

She nodded, face pale. "What's he planning to do?"

I had to tell her the truth. "Sammy set up a meeting with him tomorrow. He says he needs to buy quality stock, but I think he really wants to confront him about the wood alcohol going around town."

"Oh no!" she gasped, covering her mouth. "Can't you see Sammy losing his head, accusing Black Jack of selling bathtub gin?"

"Yes, I can. Now you know why I'm so worried," I sighed. "But am I doing the right thing, giving him cash that's not mine?"

Amanda jumped up, arms waving like a railroad crossing.

"Jazz, you've got to help Sammy. He's your brother! What if he shows up empty-handed? He could get killed!"

"I'll help Sammy in any way I can. Don't worry, I've got a plan."
What plan? So far my bright idea involved playing dress-up with
Nathan, then hide-and-go-seek with Sammy and Black Jack.

When I told her our not-so-brilliant strategy, Amanda looked
skeptical. "That's such a screwy plan, it might work. But please be
careful, Jazz. I don't want any of you getting killed."

The next day, on the way to work, I heard our neighborhood
newsie belt out the headline: "Local gang behind ice man hit! Read all
about it!" Anxious to read Mack's article, I took a paper off his stack
and handed him a few extra cents. Poor kid looked like a ragamuffin
with his dirty, stained clothes and face, but he sure knew how to
attract attention.

Mack's story was on the front page, with all the graphic details,
and a 36-point headline: GANGSTERS ON THIN ICE IN ICE
MAN SLAYING. Clever. Below it was this subhead: GALVESTON
GANGS CONTROL ISLAND WITH MONEY AND MURDER.

Talk about sensational. Skimming the article, I couldn't help but
admire Mack and Mr. Thomas. They had guts, all right. Not only did
the article give names, it even included photos of all the big guns:
Ollie Quinn, Johnny Jack, Dutch Voight, George Musey, the Maceos.

I was relieved Mack added the fact that Sammy had been falsely
accused, and released the next day since he was no longer a suspect.

As I approached the *Gazette* building, I noticed Golliwog on the
steps, pawing at a rolled-up newspaper. Strange since Golliwog was
so skittish, she rarely made an appearance this close to the front
entrance. I bent down to pick up the paper when I saw it: a long,
thin, hairy tail sticking out. Jumping back, I let out a scream, almost
falling off the steps.

"Hey Finn," I asked the newsie, upset. "Can you see what's in
that rolled-up paper?"

"Aw, don't be a 'fraidy cat," Finn said, putting down his stack of
newspapers. He kicked at the paper with his foot, then bent down,
unfolded the paper and let out a loud yelp: A huge dead gray rat
rolled out, its throat slit open, blood splattering most of the
newsprint. As I jumped back, I barely made out the blood-soaked
headline: GANGS ON THIN ICE IN ICE MAN SLAYING.

CHAPTER FORTY-EIGHT

This time, I screamed so loudly they could hear me in Houston. I clutched my stomach, ready to upchuck as I stared at the big, bloody, hairy rat. My worst fears: rats, snakes and cockroaches. Golliwog ran off to hide in the alley, scared by the commotion.

"Who did this?" I demanded, starting to shake. "Did you see who put the paper here, with that disgusting dead rat?"

Finn, the newsie shrugged, his hands smeared with newsprint. "Hey, don't ask me. I ain't the doorman. I just sell papers."

Carefully I stepped around the bloodied newspaper and went inside, looking for someone to clear off the step. "Can anyone help me?" I called out. All these hard-boiled reporters around, but they wouldn't touch a rat with a ten-foot pole. I admit, I was deathly afraid of rats, especially when they showed up mutilated at our door.

"What is it, Jasmine?" Mrs. Harper rushed by my desk. "I heard you scream."

"I wouldn't go outside now. Wait a while," I warned her, frantically motioning for Pete, the cub reporter, to help me discard the disgusting dead rat.

"Why not?" She marched over to the door, but stopped short when she saw the bloody bundle. "Oh, my word. What in Lord's name is that thing?" Mrs. Harper leaned against me, about to faint, so I took her arm and helped her to her desk. She sat down, her face pale. "Is that what I think it is? A dead animal?"

I nodded. "A rat with its throat slit. It was on the steps, wrapped in the front page of today's paper." I lowered my voice. "I assume it was a warning to Mack. The gangsters aren't too subtle, are they?"

"The message is deafening." Mrs. Harper dabbed her brow with a hanky. "Mack hasn't come in yet, has he? We can't invite that kind of controversy. I'd best have a talk with Mr. Thomas."

She stood up, smoothed out her navy linen suit and entered his office without knocking. I hid by the door, listening as they got into a heated discussion. Wish I could be a fly on the wall!

Glancing outside, I noticed poor Pete seemed confused as he held the crumpled newspaper, unsure what to do with the rat's remains. I rushed out the door with a small trash bin, holding my nose. I turned away in time to see Mack, followed by Nathan, coming up the sidewalk.

"What's all the ruckus? Selling lots of papers, kid?" Mack asked the newsie with a grin.

"Sure, Mack." Finn saluted. "Your name always sells papers."

"So why the long faces?" He frowned. "What's the matter, Jazz? Something wrong?"

"I'll say!" I cringed, pointing to the bloodied newspaper and rat inside the trash bin. "You got an anonymous message. They left this…uh…calling card...on the front step."

"Ha!" Mack glanced in the bin, then raised his fist in victory. "Seems I hit a nerve. Serves those bastards right!"

I stared at Mack in amazement. The sight of the dead rat seemed to give him a thrill.

"Mack, maybe you should take the day off." Nathan eyed the rat. "Lie low for a while."

"You mean run away like a scared rat with my tail between my legs? Hell, no!"

Nathan and I exchanged looks, no doubt thinking the same thing. How long before Mack turned up dead, with his throat slit? The symbolism was clear, if not gruesome.

Mack marched up the steps like a soldier ready for combat. But he needed more than a typewriter if he wanted to fight off Galveston's liquor lords. Sure, the pen was mightier than the sword, but the gangs had secret weapons.

With great flourish, he hung his safari hat on his hat rack, sat down and popped open the paper, clearly pleased with himself. Besides Mr. Thomas, Mack was the only staff member with his own personal hat rack by his desk.

"Mack! I need a word." Mr. Thomas motioned for Mack to come to his office, but he dragged his feet like a naughty schoolboy. His shoulders stiffened, his back up, ready to duel. The staff watched in silence while Mack argued back and forth with Mr. Thomas. As Mack's arms flew about and Mr. Thomas pounded on his desk, we overheard a few colorful words, unfit for a family newspaper.

Then, with his head held high, Mack stomped back to his desk. He stuffed several folders and papers into his satchel and grabbed his hat, almost knocking over his hat rack.

"What happened?" Nathan asked Mack. "Leaving so soon?"

"I'm going on vacation," he announced as he stormed out. "Whether I like it or not."

"Mack got the message loud and clear," Nathan told the staff after he'd left. "You don't rat out your friends, and never squeal on your enemies."

After the newsroom emptied and the drama died down, I pulled Nathan aside. The bloody rat made me even more determined to help Sammy. "Got everything ready for tonight?"

"Maybe this stake-out isn't a good idea. That rat made me want to throw up," he admitted.

"Those gangsters mean business. If they can mangle a rat to make a point... I hate to think what they could do to poor Mack, or Sammy." I shuddered. "I swear, it gave me the screaming meemies."

"Sure you won't change your mind?" Nathan seemed hopeful.

"We can't abandon Sammy now," I insisted. "All we have to do is watch his back, make sure he's not in any danger."

"That's all? OK, if you're serious, then I'm in." He put up his hands, surrendering.

I returned to my desk, neck tense, trying to think. Did I really expect to help Sammy? We didn't exactly have any experience chasing off criminals. If Black Jack or his goons saw us, Sammy might be in even more danger. And the one person I wanted to ask for advice had just left "on vacation."

As I tried to concentrate on work, Mrs. Harper placed an embossed ivory invitation on my desk. "Thank you for trying to help today, Jasmine. I know it's short notice, but I wondered if you'd like to attend a special charity event this evening. I don't feel up to it, especially after that spectacle. Perhaps Agent Burton might be free to escort you?"

She was about as subtle as the gangs. Did a dead rat bring on this change of heart?

"Tonight?" Normally, I enjoyed charity events, especially since Mrs. Harper rarely allowed me to attend on my own. But why tonight, of all nights?

"Yes, tonight." She snatched the invitation and turned to leave. "If you have some prior engagement, I'm sure I can find someone else who'd love to go in your place."

Did I have a choice? "I'll be glad to go." I smiled to pacify her. The event lasted from 6:00 to 8:00 p.m. so I could try to leave early. Afterwards I could stop by the Oasis and give Sammy the money. His note said 9:00 p.m., after dark, so I'd have plenty of time before he met with Black Jack.

"Very good. Oh, and be sure to ask Nathan to come along," she said. "We'll need some photos of the event. It should be nice—it'll be held at the Galvez Hotel."

"What's the occasion?" I asked, looking over the invitation. I'd been so preoccupied that I hadn't even read the fine print.

"It's a fund-raiser for the Galveston Children's Orphanage." She beamed. "Lone Star Bank is going to present the orphanage director with a nice big check. Such a worthy cause."

Lone Star Bank? Interesting. Perhaps I was wrong about the bankers. It might explain why Mr. Jones and Mr. Clark met with the gangsters at the Surf Club: to solicit charity donations.

Mrs. Harper looked me up and down with disapproval, noting my sleeveless pink cotton frock. "You might want to dress up, dear. Most of Galveston society will be there and you'll want to look your best when you represent the *Gazette*."

"Of course, Mrs. Harper." I felt like her humble handmaiden.

When I told Nathan about our new assignment, he asked, "What about our plans? Won't that be cutting it close?"

"We'll have to make an early exit." I didn't want to disappoint Mrs. Harper *or* Sammy. Better to cut the night short and give him the cash in plenty of time for his meeting.

That evening, Nathan came to pick me up in his Model T, looking natty in a pin-striped seersucker suit and tie. "You're the bee's knees! You look too pretty to be a crime-fighter."

"Thanks." I smiled, glad he noticed. Heaven forbid I embarrass Mrs. Harper and the *Gazette* in a plain Jane frock! I'd dressed to the nines, wearing a pale peach and pink floral print handkerchief-hem gown with ruffles at the neck that I'd bought on sale, topped with a floppy peach straw hat. The money was safely tucked away in my leather clutch, bulging at the seams. I felt nervous carrying so much cash on me, but where else could I hide it?

"Let's only stay an hour or so, OK?" I told Nathan.

"Fine with me. Hobnobbing with a bunch of rich stiffs isn't my idea of fun."

"You said it!" I agreed, then whispered: "Did you bring a gun?"

He nodded. "Don't worry, it's hidden in the glove box." Better to be safe than sorry. Gangsters and bootleggers came armed with a full arsenal, but one gun was better than nothing.

When we arrived at the elegant Hotel Galvez, my heart skidded as I noticed a gold Bentley parked right in front. Could it be the same Bentley that followed me on Sunday, or was it a coincidence?

By the carriage entrance, a valet opened my door, but Nathan waved him away, no doubt worried about the gun hidden in the glove compartment.

Inside the hotel, I admired the Galvez's majestic lobby, with its graceful arches and columns. "I'm with the *Gazette*," I told an elderly matron, who examined my invitation.

"I see." She frowned and thrust out her triple chins. "A reporter. I assume you have an escort?"

Horrors, a reporter! What a scandal for a young single woman to be seen unescorted at a tony charity event. "Yes, he's parking the Bentley," I sniffed, stifling a smile. "He doesn't like strangers handling his precious new car." What an old bluenose—with silver-blue hair to match.

I observed the posh crowd, pretending I, too, was rich and powerful. Arched windows faced the Seawall, sunlight radiating off the sparkling chandeliers. As I took notes, I recognized the familiar faces whose photos often turned up in the society section.

A pianist in a bow tie and tails played classical music softly on a grand piano. Negro waiters in black suits served the crowd, holding trays of hors-d'oeuvres, finger sandwiches and fresh fruit. Several couples in long gowns and tuxedoes milled around, holding crystal glasses. Surely they were drinking water and soda pop in public, not cocktails? I was so nervous about Sammy's meeting with Black Jack that I needed a drink, but made do with a Dr. Pepper.

When a Negro waiter offered me a tray of apricot tarts, finger sandwiches and candied almonds, I gladly helped myself. Nibbling on my snacks, I wandered through the hoity-toity crowd, but stopped short when I spied a group of men in slick suits and even slicker hair.

Beach Gang leaders Ollie Quinn and Dutch Voight held court with Rose and Sam Maceo, all dressed in their finery, perfectly comfortable to be seen out and about in old Galveston society. The mobsters were having a heated discussion on the veranda, raising their voices and hands for emphasis.

Nathan appeared at my elbow, and cocked his head at the gangsters lingering on the balcony. "This looks more like a mob convention than a charity event."

"Or a barbershop quartet." I surveyed the room, filled with old and new money. "I'll bet half of Galveston society is here."

I admit, I was disappointed that I didn't see Agent Burton in the crowd. I hoped to run into him since I'd never had a chance to properly thank him for helping Buzz and Sammy.

"Say, let's try to get the old geezer to play some jazz." Nathan elbowed me in the ribs. "Wouldn't it be fun if we started doing the Charleston, just to liven things up?"

I stifled a laugh, trying to picture the stuffy crowd's reaction. "I dare you!"

"Watch me," Nathan said, doing an improvisational tap dance.

"Nathan!" I pulled on his arm. "Be serious. We represent the *Gazette*, remember?"

"Oh, that old rag," he joked. "I forgot we have to work."

"I wonder if Clark and Jones are here?" I whispered: "Did I tell you they met with the Beach Gang at the Surf Club?" In order to win public approval, the gang leaders were known for their generosity and goodwill toward charities. Self-serving, but the local benefactors didn't complain.

I scanned the crowd, holding my clutch tight. "There's Mr. Clark, talking to a lady in black." The woman, dressed in black from head to toe, stood out in this crowd of summery pastel frocks and pale suits. I moved closer to get a better look, blinking in surprise. "What is Mrs. Andrews doing here?" She looked stylish in her black mourning gown, wearing a black hat adorned with an ostrich plume.

"Maybe she's active in this charity?" Nathan suggested.

I nodded. "That makes sense since Andrews was an orphan. But I'm surprised to see her at a social event so soon after his death."

I felt a pang of guilt as I thought about the bag of cash we'd found, money that he might have obtained illegally, but cash she so desperately needed.

"An attractive lady like her shouldn't be in mourning for the rest of her life," Nathan said.

I considered that notion. "You're right. Good for her."

Nathan and I blended in, nodding at a few people we knew, nibbling on snacks and drinking Coca-Colas. No doubt many folks were adding a few shots of rum or bourbon to their soda pop from secret flasks. When it came to dodging the law, manufacturers became quite creative, hiding tiny flasks in canes, hats, garters, fake cameras, even lingerie.

I nodded to Mr. Clark, who shook my hand as he passed. "Nice article on Andrews."

"Thanks." I smiled, glad he'd remembered. Now was my chance to talk to Alice alone, so I told Nathan, "Excuse me while I mingle. Why don't you take a few photos?"

My heart pounded as I approached. What could I say—that her husband had secretly stashed a bag of stolen cash at the train station, and was planning a quick get-away? What else had he hidden?

"So nice to see you, Mrs. Andrews." I touched her arm. "I hope you're doing well."

"As well as can be expected." She shook my hand. "I wanted to make an appearance tonight for Horace's sake. Phillip asked me to attend since the Children's Orphanage was our favorite cause. He always had an affinity for orphans and the less privileged."

Did that include Buzz, his own son, I wondered?

"I'm sure he'd be proud you're attending in his honor."

"Thank you. Do you have any news for me?" she whispered.

I nodded, taking her aside to a quiet corner. "Do you remember the matchbook you gave me from the Hollywood Dinner Club?"

"Yes, of course." Her face blanched. "Did you find out about that woman, that Rose?"

I hated to break the news to her. "No, but I'm sure you've heard of the Maceo brothers? You may know they own the Hollywood Dinner Club. In fact, they're here tonight."

She gasped, holding a gloved hand to her cheek. "Those gangsters? Here?"

I almost hushed her, but luckily the Beach Gang was still outside on the veranda. "Did you know that the nickname for Rosario Maceo is Rose?"

She blanched. "Goodness, I'd almost prefer a lady friend over a hardened criminal. I suppose it makes sense if they own the club. Perhaps it is good news, after all. Thank you, Jasmine."

I tried to soften the blow. "You may not realize that they're major contributors to local charities, including the orphanage. I'm sure that's why Horace had his number."

"I never thought of that possibility." She smiled at me with relief, then moved closer. "What else have you found? Any luck with the key or ledger?"

"I'm still working on it. I need more time." More time to incriminate her husband?

Then I heard clapping and a loud voice called out, "Attention, everyone!" Across the lobby, I saw Mr. Clark standing by the piano.

"Good evening. I'm Phillip Clark, vice president of Lone Star Bank. I'd like to thank you all for attending this fund-raiser for the Galveston Children's Orphanage. This was a favorite cause of our good friend, the late Horace Andrews. Not only is he here in spirit, he's represented by his lovely wife, Mrs. Alice Andrews."

When the crowd applauded, she gave a slight bow, her face flushed, clearly surprised but pleased.

I noticed Ollie Quinn and the Maceos clapping near the front, probably the real patrons. Like most people, I thought only the worst of the gangsters. Despite their shady business dealings—and alleged murders—society quickly forgave and forgot their wrongdoings. Money spoke volumes in Galveston, no matter who or what was the source. How ironic that both halves of Galveston society were now under one roof, socializing at the same charity event.

Clark continued: "On behalf of us here at Lone Star Bank, we'd like to contribute a check to the orphanage for their good work. Here to accept the donation is Mrs. Eunice Rosenberg."

Plump and pink, the flustered matron accepted the check with delight. However grateful, a riveting speaker she was not. After a few minutes of nonstop rambling, I wanted to tear my hair out.

By now it was almost 8:00 p.m.—Sammy's meeting with Black Jack started in an hour. Not that I expected bootleggers to be punctual, but I was already running late. I found Nathan snapping photos of two blonde debutantes who posed as if they were Hollywood starlets. What a wolf.

I tapped his shoulder. "Can you take photos of Mrs. Rosenberg before we go?"

"So soon?" His face fell. "See you later, ladies. Duty calls."

Mrs. Rosenberg beamed like a bride while Nathan took the obligatory photos of Mr. Clark handing her the check. Afterwards, Nathan said, "I'll get the car and meet you by the back entrance."

"I'll step into the powder room first." As I turned a corner down a side hall, a short dark-haired Italian man approached me, blocking my way.

"Miss Cross? Do you remember me?" He looked familiar.

I blinked at him. "Aren't you the Surf Club host? How do you know my name?"

"Are you enjoying the evening?" He asked politely, ignoring my question.

My heart began to race. What did he want? "Yes, I am. How about you?"

"I hoped you'd be here." His friendly façade changed in an instant, like Texas weather. He reached out and grabbed my wrist so tight, I winced in pain.

"Stop it, you're hurting me!" I tried to yank my arm free, but his nails dug into my skin. I clutched my bag behind me, out of sight. Did he know about the cash? Was he trying to rob me?

His voice was a low growl. "Give your boyfriend a message from the Beach Gang."

Did he mean Agent Burton? Heart hammering, I attempted to scream, but he covered my mouth with his hand, twisting my arm behind my back. Where was everyone? Why didn't anyone help me?

"Tell Agent Burton to stay away from our turf." Roughly he pushed me up against the wall and pressed his weight against me while I struggled to get loose from his grip. My hat flew off as he banged my head on the brick wall. "Or else."

CHAPTER FORTY-NINE

Pinpricks of pain stung the back of my head, and white dots floated before my eyes. Where was I? What happened? I tried to regain my balance as I waited for the room to stop spinning. Then the thug tipped his hat, pasted on his maitre d' smile and disappeared down the hall, vanishing like a phantom.

Still shaky, I picked up my floppy hat and fled to the ladies room to compose myself, gulping for air. Where had the thug come from so suddenly? Was he following me?

After splashing water on my face, I rushed to the exit, my legs wobbly. I tried to focus, to compose myself, but I still felt dizzy. Thank goodness Nathan sat waiting for me in his car by the carriage entrance. The gold Bentley was gone.

"What took you so long?" Nathan tapped his watch. "It's getting late. Sammy will be leaving soon."

"The host from the Surf Club attacked me in the hall." My breath came out in short bursts. "He twisted my arm and wrist so hard it still stings." I showed him the red marks on my wrist, my body still trembling. "He gave me a message for Burton, to stay away from the Beach Gang."

"That son of a bitch!" Nathan smacked his hand on the steering wheel. "I'll bet he was watching us all evening, and made sure you were alone before he attacked you." He started to open the car door, ready to bolt. "Where is he? I'll break both his arms!"

"I think he left in that Bentley." I pulled on his sleeve, touched by his chivalry. "Thanks, Nathan, but it's getting late. Let's go to the Oasis and follow Sammy to his meeting, as planned."

"Sure you're up to it?" He stared at me, clearly worried, as he started the car. "We don't have to go through with it, you know."

"I can't let Sammy down." I took a deep breath. "I'd never forgive myself if he got hurt."

"What if we get caught? Then we'll all be behind the eight ball."

Nathan gunned the engine and we got to the Oasis in record time. I told him to wait while I knocked on the door, holding my bag filled with bills. No answer. Then I remembered Dino was in Houston so they were short-handed.

When Buzz finally opened the door, I asked, "Where's Sammy?"

"He's g-g-gone." Buzz shuffled his feet.

"Gone? How can he be gone? We were supposed to meet tonight." Panicky, I pushed past Buzz and raced downstairs.

I locked eyes with Frank, who stood guard behind the bar. My words tumbled out in a rush. "Sammy was expecting me. I have something for him."

"You're too late, Jazz. He just left." He looked worried—with good reason.

"Damn it! I had to cover a charity event after work. Do you know where he went?"

Frank shrugged, refusing to meet my eyes. "Beats me."

"I know he was meeting Black Jack." I held out my clutch bag. "I brought the cash he needed."

"No need to worry, Jazz. Sammy got enough money from the bank today."

"He did? Frank, please tell me where Sammy is," I pleaded. "Maybe I can catch him in time."

"In time for what?" He slapped the counter with his palm. "Don't get involved, Jazz."

Nathan walked up, patting his side pocket. "We're only trying to help Sammy, Frank. I've got a gun, just in case."

"One gun won't help Sammy if Black Jack gets suspicious," Frank snapped. "If he catches you, it could get dangerous. He told Sammy to come alone."

Upset, I paced the floor. "He won't see us, I swear. Tell us where he went. We're wasting time!"

"On the d-d-docks!" Buzz blurted out. "Pier Twenty-one!"

"Pier Twenty-one?" My eyes darted from Buzz to Frank, trying to read their expressions. "Is that right?"

Frank nodded. "Go find Sammy. Be careful. Stay out of sight."

Nathan and I ran outside to his car, where he handed me a baggy white shirt and dark trousers. "I'll change in the car, but no peeking!" I started inching my dress up, exposing my peach silk slip, fumbling with his white shirt.

Nathan watched me in amusement. "I've never seen you in your lingerie before. Nice."

"Keep your eyes on the road!" Embarrassed, I yanked on his trousers, but had to roll up the legs like cuffs. Then I looked down at my girly pink shoes with bows. "I forgot about my shoes!"

"Don't worry, it'll be dark soon. No one will notice your shoes. But I did remember to bring this cap." I stuffed my hair under the cap, wiped off my pink lipstick and rouge, then took a quick look in the mirror. With my bare face and cap in place, I didn't look that different from a newsie. "That's more like it!" Nathan beamed at me. "I swear, you *could* be my kid brother."

Guess he meant it as a compliment. "Swell. What about you? You don't exactly look like a skid row bum."

"I'll fix that." He removed his tie, unbuttoned his shirt and messed up his sandy hair so he resembled a ragamuffin. As we approached the piers, Nathan slowed down and turned off his headlights. Several weather-beaten boats banged against the docks while the salty sea air whipped and howled, sounding like a lonely coyote. Shivering, I glanced around, searching for lights as we got near Pier 20, a remote area of the island facing Galveston Bay.

My heart leapt when I saw the Packard. "There's Sammy's car," I said, pointing. "They can't be far. Do you hear anything?"

"Not yet." Nathan parked near his car, then we crouched behind it, looking around for any activity. By now, the sun was setting and the half-moon lent a faint glow. A few seagulls squawked overhead, circling the piers, dipping low into the bay for fish.

Slowly we crossed the railroad tracks until we saw a large wooden warehouse located between Pier 20 and Pier 21. The worn structure looked abandoned and leaned slightly, probably damaged by hurricane winds.

Nathan went ahead, down the worn wooden docks toward Pier 21. Bending down low, we crept along the docks, past the tug boats and fishing boats tied there for the night, the bright stars guiding our way. A row of sailboats were tethered to the docks, bumping in the wind. In the moonlight, I made out a few names: Belle Weather, Angel Face, Bloody Mary. A white seagull perched on a pier, silhouetted against the deepening night sky.

As we passed Pier 20, I pulled on Nathan's arm. "I hear voices," I whispered, pointing toward the bay. "Over there." A large boat had docked between the piers, its motor quiet, as if resting for the night.

Like burglars, we tiptoed by the side of a dilapidated warehouse on the docks, trying to get closer to the boat. Worn boards creaked beneath my feet, and I stumbled over a thick rope, strewn carelessly across the pier. Was it too late to turn back?

Luckily, I noticed a few big oak barrels by a warehouse, wide enough to hide behind. I saw a faint light on one of the piers, and two men walking up a plank to the ship. They each reappeared with a wooden crate and entered the warehouse by the docks.

Crates full of liquor, I assumed. Except for the bootleggers, the battered building seemed empty, isolated. We crept along the side away from the bay, hiding behind the barrels. The front entrance facing the bay was wide open, and three men came out of the shadows to load the crates, assembly-line, into the warehouse.

No doubt, it had to be Black Jack and his thugs. I was amazed they were so bold—docking before 9:00 p.m.—but then week nights weren't known for much gang activity. The whole area seemed quiet, too quiet, and I figured Black Jack had probably paid off the cops to look the other way. I felt guilty for not telling Burton, wondering if he had any idea about Black Jack's drop tonight. But wasn't that his job—to know these things?

A tugboat sounded its horn as it slowly chugged by, a beam of light illuminating the murky water. Immediately one man turned off the kerosene lamp atop an oak barrel on the docks. The other men froze in place. Inching forward, I squatted behind some barrels by the warehouse and peered around the side, trying to get a better look.

I saw Sammy standing on the dock, talking to a big burly man with a black beard and a scarf wrapped around his neck. To me, he resembled an old-fashioned pirate, like a swashbuckling Jean Lafitte, Galveston's famous buccaneer.

"There's Sammy," I whispered. "That must be Black Jack."

"I see them. Everything looks OK to me." Nathan crouched by me, his breath hot on my neck.

"So far." I tried to listen, but only heard every third or fourth word—words like cash, supply, booze and bars. I edged forward along the building, never taking my eyes off the men on the docks. As we approached the side, the wind carried their voices over the bay. I pressed up against the wall behind a barrel, moving closer, straining to hear Sammy arguing with Black Jack.

"What's your beef?" the pirate roared. "Don't you trust me?"

"Sure," Sammy said. "I just want to sample the stuff first before I dole out any dough."

Black Jack pointed to one of the men. "Hey, Rico, go get him a bottle of that Cuban rum. The new stuff." Black Jack patted Sammy on the back. "Only the best for my old friend."

Sammy took a swig from the bottle. "This is more like it. I want the real deal—none of that home-brewed hooch going around. A friend nearly died in my bar drinking that rotten rotgut. Know anything about that?"

"What?" Black Jack bristled. "You accusing me?"

"Just wanna make sure you run a clean operation." Sammy stood his ground.

"What's the big idea?" Black Jack hooked his thumbs in his belt, and planted his boots in front of Sammy.

A tall man with a snake tattoo snuck up behind Sammy, grabbing his neck, pinning his arms back in one motion. I covered my mouth with both hands, trying not to scream.

"Ask your henchmen," Sammy snapped, breaking free of the man's grip. "I hear they're doctoring up your booze with all kinds of shit, and pocketing the change. Sounds to me they got greedy."

Four burly men surrounded Sammy, their arms folded over their chests. A tall lean man held up a kerosene lamp that flickered across the docks, casting an eerie glow. Even in the dark, I saw the fury on Black Jack's face, his head swiveling back and forth from Sammy to his goons. He circled the men, glaring at each one. "Is that true? You mucking up my goods?"

"Hell, no," said one guy, shoving Sammy. "Who you gonna believe? Me or this piker?"

Sammy grabbed the man by the throat and lifted him up off his feet. "What did you call me? You dirty grifter!"

In a flash, a tattooed man yanked Sammy's arms back while the others punched him in the gut, until he doubled over.

My heart seized: Sammy was going to get himself killed if we didn't act now. Did Nathan have his gun ready? I elbowed him, but he put his finger to his lips. Black Jack stood by watching without emotion, arms folded across his massive chest.

My legs started to tremble as I crouched down lower. I squeezed my eyes shut, saying to Nathan, "Do something!"

Nathan patted his pants pocket concealing his gun. "Not yet. We're too far from the ship." He was right. Shooting in the dark could get us all killed.

With a start, I made out two familiar frames, one tall, one short: Mutt and Jeff, the two goons who showed up at all the gangs' hot spots. Now it began to make sense: They didn't work for the Beach gang, they were Black Jack's men.

"Had enough?" Jeff yelled in Sammy's face. "Wait—I've seen you before. In the papers. I heard you got pinched for murder, but a Fed tried to bail you out." Some damn cop must have told them about Agent Burton. Now I wished I'd never asked for his help.

"That's not true!" Sammy backed away as the men circled around him. "They let me out 'cause I was innocent. I'm no killer."

"So you working for the Feds or what?" Mutt yelled, looking around. "Are they here?"

A tall man with weathered skin pushed Sammy down onto the docks, and kicked him while the others watched, laughing and taking turns swigging from the bottle. "Get off me!" Sammy yelled as he rocked back and forth, trying to avoid the blows, blocking his face with his arms.

I bit my lip, grimacing as I half-watched the scene unfold, paralyzed with fear. We had to do something—but what?

Nathan pulled out his gun and cradled it in his hands. I covered my face, afraid to look, but my eyes popped open when I heard scratching noises: A huge rat crawled out of the barrel, inches away, its beady eyes shining. Not again.

Without thinking, I jumped back and let out a loud scream.

"What was that?" a deep voice said. "Sounds like a dame."

Oh no—I'd blown our cover. Nathan put his hand over my mouth, but it was too late. The thugs released Sammy and moved toward us in the dark. Black Jack grabbed Sammy while two men walked around to the side, and two more approached the front entrance. Breathing hard, Nathan yanked on my arm and pulled me into the warehouse.

Luckily the moon ducked behind a cloud, dimming the docks. Mutt and Jeff entered the warehouse, one holding up a kerosene lamp that swayed back and forth as we inched along the back of the building. Squatting down, we tried to hide behind tall stacks of crates and boxes marked 'COTTON,' one of Galveston's biggest exports.

A kerosene lamp sat on the floor, illuminating several open crates filled with bottles. Dozens of empty liquor bottles were lined up next to a barrel with a spout, near a pile of new Johnnie Walker and Jack Daniels whiskey labels.

So Mack was right. That's exactly what they were doing: filling up empty liquor bottles with diluted and doctored whiskey, adding new labels and passing them off as the real deal. Talk about evidence!

Had Sammy seen this two-bit operation? I crept toward the barrel, grabbed a few labels and shoved them in my pocket, hoping to show Burton later—if we made it out alive.

Unfortunately, Sammy had no idea we were there and he was in no position to help us. All anyone knew was that some loud-mouthed "dame" was watching their operation.

I began to feel woozy and weak from the heat and humidity, easily 100 degrees. Disoriented, I looked around, but couldn't find Nathan. What was he going to do—shoot them in the dark? I waited, hoping they didn't notice us in the back, but it was deathly quiet. Where were they? Had they already gone?

Slowly, I crept behind some crates along the side wall toward the front entrance, feeling my way as I inched forward, my whole body trembling. I craned my neck around the side, looking for signs of life.

Without warning, a hand jerked me up by my collar, choking me. My heart jack-hammered so hard my chest hurt.

"What have we here?" The tall, tattooed man leered at me, his crooked teeth stained by tobacco. "A young stowaway."

CHAPTER FIFTY

I couldn't breathe, couldn't speak. Gasping for air, I tried to reply but my mouth felt full of straw. Panicking, I tugged on my collar, trying to loosen the man's grip, but he just lifted me higher. "What are you doing here, boy—spying on us?" For a moment, I was confused, then I remembered I was wearing Nathan's clothes.

Crazy thoughts raced through my mind. If he thought I was a half-wit or a child, maybe I was safe. If I refused to talk, he might assume I was a mute or a foreigner and let me go. Then as quickly as he picked me up, he dropped me hard on the wooden floor. I bit my lip, wincing in pain. Worse, my cap fell off and my dark hair tumbled out. I turned away, shielding my face with my hands.

"Well, what d'ya know?" The man smiled slyly. "It's a girl."

A shock of recognition jolted through me when I saw him up close: He was the same leather-faced man who tried to crush my hand at the Oasis and swipe Andrews' flask. He lunged at me and hooked his finger in my open collar, trying to rip off my shirt. Two top buttons popped off and I fell backwards onto the wood floor.

His tattoo gleamed in the dim yellow light of the kerosene lamp: A voluptuous naked woman, with long flowing hair, intertwined with a snake. How fitting: Eve and the serpent. He started to grope me, but I kicked his chest, digging in my heels, managing to push him off.

"Damn you!" Staggering backwards, he fell against a stack of crates, knocking over a few bottles. I crawled across the uneven wooden floor, splinters piercing my palms and knees through the thin pants. The bully reached for me, tugging on my pants' hem, but the belt held tight. Desperate to escape, I kicked my legs in the air, silently cheering when my heel smashed into his chin.

"So you like it rough?" he sputtered. "I can play rough, too."

"Leave me alone!" I screamed, hoping Nathan or Sammy would hear me. The brute outweighed me by at least one-hundred pounds and I wasn't sure how long I could fight him off.

"I like a spitfire," he smirked, pawing at my shirt and pants while I clawed at his face.

"Let her go!" Nathan appeared out of the dark, holding a gun, his hand shaking. I was terrified, but I felt a flush of admiration for his bravado, even if futile.

"What's it to you?" He scowled. "Just trying to have some fun."

"Fun? Looks more like an attack to me."

Behind Nathan, I saw a second man creep up.

"Watch your back!" I screamed. Nathan turned around and pointed the gun at the goon's scrawny chest.

"Don't shoot!" the second man said, clearly afraid, his hands held high, staring at the gun. Luckily he appeared to be unarmed, or else he was pretending. Seeing his chance, the bully grabbed me by the waist, his dirty nails digging into my ribs.

"Get your hands off me!" I swung around and scratched at his face, but he just laughed.

"Drop that gun or you'll see what happens to your girlfriend," he ordered Nathan. I tried to pry his grimy fingers loose, but he only gripped me tighter, making it hard to breathe.

"Don't do it!" I yelled. In that split second, I realized how much I depended on Nathan.

"You're a tough guy, aren't you?" Nathan snapped. "Picking on girls half your size." He pointed the gun at the tattooed man, eyes darting back and forth at us, arm outstretched.

"Put me down!" Instinctively, I began kicking wildly, and managed to hit the jerk on his kneecap. He stumbled backwards, holding his knee, his face twisted in pain.

"You little bitch!" He tried to pull my shirt tail, but I yanked free and ran toward the light.

"Come on, Nathan!" I yelled as I made a beeline for the kerosene lamp. I gave it a hard kick and watched as the glass shattered in thousands of tiny pieces, catching the light as they fell.

Immediately a flash of fire erupted and flames spread across the wooden floor like molten lava. My face felt hot, my throat raw, while I jumped away from the flames. The hoods stared at the fire, blinking, clearly dazed.

"Holy shit! Get the booze!" The men seemed to forget about us as they rushed to the back, stomping on the floor to put out the fire.

Flames leapt near the ceiling and I heard snapping and popping noises and loud shouts as the other two men rushed inside. Frantic, they began grabbing the crates of liquor from the front, and carrying them outside. Black smoke began filling the back of the warehouse, reaching the stacks of crates against the left wall.

Sweat dripped down my face as I crept along the right side, away from the flames, shielding my eyes from the bright glare. Dizzy from the heat, I inched toward the entrance, hiding behind barrels and crates not yet consumed by the blaze. My eyes and nose stung from the smoke and embers, but I strained to see past the flames into the back of the warehouse. I tried to swallow, my throat dry, but only tasted soot and smoke.

What happened to Nathan? Dare I go back and risk getting caught again? Or should I try to help Sammy? I edged closer to the front entrance, waiting for a chance to escape.

Outside, Black Jack had released Sammy and was shouting orders to his men: "Grab the liquor! Load up the ship! Hurry!"

Couched down behind the crates, I wiped my face with Nathan's shirt, now covered in grime and soot. Sweat dripped down my forehead, into my eyes. I squeezed them shut, temporarily blinded.

A rough hand shook my shoulder and I twisted around, my fists pumping air. Nathan leaned over me, his shirt torn and wet with sweat, his face blackened by ashes.

"Nathan, you're safe! I was so worried."

"I'm fine," he gasped, breathing hard. "Let's go get Sammy." He grabbed my hand and pulled me up, and together we darted toward the docks. Sammy was loading up crates of booze, and already had a short stack sitting on the dock. He looked like he'd been worked over by pros.

"Are you OK?" Stupid question. Sammy's face was swollen and bruised, and a fresh black eye had reappeared. A few bloody cuts and scratches covered his neck and arms.

Sammy did a double-take while he looked us up and down, both covered in soot and ashes. "Jazz, is that you? What in hell are you doing here?" He seemed dazed, disoriented. No wonder after that beating he suffered. "Why are you dressed like a boy?"

"These are Nathan's clothes. Guess it wasn't much of a disguise." I yanked on his arm. "Hurry, let's get out of here!"

I fanned away the smoke, calling out to Nathan. "Come on, let's go! It's too dangerous!"

"You two go ahead," he nodded, the fire reflected in his blue eyes, his face. "I need to get my camera out of the car. I've got photos to take."

"You sure?" I questioned his bravado. "It's not worth risking your life for a few photos."

"It is to me," Nathan said. For a moment, we watched on the pier, transfixed, as the flames leapt higher and higher through the warehouse. Looks like he wouldn't need a flash after all.

Then I heard a motor start and saw the tattooed man untying the ship. Black Jack was on board, pulling up the plank. "What's he doing? Leaving his men inside the warehouse?" I pointed to the ship.

"He may be cruel, but he's no fool," Sammy said, picking up two crates of liquor.

"Forget the booze!" I told him as we dashed away from the dock. "We don't need it."

"Like hell I don't. It's evidence. These crates might save my ass, and my bar."

Guess he was right. I grabbed a couple of bottles and as we made our way to Sammy's roadster, I saw a familiar car drive up and park. My heart stopped when I saw Agent Burton bolt toward the fire, stopping in his tracks when he saw me and Sammy.

"Jasmine, is that you? Sammy, what happened to you? What in hell are you doing here?"

"Black Jack is trying to escape, and his gang is inside." I gulped hot air, trying to breathe. "He's got tons of liquor stashed in the warehouse, and it might explode any minute."

Burton waved us away. "Get out of here before you get hurt!"

"Nathan is still there. You've got to help get him out!" I gasped, flinging my arms toward the warehouse. "Where's the fire brigade? The cops? What's taking so long?"

"They're on their way," he called out, darting to the warehouse. "Now go!"

We rushed out to Sammy's roadster, looking over our shoulders. Ashes swirled in the air, stinging my skin, burning my face. I tried to cough, but my throat felt itchy, raw.

"I hate to leave Nathan and Burton alone. They could get seriously hurt," I told Sammy as we watched the flames grow higher, bursts of light reflected on his car, his eyes.

"What else can we do?" Sammy wiped his bruised, sweaty face with his dirty sleeve. "I hope the firemen get here quick."

"You and me both." While the fire roared, I saw the ship easing away from the dock. Loud shots rang out as Burton ran down the dock to Pier 22, his arm outstretched, firing at the ship.

Like a flash of lightning, Mutt and Jeff suddenly raced out of the warehouse toward Burton, screaming like hell, their clothes on fire.

"Look out!" I yelled, but my voice was drowned out by the noise and roaring flames. Shuddering, I saw Black Jack's goons bolt past Burton and jump into the bay, their arms and legs flailing like windmills. Criminals or not, I hoped everyone would survive.

Watching from the street, I heard a loud explosion and black smoke billowed out, engulfing the warehouse in neon yellow and orange flames. Bits and pieces of debris spewed out of the warehouse—shattered glass, strips of metal, pieces of charred wood—flying out so fast that it looked like a hurricane hit.

CHAPTER FIFTY-ONE

Hiding behind Sammy's car, I let out a loud scream, covering my head until the blast subsided. I'd been screaming a lot lately.

After the fire died down, I dashed toward the warehouse. "I'll go see if anyone is hurt," I yelled, but Sammy caught up and held onto my shirt tail, pulling me back.

"Are you nuts? Let's go before more cops show up. They may try to pin the blame on me. Who knows who Black Jack paid off to keep quiet?"

"But what if Nathan and James are hurt or injured?" It was the only time I'd used Burton's first name.

"We can call the medics from the Oasis." Sammy pushed me forward. "Come on, get in the car. Now."

Too tired to argue, I obeyed his order. Sammy loaded the crates of liquor and slammed the trunk just as a fire truck drove up, followed by a police car. I leaned out and yelled: "There was a huge explosion at the warehouse. People may still be inside. Be careful—it's full of liquor!"

A young cop with dark hair looked me over, no doubt taking note of my smudged clothes and face, puzzled. "Who are you? What are you doing here?" he asked, suspicious.

Typical flatfoot, following protocol. "I'm trying to help. Please hurry! My friends may be in danger!"

Sammy shielded his face, but the cops didn't pay any attention, too distracted by the fire and noise. The firemen and police raced up the pier to the dock, but I couldn't see much in the cloud of smoke.

I felt so guilty leaving Nathan and Burton behind, but they were grown men, with brains and wits and more guts than I had. I wished I could go back to help them, make sure they were alright. After all, didn't I cause the fire—and the explosion? If anyone was hurt, it was my fault. Bootleggers or gangsters or cops, no one deserved to die that way—especially not my friends.

Sammy and I sat in the car in stunned silence, taking everything in, trying to catch our breath. What seemed like hours had all taken place in a few minutes.

Finally Sammy piped up, gunning the engine, escaping the fire. "What in hell were you and Nathan doing here, Jazz? Don't you know how dangerous this is? What were you thinking?"

I could ask him the same question.

"I wanted to bring you the cash, make sure you were OK. Those goons almost killed you." I rarely lost my temper with Sammy, but seeing him roughed up upset me to no end.

"Hate to admit it, you kids may have saved my life." He rubbed his jaw, stopping to let a horse and buggy pass. "When I tried to talk to Black Jack alone, his men ganged up on me. This new guy— Orville?—is calling all the shots. Seems Black Jack got too cocky and careless. Maybe he's throwing back too much of his own booze. Lost control over his whole operation."

Was he actually grateful? "I doubt there'll be much of an operation now. You saw the warehouse go up in flames, along with the liquor. It may take a while to find new inventory."

"The good news is I still have my money and a few crates of booze to boot. But this time I'm testing it before I serve it in my bar." Sammy gave me a lopsided grin.

He parked the Packard in the alley behind the Oasis, for once clear of cars and bums. I'd bet everyone in town had heard the explosion and went to gawk. Nothing like a deadly fire to liven up the night.

"We'd better go get cleaned up." Sammy attempted to smile. "Ouch, my face hurts."

"Why don't we stop by the hospital first? Get checked out? You look like a punching bag!"

"Naw. I'm fine. That beating taught me a lesson." He rubbed his eyes with his shirt tail, smearing more dirt on his sweaty face.

"Like what?" He was so stubborn, I doubted one beating would really change his ways.

"Like, don't stick my nose where it doesn't belong." He gave me a stern look. "Leave well enough alone. Don't bite the hand…"

"OK, that's enough clichés for one day. I got the telegram. Anything else?"

"This one's made for you." He nodded, and shook his finger in my face. "Mind your own business."

"Thanks for the advice." I smiled, so glad he was safe now. "Even if I've heard it before. Hundreds of times." At least they hadn't beaten Sammy's wry sense of humor out of him.

"Say, I recognized two of those guys, the Mutt and Jeff characters. I've seen them around town a lot lately…at the Oasis, the Lotus fire and Joe's Bar. Have you dealt with them before?"

"Those assholes?" He scowled. "I found out they're trying to sell that cut-rate crap to all the local bars, but using Black Jack's name as their calling card. Rumor is, they started the Lotus Club fire when Johnny Jack turned them down flat. Too bad he lost half his Cuban rum in the blaze. I bet those two palookas set me up, since I refused to buy their rotgut."

"So you finally found out who was behind the moonshine. Frankly, I didn't think they were bright enough to pull it off."

Finally, the pieces began to fit. No wonder they beat up Mack, and tried to finger Sammy—they didn't want anyone to expose their deadly scam, especially to their boss. "Did Black Jack actually spill the beans to you?"

"Let's just say I scared it out of them." He tried to smile. "Or maybe I figured it out after they beat the shit out of me. I just hope they're gone for good." Maybe it was worth all this trouble—if Burton and Nathan returned, safe and sound.

At the Oasis, Sammy got out and tugged on the door, but it wouldn't budge. "That's strange." He removed his keys and unlocked the door, calling out: "Frank? Buzz?" Then he rushed down the stairs, knocking over a wine bottle on the steps.

The Oasis was unusually quiet, a stark contrast from the warehouse blast just minutes earlier. I hoped everyone was OK, the fire contained by now. I stopped to stand the bottle upright but my ribs hurt when I bent over, so I rested on the steps for a moment.

Then I heard Sammy exclaim, "What's the big idea? What in hell are you doing here?"

"What happened to you?" a familiar voice said. "Looks like you got hit by an ice truck."

Ice truck? I paused on the steps and peered into the room, staring at the reflection in the large beveled mirror.

A handsome man in a smart suit and hat stood in the empty bar. My breath caught in my throat: It was Phillip Clark, the new vice president of Lone Star Bank, and he was pointing a gun at Sammy.

CHAPTER FIFTY-TWO

Why was Phillip Clark threatening Sammy with a gun? I pressed my back against the wall, trying to stay out of sight, watching the two men face off, their images reflected in the beveled bar mirror.

While the men traded barbs, I strained to listen, trying to comprehend. Compared to Sammy, Clark was short and slender, but he did have one big advantage: a handgun.

"Get that thing out of my face." Sammy pushed the gun away. "What do you want?"

"Careful, it's loaded." Clark held the weapon higher. "Tell me, where's that ledger?"

"What ledger?" Sammy looked blank. "I don't know what you're talking about."

"Says you! How else would you get into your account today?" Clark strutted around Sammy, waving the gun. "I let you have all of that cash and this is the thanks I get?"

I held my breath, my pulse racing. After his beating, I doubted Sammy could hold his own against Clark, especially since he was armed. And I was no help, hiding here on the stairs. Too bad Sammy's gun was hidden under the floorboards in his office.

"It's my goddamned money. And I've known the account number all along," Sammy lied.

"Bullshit. I know for a fact Horace handled all those accounts." Clark waved his gun at Sammy, stomping around the hardwood floor like an agitated bronco ready to buck.

Sammy played dumb. "What's so important about that ledger?"

"None of your business." Clark slowly edged toward Sammy.

"It *is* my business since you're in my bar pointing a gun at my head." He faced down Clark, ignoring the gun as if it didn't faze him.

"How do you know so much about this ledger?"

"Got it straight from the horse's mouth—or should I say, Horace's mouth." Clark snickered at his pun. "He got plastered one night at a poker game, and told me all about his money-making scheme. I wanted in, but he wouldn't let me share in his good fortune. Greedy bastard."

"Who's the greedy bastard now? Even if I knew anything, why should I tell you?"

My nails dug into my palms as I listened, trying to keep still.

"It's your funeral. My new clients and I are *very* interested in that ledger. You may have heard of them: Rose, Ollie, Johnny Jack, Dutch. Bet you don't want them as your enemies."

The two men circled each other like angry pit bulls. "The ledger has to be here. I've already searched Andrews' office and house. This was the last place he came before his untimely demise."

Beads of sweat dotted my face. So Clark was behind the break-in at the Andrews' house?

"How would you know?" Sammy's olive eyes flashed in anger.

"Word gets around. He was supposed to be at the Hollywood that night for a high-stakes poker game, but came here instead. Why is that?" He challenged Sammy.

"Beats me." Sammy shrugged. "We were friends, that's all."

"Since you were such good friends, did you know he'd embezzled five grand from Lone Star Bank? But we can't find it." Clark raised his brows. "Any idea where he stashed the cash?"

My heart skipped a beat. So I was right about Horace: He must have embezzled the money from Lone Star and hid it in the train locker. I remembered fingering the crisp, clean tens and twenties in the satchel, newly-minted bills fresh from the bank.

"Bullshit!" Sammy worked his jaw. "He'd never steal from his own bank. If that's true, why are you here with a gun? Maybe *you're* the one who stole the jack."

I sucked in air. Sammy was going to get himself killed if he didn't keep his mouth shut.

"I'll ask you again: Where is that ledger? The cash? Alice knows nothing and from what I hear, she hasn't been living high on the hog lately. Poor dear Alice is in debt up to her eyebrows, grieving in that fancy mansion." Clark said it with obvious contempt. "I know Horace hid the money somewhere and the ledger is the key. I've searched your office and bar but no one here is talking."

In the mirror, I saw Sammy shaking his fist at Clark, eyes blazing. "What did you do to my help? Where are they? If you touched one hair on their heads…"

"Don't worry, they're fine. For now," Clark taunted him. "But unless you talk…"

Sammy raised his chin in defiance. "Say I know where the ledger is. What's in it for me?"

Did I hear right? My body locked up as I strained to listen.

"What do you want?" Clark lowered his arm, pointing the gun at Sammy's chest.

"Half of everything. Split fifty-fifty," Sammy said evenly.

What? Was he really trying to work out a deal with Clark or was he bluffing? With Sammy, it was hard to tell. Either option could get him killed.

"Forget it!" Clark snapped to attention. "That's my money! He got lucky at a poker game and cleaned me out. I planned to win my cash back that night at the Hollywood, but as you know Horace never showed."

"*Your* money?" Sammy played it cool. "You said Horace embezzled it from the bank."

"Let's just say I gave myself a temporary loan." Clark shrugged. "Horace threatened to turn me in if I didn't return the cash, pay him back in full. All I needed was one good game to settle the score."

My head throbbed. So it was *Clark* who'd embezzled the money, after all. But why was he confessing all this to Sammy—did he plan to kill him too?

"What if you lost?" Sammy said. "No doubt you were going to set him up, let him take the fall."

"So what? He deserved it, that smug son of a bitch. The bank even promoted him, gave him a fancy new title: 'Vice President of New Accounts.' What hogwash. It wasn't right!" Clark waved his gun in the air wildly.

I froze in place, not daring to move or breathe.

"And you think killing him was the answer?" Sammy shook his head, disgusted. "So Horace suspected you all along. I'll bet he planned to tell me everything that night before he died."

"Kill him? It was an accident." Clark forced the gun barrel under Sammy's neck. "The way he guzzled that gasoline, poor sap…Never knew what hit him."

I wanted to create a diversion, to distract Clark, but that could backfire, literally. As I watched the scene unfold, it all began to make sense. Thank goodness Alice Andrews wasn't involved. She was an innocent bystander, a victim, but because of Clark, I'd even begun to suspect her as well.

Sammy's eyes narrowed. "What did you do to him?"

"Who, me?" Clark feigned innocence. "I just wanted to knock Horace off his game for a while, teach him a lesson. Win my money back, fair and square. For all they know, he drank that bootleg booze right here. Who will the cops believe—me or a two-bit barkeep?"

Clark moved toward him, panic in his voice. "Damn it, tell me where he hid that ledger—or else!"

"Why should I tell you anything?" Sammy crossed his arms.

"You're not exactly in a position to argue, are you?"

Clark swung the gun hard across Sammy's temple, knocking him against the bar counter. Sammy touched his head, blood oozing, dripping down his face. I let out a gasp, and covered my mouth with both hands to keep from screaming out loud.

Panicking, I looked around for something, anything, to disarm Clark. Luckily, I spied the wine bottle nearby. If I could only reach it without attracting attention.

While Sammy struggled to regain his balance, Clark cocked his gun at his bleeding temple. "How about I give you a taste of your own medicine? Or should I say methanol? No one will think twice if a lowlife like you winds up dying of wood alcohol poisoning, here in your own bar. Especially not the cops. Occupational hazard, I'd say."

Clark reached into his left pocket. "In fact, I seem to have a full flask right here. Want a sample?"

I held my breath. That bastard had poisoned his own friend with methanol, and now he was trying to poison Sammy.

Sammy attempted to push Clark away, but lost his footing. Clark held the gun against Sammy's throat while he fumbled with the flask. Heart hammering, I watched the two men struggle, afraid that the gun might go off. How could I stand here doing nothing? Quietly as possible, I reached for the bottle, aiming for a clear shot at Clark.

"Let go of me!" Sammy tried to push Clark's hand away, but he'd managed to screw the cap off the flask. Clark held it above Sammy's head while he tried to block Clark with his forearm. Clear liquid splashed out onto Sammy's face, his neck.

Holding the wine bottle like a spear, I took aim at Clark's back, throwing it with all my force. I hoped all those games of softball that I'd played as a kid would pay off.

The bottle hit between Clark's shoulder blades and smashed to the floor, the red wine seeping into the wood like blood.

"What in hell?" Stumbling, Clark whirled around, glancing around the bar in shock, enabling Sammy to grab his arm with the gun. A loud shot rang out, followed by silence.

What had I done? Who got shot? Heart thudding, I crouched on the stairs, numb.

Suddenly Sammy jumped on Clark and wrestled him to the floor, knocking the gun out of his hand. Clark scrambled for the gun but I bounded down the steps, cutting him off.

"Where did you come from?" Clark lunged for my ankles, tugging on my pants leg. I managed to move away, stepping hard on his right hand with all my weight and kicked the gun out of reach. Hands shaking, I picked up the gun, pointing the barrel at his chest.

"Put that gun down!" Clark yelled. He glanced at my shoes, puzzled, then his face twisted in a smirk. "Well, I'll be. Where'd you come from, little lady? Sammy, I didn't expect a dame to do your dirty work." He grinned at me, the slimy smile of a snake oil salesman. "Darling, if you help me escape, we can split the take and we'll both be rich."

Clearly Clark didn't recognize me, no doubt because I was dirty and disheveled and still in men's clothes. "No, thanks. Tell Alice Andrews how you killed her husband by mistake. Admit to his wife that you poisoned him on purpose, then pretended it was an *accident*."

My voice rose, my hands shook as I tried to steady the gun. One wrong move and it might go off again. I'd never held a gun in my life and now wasn't a good time to start.

"Where's the proof? It's your word against mine." Clark started inching toward me, eyes fixated on the gun. "Besides, Alice was too good for him. She deserved better than a lying, cheating nobody."

"Oh, yeah? Tell it to the cops." Enraged, Sammy began punching Clark in the face, hard and steady, like a machine.

Clark clawed at Sammy, yelling, "Get off of me, you bastard!"

Sammy once told me he'd boxed as a youth for extra cash, but I'd never seen him in action. Clark's nose was bleeding, his eyes red and swollen, face wet with sweat. My stomach started to wretch, nauseous, and I turned away.

"Sammy, stop it!" I yelled, shaking him to snap him out of his rage. "He's out like a light."

Sammy stood up, swaying as if sleepwalking, and dropped in a chair, touching his temple.

"Are you hurt?" I examined the injuries on his face, handing him a glass of water while he caught his breath.

Still shaking, I searched the bar, the kitchen, then the office. There I found Buzz and Frank, tied back to back with rope, socks in their mouths, their wrists bound. What a relief!

Quickly I untied them and helped Buzz stand up. Thank God they seemed fine, frightened but unharmed. "What happened? Are you OK?"

"Thanks, Jazz." Frank got to his feet, rubbing his wrists. "We're just shaken up, that's all."

"Is S-S-Sammy hurt?" Buzz asked. "I heard a g-g-gunshot!"

"He's a little banged up, but he's alright." I patted his back. "Go see for yourself."

Sammy rolled Clark over, giving him a final kick. "Help me tie him up," he ordered Frank and Buzz. "No good piece of shit. Jazz, call the police station. Get the cops down here to take this trash out of my bar. Find out if our boys made it out in one piece."

"I sure hope so." I hated to think the worst. "What about the gun?" I asked Sammy. "I heard a shot."

Not a smart idea, aiming a gun at a bank vice president, even if he was a murderer. Clark was laid out like a worn welcome mat, his eyes and face swollen, bloody—eerily near the spot where Andrews had passed out ten days earlier.

Sammy flashed a weak smile, motioning toward our wooden mascot. "Looks like Doria got a new beauty mark."

An hour or so later, the cops had arrested Clark and taken him to the police station for questioning, the gun and flask bagged as evidence. Medics took Sammy to John Sealy Hospital to be examined, ignoring his protests.

Now I sat with Agent Burton inside his car in front of the Oasis, trying to catch my breath. Burton seemed a bit banged up, soot and dirt clinging to his suit.

"What happened at the docks? How's Nathan? Did anyone get hurt?" I held my breath.

"The medics took some guys to the hospital. Nathan is being treated for smoke inhalation. He got damn close to that fire."

"That's all?" I breathed a sigh of relief. "Figures. I hope he's OK. Nathan will do anything for a great shot."

Now I couldn't wait to go back to the newsroom, eager to tell Mr. Thomas all the details about our run-in with Black Jack and his goons. Not even Mack could make that claim. And with Nathan's close-up photos of the bootleggers and the warehouse fire, the article was bound to make front-page news.

"Thanks to you and Nathan, Black Jack is out of business, temporarily, at least in Galveston. He and a couple of men got away, but we have the other two in custody." Was it Mutt and Jeff?

Burton flashed me a grin. "You single-handedly managed to bring down Black Jack's bootlegging operation with that fire."

Was he kidding? "Some crook will take his place in no time."

I figured he was razzing me, but I was glad he gave us some credit. "At least we slowed him down for a while." I reached in my pockets and held out the whiskey labels I swiped from the warehouse, wrinkled and smudged, but still intact. "Take a look at these labels. Seems his thugs were the ones passing off doctored-up hooch as Johnnie Walker and Jack Daniels."

"This is solid evidence." Burton looked impressed. "I doubt Black Jack will show his face here anytime soon. His whole dirty operation went up in flames."

"Literally." I felt a flash of pride. Working up my nerve, I fiddled with Nathan's shirt, streaked with soot. "I hate to bring this up now, but do you remember the host at the Surf Club?"

"You mean our Champagne server? That little shrimp with the beady eyes? Yes, why?" Burton didn't appear fazed one bit.

"He cornered me at the Hotel Galvez tonight, and gave me a message for you: 'Stay away from the Beach Gang.'"

"What? Why'd he threaten *you*?" Burton fumed. "Are you OK?"

"I will be when this is all over and Clark is in jail." I relaxed my fists, tight as knots.

"What happened? And how did you get messed up in all this?"

"Do you want the long or short version?" I asked, mentally trying to edit my account. How much could I reveal without lying or incriminating Sammy or anyone else, including myself?

"I'd like to hear the whole story, from the start." He gave me a lazy smile. "I have all the time in the world."

The whole story? Still dazed, I filled him in, beginning with Andrews and his poisoned flask, the pharmacist's findings, Sammy's run-in with Black Jack and then Clark's confession. Some facts could wait. Did Burton need to know about the bag of cash right now?

To be polite, I paused to ask, "What about Clark?"

"We'll get more out of Clark if he's still scared and hurt. The hospital visit can wait. With Andrews' flask and Clark's gun, we can charge him with attempted murder or manslaughter."

"*Attempted* murder? He killed Horace in cold blood! Even if he claims it was an accident." My breath came out in gulps. "He might have killed Sammy, if I hadn't…" Did I need to spell it out? "About his gun…you may find an extra set of fingerprints or two."

"Why am I not surprised?" Burton pushed some hair away from my face. "I'm glad you're not hurt. Sounds like you were involved with some dangerous characters."

"Including you." I smiled at his worried expression. "I just hope Clark gets convicted. I'll help in any way I can."

"You've done enough for one day. We'll also charge him with embezzlement, if we can locate the five-thousand." He raised his brows. "Any idea where it could be?"

"I might have a clue," I admitted. Of course, I'd turn over the five-thousand in new bills to the bank, yet I was tempted to give Mrs. Andrews the rest. Wouldn't it be nice to see the look on her face when I handed her Horace's bag filled with $6000. dollars in cash?

Alice definitely needed the dough a lot more than the gangsters, and I'd keep quiet about how Horace had "earned" his extra income.

Then I remembered all the bills still stuffed in my pockets. Sammy could easily use the grand to take care of Buzz.

Yet I was ambivalent: Was it right to play Robin Hood? Was it wrong to want to help my family and friends? I was afraid the gangs might get wise, and come after us, looking for the money.

If I told Burton, I hoped they'd do the right thing and give the rest to Alice Andrews. What to do? So much had happened recently, I couldn't think straight.

"There's a reward, in case you do locate the loot." Burton watched my reaction.

"A reward? How much?" I perked up.

"How does one-hundred dollars sound?" He smiled at my excited expression. "I'll drive you home, and fill you in on the way."

A hundred bucks! More than enough to cover Eva's rent for a few months. Perhaps we'd even splurge on two fancy new frocks or a scenic beaded purse or tango compact?

"Swell! I'll be glad to share the reward with Nathan."

"He'll also get a reward." Burton started his car and gave me a sudden kiss on the cheek. "Now we have a real reason to celebrate."

Self-conscious, I tried to wipe the soot off my face and neck. "What was that for? I must look a fright!" I blushed. "Boy, do I need a bath and a change of clothes!"

"You said it," he teased. "Not me."

Gee, thanks. On the way home, I kept firing off questions, but Burton only said, "Let's talk more later. Say, over a bottle of French Champagne?"

So he'd kept the bottle, instead of turning it over to the cops.

"It's a date." I smiled at the thought.

Meanwhile, I couldn't wait to start writing up the article on Black Jack's gang and the warehouse fire. Maybe Mack would even give me a few pointers. I hoped Nathan had taken plenty of dramatic photos to illustrate our future Pulitzer Prize-winning story.

I tried to imagine the headline, above the fold, of course: GAZETTE STAFFERS HELP CAPTURE KILLER BANKER AND DANGEROUS BOOTLEGGERS.

Sure, I was stretching the truth a bit, but we did try our best. Still, wouldn't it be swell if I finally got my own front-page byline?

1920s JAZZ AGE SLANG

All wet - Wrong, incorrect ("You're all wet!" "That's nuts!")

And how! - I strongly agree!

Applesauce! – Nonsense, Horsefeathers (e.g. "That's ridiculous!")

Attaboy! - Well done! Bravo! Also: Attagirl!

Baby grand - A heavily-built man

Balled up - Confused, Unsure

Baloney - Nonsense, Hogwash, Bullshit

Bathtub Booze - Home-brewed liquor, Hooch (often in tubs)

Bearcat - A hot-blooded or fiery girl

"Beat it!" - Scram, Get lost

Bee's Knees - An extraordinary person, thing or idea

Berries - Attractive or pleasing; Swell ("It's the berries!")

Big Cheese - Big shot, an important or influential person

Blotto - Very drunk, Smashed

Blow - (a) A wild, crazy party (b) To leave

Bluenose - A prim, puritanical person; a prude, a killjoy

Bohunk - A racist name for Eastern Europeans, a dumb guy

Bootleg - Illegal liquor, Hooch, Booze

Breezer (1925) - A convertible car

Bruno - Tough Guy, Enforcer

Bug-eyed Betty - An unattractive girl or student

Bum's rush - Ejection by force from an establishment

Bump Off - To murder, to kill

Cake-eater - A lady's man, a gigolo; an effeminate male

Carry a Torch - To have a crush on someone

Cat's Meow/Whiskers - Splendid, Stylish, Swell

Cat's Pajamas - Terrific, Wonderful, Great

Clams - Money, Dollars, Bucks

Coffin varnish - Bootleg liquor, Hooch (often poisonous)

Copacetic - Excellent, all in order

Crush - An infatuation, attraction

Dame/Doll - A female, woman, girl

Dogs - Feet

Dolled up - Dressed up in "glad rags"

Don't know from nothing - Don't have any information

Don't take any wooden nickels - Don't do anything stupid

Dough - Money, Cash

Drugstore Cowboy - A guy who picks up girls in public places

Dry up - Shut up; Get lost
Ducky - Fine, very good (Also: Peachy)
Dumb Dora - An idiot, a dumbbell; a stupid female
Egg - Nice person, One who likes the big life
Fall Guy - Victim of a frame
Fella - Fellow, man, guy (very common in the 1920s)
Fire extinguisher - A chaperone, a fifth wheel
Flat Tire - A dull, boring date (Also: Pill, Pickle, Oilcan)
Frame - To give false evidence, to set up someone
Gams - A woman's legs
Gate Crasher - A party crasher, an uninvited guest
Giggle Water - Liquor, Hooch, Booze, Alcohol
Gin Joint/Gin Mill - A bar, a speakeasy
Glad rags - "Going out on the town" clothes, Fancy dress attire
Go chase yourself - "Get lost, beat it, scram"
Hard Boiled - A tough, strong guy (e.g. "He sure is hard-boiled!")
Hayburner - (a) A gas-guzzling car (b) A losing racehorse
Heebie-jeebies (1926) - The shakes, the jitters, (from a hit song)
High-hat - Snobby, snooty
Holding the bag - To be cheated or blamed for something
Hooch - Bootleg liquor, illegal alcohol
Hood - Hoodlum, Gangster, Thug
Hooey - Bullshit, Nonsense, Baloney (1925 to 1930)
Hoofer - Dancer, Chorus girl
Hotsy-Totsy - Attractive, Pleasing
Jack - Cash, Money
Jake - Great, Fine, OK (i.e. "Everything's jake.")
Jeepers creepers – Exclamation of surprise ("Jesus Christ!")
Joe Brooks - A well-groomed man, natty dresser, student
Juice Joint - A speakeasy, bar
Keen - Attractive or appealing
Killjoy - Dud, a dull, boring person, a party pooper, a spoilsport
Lollygagger - (a) A flirtatious male (b) A lazy or idle person
Lounge Lizard - A gigolo; a flirtatious, sexually-active male
Mick - A derogatory term for an Irishman
Milquetoast (1924): A very timid person; a hen-pecked male
  (from the comic book character Casper Milquetoast)
Mrs. Grundy - A prude or killjoy; a prim, prissy (older) woman
Moll - (Gun Moll) A gangster's girlfriend
Neck - Make-out, kiss with passion

"Oh yeah?" - Expression of doubt ("Is that so?")
On a toot – On a drinking binge, Bar-hopping
On the lam - Fleeing from police
On the level - Legitimate, Honest
On the trolley – In the know, Savvy ("You're on the trolley!")
On the up and up - Trustworthy, Honest
Ossified – Drunk, Plastered
Palooka - A derogatory term for a low-class or dumb person
(Re: Comic strip character Joe Palooka, a poor immigrant)
Piker - (a) Cheapskate (b) Coward
Pitch a little woo - To flirt, try to charm and attract the opposite sex
Rag-a-muffin - An unkempt, dirty and disheveled person/child
Razz - To tease, to insult or make fun of
Rhatz! - "Too bad!" or "Darn it!"
Ritzy - Elegant, High-class, "Putting on the Ritz" (Re: Ritz Hotel)
Rotgut - Cheap hooch, inferior alcohol, poisonous bootleg liquor
Rummy - A drunken bum, an intoxicated man, a wino
Sap - A fool, an idiot; very common term in the 1920s
"Says you!" - A reaction of disbelief or doubt (also "Hogwash!")
Screaming meemies - The shakes, the jitters, to be afraid
Screwy - Crazy, Nuts ("You're screwy!")
Sheba - An attractive and sexy woman; girlfriend
(popularized by the film "Queen of Sheba")
Sheik - A handsome man with sex appeal
(from Rudolph Valentino's film "The Sheik")
Scram – "Get out," "Beat it," to leave immediately
Speakeasy - An illicit bar selling bootleg liquor
Spiffy - An elegant appearance, well-dressed, fine
Stuck On - Having a crush on, attracted to
Sugar Daddy - A rich, older gentleman (usually married)
Swanky - Elegant, Ritzy
Swell - Wonderful, Great, Fine, A-OK
Take for a Ride -To try to kill someone (bump them off)
Torpedo - A hired gun, a hit man
Upchuck - To vomit, especially after drinking too much
Wet Blanket - A dud, a dull date or person, a party pooper
Whoopee - (Make whoopee) To have fun/a good time, to party
"You don't say!" – i.e. "Is that so?" "Oh, really? I didn't know"
"You slay me!" -"You're hilarious!" or "That's funny!"
Zozzled - Drunk, intoxicated, (Also: Plastered, Smashed)

BIOGRAPHY

Ellen Mansoor Collier is a Houston-based freelance writer and editor whose articles, essays and short stories have been published in a variety of national magazines. Formerly she's worked as a magazine editor and writer, and in advertising/marketing and public relations. A flapper at heart, she's the owner of DECODAME (www.art-decodame.com), specializing in Deco to retro vintage items.

She graduated from the University of Texas at Austin with a degree in Magazine Journalism, where she lived in a c. 1926 dorm her freshman year. She worked as an editor on UTmost magazine and was active in Women in Communications (W.I.C.I.), serving as President her senior year.

FLAPPERS, FLASKS AND FOUL PLAY (2012) is the first novel in her "Jazz Age Mystery" series, followed by BATHING BEAUTIES, BOOZE AND BULLETS (2013) and GOLD DIGGERS, GAMBLERS And GUNS (2014).

DEDICATION

Thanks to Gary, my wonderful husband, who has helped and supported me from day one and read virtually every draft of this novel. To my mother, May Mansoor Munn, also a writer, who inspired me to write at a young age and often offered words of wisdom, and to my late father, Isa Mansoor, who always encouraged me to do my best.

ACKNOWLEDGEMENTS

I owe a debt of gratitude to Karen Muller, who read and meticulously edited the first and last drafts of FLAPPERS.

Many thanks go to *Texas Monthly* contributor Gary Cartwright, author of *Galveston: A History of the Island*, whose painstaking research made Galveston's past come alive.

For my cover art, I'm delighted to credit George Barbier, the fabulous French Deco artist (1882-1932). My talented brother, Jeff J. Mansoor, created the great graphics for the title and back cover.

I'm especially grateful to the friends and family members who read drafts of my novel and offered suggestions and encouragement.

(Thanks to Gary, Mom, Karen, Jeff and Rana!)

Made in the USA
Charleston, SC
28 August 2014